THE
STORM OF
LIFE

THE

STORM

OF

LIFE

AMY ROSE CAPETTA

VIKING

VIKING
An imprint of Penguin Random House LLC, New York

First published in the United States of America by Viking,
an imprint of Penguin Random House LLC, 2020

Visit us online at penguinrandomhouse.com

LIBRARY OF CONGRESS CATALOGING-IN-PUBLICATION DATA IS AVAILABLE
ISBN 9780451478474

Printed and bound in Canada   Set in Manticore   Book design by Kate Renner

10 9 8 7 6 5 4 3 2 1

For everyone
who is more than the words they were given
more than the fates that were foretold
more than the bodies they were born in

for the ones who are storms
bringing change

and especially, for the one who is my sky

The End

When I was a little girl, my father's tours of Vinalia carried him far from home. While he conducted di Sangro business in the darkest corners of the finest palazzos, I sat on his black walnut chair, a crown of violets in the bramble of my curls, and made decrees.

I told my brother Luca that he was the bravest young man in my kingdom, which was true—my kingdom was no wider than Father's study, though it ran as deep as my stepmother's old stories.

I told my little sister Carina, barely born, that she must be a great strega. With her pickled face, solemn eyes, and perfectly timed wails, she seemed both young and old, wise and wicked.

I told my older sister, Mirella, that she'd been declared the queen of a neighboring kingdom, and I would trade with her if she had my favorite almond paste sweets.

I did not tell my brother Beniamo anything.

One day at the turn of winter, as the cold made its first advances into the castle, I sat alone at Father's desk, working on a scrap of Mirella's drawing paper with a stick of charcoal from the kitchen fire. I wrote out rules for my subjects, my hands smudged black, my mind burning with the bright frenzy of creating a kingdom. The magic inside me liked this business as much as I did.

It had been with me for nearly a year, since the night I went downstairs for a glass of milk and saw a man murdered on the stairs. The magic I'd inherited from this stranger ached to be used, but I couldn't transform objects openly. My family might be frightened or jealous; they might scoff at me or stubbornly choose not to believe. So instead of showing them the whole of who I was, I snuck to the fields on the mountainside, changing ice to white linen sheets. As summer breathed hot down our necks, I turned white poppies to snow that melted in my hands and trickled it down the back of my stuffy red di Sangro dresses.

The scrape of a foot against stone pulled my attention up from the papers on Father's desk. I'd been so deep inside of my schemes that I hadn't heard the door as it opened. Beniamo stood on the threshold, watching me. Honeyed light from the hallway clung to his dark curls, and if I did not know him a bit, I would have thought he looked like a saint.

"What are you playing, Teodora?" he asked.

I wasn't playing a game. I was perfectly serious.

"Nothing."

He'll hurt us, the magic whispered. *Stop him.*

I'd never changed a person before, and my magic was suddenly hungry to try it. But if I changed Beniamo, Father would disown me: strip me of my di Sangro name, send me away from the home and family that I loved.

"*Not now*," I whispered hotly to the magic.

"Are you talking in church words?" Beniamo asked. I

hadn't known I was doing that until he pointed it out. "You wish to be a priest *and* a king? Isn't one stupid dream enough to fill your day?"

I shoved the magic down. Shame and anger rose to fill its place, a natural spring pushing up to my cheeks. I vowed that I would never speak aloud to my magic.

"You know you can't rule anything, don't you?" Beniamo asked, his voice burning low and steady. He waited for me to give an answer that he could transform into the proper punishment. I wondered what a queen would do.

"This is my kingdom," I said in an ironclad whisper.

"Yours? What if it's invaded?" Beniamo crossed the room swiftly. Things were moving now, and I could not slow them, could not stop them. I locked my legs around the posts of the chair, edges biting through my stockings and into my skin.

Beniamo pushed me, toppling the black walnut throne.

I rolled free, and Beniamo kicked me in the chest. Once, twice. I curled around the broken feeling, gathering the pieces. It wasn't safe to cry out. Beniamo would enjoy it too much. He would kick me harder, to hear me shout again.

I watched from my place on the floor as his boots strode toward the crown of violets that had fallen from my hair. Beniamo smashed the deeply blue flowers beneath his heel. I had spent hours on the mountainside picking the ones with perfect cups of black in the center.

"You have been unseated, sister," Beniamo said, laughing as he dropped the ruined crown back on my head. He stepped back and studied me with a flat expression. "I'm only preparing you for the rest of your life. You should kneel and thank me."

I must not have acted quickly enough, because he kicked me once more, a sharp toe to the shins.

I whimpered, stuffing a louder cry back down my throat.

"Go on," he said.

I pushed the heels of my hands against the floor. My knees scraped the stone as I shifted, and because I could not look at his face without giving away the force of my hatred, I stared at my brother's stomach, thinking about how soft and unprotected it looked. "Thank you," I spat, the words as bitter as blood in my mouth.

And I started counting the days until I would never have to kneel again.

One

Defiance Doesn't Come for Free

Cielo and I left at dawn, before the black crepe sky shed its mourning colors. We'd barely stayed long enough for me to learn the name of the town we now fled. Pavetta, or maybe Paletta. By day, each new place Cielo and I passed through offered memorable features—a jewel-colored piazza, a fortress that stubbornly carried the weight of a dead empire, a church whose stone walls wept grime that the villagers called God's Tears.

This was no grand tour of Vinalia, though.

We were warning every strega we could find of the Capo's plan to use their magic in the war he'd stirred up. Wherever we went, a growing number of doorways bore the green-and-black flag of the Capo's unified nation. I spotted one over the door of a palazzo and resisted the urge to turn my magic on that flag, frying it crisp as a sage leaf.

Now that I'd taken on more than my share of magic, things were different. I had to be careful in a new way, tiptoeing around my own power. It worked on a much grander and more unruly scale, and it didn't always wait for my command.

The town ended abruptly, and we left Pavetta and its half dozen streghe behind. Cielo had helped me pick them out on market day, her eyes sharp as hooks, fishing through the crowd for others with magic. She'd mostly stayed in girlish form since leaving Chieza, which meant we were easier prey for bandits on the road, but also that strangers were more likely to speak with us, delighted and defenseless, when Cielo offered them even the smallest fraction of a smile.

All smiles died a swift death when we told them of the Capo's plan to use their magic as a sacrifice, feeding the might of a small number of streghe. *His* streghe.

That was the magic I carried now: the death inheritance of two sisters who had given themselves over to the Capo's schemes and taken the lives of our own kind. One had her throat slit by the Capo himself. One fell into the earth after I tore it open beneath her. As Cielo and I chased rumors of streghe, and I hunted down the worst of the criminals I had let escape from the di Sangro castle, I kept thinking of Azzurra's wild attacks on my home, her unshakable love for her sister, the guilt I felt at killing a fellow strega instead of finding some way to save her.

My magic had always craved greater strength, but now that I bore the death-passed magic of dozens of streghe, it didn't feel like I held a single, seamless power inside of me. It was a collection of splintered pieces.

"Do you think the streghe we met in the market yesterday will heed our warning?" I asked.

Cielo pulled her cloak, one of our few possessions, tighter against the newborn cold. We'd left summer behind in Amalia. "Who knows with the northern streghe? They are ferociously independent."

If Cielo thought that, I felt little hope.

We kept moving—north as far as I could tell. Cielo tested

the winds by becoming one, flicking the pages of the book she used to control her changes. Not that the strega's magic was obeying the rules now, either. Only an act of unchecked power had been able to break me away from servitude to the Capo. I was the reason Cielo had lost control of the magic she'd worked for years to bring to heel.

We had lost so much to gain each other.

The wind that was Cielo swirled around me, raking through my hair, toying with the hem of my dress, sliding under my collar and working its warm, sure way down the valley between my breasts.

A blush started in my cheeks and then went on a rampage. "Not now," I said roughly.

I ran my hands down my dress, pretending to smooth it from the ruffling of the wind but really savoring memories of Cielo's hands, Cielo's mouth, Cielo's skin.

The wind breathed over the book, flipping it to a well-worn page that turned Cielo back into the boyish version I had first met on the mountain those months ago. He stood up, naked and grinning, and I tossed a pack directly at his stomach.

"We need to lay a course," I said as he removed a shirt from the pack and shook out the wrinkles.

He hopped into his pants and then removed the green-and-purple traveling cloak that had snared my attention the first time we met. As it turned out, the web of stitching on the back was not just a rich design—it formed a map of Vinalia, including the locations of all streghe known to Cielo.

"We're here," Cielo said, jabbing a finger at the silk.

Pavetta—or Paletta—sat in the western foothills, as far as we could walk before the Uccelli dwindled to nothing, soon to be replaced by the sharp angles and snowy creases of the Neviane. My mind filled with those peaks and the war the Capo waged there.

"Let's see if we can make it to the hazelnut fields of Alieto by midday," Cielo said. "From there, it's only a short hike to—"

"No," I said, stabbing through the heart of Cielo's plans. "We should be doing more than skulking from village to village, warning a few streghe at a time, always afraid we're about to be caught. Unless we find some way to unite the people, *our* people, the Capo will be able to pick them off."

My hands slid into knots, and Cielo eased them back open. "Don't think of him."

"He's *your* uncle," I muttered.

"I take no responsibility for that," Cielo said. "I didn't choose my uncle any more than you picked Beniamo from a batch of possible brothers." Even the mention of Beniamo felt like an attack, and I cringed away from it. When I blinked, light alternated with fractured bits of memory—turning my brother into an owl, watching him come back more vicious than before. The last time I'd seen him, he'd vowed to make my life an endless parade of pain and loss.

"You're shaking," Cielo said, taking me by the shoulders.

"I'm not." I forced myself to stillness and then realized I hadn't been the only thing shuddering. The ground shivered subtly beneath our feet.

I hoped this was one of the earthquakes that seized the Uccelli on a monthly basis, gave the mountains a quick shake, and then died. But the feeling grew steadily, and so did the dread in my chest. Cielo dropped to one knee and spread the cloak over the ground. It jolted and danced.

"Someone's coming." Without so much as touching the book, Cielo split into a flock of birds. Dark wings rose into a sky as pale as a fevered brow.

I called on my own magic and found it restless. It hissed, angry that I had been holding back for so long. When I pulled, there was no smooth and ready response. Instead, I grasped for sharp edges. There were so many of them, so many different ways to hurt.

I turned to the mountain and focused on its smooth hide. *I need a place where I won't be seen.*

A dozen spots on the mountain burst as if they'd been hit by cannon fire. Above me, the flock of Cielo-birds crowed.

Not very inconspicuous, I told the magic.

It buzzed a rude, angry response. It had become a chorus of discontent, always pressing me to do more. I rushed to a pockmark in the mountain's newly pitted face and settled behind a great stone that gave me a perch to spy from. Just as I rounded the corner, the road came alive with dust.

Men marched across the foothills of the Uccelli, wearing green and black. They were moving north from the Capo's beloved capital of Amalia to the brutish cold of the Neviane, their necks slung with scarves, their sweat evident under winter coats, even from here. The Eterrans had chosen to swarm over the northern mountains: the least forgiving approach, but their navy was tied up in constant skirmishes with the Sfidese. Keeping their army alive meant trusting the known passes through the Neviane, and only one was large enough to allow a great number of troops through its harsh, rocky embrace. It sat just north of the town of Zarisi. These Vinalians were marching toward the pass, pouring over the fields, a river of bodies. There had to be at least two thousand trampling crops and fallow fields alike. They kept their eyes ahead on the glory of coming battles.

I thought about changing them now, to spare them the pain and death of this ridiculous war. The Capo shouldn't have so many lives at his disposal. I could save them all in one great sweep.

Turn them into a field of toy soldiers, the magic said.

Would that be mercy? What would I do when the Capo, bereft of soldiers, lost the war? When the Eterrans broke into the country and took whatever they pleased? It was no secret that the northern invaders had their eyes on our rich fields. They wished to claim our glories in science, art—possibly even magic. Eterrans were empire builders. For a few centuries they had been focused on spreading over the seas to the virgin continent, but they'd lost most of their colonies there to war. Now they had their eyes on Vinalia, and they were well practiced in taking what was not theirs.

I remembered that moment of being forced into the Capo's army—my body, my magic, belonging to him.

Would Eterra try to claim the streghe? Would our magic be the first thing they stole?

The Capo had exposed us to the world and then brought on a war in the name of his own glory. My rage took flight, but I kept still. These troops might not have been sent to scout for the two streghe who had set magical fire to Amalia, but if they caught us along the way, it would certainly earn them the Capo's gratitude.

One of Cielo's flock landed at my feet.

"He's sending more troops," I whispered. "You know what that means."

The bird tapped its beak on the rock, with the impatience

that Cielo possessed in all forms. Above, several of the Cielo-birds flew ahead to note the path the soldiers took toward the Neviane.

Pavetta had been dripping with whispers of the war. The Capo was losing battle after battle, even though our men fought bravely. Everyone knew the Eterrans came from a cold, drizzly land where they spent all their time indoors plotting conquests. Soon they would take the pass at Zarisi.

Vinalia was on the verge of losing its first war.

🜚

HOURS LATER, WHEN THE SOLDIERS WERE ONLY A SMUDGE IN the distance, Cielo's flock came together, wings blurring and molding into a tall, black-haired, distinctly human sil-houette. Cielo's skin had finally taken on a hint of color by the end of summer, but my strega was still startlingly pale. I wondered what Cielo would look like in winter—if we ever lived to see one together.

"We have to stop them," I said.

Maybe I should have waited until Cielo was clothed for such a grand statement, but it couldn't wait.

"You escaped the Capo's service only months ago," Cielo said, crossing his arms over his chest, as if that covered anything—notable. "I thought you didn't want to be any-where near the front." I worked hard to keep my focus on Cielo's eyes, which had gone mostly gray, a color that came out of hiding when the strega was in a heightened state. Anger, sadness, passion of any sort.

Cielo took a step toward me, capturing my chin between

two fingers. My breath changed, as pitched and short as if I were climbing a mountain.

"I refuse to win wars for the Capo, but I can't allow . . . *this*." I shook my fingers at the troops marching toward the Neviane.

"Those men are allowed to do whatever they please, including join armies, Teodora," Cielo said.

"What about streghe, then? Now that magic is no longer a secret, who knows how we will be treated by an invading power? They might want to rid the world of our magic or claim it as their own. The Eterrans could break through the pass and march on Amalia at any time. We have to act quickly."

Cielo's fingers worked at my buttons, slipping me out of the tired, dirty shell of my traveling clothes. "I was thinking that, too."

Cielo took a single step closer, and full contact came with a sigh that my throat released gratefully. The feeling of Cielo's skin would have been enough to distract anyone except a di Sangro. I pressed down harder on my point. "If we had more streghe on our side, we could win the war ourselves. It would show Vinalians that we're to be trusted. And the Capo is not."

"A strega army," Cielo said, trailing a finger where he had just undone my buttons, tracing and retracing. "Is that what you dream about at night? You make such triumphant little noises."

My dreams had *not* been warlike, but I got the sense Cielo already knew that.

"It wouldn't be an army," I insisted, my voice thick in my throat as Cielo's hands settled over my hips. "More of a campaign."

"Ah, yes," Cielo said. "Should I salute you now or later, General di Sangro?"

I leaned over and bit his shoulder, an attempt at punishment that he seemed to take as a reward. His eyes flared delightedly, and his fingers doubled the strength of their grip.

"There's the slightest hint of a problem," Cielo said. "Streghe usually turn down social invitations, especially ones that might end in their death."

My mind stormed through possibilities, but my usual di Sangro ways wouldn't help in this matter. "If I threaten or bribe streghe into joining me, I'm no better than the Capo."

"You are better in every way that can be named or numbered," Cielo said, stepping back to look at me. "If they ever paint your portrait, and I have no doubt they will, it should look exactly like this." He nodded at how my hands capped my hips. "Goddess, naked and arguing. Now please stop talking about the Capo. It's ruining the moment."

"What moment?" I asked, pretending at innocence.

Shyness moved over Cielo's face, changing it as surely as clouds cast their spell over the sky. "I believe it's time to put the magic we've purchased in town to good use. I'll . . . ah . . . just need a moment." The strega reached for his cloak and the hidden pockets of the inner lining.

"Don't you have it?" My body was in a charmed state, but my voice sounded far away. Teodora di Sangro couldn't be here, in a cave formed by magic, a lifetime's expectations of marriage to a noble young man shed as simply as my clothing.

Not that Cielo and I had been anything close to virtuous in the past months. But there was a bridge we hadn't crossed yet, mostly because of the looming toll neither of us wished to pay.

"Of course I have it," Cielo said, thrusting his hand in each pocket, more frantic as each turned up empty. "I wouldn't come all this way and then lose such a necessary thing. This is *not* the time or place to have children." He looked around with a scornful air. "I know I'm not an expert in families, but I believe a nursery should have walls. And fewer nightmarish shadows."

In Pavetta, we had visited a strega Cielo knew of, with knuckles as large and shiny as walnuts. She kept a shop of herbs and poultices—or at least, that was what she sold to most people who knocked.

When Cielo and I asked for her help, she looked back and forth between us, no doubt trying to figure out which one the magic was for. Her eyes settled on Cielo, whose girlish form was carved of confidence.

I missed my boyish form, even more now that I didn't need it simply to command the respect of the five families. If I shifted into another variation of myself now, it would be for me alone, a tempting notion. But with the unwieldy new power in my body, I was afraid to work the reversal of magic needed to shift. And the truth that I'd found in Amalia, the warm glowing knowledge that I held close to me now, was that my body could bring me comfort or frustration, distance or delight, but it didn't dictate who I was. That boyish side was with me, no matter how I looked to the world. No matter what rested between my legs.

Yet people like the strega in Pavetta saw only one side of things—and what she saw were girls, at least one of whom wanted to avoid bearing children.

"If you tell certain people about this, I'll be arrested. Or worse."

"Don't worry," Cielo said. "*Certain people* can leap off a cliff."

"Use it before, not after, you hear me? The effects should last for six moons. You'll bleed less, too."

Now Cielo unwrapped the package the old woman had given us, his hands gentle and slow. It contained six vials of milk, each a slightly different color, ranging from an icy bluish white to the near tan of an eggshell.

"What now?" I asked.

"You're supposed to drink one," Cielo said.

I nodded as I inched the first vial out from its small loop of cloth.

I sent thoughts of my sister Mirella, who must have given birth to her first child by now, scurrying away.

"What if it's stronger the more you take?" I ask. "Won't milk spoil if we leave it for so long? Should I drink two?"

Cielo shook his head, and his certainty felt like the solid rock beneath my feet. "You might sicken if you take too much. The milk won't curdle—it's magic. And we want these to last. Who knows how long it will be until we pass through Pavella again?"

"*Pavella*," I said, hammering the town's name into place in my head. We had been wandering Vinalia in such a frantic haze that I did not know where my feet took me anymore. But when Cielo's hands settled on my thighs, softly stroking as I downed the tangy-sweet milk, I knew precisely where I was.

I could draw the shape of what I wanted.

I pushed Cielo down onto the stones, on top of his silky

cloak. I slid myself onto him, and he lifted his hips slowly, eyes half-closed, a catlike rumble of warmth in his throat. I kissed him on a rush of pure delight, and then I kissed him with a great wildfire need, and then I couldn't hold back a second longer. I hovered over him, aligning our bodies. When I stared down at Cielo's nervous smile, I felt too small to hold the sum of every feeling that had been building as we waited for this moment—anticipation and wild joy and a single prick of fear.

It overwhelmed my blood.

It called out to my magic.

Power came crashing out of me. The mountain above us had been weakened by the holes I'd blown in it, and now it ground its stones together, a great gnashing of teeth.

"I believe our rocky friend is displeased," Cielo said. His voice was delicate and not particularly urgent, but I knew we needed to move. The more danger we faced, the politer the strega grew.

Cielo grabbed his book and cloak, while I took hold of whatever clothes I could. Stones began to fall from the cave's ceiling, and I was almost crushed to powder as I doubled back to grab the precious vials of milk.

I left the cave, following Cielo, his bare ass showing under the shirt he'd hastily tugged on. We pelted for the safety of the fields as rocks roared down behind us. Only when I felt certain we wouldn't be caught in an avalanche did I grab Cielo's hand and pull him to a panting stop.

We turned and found that the mountain was now a crater, puffing granite dust.

As if that wasn't enough, my body announced that it was

not delighted at being cut off from the pleasure I had been so intent on. By the depths of Cielo's frown, I gathered that he felt the same.

"Well," Cielo said, surveying the wreckage. "At the very least, we have made our mark on Vinalia."

"People will believe it was an earthquake," I said with conviction that did not sink its roots all the way to my heart. Any strega who saw the remains of that mountain would know it had been touched by magic. I hoped the Capo hadn't been able to recruit new streghe who would be able to track us.

I could not keep my magic quiet anymore.

The hazelnut fields on the route to Alieto were home to rows of skinny trees, their bodies split into forked trunks. We were headed west, even though I knew that our true business lay to the north. The sight of those soldiers had turned the war from a vague danger looming over our heads to a blade poised at our necks. But Cielo was right—streghe didn't have a good enough reason to come out from the shadows and fight.

"If we could get the five families on our side, the streghe would follow," I said, my mind refusing to let go of the grand plotting that might save us. My magic had grown to epic proportions, and my scheming rushed to keep up.

"If you could get the five families on your side, you never would have left the di Sangro castle," Cielo reminded me.

The five families would rather let the Capo crumble

Vinalia to ruins than accept women as leaders, and streghe in their ranks. Cielo was as honest as he was frustrating, and what's more, he didn't seem to notice. He was sniffing at the hazelnut trees as if they might yield lunch.

"Father could be won over if he felt it was safer to live openly as a strega," I said. "There's no way he's the only one in the five families with magic. There must be others who are hiding it, like I was for half of my life." And I might be able to help them live openly, without paying as steep a price as I had. "I'm sure there are others. Think of *the brilliant death*."

"And the bodies that pile up wherever the five families take a stroll," Cielo added.

I swerved around the obvious invitation to fight. "Sniffing out streghe in these little towns has given us practice. We could do the same with the five families, and then Father would have no ground left to deny his magic. All I need is a meeting of the families, some kind of wartime conference or festival or . . ."

"Wedding?" Cielo asked.

"Yes. Exactly."

The strega's nose scrunched in a highly suspicious manner.

"What do you know?" I asked, turning the force of my attention on Cielo, and leaking magic. The trees around us no longer bore leaves, but a collection of knives that glistened under the midday sun.

"Well, that's a new form of intimidation," Cielo said sotto voce. "While you were busy talking to that strega who changes warts into wishes, and wishes into warts, I *might* have been at the tavern, and over a very nice plate of boar ragù I *might* have heard that a daughter of the five families is to be married in three days."

21

"That could be any number of girls," I said, though my mind stuck to one with the stubbornness of a thistle. Cielo gave me a look that said he knew more than he was telling. "Even if Mirella is the one getting married, you know I can't go to my sister's wedding. I would kill Ambrogio all over again."

"That is where the story takes one of those interesting turns that spits you out into an entirely new landscape," Cielo said. "Mirella isn't marrying Ambrogio Otto. If the gossip of a slightly drunk traveler and a barely interested tavern keeper is to be believed, a girl who has recently given birth to an Otto baby is marrying an altogether *different* son of the five families who lives in Castel di Volpe."

"*Vanni?*"

"It looks that way, if you squint at it hard enough."

Vanni Moschella was not the worst of the young, newly minted family heads I'd met in Amalia, but when I tried to pair his bright red hair and merry ways with my darkly lovely and ever-careful older sister, my imagination stumbled. Of course, I had no way of keeping up with the changes in my sister—or any other di Sangro, for that matter—since our lives had been blasted apart. I had moved away from my old self in leaps during that time, my magic and my days utterly transformed.

Why shouldn't Mirella, who was newly a mother, be several degrees different by now?

Frustrated at knowing so little about my family's lives, I swung back to Cielo. "You knew that my sister was about to be married to Vanni Moschella, and you didn't say a thing?"

"I thought it would dredge up the muck of certain memories," Cielo said. "Things that you didn't wish to dwell on."

Father.

My hand went to my neck, where I used to wear a small ring of iron on a leather cord—a shard of Father's magic. It had been formed on the night my mother died. Father's healing powers had failed to save her after she gave birth to me. When his heart broke, so did his magic, creating the shard: a trapped piece of his power that anyone could use.

It would have helped me to feel it there now.

But how could the memory of his cracked heart heal mine? The great Niccolò di Sangro had loved me enough to want me as the next head of the family but not as a strega. Not when the world saw me as a daughter instead of a son.

I'd given away Father's necklace to help Cielo in Amalia. One more piece of my life, my story, that I would never get back.

But for the first time in months I felt hope stirring through the broken shards of my life, looking for new ways they might fit together. If I found streghe within the five families, I might be able to convince Father to finally accept his magic, giving his healing abilities a chance to flourish. And if that worked—who knew what was possible?

"Cielo," I said, "how do you feel about weddings?"

"I've never been to one," he admitted. "Streghe don't have great big affairs that are aired like so much laundry. But a wedding *night* might be interesting. I've heard there's infinite carousing, and everyone ends up in someone else's bed." Cielo gave me a smile that made his hopes clear. More than clear, in fact—vivid. The memory of what had almost happened under the mountain came back in relentless, dizzying detail. My thoughts burned as I pictured all the ways we might make use of an actual bed.

"This is a five families wedding," I said, letting us both

down before our hopes built past reason. "There will be drinking and dancing, but you're more likely to find a knife in your throat than a visitor in your bed."

Cielo sighed, then waved a wilted hand. "Two out of three will suffice." And with that, he whirled off his cloak and drew a new constellation of silken threads, a shining road to Castel di Volpe.

☽✦☾

THE MOSCHELLA LANDS RAN AS FAR NORTH AS THE BOLD ROCK faces of the Neviane, but in the south they were capped by the long, placid stretches of Lake Dietà. Cielo and I reached its shores as night smothered the day.

We camped by the lake, just inside the bounds of the woods. Cielo turned into a fire and burned a quick supper of fish, and then we formed a warm nest of our cloaks and traveling packs. The strega slid close to me, but I feared that if I slept with my body where it preferred to be, pressed against Cielo's, I would burn with magic and we would wake up beside a lake of flames. I kept a careful space between Cielo's back and my chest, filling it with frustrated sighs.

When I woke, I felt cold and slightly irritated, but at least the lake was properly blue.

Cielo—who had slipped back into girlish form—joined me at the water's edge, pitching a small stone that broke the surface of the water. It healed over in an instant, a property that my soul envied.

"Lake Dietà is known for its brilliance," Cielo informed me. "Though, much like dazzlingly bright humans, it becomes hard to look at for long."

"It's a good thing we're not terribly smart," I said, thinking of what we were about to attempt, breaking into a wedding hosted by the five families. Declaring that I was a di Sangro would only get me killed faster if a guard loyal to the Moschella family chose not to believe me. "Do you think we should approach Castel di Volpe by land or water?"

"I think we should go to Alieto, which I've made as clear as the finest Amalian glass." Cielo's hand lit on my shoulder, a nervous bird ready to fly at the first sign of trouble. "But I know how much it means to make peace with your family."

"This isn't about my family," I said. "This is about saving all the streghe in Vinalia."

Cielo gave me a look she had refined until it was both dubious and attractive, eyebrows round as triumphal arches.

"Well?" I asked. "What's our best approach?"

I hated giving over the reins of a scheme, but Cielo knew the Moschella territory better than I did. With the exception of the Uccelli, Cielo knew *all* of Vinalia better, thanks to a patchwork childhood spent in the homes of many streghe, while I had been shut in the di Sangro castle like a treasure in a stone box, hoarded and kept safe. That sort of safety did me no good now. I had been able to survive the Capo's court, but while traveling in the open country I often felt as useful as a slipper carved from marble.

"We should go over the lake," Cielo said. "Not as fishermen, though. I don't look good in those big, dour coats or the flapping hats they wear." Cielo pulled out the book. "Do you think you can still manage a reversal?"

My magic ached to try it, but I'd just seen that a loss of control could be catastrophic. If I used the same power to change myself, the results might be even worse. Unless I made these inherited pieces work together, I could crumble like that mountain had.

"Can't you change me yourself?" I asked. Cielo had used a reversal on me in the Uccelli, an intimate bit of magic that I was eager to re-create.

The excitement on Cielo's face was immediately doused. "That sort of fun is exactly what triggered your last outburst of magic, and I doubt you'll want to draw eyes to your sister's wedding."

"I'm not sure I can . . ."

Cielo had already turned away and was opening the book with a *flick*. I knew that sound so well, and the way it seemed to make the world shiver in anticipation. In Cielo's place, a rush of blue-gray-green water unspooled down the rocks, flowing toward the lake. The leather book bobbed along the surface.

Cielo made it look so simple.

"Fine," I muttered. "Let's take this one step at a time." The first thing I needed to work a reversal of my magic was a reflection. I took a few steps to the water's edge and looked down at myself in a shallow pool crowned with sharp rocks. The girl beneath my feet bore a scattering of deepest brown beauty marks on sun-browned skin. The lines of her arms and legs were hardened by travel. She had wide hips, abundant nutmeg-colored hair, a rocky slope of a nose. Until I'd learned to change myself with a reversal, this body had bothered me. Now I had a fond spot in my heart for its softness, its stubbornness.

"Next step," I said. "Distance."

I had to think of this reflected image, not as myself, but

as another person altogether. That girl in the pool *was* a stranger in some ways. She was no longer a di Sangro since she had left her home in a whirlwind of defiance and disgrace. She spent her days seeking out allies instead of her family's enemies. She only had two things left to her name: Cielo, and the magic simmering under her skin.

"*Change this person, please,*" I said. Carefully. Politely. I didn't want to demand more of Delfina's magic than the world had already taken. I didn't want Azzurra's magic to balk at a show of disrespect. And what of all the other streghe who had been lured in by the Capo? I could only imagine how angry my magic would be if I'd died for his cause.

Power overtook me, fierce and rushing.

What if I became an ocean and drowned all of Vinalia? What if Mirella's wedding was swept away to sea?

I felt a snapping, all of the stays on a corset loosed at once. But the corset was my body, and I flowed away from it, joining the rest of the water.

Now that I'd worked a reversal successfully, I was upset that I'd waited so long to try. I loved being free like this, neither girl nor boy. There was so much waiting past the boundaries of what people understood, past the lines of the body I was born in.

Traveling in this form was loose and light, with a sense of blurring at the edges. I felt myself split around the rocks and creatures of the lake, always coming back together. I avoided the wooden hulls of fishing boats and kept moving until I reached a finger of land crooked out into the water. At the very end was a castle.

I pressed toward it, and at the same time the hands of memory pulled me backward. The di Sangro castle was different in every detail—spilling and sprawling where this was neat and trim, round battlements where these were in the swallowtail style—but they called to me in the same voice, speaking of home and comfort, banked fires and pots simmering with broth. There was one true difference: the di Sangro castle no longer stood.

Azzurra's magic had ended it.

The magic I now carried.

I shivered against a thread of cold in the water. In this form, I could feel the edges of myself as well as the currents that moved through me. I could feel that Cielo was flowing behind me now, a rush of water following in my wake.

My human senses weren't entirely gone—I was both water and Teo at once. I could smell fish and see the approaching walls of the castle. I could point myself toward a series of small half-moon openings along the bottom of the walls, where water flowed in to be used by the castle servants. Each opening was fitted with a grate, and though few would ever have cause to see the ironwork, it looped and flowered in a way that Fiorenza, my beauty-loving stepmother, would have appreciated.

No matter where I went or what form I was in, I brought her sense of *the brilliant life* with me.

I slid over and around a grate. After a plunge into damp and darkness, I became part of a small underground river diving below the castle. The passage was low, the water pushing its narrow way through the dark until it reached an open room with a high stone platform on one side. I let go of the reversal and came back into my girlish body with a cold shock. The platform scraped against my fingertips, but the current had the hold of a cruel lover, ripping me away. I reached, arm over arm, against a tide that slammed the river into another iron grate.

"Cielo," I said, pulling myself up onto the stones and seeking out anything that could be used to cover me. "We made it."

The underground river spat out Cielo's book, and the cloak followed, wet silk splayed on the stones. Cielo appeared last, caught in the current of the river. Girlish body, then boyish, struggling toward the stone platform, dragged down by changes that came too quickly to be controlled.

"Hold steady," I said.

My body, racked with cold, told me not to get back in the water. I resisted its good advice, dipping down to my waist and straining every thread of muscle until Cielo and I were almost touching. Our fingertips brushed, but then he changed again and went under. Cielo came back up in girlish form, halfway to the grate. If she reached it, she would bash mercilessly into the iron.

I had seen Cielo flick back and forth like this only once, when facing painful memories of her mother. "Tell me what's wrong," I shouted.

"Your family," Cielo gasped.

"They won't harm you!" I promised. "We don't actually stab everyone we see."

"It's . . . not that," Cielo said, fluttering back and forth in a single moment. "I have to *meet* them."

Understanding came, an overwhelming wash of sadness. "And you don't know who to be."

Cielo nodded, and her chin dipped below water level. I wanted to tell Cielo that my family would see one truth no matter Cielo's outer form—that I loved the strega deeply—

but as her body sped toward the metal grate, those words dissolved on my tongue.

My family hadn't accepted me as I was. How could I promise they would accept Cielo? They had been willing to break my heart, and I was one of their own.

"*Please*," I begged my magic in the moment before Cielo met the grate. "*Something soft.*"

The magic turned the water around Cielo into a tangle of soft blue-green bedsheets, saving Cielo's body from the worst of the impact. She still met the grate with a dull thud, shaking the bones of the Moschella castle.

Guilt trampled Cielo's usual proud expression.

Footsteps sounded on the stone stairs, and I threw Cielo's cloak over me as a trio of guards came into view. The five families had anticipated trouble at the wedding. Did they fear Beniamo's arrival as much as I did? Or was it Ambrogio and the Otto family they wanted to keep away?

The guards took in the scene in front of them—one girl in a flimsy cloak, another in the river, one shoulder up against the grate, her pale body swirled up in blue-green sheets.

I gave them a quick eyeing as well. Hired guards came in three categories: the eyes, ears, and hands of the five families. Here was one narrowed set of eyes, slicing the room to the smallest morsels of information. Here was a slight man who walked without sound, gathering the gossip that the world was always offering up, if you knew how to listen. And here was a thick set of fingers, ready to wrap around the nearest neck and squeeze.

The last of the three men moved to the edge of the stone platform, offering a hand to Cielo and pulling her in with ease. Cielo drew away from the man as soon as she reached the safety of the platform, wiping the places he'd touched her as if they were slicked with slime. "How generous of you to save me from drowning before cutting my throat."

"What do we have?" the ears asked, his voice soft as combed velvet.

"I am the bride's sister," I said, claiming all of their attention, mostly to keep it away from Cielo.

"Why didn't you take the bridge?" the ears asked.

"I didn't wish to be obvious," I said. "My arrival is a surprise and using the bridge in plain sight of the tower Mirella resides in—the one with the view of the church and the town below—would have ruined it." I had made a calculated guess about the rooms Mirella would choose, based on the one she'd picked in our own castle and the assumption that Vanni wanted to please her.

The guards traded looks.

"She talks like one of them," the ears whispered.

"But she doesn't wear their color, and there's no token to show she's di Sangro born," the eyes said.

"You don't think *she's* the one they're talking about?" the ears asked. Those words plucked at the air, sending ripples that hit my cold skin and raised bumps.

"Too pretty to be one of those magic types," the eyes said, as if he had the right, given by God himself, to decide how pretty I was—and what that meant I could or could not be.

The magic slid viciously under my skin. "If I'm not a di Sangro, and I'm not a strega, what would you call me?"

The ears slid over to me, peeling back the corner of the damp cloak and helping himself to a generous glance of my body. "Good enough for the night."

"I'll take the tall one," the eyes said, with a thin slit of a smile. "To the wedding, I mean."

The two men laughed as the one with two cuts of raw meat for hands waited to be told what to do.

Cielo nodded over the head of the rather short man standing in front of me. "You have my permission to turn them into mushrooms," she said. "Not the delicious truffly sort, either. Short, damp, foul smelling."

I whirled toward Cielo, my bare heel slick on the stones. "I don't need permission. I do like your idea, though."

The guards drew their knives, and I savored the moment when it became clear they had no clue where to point them. They could draw forth my blood, but they couldn't cut out my magic. It was firmly knotted to my entire being.

I turned to the eyes first, eager to put a stop to the way he stared at Cielo. Magic flew from me, and where the man had stood, a hundred tiny mushrooms—with dark gills and caps as white as fear-bright eyes—sprouted between the stones. In the time it took me to blink, they spread. Soon they would overtake the room.

Cielo sent me a coded stare, asking if I was worried.

I looked to the ears, who had started to beg softly for mercy.

"Carry this message to the leaders of the five families," I said. "Eyes, ears, and hands might seem like plenty of protection. But what if your enemy can look like anything, sound like a rustle of wind in the tapestries, and slide out of your grasp?"

The ears turned and ran, his feet soundless on the stones.

I spun to the last of the three men. "Now," I said to the hands, who was slowly backing away, palms folded and raised to heaven as if someone up there might help him. "Since I've proven I'm the strega the five families are whispering about, take me to my sister."

❦

As it turned out, I had chosen wisely. Mirella kept a small set of rooms in the Moschella castle, in a tower that did not point out toward the lake but cast its gaze over the town. Castel di Volpe was a fishing village woven from stone streets, with roofs of overlapping white and sienna tiles that bore patches of mossy green.

"Is this really your sister?" the guard asked, ready to cuff my arms at a single word from Mirella.

Her face was a lantern, pure brightness against the gray cast of the afternoon. Mirella's sisterly love was a nearly blinding force—and so was her disappointment in me. They shone together, and I wondered if I could ever change the way she looked at me, since I'd drawn disaster down on the di Sangro castle and then run away.

She would not care that I had to save the streghe of Vinalia. Mirella would tell me that family should come first. Standing in her presence, shivering from love and regret and the frozen caress of an underground river, I nearly agreed.

She nodded at the guard, dismissing him. Then she slid a single hair back into place in her long, elaborate braid. "You're here, Teodora," she said, as if those words were highly volatile, a compound in one of Luca's less safe experiments.

She paced as one of our cousins, a di Sangro I vaguely remembered playing with as a child, rushed to adorn Mirella's face with powder. "Let's pretend that your appearance will make everyone gathered today delighted, because it is my wedding and I will *tell* them they are delighted."

Cielo leaned toward me. "I feel like I understand you fully now," she said in a dizzy whisper. "It's like finally seeing a book sitting on the shelf with the rest of its series."

Mirella marched forward, too caught up in her own pronouncements to pay attention to Cielo. "Let's also ignore, for the moment, that the five families have declared this a day free from streghe and magic."

"What?" I cried. "Were they trying to keep me away?" I choked down the next question—*was this Father's doing?*

"Not everything in heaven and earth is about you, Teodora," Mirella said, with a sweetness that cut against her words, honey and vinegar in the same bite.

"Interesting," I mumbled. "A few scant months ago, I would have said the same about you." Mirella's wedding to Ambrogio had been the center of our family's lives for almost a year, the sun around which everything else revolved.

Of course, I had ruined that as surely as I'd crumbled the castle itself.

Mirella sat down on a beautiful chair, each leg carved into the likeness of a fox that could be seen echoed throughout Castel di Volpe. "The ban against magic was decided by four of the five families, the Otto family being left out of this happy occasion." The control in her voice was impressive, but she would not meet my eyes.

"Ambrogio must be . . . irked," Cielo said, "if we're all using our talents for understatement." The strega was as good at holding back her honesty as I was at bottling my magic.

Mirella stood, and though her height was not great, and her body had taken on a sweetly curved shape from carrying a child, her expression was so severe I thought even the Order of Prai would fear her. "If you speak that name again, I will have you thrown out of my sight. I don't care how much magic you have at your disposal, Cielo Malfara, and I don't care who your uncle is, either."

I had never seen Cielo turn such an unnatural shade.

"I wish Mirella would lend me a canvas," I whispered to the strega. "I should paint you right now. Goddess, wearing a bedsheet and a face of pure mortification."

"How do you know my name?" Cielo asked, shaking off my teasing words and getting back to the mysteries at hand.

"We might not get our gossip fresh in the Uccelli, but it does reach us eventually," Mirella said. "Stories of how you two escaped Amalia were the centerpiece of every passeggiata for a month."

Cielo's anger turned her beautifully righteous—even as her bedsheets slipped a bit. "If everyone knows a di Sangro daughter is a famous strega, why the decision against magic?" she asked, a challenge rising through her voice like steam.

"The families wish to make sure that my match to Vanni is free from *influence*," Mirella said.

"You mean, unlike the one to Ambrogio?" I asked, catching on ten seconds later than I should have. I was out of practice at the art of insinuation. Father must have told everyone that Ambrogio had used his association with the Capo and his streghe to lure Mirella into bed. If magic had been involved, it gave her a window to escape her engagement, where most families would have forced the marriage as quickly as possible.

I had to admire this plan for its brilliance in releasing Mirella from an unbreakable bond to a horrible man, as much as I loathed the light it cast on the magic of streghe. Is this how people would treat us now—blaming us for their own troubles, twisting our magic into excuses, and then calling *us* untrustworthy?

Two parts of me tugged against each other, causing magic to rise in a flash flood. I bit down on my lip, and the ground beneath my feet grew slippery. With a glance down at a fast-spreading stain at the hem of Cielo's cloack, I realized that I'd melted the carpet into water. Mirella snatched herself back, gathering her dressing gown and glaring at me.

My di Sangro cousin, who had been trying to stay invisible in the corner, looked down at the floor with a hand held to her mouth.

"Don't look so scandalized," Cielo warned my cousin, "or Teo will turn you into a little boat."

"You'll do nothing of the kind," Mirella said, moving to an ornate wooden crib in the corner. "You will not use magic today, not until the moment you leave Castel di Volpe."

I thought about the true reason we'd come: to find streghe and recruit the aid of the five families. We didn't exactly need to use magic to find them, just Cielo's heightened sense of who *carried* magic. "I can agree to that."

"You are here today as my sister," Mirella said as she lofted a set of blankets from the crib. "And his godmother." She angled the bundle toward us, and I was caught unguarded by the sight of a newborn's face. He scowled at me with eyes that reminded me, startlingly, of Luca's—not yet deepened to brown, but already solemn. I could not see Ambrogio in him at all. He had been overwhelmed by di Sangro features.

Mirella settled the bundle of blankets and baby in my

arms. "His name is Luciano di Sangro," she said, with dazzling pride.

"Luciano," I repeated, my voice scratchy with the wool of some emotion I could not name. Ferocious happiness balanced with the invocation of our half brother, Luca, buried in a roadside grave, and our mother, Luciana, a woman I did not remember and yet loved with all my heart. So many pieces of our family were tucked away in that name. It made me feel like a di Sangro again, even though I'd banished myself. But godmothers were no small business in Vinalia. Had Mirella gone against Father's wishes to choose me? "How can I be his godmother? Hasn't he been baptized yet?"

"We've made it part of the wedding ceremony," Mirella said.

"What if . . . what if I hadn't come today?"

Mirella put a hand on my shoulder, as if she was proving to herself that I was solid—and standing still long enough to accept. "Here you are." I marveled at her trust in me, and at the same time guilt grew thick vines in my chest. Mirella could never know the true reason I had come here today. I wished that celebrating her marriage and Luciano's birth were the only two items on my agenda, but my life was not that simple.

"We will add Vanni's name after the wedding," she said, bobbing the child and putting her nose to his smooth, perfect cheek. "This boy was born a di Sangro, and Father wants to keep it that way."

"Of course he does," I muttered. After I refused to stay in the Uccelli, in a body that looked boyish enough, Father desperately needed an heir.

I looked back down at Luciano to find his gaze fixed on

Cielo's face. She was beaming an astounded smile at the baby.

"Who are you to my sister?" Mirella asked, finally swinging her attention back to Cielo.

"I am whoever will be allowed to attend your wedding at Teo's side," Cielo said.

Mirella blinked at Cielo's use of my family nickname. "And you trust this person absolutely?" she asked me.

"If I didn't, would she be standing so close to your son?"

Mirella nodded and took the baby back from me, babbling at the tiny child in an invented language—or perhaps the oldest language of all. Luciano grabbed for a strand of Mirella's hair that had fallen free.

"I have to keep up with preparations," she told me, and then nodded to our cousin. "Sofia, will you show them the way to the thermal baths? And make sure they're given suitable clothes for the evening?"

The three of us left the room. As soon as the door closed, Cielo flickered back to boyish form. Apparently, my strega was still nervous. Sofia stared at Cielo's body, less with the look of a devout woman witnessing a miracle than the appetite of a starved traveler sitting down to a good supper.

"Oh, I've done it again, haven't I?" Cielo flickered back into girlish form, and Sofia's eyes lingered.

"To reach the baths, you take the back stairs and the walk that circles the castle," she said without moving her gaze an inch. "I'll have dresses sent after you."

"How will you fit us?" I asked.

"I've been a seamstress as long as I've been able to hold a needle, Signorina," she said. Even if this cousin ranked below us, I found the use of a formal addresses ill-fitting. I had just slept in the open country the night before. Traveling as a strega made me want to shed as many layers of pretention as possible.

"Call me Teodora," I said, stopping short of offering Teo. I did not want her feeling *too* familiar, not with the way she was wolfishly devouring the sight of Cielo.

I pulled Cielo down the hall, toward the stairs. "We've found our first strega," she whispered.

"Mirella?" I asked, hope welling fast. It would be a blessing to have my sister at my side as I faced the Eterrans and the Capo.

"Not even a bit," Cielo said. "That girl with the powder puff and the di Sangro scowl."

"The one who was looking at you with her eyes leaping out of her face?"

"Was she?" Cielo asked, smoothing her bedsheet as if it were the latest fashion from Vari.

A small growl formed in my throat. I wanted an army of streghe, not an army of Cielo's admirers. "At least we have one potential alliance in our pocket, and that was *before* you bathed," I said. "Let's see how many streghe you can lure when you don't smell like the bottom of a lake."

3

The thermal baths that lay within the walls of Castel di Volpe were lush with steam, scented by jasmine blossoms, and they somehow made mud seem like a luxury. As Cielo and I were both in girlish forms, we were allowed to bathe together.

The sight of Cielo's body dipping into the slate-gray pools sent me into a haze of pleasure, thick and warm enough to rival the mist that rose from the water's surface. Only the presence of other bathers stopped me from slipping toward Cielo and finding my watery way into her lap.

When we were finally roused from our places to make way for new bathers, I found a red dress waiting for me. A servant helped me step into a lace skirt that had come all the way from the country of Sevice, and then laced the front and back of a matching corset.

I finished first and waited for Cielo to dress, looking past the castle walk out to the lake. Did the five families have guards along the shore? Even as I savored the feel of the gorgeous dress against my skin, I calculated the number of men that would be needed to keep my brother away. He had been vicious when he was only a boy. Now he had the senses of an owl and a taste for heartless killing.

Cielo's voice rose from the other side of the door as she dressed. "You know, I rarely have patience for these garments. They're so fussy, I start to feel fussy, as if the property has passed from the dress to my skin. But I suppose there's not much to be done about it, unless you think Mirella will let me wear boots to the wedding? No one will see them under the bell of this skirt. It could swallow a continent." There was a groan, and I wondered if Cielo had been attacked, or only fastened into a tight set of buttons. "As deeply charming as it is on you, I'm glad that I wasn't made to wear di Sangro red. That bloody hue would make me look like one long gash." She emerged, fiddling with the low-cut neckline of her dress. The velvet was so soft, it called out to my fingers. My canny seamstress cousin had chosen a green that verged on black, the color of the deepest woods, making Cielo's skin shine like snowy fields. The skirt was studded all over with seed pearls.

"You look . . ." My throat corked itself, and my breath was trapped.

"Like a noble pincushion?" Cielo finished.

That was the moment Father overtook us on the castle walk.

If I hadn't been keeping track of the time, I would have believed he was ten years older than when I'd seen him last. His hair had both thinned and grayed, turning almost as cloudy as his expression.

"Teodora?" he said. That one word, in his most deeply suspicious tone, told me that he'd been convinced his second daughter wouldn't come to the wedding. It felt like even now, as I stood in front of him, Father wasn't sure I was who I claimed to be.

I'd ruined his picture of me, the one I'd been drawing my entire life: the portrait of a loyal daughter who cared only for di Sangro matters.

The impossible truth was, I still cared about those things. But I could no longer pretend they were all I wanted.

My eyes stayed impressively dry. "Father."

I thought we would have an encore to the discussion that had chased me away from the di Sangro castle—or else Father would inform me that he no longer needed my services now that Luciano had been born. Instead, he gathered up all of his displeasure and dumped it on Cielo. "So you are the one who stole my daughter."

Cielo's cheeks pulled into a tight, false smile. "Oh, Teo did all the stealing. I only lit the capital city on fire for her."

Father clearly had no response prepared for that. He slid his jaw to one side, then the other, making us suffer his silence. Then he mumbled something about finding Fiorenza and went on his stormy way down the castle walk.

I let out a low hiss of a sigh. Father and Cielo had met, and we had lived to tell the uncomfortable tale. I could only imagine what Father would have added to his accusations if Cielo had been more boyish in appearance. Which showed how little Father knew me—Cielo was just as dangerous to my virtue in this form.

We walked past the castle and toward the ancient-looking abbey. Guests were streaming in from all directions, and I found my little sisters, Carina and Adela, weaving around people like bright ribbons. Adela was still as tiny and commanding as ever, but Carina had taken a leap toward womanhood in the months that I'd been gone. I startled to see how the dark red dress of her childhood pulled at certain necessary seams.

Everyone flowed into the abbey and found seats in the shining walnut pews. The nave of the church was enough to fit both the entire Moschella and di Sangro families, important members of the Rao and Altimari clans, and half the village of Castel di Volpe.

Mirella and Vanni stood at the altar, Mirella's face covered in a heavy fall of lace. Vanni's was bare and shining under his red curls. His soft brown eyes glowed as he stared at my sister—and nowhere else.

Vanni loved her.

It came as a welcome shock, settling through me like a sip of mulled wine when I had expected cold water.

Cielo swept a glance over the crowd. "Should I be looking for streghe?"

"Not now."

I wanted to watch Mirella's wedding, even if the scene left a scraped hollow where my heart should be. I didn't understand the pain at first. My sister was marrying well, and I was escaping the fate of a di Sangro daughter, the sort of narrow match I had never wanted. But it was a cruel twist of the knife, knowing that I would never be able to stand with Cielo like this, in front of my family and all the world, as well as God. The church would never marry two streghe.

There was so much Cielo and I would never have, simply because of who we were. *What* we were.

And I wanted to marry Cielo. Not today, but someday.

Not with quite so much pomp, and yet, I wished to be sealed together with the strega in an unbreakable way.

"Are you all right, Teo?" Cielo whispered. "I know the whole thing is a bit tedious, but you look like you're in actual pain."

My eyes grappled with selfish tears. My hand reached for the strega's, even though I never took my eyes off the ceremony. I didn't want Cielo to know how much this scene hurt me. What if the strega believed that my interest in marriage was a silly vestige of my di Sangro upbringing? Worse—what if it seemed to Cielo that I thought our love was not enough on its own?

The priest called on the godparents of Luciano di Sangro, and I bowed my head as I rushed down the aisle. Usually, godparents were a married couple, but my family would never have accepted Cielo. Instead, I took my place opposite Vanni's next-oldest brother, another red-haired Moschella boy, whose pale skin bore none of Vanni's delicate olive tones. His eyes held the dull fear of a goat that had gotten into the wrong pasture.

I had to curl my tongue to keep from asking how I would raise a child with such a person if the situation arose. The priest intoned sacred words as I dipped Luciano's soft head into the water, and his face turned a deep, painful red. When I pulled him up, he wailed at my betrayal.

I wanted to tell him this was only the beginning of the ways his family would hurt him and call it love. I wanted to promise him he would be safe, that I would fight every power in Vinalia and beyond to make sure of it. Those two feelings staged a pitched battle in my heart, and Mirella and Vanni looked at me with alarm. At first, I thought I had used magic without meaning to, right there at the heart of their wedding ceremony. But it was nothing so damning. My tears had broken free.

I was crying into the holy water.

The priest looked down at me with pity. This priest did not wear the charcoal robes of the religious order that had turned hating streghe into a vocation, but he was still a member of the church that allowed such things. What if he knew who I really was? Would he snatch the baby away from my blasphemous hands?

Vanni's and Mirella's vows came quick on the heels of the baptism, Mirella's head bowed under lace that, for all of its airy beauty, looked stifling. But as soon as Vanni lifted it, her smile came out like the sun from behind a bank of clouds.

I did not know if my sister loved Vanni, but in that moment, her happiness was plain. Still, as I shifted the baby in my arms, I felt an old pain like a stitch that wanted to burst. I was holding my breath, waiting for the moment when Beniamo appeared in the doorway and tore all of this to pieces.

Bells tolled the first notes of celebration. Vanni leaned forward to kiss Mirella with one long, unbroken breath.

❧

FESTIVITIES CASCADED THROUGH THE MOSCHELLA CASTLE, spilling over the bridges into the town beyond. The pounding heart of the party was in the great hall, a place filled with laughter and food and wild dancing.

"It's time now," I said as Cielo and I made the rounds with our wine goblets. She tipped hers all the way back, and

I winced. I knew Cielo felt nervous around my family, but finding a bottomless cask wasn't the solution.

"What about him?" I asked, pointing at Vanni's great-uncle as he passed. "Her?" I whispered, pointing out the Moschella matriarch. Now that I was a strega, I felt eager to claim everyone I saw as one of our number.

"Not a strega," Cielo said. "No, no, absolutely not."

"Who *is*, then?" I asked.

Cielo pointed at the girl who had just come in on the arm of Lorenzo Altimari, head of the family that ran the island of Salvi. His deep brown skin and tight curls glowed in the light of the chandeliers, and Mimì looked wondrous in a bright blue gown. I knew Mimì—not well enough to claim her as a friend, but well enough to wish that I could.

"Really?" I asked. "You're certain?"

Cielo nodded richly, knowingly. "Oh, she's got power tucked away under that gracious manner."

"I don't know how she will feel about being asked to fight for the good of the streghe," I said. "What if her loyalty is to Salvi first?"

"My loyalty is to this wine first, so you will have to ask her yourself." Cielo hiccupped, and I held my breath, afraid that she would accidentally change into a bunch of grapes. When her form held, I let out a small sigh and took my own glass of wine over to greet Mimì and Lorenzo.

Lorenzo clapped me to him, the same way he had when I was the di Sangro heir in the capital—and a boy.

"Teodora," Mimì said, dropping a curtsy.

I couldn't see anything past her brilliant gown and matching smile. The scar running a thin line from beneath her eye, curving all the way to her chin, stood out pale against her dark brown skin. Her hair was pinned in a half circle along the back of her head, a waterfall of tight curls spilling artfully over one shoulder.

"You should call me Teo," I said.

"I've heard that you've been busy since last we met," she said. "I'm sorry that your work has not yet brought you to Salvi."

Did she know what Cielo and I had been up to in the towns we visited? Had she known I was a strega since the night we met at the Capo's ball? When I flicked through memories, I saw she had been warm with me in a way that went past the strict measures of politeness.

Knowing someone was a strega made me feel an immediate bond, a tightening of strings that lashed us together in an invisible storm.

"You missed our betrothal festivities," Lorenzo said, beaming as if the sun needed an understudy.

"Lorenzo finally talked his mother into liking me," Mimì said, but I knew that it was more than that. Lorenzo had been slated for a marriage to a girl from the five families when last I saw him.

Between Ambrogio's betrayal, Father's scramble for an heir, and now this, the families were weakening every day. My loyalty to them flared like an old wound. And yet I could not begrudge Lorenzo and Mimì the same happiness that I'd sought with Cielo.

"We'll have to celebrate all over again," I said. Before I could find a way to bring up the subject of streghe and the impending attack on the pass at Zarisi, Lorenzo shot a hand out to my arm. "Oh, look," he said, with a rare attempt at sarcasm. "Your greatest admirer is here."

He pointed to a table I'd noticed the moment we came into the room, filled with honey-drizzled figs and small olive oil cakes flavored with blood orange, pistachios, and specks of the darkest chocolate. As someone who had lived on a traveler's meager rations for months, I coveted each and every one of those cakes.

But Pasquale Rao was lording over the sweets, looking deeply pleased with himself. Favianne, his bride-to-be, was not at his side. I imagined she was turning the deep blue tide of her stare onto some unsuspecting noble.

I flushed to remember how well that trick had worked on me.

It looked as if Favianne wasn't the only one exploring new flirtations. Pasquale addressed most of his words to a slender girl in a gown of silver, shot through with sunbursts of gold. Her long black hair was set in curls as large and shiny as cut-glass tumblers. The set of her features and the bronze tone of her skin suggested she was Ovetian, or a Vinalian descended from that part of the world. The Moschella lands were the farthest north in Vinalia, and their family did the most overland trading. One of the Moschella men might easily have left in search of fine paper and gold to trade for our wine and bittersweet fruits and fallen in love with an Ovetian woman along the way.

"Who is that girl?" I asked. "I've never seen her before."

"That, my unexpected sister," Vanni said, appearing suddenly to hook his arm through mine, "*that* is Elettra." My stare must have been blank, because he rushed to provide details. "The soprano who gave such fine concerts in Amalia? I thought your sister would want to see her sing."

Vanni had remembered that Mirella craved the sounds of

opera more than the taste of any delicacy or the touch of the finest silk. Another sign that he cared for Mirella better than Ambrogio Otto had ever been capable of doing.

Cielo's hand nipped at my shoulder, and she drew me close to whisper, "In case your sense of magic is overwhelmed by the scent of every fish from Lake Dietà, all of which seem to have been fried for this happy occasion, the singer is a strega."

"So we have Mimì, a cousin I barely know, and a rising star of the Vinalian opera. That won't be enough. We need someone powerful. A key member of the Moschella line, maybe?"

"You act as if the others aren't important," Cielo said tightly. It was easy to trace the strega's bitterness back to the source. Until Cielo had found out that her father was the Capo's brother, Cielo had *been* one of those unimportant streghe. She had lived most of her life that way—in fact, she had preferred it.

"I have to think of things from Father's perspective," I said.

"Well, please inform me when Niccolò has left and I have Teo back again," Cielo said. She turned, casting her eyes over a large number of men with light olive skin, softly molded features, and curly red hair.

"Which of you is the most powerful?" she asked, a little too loudly.

I cuffed her arm with my hand, and she spun back to me, the motion blurry with wine and feeling.

"Are you looking for someone to dance with?" Vanni asked, bounding into our tense moment. "I'd be happy to find you my second cousin Nino, who will dip the courtliest bow you've ever seen or throw you over his shoulder, according to your likes."

Vanni started, realizing all at once who he was talking to—the servant I had kept at my side in the Capo's court. "The last time we met, you were less . . ." Vanni's hands sketched a healthy set of curves in the air. "Well, I'm glad to see you again, no matter what the shape. This is a regular reunion!" Only Vanni Moschella would think to celebrate our week in Amalia as the best of old times. He tipped his glass. "To your health."

"To your wife," Cielo said.

"To Mirella!" Vanni shouted with iron lungs, and the room roared its agreement.

"To the di Sangro women!" Cielo cried, lofting her glass high. "And their particular strain of magic."

The room stopped, everyone paused in the midst of a sip or a word. Even the bows of the violinists paused over their strings.

"Yes," Father said, picking up the toast across the room. "To the di Sangro women, may they all make matches to those who are worthy."

Apparently, my feelings for Cielo hadn't escaped Father's notice, even with Cielo in girlish form.

Fiorenza stepped right in front of Father, stretched her arm to its fullest length, and shouted, "Now drink!"

I took a long sip and coughed. This northern wine had a bite. I muscled it down, hoping to soften the edges of my embarrassment. As I settled my cup on a nearby table, Fiorenza sent me a look that was half apology, half warning that Father's mood was not bound to improve. Father nodded at the musicians, and at the cue of the wise Niccolò di Sangro they began to play an extravagant waltz. Elettra slid into place at the head of the orchestra, and as the music swelled and the cheers of the crowd thickened, the soprano's voice rose above the fray. Her hands moved languidly through the air as her mouth shaped pure, trembling vowels that rippled with vibrato. Each note was clear yet tinted with emotion, like the vibrantly steeped colors of stained glass. I felt, at once, the happiest I'd been in years.

Was Elettra's magic tied to her music?

I grabbed Cielo's arm and pulled her into the dance, coupled with her as the men and women around us whirled in tight pairs.

"What are you doing, Teo?" Cielo asked, a knot of confusion between her dark eyebrows.

"I promised not to use magic," I said, "but that doesn't mean I have to lie about who I am."

Cielo looked fearful and proud. Her steps were a clumsy guess at a dance she had probably never done, so I kept my hands on her waist, taking the man's part as I had at the ball in Amalia. As Cielo and I worked our way across the room in the twisting boxes of a complicated waltz, we passed Father and Fiorenza at the edge of the great hall.

"Who is that stranger cavorting with our daughter?" Father asked.

"Oh, she's *yours* again?" Cielo bit out.

Father didn't catch Cielo's wine-scented mumble, or if he did, he chose to ignore it. I waited for magic to burst out of me or for Cielo to flicker in and out of her body.

Instead, the music broke.

People clapped uncertainly. It hadn't sounded like the end of a song. Elettra's voice held a low, quavering note, and worry scratched at my heart. I grabbed another glass of wine, wishing that I could use magic to change it into a knife. I kept my promise to Mirella, breaking the glass and leaving myself with the lesser weapon of a shattered stem. I waited for Beniamo to storm through the doors, Ambrogio to march in and demand my sister. At first, I did not understand that the room was being overtaken by figures in dark leather.

And then I understood too well.

I had no talent for searching out streghe, but their magic weighted the air. It was like smelling death on the wind, salted and rotten, forcing its way into my senses.

"Soldiers of Erras," Cielo whispered.

These were the streghe who believed that leaving magic unused was a sin against the old gods. I had seen a soldier of Erras in the flesh only once before, the night when Father had killed a man on the stairs, and his magic had passed to me.

"Father," I murmured, running toward him, around the confused and newly terrified guests. He was in great danger if these streghe had come for him, hoping to reclaim the magic that he left untouched.

I shouldered past clusters of people, their sweat from dancing taking on the sharp tang of fear. The great doors were closed by the soldiers of Erras, and my heart banged out an echo. Father was only a few steps away. He stared at me as if we'd reached the last note of our song.

"No," I said. "No."

Hands fastened around me, an unseen person pulling me backward by the waist. I dragged my heels and rioted in this soldier's arms, but I could not change my course. They would grab Father while I was pinned and powerless.

A blade caressed my neck. It did not cut—it did worse than that. It whispered what it wanted.

My life. My magic.

I slid my eyes all over the room and found Cielo held down by two men, knives pointed at her leather book and her heart.

I'd gotten it wrong.

The soldiers of Erras didn't care about Niccolò di Sangro tonight.

They wanted us.

The stranger held the knife at my back, driving me to the center of the room.

Destroy them, my magic said.

The soldiers of Erras had brought magic to Mirella's wedding in order to capture me. I would die sooner than let them hurt anyone.

Their presence carved a circle from the crowd. My family, the Moschella family, and all of their guests drew back. Everyone seemed to know the steps of this dance, without having to be told.

I counted at least three figures clad in leather. One of them pointed a scarred pistol at the crowd. Another ransacked the table of desserts, which I had considered doing only a few minutes earlier. He broke apart the olive oil cakes and stuffed figs and cheese into his mouth, eating with the fury of a man who has left the rules of society far behind.

These were not the well-fed nobles I had feared in the Capo's court. They were lean and hard and hungry. *At least three of them to change*, I told my magic. There were probably more if I turned my head, but the knife returned to its original place at my neck, stealing that possibility.

I would have to abandon my promise to Mirella and use magic. It came with risks. If I wasn't precise, it might change everyone around me, instead of just the soldiers.

The slight woman at my side pressed the knife deeper into my throat until it found my pulse. Even through my terror, I knew that the edge felt strange, unlike any metal I was familiar with. I slid my eyes to look closer and found that it wasn't metal at all but pure bone, carved from blunt form into a sharp threat. I wasn't sure why this strega relied on such a knife instead of her magic. Unless all she wanted was to kill me, using *the brilliant death* to take my power.

Destroy them, my magic said. *Now*.

The throbbing at a single point in my neck overpowered any other feeling in my body.

I called on my magic, and it rose, and gathered, and then—

A steady hiss of the old language stopped it.

Your magic was born as nothing but a little girl's trick, a way to show off for Father, and now that it has grown so much bigger, you have grown smaller. Afraid. You took stolen magic and it's breaking you.

At first I assumed that the strega holding me captive had decided to insult me in the old language—with information a soldier of Erras couldn't possibly know. But there was no voice stirring in the air, no breath hitting my skin. There were only the words in the old language, a steady poisonous drip.

You are powerful and useless, which is worse than being powerless.

The words seemed to be sliding along the blade's sharp edge, cutting through my thoughts, straight to my magic.

Change these people, I demanded.

My magic rustled, shivered, stayed silent.

We need to save Cielo, I implored. *And Father. Everyone we care about in the world, not to mention ourselves.*

But this bone knife had a way to keep my magic from rising up. It held some kind of counter-magic strong enough to subdue the power of many streghe crammed into my body. I thought of the gold ring the Capo wore, the one that could turn magic back into useless wishes. This was different, though. It did not negate the power I sent out into the world. It reached inside of me and stopped me from using it in the first place.

Across the room, Cielo struggled against another white knife. It must have possessed the same strange power. Cielo flickered once—girlish form, boyish form—but as I waited for those changes to gust into a whirlwind, my strega grew sluggish.

And then went unnaturally still.

"Cielo!" I cried, pushing against the knife. A few drops of blood slithered down my neck and into my dress. Everyone around me gasped, drawing my attention away from Cielo and the soldiers of Erras and back to our audience.

My friends, my family.

They were about to watch us die.

"These two have crossed the Capo," the woman at my side called out, her voice as leathery as her clothes, both hard and supple. "We have carved out a deal with this new leader of Vinalia, so to cross him is to cross us."

"And who are you, exactly?" Vanni's mother, the matriarch of the Moschella family, cried out.

"You may call me Dantae," the woman said, the deep stitch of a dimple appearing in her cheek. Her expression would have been a smirk if there'd been any humor in it. "These two," she said, "carry magic stolen from the Capo. He would like it returned."

I almost snorted, but I could see Cielo mocking me already. *You forced your throat into the blade with a snort? What a very di Sangro way to die.*

I settled for a hard roll of the eyes. "That magic was stolen to start with," I said, forcing myself to speak so the room would know—so the world would have the truth. "The Capo tricked dozens of streghe, killed them, and gathered their power."

I hadn't agreed to the Capo's foul deeds, but now their legacy lived in my blood. Unless I used this magic to change things—*truly* change them—I would never forgive myself. The world would stay broken, split along the same old lines. But the bone knife had whispered words that stuck in my softest spots. I was afraid.

To cause more suffering. To lose more than I already had.

My magic wasn't the only thing that had grown beyond measure. So had the possibilities for pain.

"Regardless of how that magic was made, the Capo owns it," Dantae said calmly.

"Is that what it means to own something now?" I asked. "To ruin lives and claim the rewards?"

Dantae shrugged. She clearly did not care about the Capo or his interests—which meant she cared about whatever he was offering her.

"This one . . ." She used the whispering point of the bone knife to flick back the hair around my ear, and then leaned in close. I could feel the presence of her magic beneath the blade's, like a subtle flavor hiding inside of a bolder one.

"The Capo wants to see you punished for crimes against the Vinalian empire."

Empire.

There was the Capo's plan laid bare. He would stir Eterra—the world's most infamous empire—to war. It was the quickest way to prove that he could create an empire of his own. He would sacrifice streghe and their magic. He did not care how many died to bring a Vinalian empire to life.

This was the kind of gutting, greedy magic that some claimed streghe brought to Vinalia. The Capo was not a strega, though. He was simply a man who believed his dream was important enough to pay for in blood and pain and loss.

Dantae turned to face the wedding guests, spinning a circle with her arms outstretched. She was smaller than me in every way, but she had no trouble filling space with her confidence. I wondered if she had been some kind of stage performer before she donned the righteous mantle of the soldiers of Erras. "Do any of you disagree that these two have wronged the leader of Vinalia?"

Fiorenza took a step forward.

My pride and panic twisted into a single wick, burning fast.

They were going to kill her. Dantae took the knife away from my throat, and I felt the point of another at my back, one of her compatriots quick to take her place.

But the knife behind me felt different, duller.

Dantae leveled the bone knife, pointing it at Fiorenza. "Mothers are so predictable," she said with a sigh worthy of the great stages of Eterra.

Fiorenza's amber eyes lit a path to me. She was the mother who had raised me, loved me without question, guided me without faltering. There had been times when I felt guilty for loving her so much, because the woman who gave birth to me had to die for Fiorenza to become part of my life. But I could not imagine it without her. Before I knew there were streghe in the world, I trusted that it held magic because of her. She was the lantern that had come into the darkness of the Uccelli, banishing the deepest shadows from my heart.

When I tried to change the knife in Dantae's hand, to toss magic out of my body like a rope that would save Fiorenza, it fell apart, sad and frayed. The bone knife had a lasting effect—even when it wasn't at my throat.

"You really shouldn't have stepped forward, you know," Dantae said. "Defiance doesn't come for free."

"Name your price, then," Fiorenza said.

I held my breath as Dantae stalked forward. She pointed the knife at the low-dipping neckline of Fiorenza's dress, where it hovered a few inches above her heart. Fiorenza pressed her lips together, but she did not flinch.

Father moved to her side, pale. Could he feel the influence of the knife? What did it whisper to him?

Dantae tapped the flat of the bone knife against Fiorenza's skin. "I'll take Teodora with me today, whether or not you live to see it. But as you have no magic, it would be a wasted death for my people, who need to stay strong more than ever. Now, what would quiet a brave woman like you and keep the others in line?"

Dantae smiled and whisked the blade away from Fiorenza's breast. "The five families are so tightly knit, are they not? I think that today the price will be one of your own." She turned the knife on the crowd, running it along the line of guests, causing a ripple of fear.

She settled on my cousin Sofia, the one who had helped Mirella prepare for the wedding. The seamstress that Cielo said was a strega. Dantae lured the girl forward, beckoning as if the knife were a long, bony finger.

"Here," she said, turning the handle around, offering the blade to my cousin. "Do what you know is right."

My cousin swallowed and accepted the bone handle. Her eyes fluttered, and then a look of concentration washed over her. She was listening. Not to any person in this room—to the knife. Was it asking her to kill me, so Dantae's hands stayed clean?

The girl twisted her grip on the handle, pointed the knife at her own stomach, and stabbed it deep.

As she slumped, my mind blazed a trail back to the memory of Cielo's mother dead by the work of her own knife.

"No," I shouted.

I might not have known this girl well, but she was family twice over—a di Sangro and a strega.

Dantae crouched over the girl where she'd fallen, sweeping a bit of hair away from her face as blood flowered dark on her dress. "Don't fear this moment," Dantae said. "It's the way of things. It's the way of magic." I shuddered at the sight of the knife still in my cousin's gut. At the touch of tenderness in Dantae's voice.

Sofia's wild gasping stopped.

Now that my cousin was dead, Dantae strode over her body, treating it as a simple obstacle. A log in a stream. "This girl's life and her magic are now mine," Dantae announced as she returned to her place at my side. She placed the knife back at my throat, keeping her voice at a hearty volume for the crowds. "Now that you know what we can do—what we can *take*—does anyone wish to continue our argument?"

My eyes went to the other streghe in the room. Lorenzo was gripping Mimì's elbow, looking for a way out. Mimì had gone glassy with fear. Elettra slipped behind several of the orchestra members, only a glimpse of her shining gown still visible, like starlight through the trees.

Now that the bone knife was no longer near Father, fury gathered around his eyes. This was not how his daughter's wedding day was meant to unfold. That di Sangro temper would not give way to sadness—not even if I died. If Father mourned me, he would bury the grief inside of him for years, the same as he did with his magic.

In a single dark moment, I thought of a way we might survive.

"Kill me," I said to the woman at my side, making sure my whisper had enough life in it to reach the crowd. Dantae was not the only one who could put on a show when it was needed. "If you must, do it now."

"I don't remember asking for a final request," Dantae said, clapping on a smile.

"The Capo wants me dead, and I do not want to fight him anymore. I'm not strong enough." The words slicked my mouth with bitterness, and the taste brought me back to the day Beniamo had me on my knees—the first time I had to lie to keep myself safe from the greed of men. I willed my voice to flutter, and it did not take much convincing. "Let me die here, with the people who love me."

Do they? the knife asked as it slid back and forth, anticipating the cut. *Do they love you enough to claim you, no matter what?* My mind went hot with anger that had nothing to do with dying.

"Fine," the woman said. "Kill you here, kill you elsewhere, it's all the same to me."

And with that, she dug the knife across my throat.

The cut was so clean and quick that at first all I felt was a blessed warmth. My blood, rising. It left me in gouts, and then a shocking cold set in. I shook as hard as I would have standing in the Uccelli in the heart of winter, wearing nothing but my red nightdress.

I hit the floor and watched the sideways world, through a flurry of last breaths and strained heartbeats. My blood was eager to cover the floor, pushing its borders farther and farther, a country made of blood, soiling the hems of anyone who stood too close.

My hands went to my neck as if they could push the life back inside of my body.

"Go," I spat up at the soldiers of Erras, my words tainted with blood. "Let me die in peace."

"Fine," Dantae said, her not-quite-a-smirk looming above me. "Easier if I don't have to fight you and that black-haired whelp all the way back to the Neviane, to be honest. Your magic will find me either way."

Did that mean Cielo's throat had been cut too? I writhed to look, but all I saw was a blockade of bodies. I hadn't heard Cielo cry out—but I'd been so occupied with the sound of my own screams.

My pain threatened to steal away all sense, but I fought to keep a grip on my thoughts. How could Dantae be so sure our magic would make its way back to her? Did she have some way of channeling *the brilliant death*? One more thing I would never know unless my impossible plan worked. But that hope seemed far away, like the sound of my own heart-beat fading into the distance.

The soldiers of Erras stepped over my body. I reached for Father, my fingers sticky with my blood. He came to my side.

"Please," I whispered, the word barely making a dent on the world.

Father shook his head. He knew what I was asking for—and he was refusing. My weakened heart took the blow and almost gave way.

This was my plan. This was the *only* plan.

"I don't have enough for this," he whispered, not naming what he could do. He still wouldn't say the word *magic*. Father hadn't trusted his abilities since the day I was born, when he failed to save Mother.

"You didn't let her die," I said. "You tried." I had grown up never asking Father for anything. I had no right. I did not wish to impose on him when the world asked so much. And yet the word crawled up from my wounded throat, pushed itself to my lips. *"Try."*

He touched my neck, coating his hands in my blood, pulling me close as he spoke warm, soothing words. At first, they were a loose scattering of pebbles. I followed the trail of Father's voice, step after step after step.

He was telling me a story.

A strega story.

Meaning dawned on me, as large as the sky overhead, as bright as the sun rising in sharp rays over the mountains.

"'The Bird Prince,'" I said, my mouth sweet and sticky with blood. It had always been one of my favorites. The words brought me back from a smooth, dark place where nothing mattered, nothing *meant* anything. Breath raged into my throat, painful and raw, the kind of pain that proved I was alive.

I staggered to my feet.

Father looked gray and threadbare kneeling in a puddle of my blood. It seemed small now, as if all of the life that had leaked out of me hadn't amounted to much. Everyone in the five families was staring at us. At Niccolò di Sangro.

They knew what he was now—a strega. A healer with a low, haunted voice that could knit bones and skin back together with a story. My little sister Adela looked on with amazement. Fiorenza watched with the steadiness of a woman who had paid close attention to her family and grown immune to surprise. But most were glaring at Father as if he had been lying to them for years, for decades.

He kept his eyes on me. He had never been able to face the judgment of the five families, and today was no exception.

I crossed the room to Cielo. He was huddled around the book, his blood seeping into the pure white pages. His black hair splayed across the floor, as limp as a half-hearted apology. His eyes had gone elsewhere, leaving me behind.

It did not matter how many people surrounded me. If Cielo died, I would be alone.

I whirled back toward Father with a new demand on my lips. "Save him."

"Impossible," Father said, putting his hands to his knees as he rose. I understood his exhaustion, his uncertainty, but there was something else lurking in his tone—a resistance that hadn't been there when I was lying prone on the floor, leaving the world one breath at a time.

"I need Cielo," I said, this moment pushing the truth out, even though I knew my father wasn't ready to hear it.

"This person is leading you astray, Teodora," he whispered.

"You think Cielo is the problem?" I said with a vicious laugh. "The world is ripe with enemies, and you pick the strega who shares my bed to blame?" Father's face hardened. I had gone too far—revealed too much. But I was tired of keeping my story down. Hiding it shamefully, as my magic hid now.

Father shook his head, putting two fingers to the knot at his brow. "Today should have been a simple day. No magic. No death."

Cielo's breath rattled like a key in a lock that didn't quite fit.

"He's in pain," I cried.

And so was I. Losing my strega only months after finding that such a person existed was unthinkable. I could only imagine how my heart would split—the shards of magic that I would leave behind.

Father's nod was heavy with consideration. "I will ease it," he said, spreading his fingers over Cielo's chest. "Make things . . . peaceful."

I ripped his fingers away as another truth knitted itself together. Father hadn't killed that man on the stairs all those years ago just by stabbing him. Niccolò di Sangro was a strega, and on that deep winter night, I had seen him use a reversal. Instead of telling a story that summoned healing, he had offered a deep silence, drawing the marrow out of life.

I would not let him do that to Cielo.

"This *person* is a strega," I said, falling back on a language Father understood—threats. "And not any simple strega.

Cielo's magic is the strongest, most potent, most sought after in all of Vinalia. People will keep coming for us. They will *always* come for us." My own words hit me, a fresh wave of terror.

"All the more reason to keep you safe," Father said, his decision still firmly in place.

"Would you take all that power in when Cielo dies?" I asked, prying wildly at his conviction, no longer in control. "Would you chance it going to someone else in the family? Another one of your children? Your grandchild?" I looked around the room for Mirella and Luciano, but I could not find them in the crowd.

I hated every word of the argument I was making, but to save Cielo, I would say anything. "The last time you let a strega die, I was the one who took on his magic. Do you want that to happen again?"

Father's eyes went wide, as if he'd been poisoned with understanding. As if turning me into a strega—a person so much like him—was the worst thing he'd ever done.

Cielo cried out as his body flicked to girlish form and then slowly changed back. Agony infused Cielo's magic.

Father knelt roughly at Cielo's side. Niccolò di Sangro looked older than he ever had before, and Cielo looked young, a child, as Father spun another strega story for him, a live-giving stream of words. Cielo's long, shadowy eyelashes fluttered.

He looked up into my father's face. I thought Cielo would spit out some remark about how long it had taken Father to heal him. "Signore," he said, voice rusted over. "A thousand thanks."

Father wiped Cielo's blood off his hands and stood. Cielo

bounded to his feet twice as quickly as Father had. I rushed
to him, but Cielo held up a hand, his throat working hard to
swallow. "Before we lose another moment, I need to talk to
those death mongers who call themselves streghe," he said,
"and soil the good name of every cow who died to make their
leather."

"Really?" I felt my face souring. "You always say I'm so
bent on revenge that it will change my shape altogether."

"You are," Cielo said. "But this isn't a matter of revenge.
It's about those knives."

Carina ran through the crowd, breaking past the line
that separated us from everyone else. She tugged at Father's
sleeve. "It's all right, wildflower," Father said, patting her
head, trying to put her fears back in place. "Teo is going to
live, and so is her . . . friend."

"No, no." She pulled Father down to her height. I could
read my sister's lips, white as strawberries picked out of season. "Luciano is missing."

I started running, with death's shadow still clinging to
my heels.

꒰ ❀ ꒱

THE TOWN ON THE FAR SIDE OF THE MOAT MUST NOT HAVE KNOWN
about the trouble in the castle, because festival lights burned
a hole in the dark. Cielo and I split the quiet of the castle
walk with our bootheels and the harsh breath that came of
recently having our throats slit. As we searched for Luciano,
I gathered the facts that had been hard to see with the distraction of a knife at my neck.

The soldiers of Erras had tossed in their lots with the

Capo—he had probably been wooing them for years. Whatever he had promised had to be worth more than the dirty little bargain he'd made with the streghe he stole from the streets of Amalia. The Capo had also courted Ambrogio and won him over with the promise of power and the di Sangro lands. Now, to keep one of the five families in his well-lined pockets, the Capo had said he would reclaim the child for Ambrogio, ripping it away from Mirella. The soldiers of Erras had been sent on two errands tonight: Dantae had put on her little circus of violence while one of the soldiers of Erras quietly stole the child.

"Both bridges to the village have been drawn," Cielo said.

"Of course they have," I said. "It's supposed to be safer that way."

"Did they come in by the lake?" Cielo asked. "Villains always have an array of skills, like seafaring. Although I suppose this would be lakefaring."

I shook my head. "The five families posted guards along the shore."

Cielo's eyebrows danced into a scornful position. "Guards who are immune to magic?"

"There are no sounds of a fight," I said. "But . . . what if there is a secret way for a boat to leave?"

Cielo caught up to my reasoning. "The underground river."

"It flows into the castle," I said. "Where does it come out?"

Cielo took my hand and pulled me along. Our feet scraped the stones of the castle walk, all the way back to the abbey.

"You think they took a quick moment to pray?" I ask. "They're not fond of God, from what I hear."

"Precisely," Cielo said. The smile he gave—an enigmatic

slide of the lips—might have frustrated me on any other day, but I was glad to see it now. Cielo was still alive, still mine. The embers of my excitement crackled to life at the worst possible moment.

The abbey was emptied, silent, the pews shiny with polish, long and inviting. If it hadn't been for Luciano's disappearance, I might have dragged Cielo onto the nearest one and risked damnation.

"We need a way down," Cielo said.

"What?" I asked, still dizzy with thoughts of pulling Cielo to his knees.

"These old abbeys weren't plunked in any old spot, or rather they were plunked in the oldest spots of all. Built on the bodies of temples for the worship of the old gods."

"Yes, yes." I dusted off my di Sangro lessons. "Every temple to the old gods contained a stream so truth could flow from the lips of worshippers to Veria's ears." That underground river must have been the source of the cold, clear water Luciano had been baptized in.

Cielo and I ran through the nave, every sound our bodies made clanging through the empty space. Behind the cold marble stretch of the altar, I found a wrought-iron railing bolted to the ground. A tight spiral of steps led into the damp, breathing earth. My fear closed in as I worked my way down. Cielo stayed a single step behind me.

We emerged into a world of crumbling pillars, many covered in markings I could not read. My knowledge of the old language came from hearing the priest at mass and novena and from the magic that rang through my body. It was all spoken, never set down.

A whisper slid into my ears. At first I thought it was the

bone knife, back to do its sharp work. My hand rose to my throat, finding a single line crusted over with dried blood and throbbing an echo of the pain that had almost killed me. But the knife did not return, and the rush of sound did not settle into words. I took another step into the chamber as it grew more forceful.

Water.

Cielo and I ran forward and found two small boats poised on the underground river's rumbling dark surface. Dantae stood with her heel on the prow of the first boat, the other soldiers of Erras working to untie the knots that held both in place. When Dantae spotted us, her lips went flat. "So that healer had a few breaths in his old lungs. I would have killed him if I'd known he was worth anything."

I would have rushed to Father's defense, but Luciano's cry silenced me. He was nestled in the arms of a soldier on the bank, so deep inside of a bundle of blankets, I hadn't noticed him at first.

Dantae tracked my interest like a bird of prey. "Oh, this is coming with us," she said. "His father wants him."

"Vanni is his father," I insisted—like Fiorenza was my mother. Blood formed a bond, but it proved weak and watery in the face of love.

Cielo shouldered his way in front of me, locking eyes with Dantae across the cavern made of ruins. "Tell me about the bone knife."

"Really?" I muttered. "Now?"

"I need to know," Cielo said, his eyes filled with hard flame.

"You *do* know what the knife is, little strega. Or you wouldn't have that look in your eyes." Dantae sized Cielo up and did not seem to disapprove. I hated it even more than if she had dismissed him outright. "You know, you could have grown up with us," she said. "The soldiers of Erras would have welcomed your magic with open arms."

"You mean the kind that reach all the way around so they can stab you in the back?" Cielo asked, but his muscles twitched.

Dantae's arrow had hit home—or rather, Cielo's lack of any such thing.

"We are a true brother- and sisterhood," Dantae said, with none of the performer's gloss to her words. She had a harsh voice when she wasn't shining it up for the crowds. "Nations rise and fall, men spark and fade. We are the steady flame, always burning. Magic is our common cause; death, our friend and companion. Did you know that once you find a way to invite death into your life, she can never surprise you? And now we have what we've needed for so long. We have the Bones of Erras."

"The Bones of Erras?" I asked. Those words gnawed out a space inside of me—raw, painful, empty.

Cielo clearly had an idea what they meant, because his entire face changed, fear and awe battling each other. "That's nothing more than a story."

The soldiers undid the last of the knots as Dantae's gaze flicked over my body, then Cielo's. "So were you, until a few months ago. What is real is always shifting, but what is true never changes."

"What are we all spitting riddles about?" I asked, even as my heart reached wildly toward Luciano. The man's arms tightened around him, as if he could feel what I was thinking. This standoff could not last forever.

Dantae sighed. "If you come after us, I'll have to throw the little one in the river. A tragic accident, but these things happen when a strega's magic is so wild and untrained."

Dantae would blame *me* for Luciano's death. The idea made my magic rise along with my fury. I feared I would take down the old temple, the abbey, the castle and island it sat on, the whole rotted world.

I fought to get hold of my magic, to spin it into a useful shape, but I knew that if I let it out of me now, Dantae would be right—I could change Luciano without meaning to.

A noise as loud as a cracking heart came from behind me.

I turned to find the snout of a pistol aimed at Dantae. The dragons cresting along the barrel took shape, and I recognized the weapon a second before the young man holding it came into focus. Vanni's red hair dipped across his sweating forehead as his hands plunged into his pockets for another ball to load. The first shot had gone wide, cracking the wall of the temple.

"What are you doing?" I asked.

"It looks like he's shooting at his own baby," Dantae said. "You're sure this is the man you want to steal it back for?"

The sound of feet on the stairs grew into thunder, and then Mirella burst into the temple alongside Vanni.

"Mothers," Dantae muttered. "Every. Damn. Time." She cast off, her little boat disappearing into the dark mouth at one end of the underground river, leaving the second boat to fend for itself.

Vanni's hands shattered the air with trembling as he loaded a new ball into the pistol and pushed the snout back in place. "I can't," he said. "I can't hit the man without hitting the baby, and I can't . . ."

Mirella pulled the pistol out of Vanni's hands, held her arm out at full length, and went as still as an eternally perfect statue. Only one finger moved, sliding the hammer back, pulling the trigger.

The man holding the baby stumbled backward. The ball must have stuck deep in his gut because he clutched himself just below where Luciano was cradled.

In the moment after Mirella killed him, there was only a slight tremble of shock moving through the temple, touching us all. Then the other two soldiers of Erras—one on the boat and one on the shore—leapt to grab Luciano. The man on the shore managed to wrest him away before the dead soldier fell, swallowed by the rushing water.

Without the bone knife or Dantae to interfere, my magic was mine again. The pieces swirled inside of me, blurring into something stronger and more powerful than I could stop. For the first time in months I did not *want* to stop. The fear of losing Luciano rose above every other fear, leaving me with a single purpose. Magic lashed through me like powerful rain, and I looked up to the crumbled ceiling of the temple as if turning my face up to the skies, welcoming the storm.

"Leave the baby," I whispered. *"You can have your way with the others."*

My magic lashed out, toppling the man who held Luciano. It crumbled him to ruins so he would blend with his surroundings. In less than a day, no one would know he had been human.

Cielo ripped into rushing wind form, arriving just in time to catch the baby and drift him slowly, carefully, to the ground. Luciano landed with a small murmur of delight. He was already done crying.

A di Sangro, through and through.

The second soldier of Erras had moved when I loosed my magic, and now he pitched himself headfirst at Luciano. Frantic, I called on my magic again, but before I could give it a direction, the light in the dim underground cavern flew toward Vanni—followed by everyone's stares.

Light pooled around his hands, and when he turned them over, it spun in threads of pale gold. With a cry of mingled confusion and fear, he flung handfuls of light at the soldier of Erras who had remembered his charge and was grabbing for Luciano.

The light hit him square in the chest, and the look on his face was extinguished. He blew out like a candle flame, his body wavering and then falling to the ground.

Mirella ran to the baby, throwing herself down with a cry that filled the temple, a wild prayer to a god even older than the ones this place was dedicated to.

I turned to find Vanni with his eyes wide and his fingers crosshatched over his chest, as if something delicate had taken root there. *The brilliant death* had done its fickle dance, and the dead soldier's magic had chosen Vanni for a partner.

Cielo brushed past me, a wind that shaded back into a boyish body, his side brushing against mine as he whispered, "I suppose you have your high-ranking Moschella man, after all."

Any guilt I felt at this twist in Vanni's fate was overwhelmed instantly, swallowed by the rushing waters of my plan. I had what I needed to convince the five families to fight the Capo.

Cielo strode to Vanni and clapped a hand on his shoulder. "Let me be the one to welcome you to an existence of magic, loyalty, and death. How do you feel about very cold mountains and very harsh generals?"

Vanni's eyes went a notch wider as his legs wilted at the knee.

"Don't worry," I said. "You're in good company."

He fainted just as I was about to call him a strega for the first time.

Two

In the Mouth of the Wolf

The morning after Mirella's wedding was drawn in every shade of gray, from the tainted white of the sky to the smoke that rose from the chimneys of Castel di Volpe in great tatters. In the distance, beyond rolling fields and a swollen river, rose the dove-gray rocks of the Neviane.

I stood on the castle's northern battlements as the wind pestered me, flinging my hair in great handfuls. The stones beneath me felt solid, but I clung to the corner of the nearest swallowtail stone, aware of how eternal my own home had looked before it was taken apart by a vengeful strega.

"Surely you aren't afraid of heights," Vanni said, studying my white fingers on the beige rock. "Why did you want to come up here, again?"

"Strategy," I gritted out.

I had wanted Cielo to come with me, but when I suggested it, the strega burrowed deeper into bed, flickered into girlish form, and insisted that she needed another trip to the thermal baths far more than she needed another tumble with the five families. Cielo had snuck into my bedroom after we returned from the abbey, but for all our talk of wedding night trysts, the only thing we'd had the will to do after nearly being killed by the soldiers of Erras was sleep in a brittle, tense embrace.

"I think you and I are facing the same sort of trouble," Vanni said.

"You mean magic and what to do with it and how to protect everyone we love?" I asked, looking out over the stretch of Vinalia with a fierce sort of adoration, as if I could fold the landscape, gather it to my chest, keep it safe.

"Yes, that, but . . . I was talking more about the aftermath of last night. You're not the only one Mirella is furious with. She won't even look at me. Of course, she won't look anywhere but at Luciano." I thought of my sister, dark hair dipping low like willow branches, curtaining her child from the world.

"She must have some feelings about your sudden dive into magic," I said.

Vanni nodded. I had never seen him look less certain. "I tried to talk to Mirella about what I'd done, how it felt. She wouldn't answer. And when I told her about your plan, well . . . she said I could do anything in the world as long as I kept you away from the castle until she felt safe again."

I felt that slap down to my bones—and most of the pain came from knowing that it was perfectly fair. My sister had lived through Luca's death, the destruction of the di Sangro castle, and now this. She had every right to cast me away. I was the common ingredient in all of her life's worst disasters.

Vanni looked up at the blanketed sky. "I wonder . . ." he said. "Since this magic seems to need a source of light . . ." The night before, Vanni had grasped handfuls of torchlight and turned them into flashing bombs. Now he turned his hand over and over slowly, as if carding wool. Threads of sunlight stuck to him, gathering in his palm until he had enough to fling into the moat below us. A splash the size of a small cannonball rose.

Vanni looked down at what he'd done with the faint traces of a smile.

"That is quite the ability," I said.

"And this happened because . . . what? I stood too close to a strega?"

"We're not contagious," I said with vigor. "And magic doesn't pass to just anyone," I added, forming the conviction as I spoke.

"You think it . . . chose me?" Vanni asked, looking both pleased and terrified. I knew the weight of those emotions. I had lived under their double yoke since I was nine years old. But I hadn't had someone at my side to explain them, to guide me through a world grown lovely and treacherous with magic. I wondered how much it would have changed.

"I just wanted to keep Mirella and the baby safe," Vanni whispered. "That was all that mattered. To keep anyone with foul intentions away from them."

His words latched to my heart, but before I could figure out why my chest was pounding in double time, steps rose on the stairs at the center of the tower. I turned, hoping for Cielo, and found nearly everyone else in the wedding party. It looked like half the contents of the castle had been poured onto the battlements. I had invited them, little cards slipped under their doors with hastily scrawled invitations. Father and Fiorenza, Lorenzo and Mimì, Signora Moschella with her white-streaked hair, and Pasquale with a glower that smeared his entire face. Favianne, his betrothed, was still absent. I'd included her on the card, and yet she wasn't here.

Perhaps they were no longer engaged—but then what had become of her? Was she back in the southern provinces, hunting for a new nobleman?

Elettra wafted up the stairs last, in a slightly less ornate gown than the one she'd worn at the wedding, but still dressed as if she were about to launch into a series of arpeggios instead of a meeting with the five families.

"Did you need something, Elettra?" Vanni asked. "I want to apologize again for what happened last . . ."

"No need," Elettra said, a little too brightly. "I came up here because a girl asked me to. Tall, black hair, talks in abundance?"

Hope glimmered at the edges of my thoughts. Cielo had asked Elettra to come. The strega knew about my scheme to stop the Eterran army—and also knew we would need every strega we could find.

"Teodora, please tell us what this is about," Fiorenza said.

Calling all these people here and pretending I knew what was best, promising I could cobble them together and lead them to some kind of victory, was either boldness or madness. I was leaning toward the latter as I looked around at my small collection of powerful Vinalians.

"This is the first meeting of the streghe of the five families," I said.

Father's lips tightened against the accusation. He'd been revealed the night before, because he had to save me. I was the reason he had to face his magic in the open. I had taken the life he'd so carefully constructed and dashed it to pieces.

"We've learned the truth about Signore di Sangro here, but there are *more* of you unnatural types?" Pasquale asked, crossing his arms tight over his chest, as if that simple motion would keep a strega's magic from striking him again. He did have cause to worry: I had turned him into a shoehorn once, and if he spoke out of turn too many times, I couldn't promise that I wouldn't do it again.

Pasquale took a brisk and measuring look at each of us, immediately starting a hunt. "Lorenzo is a strega," he said. "I should have guessed."

Mimì stepped forward and curtsied to Pasquale, her motions graceful but her face pure steel. "I am the strega of the Altimari family, she who bears the inheritance of the foremother, changer of states, bringer of fire and singer of rain, keeper of the earth and kin to the air."

Lorenzo turned to Mimì. ". . . You are?"

Mimì looked back at him with a tiny valley of annoyance between her eyebrows. "Do you tell me every little thing that goes on with the five families? No. You do not."

"This hardly seems *little*," Pasquale said, wedging into their conversation.

"Shut up," Lorenzo and I offered in chorus.

"I'm a strega," Vanni said, pulling himself up to his full height, which still fell short of his mother's. "Well. As of last night."

Elettra spread her hands over her skirts and took a deep breath. "As you can probably guess from the fact that I'm here, I have magic as well. In Oveto, I wouldn't be called a strega, though. Magic is known as the silver sea, and to use it, you have to be . . . well, it translates to something like a strong swimmer. But I've spent my life in Vinalia since I was eight years old. My magic grew to its full strength here. I suppose that makes me a strega as well."

"That's quite the biography, girl," Signora Moschella said. "All that, and your voice sounds like an angel on the wing."

Elettra winced, then corrected herself with a smile, like brushing velvet against the grain and smoothing it quickly.

I waited for Father to explain his magic like the rest, but he stayed quiet. "You know that Cielo and I are streghe, and my father is a healer." Niccolò di Sangro looked angrier than ever in the stark light of morning, and I wondered if the revelation of his magic had grown worse when he found that the five families, for all of their scowling, had not thrown him from the ramparts or tried to exile him for being a strega. He'd been keeping his secret longer than needed, and that could not be an easy bite to work down.

I swallowed and kept on. "I have also invited a member of each family who is *not* a strega, to be sure that the interests of the five families are fully represented."

"Four families," Vanni corrected.

"The Otto family has not been removed from our numbers," Father said, his diplomacy cutting into the last remnants of my calm. "They are simply not here today."

"Yes," I said. "One of them has *simply* betrayed us and done his best to destroy my sister's life for his gain." I sped on before Father could slide a pretty coat of polish onto such a foul truth. "As representative from Salvi, I have chosen Lorenzo Altimari," I said. Lorenzo nodded his acceptance, though his bewildered eyes were still on Mimì.

"From the southern provinces, I have chosen Pasquale Rao." I wished there had been anyone else to include from the Rao family. Pasquale's hatred of streghe was so strong that it grew pungent, wafting over the entire gathering. If Favianne had been present—and finally married to Pasquale—I would have chosen her instead, though she probably would have staged a coup before I could finish a sentence.

"From the Uccelli, I have chosen Fiorenza di Sangro," I said. Father nodded before Fiorenza had the chance. I was glad that he'd given his blessing, and molten with rage at the fact that she needed it at all.

"And from the northern provinces, I have chosen Signora Maria Moschella." The woman looked at me like I might still be slightly drunk from the festivities the night before.

I waited for an argument to swirl to life, for someone to bring up the untraditional choices I'd made, giving two women the power to speak on behalf of the families. But silence reigned over our gathering. With so many of our men dead—claimed by war and treachery and violent acts of patriotism—apparently women were finally allowed to step into the blank spaces.

"I can promise I'm a family member and not a strega," Signora Moschella said. "The only magic I've got is keeping this castle from crumbling into the lake and stopping my children from killing themselves with pure foolishness."

"Those are no small things," Fiorenza assured her—and I thought of our own home gone, and Luca dead.

"If you want assurances that streghe are safe in the five families and our lands, you have it from me," Lorenzo said. "I'm betrothed to a strega. Apparently." He looked to Fiorenza. "Any advice?"

Fiorenza looked like she wanted to adopt Lorenzo at once, but all she said was, "Keep your wits about you." I realized I had not seen my stepmother's face crack with surprise once since Father was revealed at the wedding party. I wondered how long she had suspected his abilities.

Everyone looked to Pasquale next. He was the link that might break this new chain before it was fully forged. Pasquale's lips shifted, slow and thick with a pout. No doubt he wanted to rage against the disgusting nature of streghe—but with so many present, he had to fear for his own safety. "It doesn't matter what we promise today if the Capo or the Eterrans take all of Vinalia by storm tomorrow."

"Pasquale is right," I said, confused to find those words leaving my mouth. "I believe we can stop both of those threats at once if, with your blessing, I take a small band of streghe to the Neviane." Actually, I would have preferred to take *hundreds* of streghe to the Neviane, but as Cielo and I had learned in our travels, they were as easy to herd as hornets.

Signora Moschella stepped right into the middle of the circle. "My Vanni isn't heading into that battle if the Capo has streghe ready to point their magic at you like those leather-bound bastards just did."

I waved away her fears. "The soldiers of Erras don't believe in the Capo's fever dream of a Vinalian empire. They proved it last night."

"You mean while they were slitting your throat?" Pasquale asked.

My hand flew to the crusted line of blood at my neck. "It's only a trade to them. They're not true believers. They're using the Capo."

Vanni kicked at the nearest battlement. "I'd say *well done* if they hadn't just pissed all over my wedding and tried to steal my son."

Father cleared his throat, and everyone turned to hear the verdict of the great Niccolò di Sangro. I waited for Father to say I had officially gone mad, and he would find me a nice warm spot as soon as the castle was rebuilt where he could lock me away for my own safety. Father's eyes gripped mine and did not relent. "What is your plan, exactly?"

This was the moment I'd been climbing toward, but I knew from experience that the top of the mountain is the sum of its dangers. Besides leaving a person exposed to the elements, the wrong step in any direction meant a long and deadly fall.

I took a breath and treaded carefully.

"The pass at Zarisi is the only place the Eterrans can break through into Vinalia unless they're willing to sacrifice most of their troops to ice chasms and bottomless snow pits. They're counting on being stronger than us, so they don't believe they have to be smarter as well. They'll keep to the pass." Father and Signora Moschella nodded, as if they'd reasoned their way through this much already. "Magic will allow us to attack them from well above the city, without putting us in the path of an invading army."

I looked to Vanni, who I knew was ready to back me. He didn't want the Eterrans running over the country, claiming Moschella lands. And besides, I got the sense that he was eager to test out his new magic. "Teo is right," he said. "We'll be up in the mountains, untouchable."

"I'll go," Mimì said without hesitation.

I wanted to ask why, but I was afraid it would make me look bewildered by her confidence in my plan. I would have to store my questions for later.

"Elettra?" I asked, turning to the glamorous singer, trying to imagine her as some kind of soldier and falling short. "I know this isn't your homeland, but . . ."

"The Eterrans invaded Vinalia at the first scent of magic,"

Elettra said, turning pale under her powder. "They're coming for *us*. Of course I'm going to fight."

"What of the Capo's troops? Aren't they waiting to recapture you?" Lorenzo asked me, breaking his fast of words. He usually let everyone else argue themselves out and stepped in only when he had something of the utmost importance to say. His eyes slid along my neck. "The Capo might care more about getting you back than he does about winning this battle."

Lorenzo was as close to a friend as I'd made in Amalia, but I knew that his concern was only partly for me. If I was taken, no doubt Mimì would be added to the ranks of the Capo's streghe against her will.

"We'll send Cielo ahead to scout every step of the trip, so we'll make it to Zarisi of our own free will. When we win this battle and stop war from spilling into Vinalia, the troops will be turned to our side. The Capo's might has always been his army. Without them, he will have nothing but a title he made up."

"And then what happens?" Pasquale asked with a snort that must have punished his nose as much as it hurt my ears. "We're at war over who should rule Vinalia after he's deposed."

"That sounds dangerously like you prefer the Capo," Father said. Pasquale ducked his head, acting as though Father had pitched a well-aimed stone at him. "Teodora's plan is sound because *if* it works, it rids us of the Eterrans and the Capo in one stroke."

"The Capo started this war himself," Signora Moschella declared. "Let him end it."

I hooked her by the arm and led her to a spot where she could look over the battlements. "These are the fields that will be trampled if the Eterrans break through. These are the first towns that will be taken, the first lives that will be claimed. And they will not be the last."

I hadn't wanted to do this, to make the threat this sharp, but it was pressing on all of us, whether we paid attention or pretended it wasn't there.

My fears drew panicked looks. A shared moment passed, and I could feel a decision settling over the group, like a cloak being cast over my shoulders for a long journey. "The five of you should leave today," Father said.

My triumph lasted as long as it took me to count. Cielo, Mimì, Vanni, Elettra . . .

"What about you?" I asked, the cry sounding far too much like a daughter's, and not nearly enough like a newly minted general's.

"Someone has to stay and run the five families," Father argued.

"I'll do it," Pasquale offered, far too quickly.

Fiorenza spun toward the Rao boy on the heel of her boot. "That won't be necessary, seeing that *you* gave our daughter up to the Capo at court."

"After she turned me into a common object!" Pasquale cried.

"If it helps, I can make it uncommon this time," I said.

Father's head went heavy at our squabbling, lowering inch by inch into his waiting hands. I had seen him do the same thing a hundred times with the petty lords and merchants and priests of the Uccelli.

I turned away from Pasquale, putting my di Sangro training to work against the man who'd given it to me. I acted as if Father were the only person on the battlements. I walked forward until I took up his whole view. He'd taught me to do that. *Give a man nowhere to look but your face, and he will have nothing else to trust.*

Niccolò di Sangro was armored against everything but his own logic. "Come with us," I said.

"Impossible."

"No," I insisted. If Father was going to deny me, I was not going to make it a simple task. "What you did last night was impossible. You snatched me off the path that leads to death. You brought me back safely." There were glassy scratches in my voice, the memory still cutting me inside.

"I don't want to speak about this, Teodora," he said.

"Father, we're marching into a war where both sides are against us. We're going to need a healer."

"No, you aren't," Father said, forgetting what I knew— when he acted most certain, those were the nights doubt untethered him from his mind, when he wandered the castle and muttered until I woke to the sound of his fear echoing down the stone halls. "If you are truly my daughter, you're not going to get hurt."

༄

WE LEFT THE MOSCHELLA CASTLE AFTER SUPPER, DURING WHICH I encouraged the streghe to eat as much of the oily, fried lake fish with capers and onions as their stomachs would allow. Vanni had no trouble with this concept, but Cielo glared at the fish as if it owed her a great sum of money, Elettra squared off the tiniest possible bites, and Mimì leaned over to me and muttered, "Fish should come from the sea."

Signora Moschella provided more of the olive oil cakes

from the wedding and stuffed a bag full of them for our travels. She would have laden us with half of the castle's provisions if I had let her. I had to point out, several times, and with increasing force, that we had to travel on foot into the highest reaches of the Neviane, and we could take only what we could carry.

She asked if there were any spells to make our backs stronger.

By the time we started out, the light was the heavy gold of late afternoon. Lorenzo and Mimì made the most of the bittersweet loveliness, kissing each other good-bye in the shade of the Moschella family's beloved pear trees.

Cielo stood apart as Father and Fiorenza pulled me into embraces that choked as much as they comforted. When I turned to Mirella, she had already pasted a kiss to Vanni's cheek and was hurrying back inside to Luciano.

"I suppose that's all the good-bye we're going to get," I said, and led my small band of streghe away from the castle. At least, I led most of them away. We had already crossed the bridge into the village before I realized that Mimì wasn't with us.

When I looked back at Castel di Volpe, I found she was still engaged in a vigorous round of kissing, Lorenzo's hands on her back, pulling her so close they looked like one figure in the distance.

"Aren't you going to order her to catch up, General di Sangro?" Cielo asked.

I thought about how I would feel if someone pulled me rudely away from a moment like that. My magic would most likely have taken down the bridge in order to give me another moment with Cielo before we parted.

"No," I said. "It's safer this way."

The walk to the mountains took us past the hobbled branches of the Moschella family's grape arbors, along roads thick with travelers. On a mild day in November the Moschella lands swarmed with people, all of them shouting at us to see where we were headed.

"North," I said, because that much was obvious. I felt the double edge of a blade at my back—we needed to get to Zarisi quickly *and* be prepared for a battle by the time we arrived.

That night, we stopped to camp. "I'll make the fire," I said, gathering little sticks from the ground. Elettra trailed behind, helping and hovering in a way that made me think she had something to say.

"What is it?" I asked.

"If I'm going to stay with you . . ." She must have seen fear leap onto my face at the idea that we were already about to lose one of our small company. She shook her head, tightening her hold on her sticks until one of them cracked like a delicate bone. "I would rather have you use my real name. Elettra is for singing." I let out a small, overburdened breath. Of course she had a Vinalian stage name.

"What should we call you?" I asked.

"Xiaodan," she said.

"Will you call me Teo?" I asked. It was my childhood nickname, and yet it seemed to stretch and change. Years after I'd first chosen it, *Teo* held the vestiges of a di Sangro daughter, a dash of the boy in the capital. It was the name of a powerful strega and Cielo's beloved.

Me, in every sense.

Xiaodan nodded as we circled back to the rest of the streghe and handed over our sticks to Mimì. She licked her fingers and put them to the dry wood. With a sizzle, it went up in smoke, and then orange flames unraveled into the night air.

I sat the streghe in a loose circle. Cielo hovered, still on her feet. "I'll fly ahead to make sure there's no one coming down the road for twenty miles or so. That should mean a sound night's sleep without anyone needing to stay awake and play sentry."

Before I could nod my agreement or kiss her good-bye, Cielo was flicking a page in her book and flapping dark wings.

"I know everyone is tired," I said, "but I need to see the magic we have at hand so I know exactly what is in our arsenal when we reach the pass."

"I have an idea," Mimì said, with a few brisk claps. "Let's have a rissa incantata. I don't know about any of you, but a fight would help me get rid of this nagging worry I've had since the wedding."

"Rissa incantata? I'm not familiar with strega terms, but it sounds like you want to stage a magical fight," Vanni said. "And I'm already covered in aches and bruises." He started to roll up the leg of his pants, most likely to display the ripest of his blue marks, but I held up a hand, and Vanni stopped in his tracks.

"The rissa incantata is an old strega tradition," Mimì said. "It was kept alive on Salvi, if nowhere else. We care about the old ways."

I tossed a handful of wood in the fire, and it hissed at me. "We care for them in the Uccelli, too, but I can't have my streghe fighting each other."

"*Your* streghe?" Mimì asked, putting me in check as

smoothly as sliding a piece across a game board. "The rissa isn't about seeing who comes out on top. It's a matter of matching strength to strength, and both growing stronger."

I had never heard this approach before. I'd only seen people hide their magic or steal it through death. "The Capo had streghe fighting each other," I said, and even though I'd warned a hundred streghe about what I'd learned in Amalia, the words still came out flecked with dark feeling. "He wanted them dead, and their power channeled into a single strega he could . . . use. Control."

Xiaodan shivered, the fire and the shadows turning her bright and dark in turn.

"Who has that magic now?" Mimì asked.

Vanni gulped, giving me a sideways glance. "Teo does."

My magic seethed inside of me, reminding me that it was ready. I didn't doubt that. I only doubted that I would be able to use it wisely. I was used to having a precise, limited power. I tried to calm the crash of waves inside, the power as glinting and unfathomable as the ocean by night. "All right, now that you know about my magic, let's see yours."

I had been there when Vanni's magic was born and used against the soldiers of Erras, but I could barely guess at the powers of the two girls. I got to my feet and pointed out places for Mimì and Xiaodan to stand.

Even though I'd just convinced them to come with me and attack an entire army, I checked over both shoulders before we used magic openly, a sticking worry left over from the time when strega magic was hidden. Anyone who came along the road now could see us and know that we were both powerful and real. We were part of the landscape of Vinalia as much as the grape arbors, the crowded cities, the clang of church bells.

I nodded to Mimì and Xiaodan.

"Begin."

Mimì bowed deeply at the waist.

Xiaodan's hands started up a little dance, back and forth, back and forth. "You feel very sure of yourself," she said.

Mimì spat into her palm and fire rose into the sky in a great rush. Then she knelt down, grabbed a double handful of earth, and tossed it toward Xiaodan, turning it into a wind so strong that the opera singer was blasted off her feet.

Mimì was an element changer.

Vanni coughed, trying to hide his words. "Doomed. She's doomed."

"Nicely done," Xiaodan said, getting up without a hint of frustration in her movements. In fact, she looked invigorated. "Growing up in the opera house, surrounded by musicians and set painters and those who sew fine costumes while their own skin grows thick as horn, you become used to seeing people who know their work—know it as well as their own bodies. But it is rare to encounter the work of a true artist. It does not simply look right or sound beautiful. It travels through your skin. It sinks its teeth into your soul and does not let go."

"Are you saying I'm an artist?" Mimì asked. "Or that you are?"

"I will let you decide." Xiaodan's hands moved lightly, the same sort of motions that she used when she was singing— only there was no song. It was gesture, stripped of words, a subtle dance of emotion.

Mimì grabbed at the air, and it became earth in her

hands. But instead of throwing it at Xiaodan, she made more and more and more, completely focused on her efforts.

"Are you making her do that?" I asked, thinking of Cielo's mother, Giovanna, who had been able to spin someone else's feeling toward action. It was the single most dangerous ability I had ever seen.

"I have no control over body or mind," Xiaodan said, her hands still shaping the air like clay. "All I do is sense what Mimì is feeling, then bring it to a peak. Simple, really. She was very taken with her own magic."

Mimì smiled at the earth as it poured over her. She laughed at her own power, completely uninterested in the fight she was supposed to be winning.

"Stop," I said, cutting it off before I had a strega choking on her own magic.

The movement of Xiaodan's hands died down, like winds fading back into the calm sky.

Mimì looked around, dazed. When she realized what had happened, she kicked at the mound of earth and it dissolved back into air.

"Do *we* . . . fight each other . . . next?" Vanni asked me, tripping over the question in so many places I worried he would never right himself.

"Yes, let's see that," Mimì said, plunking herself down to watch.

I hesitated even as the magic roared through me, or perhaps *because* it roared through me. "I don't know if it would be right to pit Vanni against me for his first rissa." Our magic had both taken paths through the soldiers of Erras—mine by way of the strega Father had killed in front of me, and Vanni's through the strega Mirella had killed in front of him.

Vanni likely had a great deal of power, concentrated over generations. We might have been fairly matched a year ago, but since then my magic had grown out of proportion, doubling and tripling when Delfina and Azzurra died.

I was carrying them with me—their violently gathered magic, their ruthless ends. There should have been a way to save them from the Capo and I hadn't found it. Instead, I had let both sisters be sacrificed to the plotting of powerful men. I'd walked away stronger, yet still afraid I could not stop anyone when it was most needed. This was all more than I could hold.

This magic. This war. This moment.

I felt a breath of wind on my neck, and then it took the shape of a warm kiss. Cielo had come back, sliding into her rightful place at my side. I closed my eyes without meaning to and melted backward into her touch. Being with Cielo was the one thing that felt bigger than I was in the best possible way.

"I miss Lorenzo," Mimì said with a rough sigh.

"I wonder if Mirella misses me," Vanni added, a wistful thought that I felt like he wouldn't have shared in different, more masculine company. Or perhaps the Moschella heir was shedding the nervous, boastful ways I'd seen in Amalia. Maybe he was coming to see that he could be honest, and show feeling, and still be counted among men.

Xiaodan stayed quiet—but it was the kind of quiet that grew thick, filling the air with thorns. "We've been having a rissa incantata," she finally said to Cielo. "Do you want to try your luck?"

"There is hardly any luck involved," Cielo said, "and no."

"Why not?" Xiaodan asked with a slight frown.

"Because I would sweep you all into a dustbin, slap my hands clean, and then where would we be?" Cielo walked off, content to sit with the sack of olive oil cakes for company, licking her shiny-stained fingers after each bite.

"What would happen if you two fought?" Xiaodan asked.

"We fight all the time," I said. But I could see what she meant. What would happen if Cielo's magic and mine were paired against each other in battle?

My magic hissed, fighting itself inside of me. It wanted to rise to this terrible new challenge. It also wanted to keep Cielo safe. It had always been attached to the strega, even before I was.

I walked over to Cielo, and she wrapped me in her arms and fed me bits of cake as Xiaodan drifted back toward camp. An hour later I could see that she was still awake, her knees gathered to her chest, her neck tipped back to take in the rise of the mountains.

That night I slept in Cielo's arms, as the merciless Neviane loomed above us, filling my dreams with avalanches.

6

Our little party walked five miles the next morning and each step seemed to take us straight into the sky. The rocks beneath us pushed up in ragged chunks. As if that weren't enough, a thin coating of snow slicked every surface.

At one point we stopped, for breath as much as for food and water. We handed around the water skins, and I waited until last, so by the time one reached me I was shaking free the last musty drops that tasted more of leather than water.

Cielo flicked a page in her book and shifted into a form I'd never seen my strega take, one that made a giggle flutter out of Xiaodan. Mimì raised her eyebrows all the way to her hairline as Cielo pranced from rock to rock as a chamois, with short brown fur to protect against the cold, black horns curled backward until they were almost touching the tips of the ears. The goatlike antelopes that graced these mountains had heart-shaped hooves that sent my strega leaping from rock to rock as the rest of us struggled upward at half the pace.

When we reached the next ledge, Cielo was waiting for us with a leather skin filled with fresh water.

"Where did you get this?" I asked.

"I had time to visit a nearby stream," Cielo said.

"Cheating," Vanni huffed.

Cielo's smile soured. "If you start calling one drop of magic cheating, soon enough the accusation spreads and it all becomes cheating, and the only way to be fair is to live in a dry, magicless world. Is that really what you want?"

"Well, no, but . . ." Vanni started, then went quiet. Cielo's words had flattened the life out of his protests.

"She will do that every time," I said. "So step carefully."

Just as I said that, Mimì slipped on the path behind us, crying out. "Damn every single flake of this snow to a hell with extra fire. In Salvi, we would never pretend a place like this is habitable."

Vanni fussed with his cloak, his ego clearly as bruised as Mimì's swollen ankle. The Neviane was part of his family lands, and by the look on his face, Mimì might as well have insulted his grandmother. "In Salvi, all you have are dust and a few withered orange trees."

"And not a single good opera house," Xiaodan added.

"I see that my people are too poor for you to respect," Mimì said, her argument sure-footed even when the fur-lined boots Signora Moschella had gifted her were not.

Cielo put an arm around Mimì and handed her the rest of the water. "The stream is a quarter mile in that direction," Cielo announced to the rest of us.

"That's not fair!" Vanni cried.

Cielo swirled her green-and-purple cloak around to show Vanni the stitching on the back. "This is a map of Vinalia. Please point to any spot on it that has ever obeyed the rules of fairness."

Vanni huffed toward the stream, Xiaodan a step behind him.

I hovered between the two sets of streghe, not sure where I was meant to stand. I had grown up in a noble family. My childhood home was undeniably a castle. But the Uccelli was a region as poor as Salvi, and even the di Sangro family had gone through years with barely enough to eat or clothing thick enough to keep us warm when winter snarled at our doors.

The cold of these mountains called up the times when Beniamo would take chunks of ice that grew from the trellises in the kitchen gardens and throw them at me. If he hit me, it was easy enough to blame it on winter.

The cry of an owl crowded out my memories with fear. When I looked up, all I could see was the unruffled sky.

I looked to Cielo with dread moving through me, like a hard rush of wings. "An owl should not be flying in the daytime."

"Beniamo is not an owl anymore," she said, a newly crafted balance in her words meant to chase off my fear without making me feel like an idiot. She hadn't quite mastered it yet. "It must be . . . some other bird."

"An owl's cry is distinct," I said, turning to Mimì to recruit a new ally. "Wasn't that an owl?"

Mimì pinched her face to listen, but then Vanni and Xiaodan were back from the stream, the force of their sulking so powerful it distracted me. Xiaodan was mumbling something about how she had endured more hardship than the rest of us put together, but the words were so quick and quiet that I could not pick most of them out, and when I stared at her straight on, she stopped talking at once.

I did not want to pretend that there were no differences in our company, but I feared the ones we had would grow long as cracks in ice, splitting us apart. I needed these streghe, needed one thing in my new life to stay whole.

We were less than a mile from the town of Zarisi, and the pass was only a few miles beyond. "Let's keep practicing as we travel," I said, an idea that Mimì countered with a long groan.

"I know my magic," she said. "It was passed down to me upon the death of Salvi's greatest strega when I was twelve years old. I don't need to *practice*."

"You know how to use that magic by yourself," I agreed. "But if we are to take on the whole Eterran army, we need all of our powers together, in a sort of concert." I turned to Xiaodan, hoping that as an opera singer, she would understand. "Harmonies work together. If any of our notes clash . . ."

"We die," Vanni said.

"That's not really like music," Mimì said.

"Don't you feel a tiny death when a note is out of place?" Xiaodan asked.

"No," Mimì said flatly. "I feel a large death when the world is on fire and no one is dousing it. And I would like to avoid feeling an actual death soon, so I suppose we should keep working."

"All right," I said, pointing to where Cielo climbed the rocks ahead of us, in girlish form but still with the zest and impeccable balance of the chamois. "I want you to work together to sneak up on Cielo."

"Why?" Vanni asked, clearly dreading the assignment.

I patted both of Vanni's shoulders. "If you can tip Cielo's balance, you are ready to turn the tide of any army."

WE REACHED THE TOWN OF ZARISI AT MIDDAY, AND THE NEARNESS of the pass seemed to flood our steps with importance. The town was tucked in a small crevice that could barely be called a valley, surrounded on all sides by sharply angled rock. Sun clanged down on the snow, creating a blare of reflected light. The town itself was dark and cramped, with cobbled streets and houses so thin they looked famished.

"Teo and I should go make friends with the back alleys of Zarisi," Cielo said. "The Capo's men will be all over this town."

Xiaodan started to breathe with a hitch, her chest rising against the weight of her plum wool cloak. "You should be safe," I said. "Especially with Vanni in your ranks."

Xiaodan stared at Vanni, her fingers plucking at the air; it seemed to be what she did to test the waters of someone else's emotions. She dropped her hands and frowned. "He's too afraid to protect us."

"Vanni protects us just by existing," Mimì reminded her. "That's what it means to be a man in Vinalia. The rest of us have to work harder."

Vanni made a slight blustering noise—but had no argument to back it up with.

"Meet us at the far side of town in an hour," I said to the three of them. "Grab as much food as you can."

"Olives," Cielo blurted.

"If they have them," I added.

Vanni and Xiaodan started off. Before Mimì could join them, I pulled her aside. We'd been traveling in a pack for days, and there hadn't been a single chance to speak alone. Now that I had one, my question leapt out.

"You agreed to this trip so readily back in Castel di Volpe. Why?"

Mimì crossed her arms, gripping her elbows. She felt the cold keenly, and the warmly smiling girl I had met in the Capo's court now wore a frozen grimace. "On Salvi, we don't believe in unification. It's no secret, I know, but that doesn't mean other people understand how it feels. Every day since the Capo took power has been like a funeral for our people. Salvians want Lorenzo to declare his own war against Vinalia, but to do so would be as good as herding everyone on our island to a cliff and pushing them into the sea."

"So don't declare war," I said, already feeling that my answer was wrong without knowing why.

"The people will unseat Lorenzo if he doesn't stand against the Vinalian throne," Mimì said. "The Altimari family has ruled Salvi for twenty generations, and I know that's not a good enough reason to keep a ruler in place, but . . . Lorenzo is good for Salvi."

"That's not hard to believe," I said, thinking of how he dealt with the rest of us in Amalia. "He listens to everyone— most of the young family heads listen only to their own impatience and certainty."

"And with his mother's family, Lorenzo is the first family head with Ravinian lineage in a hundred years," Mimì added. "That means something to a great many people." I knew from my time at court that Lorenzo's mother was Ravinian, and Mimì shared that heritage, though her family had been in Vinalia for a great many generations. Ravinia sat across the Mare Terrano, the northernmost country on the Rivan continent, which meant that trade and travel back and forth between the two lands were hardly rare. But seeing Ravinians in power on this side of the Terrano still was.

"If we fight tomorrow—if we win—do I have your promise that Salvi will be independent?" Mimì asked.

So that was why she wanted to be here facing the Eterrans with me. Mimì saw it as a possible way to secure Salvi, especially if we could take down the Capo. I admired her plan. I admired *her*.

Snow started falling, swirling over Mimì's head and landing in her black curls. She ignored the cold, keeping her eyes fastened on my reaction. I wanted to say *yes*, but the word stopped halfway up my throat. "That's not mine to choose."

"I suppose it's a matter for your father," Mimì said, with no small amount of scorn.

I shook my head, feeling the slice of cold along my cheekbones. "The people of Salvi should find their own way, with help from their own leaders, and not have this chosen for them in some back room or secret pact. When we take down the Eterrans and the Capo, I promise to let them decide what happens next. Though, even if Salvi is not part of Vinalia, I hope that we will stay allied."

"Of course," Mimì said. "The five families always work together."

"I wasn't speaking of the five families." My magic spiked, as if it too had felt the touch of the cold and turned harder, sharper. Clearer. "What if we are the sixth family?" I asked. "One whose members were not born but chosen by one another? A family of streghe?"

Mimì's smile, the one that had burned as bright as a

miniature sun at the court in Amalia, and again at Mirella's wedding, returned. "I have an ungodly number of cousins, but I guess I could live with a few more." She shook the snow out of her curls and drew up the burgundy hood of her cloak as she turned to face Zarisi, and the promise of the pass beyond. "Now let's hope we survive our first family outing."

❦

CIELO AND I SCRIBBLED A CRUDE PATH THROUGH THE ALLEYS OF Zarisi. If I had expected a mountain town bursting with trade and travel and soldiers, I had been wrong in all ways but one. Men in green-and-black uniforms were strewn throughout the streets, but everyone else appeared to be missing, leaving Zarisi covered in a quiet to rival the fresh snowfall.

"The villagers know the pass is in danger," I said. "They've taken their chances elsewhere." This was a sort of bad news I could hold in my hands, turn over to feel the weight of it, inspecting it from every angle.

"Vinalians are not skittish colts when it comes to invasions," I said. "Their stubbornness means they often stay put until the last minute or much later than that."

"The only ones who stay now are weighing their lives against profit each day," Cielo added. "A foul mathematics. Do you think there is still a decent bakery open? I would give my left foot for a piece of warm bread."

"Is that really all you can think about?" I asked.

"No," Cielo said. "There is also the hateful truth that I haven't had coffee in two days."

We hadn't been alone in two days, either. I backed Cielo into the wall behind us, her body against the cold stones, and apologized for the discomfort by pressing my warmth into her. One of my legs between hers, I *pushed*. "Do you feel more awake now?"

"Yes, but I will need more stirring." I kissed her and slipped my hands beneath the silky layer of her cloak. She pulled back slightly, just enough that I could smell the last of the olive oil cakes on her lips as she whispered, "Is there a way to add sugar? A dash of cream?"

"Vinalians don't foul their coffee with cream," I said.

"I am no ordinary Vinalian," Cielo said.

I added sweetness to the kiss, light touches of my lips. And then I opened my mouth, pouring my body farther into hers, my hands finding the top of her pants and plunging deep, a richness that could not be denied. As I moved my hand and Cielo's breath moved in counterpoint, I kissed my way from her lips to her chin, dripping warm kisses down her neck.

I stopped when I reached the line of blood. It had faded past red, all the way to brown. When my lips brushed that line, I felt the harsh scab.

My own neck felt suddenly exposed. My mind flinched at the memory of the knife, cutting more than skin. "What are the Bones of Erras?" I asked, hovering an inch away from Cielo, my hand as still as stone against her body.

"Nothing you need to worry about," she said, kissing my temple, arching against me, trying to convince my hand to take up its good work. But now that I was trapped in the memory beneath the abbey, I could not live fully in this moment.

Cielo let out a small slip of a groan as my body broke away from hers. She stayed against the stones, combing fingers through her mussed hair as she said, "The Bones of Erras are a story I learned from my teacher Malik, who kept little altars to the old gods all over his workshop."

"The one who was killed by the Order of Prai?" I asked.

Cielo nodded. We held still as a stray pair of soldiers came down one of the alleys that led to this dark pocket of Zarisi, which was itself a dark pocket in the mountains. The soldiers turned before they reached us.

"Do you remember how the reign of the old gods ended?" Cielo asked as their steps faded to nothing.

I reached back into my lessons, sifting through myths. "They fought each other, didn't they? Brought about their own destruction." The stories of the old gods had always seemed strange to me. They often acted more like unruly children than all-powerful deities. They quarreled with each other, plucked enemies and lovers from the ranks of mortals, and used their powers for purely selfish reasons as often as they used them for good.

"The end was a mess of blood and magic," Cielo said. "But it wasn't all of the gods who turned against each other. Only one." I shivered, even though the wind didn't reach us here under the shelter of a house's sharp eaves. "Erras decided that the rest of the gods hadn't been making the right choices, and he used his godly judgment to destroy them, one by one. He killed Melae first."

Melae was the goddess of death, splitting those who died into spirit and flesh, and so it made sense that Erras chose her. With Melae gone, death would no longer be her domain. His plan to kill the others would be easier to hide.

"When the last goddess, Veria, saw him coming, she could read the truth shining through his eyes. She knew that he meant to kill her. So she ran to the sea, lured him to the edge of the water, and called on the fury of the ocean to punish him for believing he had the right to kill the other gods. When Veria and the waves were done with him, only his bones were left behind."

"You're saying . . . those knives were made from the bones of a god?"

"I'm telling you what I've heard, which can't be believed, but which seems to be true anyway. I wouldn't take Dantae's word even if it came wrapped up in a box made of pure gold, but that knife . . ."

"What did it whisper to you?" I asked.

"Oh, the expected things. My priestly father hating me, my mother having no choice but to leave a child like me behind." My heart swelled painfully. Cielo shook her head, refusing my sadness. "Distract me. Please."

"How?" I asked, aching to help.

"You're the one who showed me this little trick," Cielo said, pulling me back to her. "Turn my bones to mercury and my mind to the darkness between stars."

This time Cielo's body ground against mine, two great forces meeting, my hips canted up toward hers, my hands bracing her sides as we pushed and pulled each other across the cobblestones.

And then there was an epic flash of light, and I had to blink twenty times in a row to clear my eyes. When my vision finally deepened from dazzling white back to its normal range of color, Cielo was looking at me with a perplexed little frown.

For a moment, I thought I'd lost control of my magic. Again.

Then Vanni leapt out from behind the corner of a house, throwing handfuls of light to the ground. Mimì appeared with a bucket of water, which she tipped along the alley and turned into a river of fire. Cielo's body split into buzzing hornets, which split again into two little hornet clouds and dove at Vanni and Mimì, who were soon swatting at their faces and swearing.

"What are you doing?" I cried.

Xiaodan appeared at my elbow, smiling. "You told us to sneak up on Cielo, overwhelming the strega with magic. Best to attack when someone is distracted."

"You couldn't have waited five more minutes?" I asked through a groan.

"Best not to let an opportunity slip by," Xiaodan said.

Cielo came back together, all of her pieces buzzing back into place. "*You*," she said, turning to me with a sting laced through her voice. "You told them to do this, Teo?"

"I didn't realize hornets could understand Vinalian," I said.

Cielo crossed her arms as if she might buzz apart otherwise.

"They needed to keep training, and you . . ."

"Are a formidable opponent?" Cielo asked. "An infamous strega?" A smile crept onto her lips for the first time in days. My strega was back and ready to play any game, win any hand. "Well," she said, brushing a bit of dirt off her shirt where I'd pushed her hard against the stones. "Now that I have acquired a reputation, I will have to keep it polished."

And with that, the life leached out of her face, draining

every inch of skin, until she vanished. Cielo's clothes, left unoccupied, rippled to the ground.

"What . . . ?" Mimì asked, spinning a hopeless circle. "Did that strega just magic right out of existence?"

Silence encroached on my heart. Cielo wouldn't go that far to win a game, and yet I worried. Once Cielo had undone all of my magic by accident. What if my strega had used too much power again and simply vanished?

I took a step, and the stones beneath my feet rippled.

I took another step, and the stones bucked. I flew forward, trying to loosen my body as I'd learned to do when I was a little girl and Beniamo cast me to the ground.

I landed, and the stones bent and softened, like warm butter.

The others were falling and staggering as well. Xiaodan was tearing at her dress as if she had been seized by a rash, and Mimì tossed a knife out of her pocket, almost hitting Vanni with a flying blade.

"What's happening?" I asked.

Above our heads, the sky tore open, like a great hungry mouth. It looked as if it could swallow all of Zarisi.

My magic crashed through me until I thought I would crumple. But I didn't know what to change, how to fix this. And besides, I'd meant to train Mimì, Vanni, and Xiaodan, not to pit my own powers against Cielo's.

"Help!" Vanni cried.

"Truce," Mimì said. "Now show yourself."

Cielo arrived back in her clothing, looking drained and even paler than usual. When the pink sprang back to her lips, she ran her fingers over them, the way I touched mine after a particularly revelatory kiss.

"What did you do?" Vanni asked. "Make a quick pact with the devil while we were out getting *your olives?*" He brandished a bag, and Cielo swiped it from Vanni with a wide smile. A moment later, Cielo had untied the bag with her long fingers, and her smile became merely a gate for olives to pass through.

She chewed as the color returned to her face, slowly. "I became gray." The streghe around me traded looks of disbelief.

"You became a *color*," I said, to make sure I understood what had happened and add it to the growing catalog of Cielo's abilities.

"Yes," Cielo said. "I really will have to add a page to the book for that one."

I sat down on the cobblestones, the cold leaching through my wool dress and into the backs of my legs.

Cielo knelt in front of me. "What's wrong?" she asked. "I thought you wanted to play." She held out an olive. I shook my head.

"I don't care about losing a game," I said. "But this is a real war we're heading into. I can't let them face the Capo, the Eterrans, and our own army. I can't risk their lives when they were just laid low by *one* strega."

Cielo's kiss was soft but insistent, the brine of her olives salting my lips. "You're forgetting that we are on the same side. This is not a matter of each strega battling alone. No more foul mathematics. This is all of us, or nothing."

"Then it will have to be all of us," Xiaodan said, her hands plucking at the strings of the world, pulling emotion from the air. "People are afraid. And it's growing stronger. Spreading."

Vanni ran to the street, but by the time he came back

carrying news, I already knew what he was going to say. Still, I unclenched my fists and waited, wanting to loosen my body the way I had when I was falling, to keep the impact from shattering me.

"What is it?" Mimì asked.

Vanni swallowed. "The Eterrans have taken the pass."

When my eyes first settled on the town of Zarisi, I'd believed it was abandoned, but as word of the Eterrans breaching the pass spread, a contagion of whispers and shouts, any villagers and profiteers who had stayed behind were inspired to leave as quickly as possible. They streamed out of shops and houses, some half-dressed and dragging on their furs.

My little band of streghe looked at me, waiting for instruction. I had lured them here, baiting their steps with grand notions of a country that could be made safer for their kind, as well as everyone they loved. I was a liar with a heart full of hollow promises. A strega whose magic could rage and reshape and ruin but not heal. A thief who had stolen people away from their lives and marched them toward death.

"What do we do now, General di Sangro?" Cielo asked.

"This isn't the way it's supposed to be! You said we'd have more time!" Vanni cried, placing the obvious in my path so I would have to trip over it yet again.

"All of my battle plans were based on defending the pass," I said. "I will have to . . . redraw them."

When I went into the dungeons of my mind, usually filled with an endless supply of di Sangro scheming, I came up with nothing but darkness. Father did not believe in outright war. He used every weapon at his disposal to avoid battles and armies. When my brothers played at being soldiers with the boys of Chieza, Father would frown at their invented victories and draw me under his arm. He would lean down and look at me as if I were wise and say, *No one wins a war, Teo. There is only a side that loses less.*

"While you're drawing up plans, you *could* sketch a line to the nearest inn with a warm bed," Vanni says. "No one knows we're here, Teo, except for the five families. It's not too late to turn around."

"Are you always this cowardly?" Mimì asked, whirling on Vanni.

Vanni looked more stung than he had when Cielo chased him as a mass of hornets. But he pushed his lips together staunchly, recovering a bit of his pride. "It's not cowardice. It's a healthy fear, and it keeps me alive. Do you know how many people in my family are confident and dead?"

I thought of Signora Moschella and her talents, including the one for keeping her children alive in the face of constant revenge, skirmishes, and assassination plots. I would have traded every drop of magic in my blood for that skill.

The magic seethed at that thought. *We are made for this*, it said. *We are here to change things.*

I had promised my magic—promised myself—that I would not let the world go on as it had. I looked down the alley at the sparse handfuls of Vinalian soldiers coming up with improbable ways to hold the streets of Zarisi as long as they could before the Eterrans overwhelmed them. The last of the villagers flowed against the tide of nature, up from the valley into the mountains.

Follow them, my magic whispered.

The last time it had given me similar instructions, it wanted me to run after Cielo. My magic was reckless, but it was often right. I did not always know how to believe the voice inside of me as much as I believed in the cruelty of the world.

"We follow the villagers," I said. "They know the safest paths."

"We give up?" Xiaodan said, looking around at Zarisi as if she were being held back in the wings when she should be making a grand entrance. She stared fearlessly in the direction of the pass, the battle a song that could not go unsung.

"We strike from the mountains, like I said we would." My magic did not like being forced into a corner. It needed a vantage point to work—it could not change the world without truly seeing it first. "The soldiers will funnel through the town, and our magic will work better if we're not fighting one man at a time."

Xiaodan nodded brightly. "We need strategy, not sweaty combat."

"Besides, the Eterrans can't spread out and attack every slope of the mountain," I said, my plan gaining speed, tumbling together as I spoke. "It would thin their forces, and the Neviane are treacherous, full of snow that will give way under your boots, burying you before you scream. Not to mention the avalanches you can start by yelling at the wrong pitch."

"So that's why everyone in town was so whispery," Vanni said with a shiver.

We started up the nearest slope, and I found myself wishing I hadn't just given breath to all the reasons we had to fear the mountains. Our steps bit through the top layer of ice, scraping along our legs and sinking deeper, until our knees were swallowed. Mimì looked disgusted, and Vanni seemed to be on the verge of another fainting spell. I braced his arm with my own. If he passed out now, he might roll downhill all the way back to Zarisi.

Xiaodan kept tossing nervous glances over her shoulder, her hands moving as if they were muddling their way through a thick stew. "Our soldiers are tired. I can feel their sadness at the breach of the pass. It feels like losing more than a battle, Teo. It feels like losing . . . *everything*."

My heart was a whirlwind, carrying me back to the day in the Uccelli when I'd lost my home, my family. It was happening again, but on a grander scale. Vinalia was my home as much as the cold stones of the di Sangro castle had ever been.

The Vinalian soldiers understood that giving up the pass meant the Eterrans had free rein to invade the rest of the country. They would most likely march straight to Amalia and declare themselves our new rulers. On the way, they would plunder our fields, and later put their fingers all over the trade in our ports. Our lives would no longer be ours, our fates at their mercy. As if that weren't enough, the Eterrans didn't believe in *the brilliant life*. They would strip this land of its magic—and not only the kind practiced by streghe. Their ways were cold, bloodless, their days without beauty or passion.

Fiorenza had told me so many times, *That is not life. It is simply an absence of death.*

My hatred for the Capo rose in great, sickening waves, and I had to swallow against bile at the back of my throat. He had brought on this invasion so he might prove his greatness. He might as well have written the Eterrans an invitation in his best handwriting.

But I could not punish the Capo. Not yet.

One enemy at a time.

"I want you to work on the Eterrans," I told Xiaodan, my voice shredded into strips by the wind and the effort of marching uphill. "If they're feeling confident, keep at them until they can barely see past their own pride."

Xiaodan nodded briskly. But when her hands went to work, they caught on something—a visible snag. "I'll need you to stop crowding the air first."

"What?" I asked, feeling dizzy as we rose higher and the battle drew closer.

"Your feelings are thick. I can't work past them." She tried to stretch her hands apart, but they hit the same blockage every time. "Fear, fear, fear," she muttered.

"Of course I'm afraid," I snapped. "What decent person would send anyone into a battle without worrying about their fates?"

Xiaodan nodded as if I'd said reasonable things, but I could tell she was holding back. Her own emotions had a way of sliding across her face in strong but fleeting glimpses, like fast-moving weather.

"What?" I asked.

"The worst of your fears all cling to one person." She nodded at the figure leading our little pack, sure steps punching through the ice, black hair swinging. "You're so afraid to lose Cielo."

I prickled along all the seams of my body. "What is Cielo afraid of?" I whispered, knowing even as I asked that this was not a fair question. It would be wrong to invade Cielo's mind that way. And yet I'd had the feeling, ever since Mirella's wedding, that Cielo was holding something in reserve.

Not lying. My strega was terrible at lying.

Xiaodan's fingers reached toward Cielo's back, running in the smooth, waving lines of a waterfall, combing through Cielo's emotions. But before she could report anything back to me, Cielo spun around and Xiaodan twisted her hands together.

If Cielo noticed, she gave no sign. She nodded at the ridge above us and to the west. "Our magical, knife-happy friends have arrived," Cielo said. Sure enough, a line of figures appeared, backlit by the sun. It hammered gilt all over the mountains. It made everything look majestic, even as the Eterran army spilled in from the north.

"Do you think those leathery bastards will stop the Eterrans?" Vanni asked. "Shouldn't we wait for them to do the job for us?"

"The soldiers of Erras don't care who wins this war," I said. "If they did, Dantae would be knee-deep in glory by now."

Cielo grabbed for her book. "I still haven't properly thanked them for the red necklaces they carved into our throats," she said, flashing a glance at my neck, which ached as soon as it was mentioned. More likely, it had always been aching, and I'd forgotten until someone brought it up. "Let me deal with them."

"No," I cried, the word knifing out of me.

Cielo's face clenched and set. Her every-colored eyes blinked once and then offered up a gritty stare.

Xiaodan's hands chopped the air as she focused on the soldiers of Erras. "It's true. They don't want to be here."

"Can you increase that feeling, please?" I asked. My phrasing was overly polite for a wartime general, but I didn't like the idea of ordering Xiaodan to feel anything.

And I knew I was taking a risk—if the soldiers of Erras worked out that their emotions were being magically toyed with, they would no doubt find us. Then we would have two battles on our hands.

Xiaodan's hands worked harder and harder. I wanted to ask her if feelings were always running through the streams of the air, invisible, and Xiaodan simply had a way of reaching a hand into the current.

The soldiers of Erras turned and disappeared over the rise. Xiaodan breathed out a gush of cold air and doubled over. Vanni clapped her on the back, and Xiaodan came back up smiling. Mimì put an arm around the slender girl. Cielo was the only one left out of the celebration, her face gathered around a hard center of disappointment.

I wanted to let Xiaodan recover fully, but we could not stop for long. The Eterran army was still rushing into place at the northern edge of Zarisi, dressed in light blue that made their soldiers look like shards of ice. Now that we'd sent away the soldiers of Erras, we were the only real power standing between those troops and the rest of Vinalia.

We took shelter behind a promontory of granite with a ledge that reached into the open air. I walked to the end, looking past the toes of my boots and the bitten edge of the rock. The world pitched down and away. This was the perfect place to work from, offering us both a hiding place and a view, even if it was a breathlessly dangerous one.

"Stay with Xiaodan," I said to Cielo. She nodded and took

Xiaodan under the silken wing of her cloak. The singer's breath was coming hard and fast.

Had the soldiers of Erras been too much for her? I could only imagine going straight from using her magic on willing, delighted audiences in the opera house to willful streghe on the battlefield.

I beckoned Vanni and Mimì to the edge of the rock. Mimì strode out, edged by death on all sides. Vanni, on the other hand, turned sideways and shuffled, with a whimper to match each step.

Mimì waited for Vanni, drawing from a deep well of sighs. I had to admit that I wanted him to move more quickly, but I knew that if I bludgeoned him with all of the terrible things that could happen, he would stop moving altogether.

When Vanni reached the end, I put a hand on each of their shoulders. "Give the Eterrans a strong blast of magic as they enter the town," I said. "Greet them the five families way."

"But that's all backstabbing," Vanni said. "This is more . . . front stabbing."

I bore down on his shoulder, friendly but firm. "You're right. The sixth family does things differently."

"What's the sixth family?" Vanni asked, turning his head to me, as if he'd finally broken the staring contest he was having with his own fear.

"I'll tell you if you take out half of the battalion," Mimì said.

Vanni and Mimì loosed their magic, Vanni snatching beams of light grown potent when they hit the reflected snow. Mimì scooped great white handfuls, and my fingers burned cold just watching her. But the snow slid to water in her hands before she sent it in fiery streams down the side of the mountain.

Light bombs exploded at the feet of the Eterrans, and Mimì's fire was not far behind.

The troops scattered and screeched. Some turned back. Others fell, blinded by light or overcome by smoke. But there were hundreds of men, and then hundreds more, and as soon as Vanni's light faded back to shades of gray, and Mimì's fire sizzled out, the Eterran troops pushed their way into Zarisi.

"I'm sorry, Teo," Xiaodan said, her voice coming from where she hid in the shadow below the promontory. "I know I said I'd work on the Eterrans, but . . ." I could hear the strain in her voice, the inner cords close to snapping.

She is exhausted, the magic said. I knew that feeling—and I knew Xiaodan would not be able to fight again until she overcame it.

"Rest," I said, trying to subdue Xiaodan's worries even as my own took on the sharp point of panic. From our perch, I could see part of the Eterran forces sheer off and head up the mountainside, toward our promontory.

They had spotted us.

"Don't bomb the climbers," I said. "If we hit the wrong place on the slope, it might take down the whole mountain."

"That's one of Teo's specialties," Cielo yelled.

Mimì gave me a quick, baffled stare.

"I'll explain later," I muttered.

I turned my attention back to the men on the slope.

Change them, I told the magic, but it was already too strong inside me. If I unleashed it on the troops below, it might spill out in every direction, changing more than I had ever asked for.

"Right now would be a nice time for one of those avalanches you mentioned," Vanni said.

I shook my head. "It involves hitting the right note, at the right volume," I said, talking myself into a valley of despair before remembering that we had Prai's most beloved opera singer with us. I looked over the edge of the rock at Xiaodan. Her magic was exhausted, but her voice was another matter.

She stared up, worry wafting across her rose-gold cheeks. She touched her fingertips to her chest, where the song welled up—the same place I touched when I thought of the magic inside of me. "I haven't sung in days," she warned. "And the weather here is not good for a soprano's vocal cords."

Vanni watched as the Eterrans stormed toward us, close enough to see the grim purpose on their faces. "Oh, believe me," he said weakly. "We'll still give you a standing ovation if you pull this off."

Xiaodan's voice stitched together a few notes, threading up and down a scale. She inched her mouth wider, and the sound flowed away from us, rippling endlessly, like bolts of rich cloth.

The Eterrans were close enough now that I could see their breath scarring the air white. Mimì closed her eyes and spat out a prayer, and Vanni took three steps back without seeming to notice. Cielo grabbed for the book, her best protection, though when her eyes caught mine, she did not change.

She stood her ground. She stayed with us.

With me.

Xiaodan's voice grew higher in pitch and more focused in tone until it narrowed to a point and seemed to puncture the air. The mountain shuddered, as if it couldn't bear that sound. And then a small knot of snow formed below us, growing larger as it fell down the slope, until it was a nightmare of white.

The men below us were close enough I could see fear in their eyes as the snow overtook them. It rumbled down the slope until it reached a crevasse, where it plummeted so deep into the earth that I didn't even see a plume of powder when it reached the bottom.

Vanni stood up and clapped, giving Xiaodan the standing ovation he'd promised, but she only shook her head sadly, her hands sliding over the air, a sweet motion like a mother smoothing over sadness with a lullaby.

I wondered if she felt the emotions of those soldiers as they plummeted. Was she trying to bring them peace? Help them rest?

She sat down and gathered her knees to her chest, the way I'd seen her do at camp the night before.

With the slope below cleared of Eterran troops and murderous snow, I could finally focus on the streets of Zarisi again. While our attention was fully claimed by the importance of saving our own lives, the Vinalian soldiers had gotten tangled with the Eterrans in the streets. My magic could not pick one side apart from the other.

Change them. Stop them. Change them. Stop them.

The magic marched inside of me, barking the same commands until I felt like I was not in charge of the battle, but a lowly soldier who had to do as she was told or face terrible consequences.

I turned to look for Cielo, to ask my magic tutor what came next, as if this were one of our harmless lessons. I did not have to go far—Cielo was running to meet me at the end of the promontory.

My strega knew me well. Cielo could see what my magic wanted, the impossible choice it urged me toward. She stood beside me and we both looked down at the battle that was quickly becoming a massacre. "No one will blame you, Teo."

"It's not a matter of blame," I whispered. "I came here to save them."

The Vinalian forces were giving way as the Eterrans pushed, relentless. The snow that had started out white was spotted pink, a surprisingly delicate color, like the apple blossoms of an early spring. When I turned to Cielo, her cheeks and lips were a much brighter shade, the blood under her fair skin a visible reminder of her life. I wanted to keep it from pouring out of her, at all costs. I wanted to pretend that Cielo staying alive was the only thing that mattered.

"If you do this, you will save the rest of the army, and everyone in Vinalia, from an invasion."

"You don't believe in that sort of thing," I mumbled through half-frozen lips. "Remember? Foul mathematics."

"True, but I am not the one who came here to stop a war."

"Teo!" Mimì cried, grabbing my attention and tugging it back to the grisly moment at hand. "What do we do now?"

My magic was rising past the point that I would be able to calm it, and with it came Father's voice, hopelessly tangled.

There is only a side that loses less.

Instead of closing my eyes, I opened them wider, refusing to blink. Instead of trying to hold back the magic, I called its name, beckoned it, brewed the storm in my soul. It was a power as great as the avalanche, and I could feel it stampeding away from me. On a single sharp intake of breath, the men in the town below us become a burst of dazzling snow.

No two flakes matched in every detail, just as none of the lives I'd taken were exactly the same. They had been rich men and poor men, Eterrans and Vinalians, great lovers of life and those who sought only to snatch it away from others. From a distance, though, they all looked the same.

For one peaceful moment, the snow hung in the air. Then it started up a wild swirl, like the snapping of wolves. The wind grew and grew, the town ravaged by winds. The narrow houses of Zarisi sighed, slumped, and started to fall.

A fresh battalion of Eterran troops came over the northern rise, but when they saw Zarisi being felled by an unnatural wind, they stopped. I did not need Xiaodan to tell me these men were afraid. I could sense it. I knew it was wrong to savor it, but I couldn't help the pleasure that spread with a delicious moment of triumph.

We can take them all, my magic said.

I almost agreed. But if the storm grew too large and I could not stop it, it would take my streghe, too. And besides, we needed witnesses to carry this story back to Eterra.

I turned to Cielo, whose black hair had become a whipping cloud. "Can you help me rein it in?"

"Are you asking me to pacify you, Teo? You know that's a fight no one could win. But I will give you something new to push against." Her slippery smile made me flush in ways that had nothing to do with wartime victory. Her body broke into ribbons of wind and raced toward the sky.

When Cielo's wind met mine in the skies above Zarisi, it pushed—softly at first, and then with growing fervor—until my resistance left me on a sigh of relief. The whirlwind died, and the only thing left was a pure mountain breeze, gathering up the snowflakes and softly, gently returning them to the sky.

"Is that snow flying . . . up?" Vanni whispered.

It was—a great glittering breath moving from the ground to the sky.

I cleared my throat and stood at the edge of the promontory, facing the Eterrans. "Remember this as the day when all tides turned." The mountains served as a natural amplifier, my voice clanging against them. I wished that everyone who had ever doubted me could see this moment. Luca, the boys of the five families, Father.

This time, I would even invite Beniamo.

"The snow has returned to the sky, as your people will return. Home, where you are wanted. Home, to people who love you. Leave us to our lives, or we will take every one of yours."

The men turned and scurried back north just as a wind wrapped around me, and then Cielo dropped at my feet, boyish and naked and shivering, so deeply bitten by cold that I could have sworn a wild animal had gotten its teeth in him.

I threw the cloak over Cielo's body, then knelt and wrapped myself around him. I wanted to fill him with my warmth.

Instead, I was startled by the force of the cold coming from his skin.

He looked past my face, up at the sky, as if it held the answers to all questions. Or maybe he was trying to be certain he'd put all the snow to bed in the thin blanket of clouds. He gave a little nod and finally turned his eyes to mine. "I've always heard people say victory or death, and every single time I thought, Why be so limiting? Why not both?"

He seized in my arms.

The hollow place where my magic had been a minute before flooded with darkness.

"Fear, fear, fear," Xiaodan muttered, or maybe it was only the wind.

8

Cielo did not die.

"You didn't even make it within a mile of death's gate-house," Mimì reminded him several times as she heated handfuls of snow and melted them, infusing her palms with warmth and pushing it into Cielo's muscles.

"Where did you learn to work this little miracle?" Cielo asked, sitting up so he could watch her.

Mimì's tight spirals of dark hair bobbed over Cielo as she moved from one of his legs to the other. "My mother was a healer, and even if that's not the form my magic took, watching her work all through my childhood gave me some ideas."

Jealousy gave itself the grand tour of my body. My father was a healer, and it had taken seventeen years for him to even admit it to me.

I had certainly never learned magic at his knee.

We were back in the flattened town of Zarisi. Beside us was a bonfire made out of plain timber from the sharply broken bones of houses. Vanni and Xiaodan had gone to pick through the piles that used to be shops and see if there was anything left worth eating. That left Mimì to tend to an injured Cielo, and me to worry over the reality that my magic had injured him in the first place.

"You're sure I'm not even a bit moribund?" Cielo asked Mimì as her palms seared his skin. "Ow! I mean, I've always thought it would be hard to know, since you only die once, so you won't know what it feels like until you've done it, and then the knowledge is too late to be useful."

"You have frostbite in two of your fingers and several of your toes," Mimì said, probably hoping a little truth, however harsh, would halt Cielo's concerns over mortality. I could have told her that was an impossible task.

"So my fingers and toes are dead," Cielo said. "That explains the feeling, actually. It's a sort of rehearsal."

"Please save all of Cielo's body parts," I said. "I need him intact."

Vanni's chuckle reached me before I saw him. He and Xiaodan had chosen that moment to turn the corner of the cobbled street, which had held up surprisingly well in the storm, leaving a perfect map of where a village used to stand.

"We all need to be in fighting shape," I said. "We don't know what we'll find in the Capo's camp. And besides," I added for Mimì's benefit, "you have no idea how much he'll complain if he loses even one of those toes."

"What does it matter?" Vanni asked, squatting to sort the items he and Xiaodan had found, pitching aside ancient parsnips, biting and grimacing at a hard ciabatta, rejecting a basket of eggs riddled with cracks, and gathering everything else in a precious little heap. "If you don't have toes in this form, just use that book of yours. Be something else."

"This body is dear to me," Cielo said, clutching it like it

might be stolen from him at any moment. "And if I lose a piece of myself in this form, it will be lost in any that boasts a similar anatomy. Do you know how many things have toes? I would be doomed to life as a snail, oozing my way from one end of Vinalia to the other. *Slowly*. Hardly helpful to your cause." I did not miss the stare he gave me.

"Be quiet, please," Mimì said, pressing Cielo back down to rest.

"Will it help me heal faster?" Cielo asked eagerly.

"It will help me not kill you," Mimì said. "So yes."

As soon as Cielo was thoroughly warmed, we made our way out of the ruins of Zarisi. Xiaodan spun a circle and tested the air with her fingers, using her magic as a sort of compass. "There are people to the west. They're . . . well, this is how people tend to feel when they've been drinking a lot. Sort of fizzy. About to fall down but happy about it."

"So they've heard about the victory," I said. "That's a good thing, at least."

"Until my beloved uncle pretends it was all his doing," Cielo said.

"*The Capo is your uncle?*" Vanni asked, which reminded me that we'd never bothered to tell the rest of the streghe. I'd thought that since Mirella knew, they must all know. But not everyone had her talent at picking through the mud of gossip for shiny bits of information that might prove useful.

The streghe were all staring at Cielo as if he'd grown several extra toes, instead of losing the slightly frozen ones.

"It's true," Cielo said shortly.

"I'm going to need more of the story than that," Mimì announced.

Cielo grimaced at me, and I could feel his pain almost as

palpably as if I were Xiaodan, plucking it out of the air between us.

"I can tell it," I said to my strega as we reached a frozen stream. I clutched his hand, and we stepped out onto the thick layer of ice. It answered with a dull, hollow sound. "If that makes things easier?"

Cielo nodded, keeping his eyes on his boots, as if the ice might crack at any moment, though it was frozen several feet deep.

When we reached the far side, I turned back to the others, still in the midst of crossing. I chose my words as carefully as I would have chosen steps on this river, come the spring thaw. "Cielo's mother was the first strega recruited by the Capo before he began his campaigns." I skipped the bit where she grew powerful killing other streghe and feeding on their power. "She fell in love with the Capo's brother, a priest in the Order of Prai." Xiaodan's eyes grew large, and Vanni slipped a bit, regaining his footing by reaching out for Mimì's arm at the last second. "And then the Capo forced her to turn her magic on his brother."

Mimì drew in a cold, sudden breath. It wasn't hard to guess that she was imagining someone ordering her to use her magic against Lorenzo.

"What happened to Cielo's mother?" Xiaodan asked as the streghe reached the bank.

I turned to Cielo, who had walked ahead a bit, probably to avoid this conversation. Still, I kept my voice pitched low.

I remembered all too well the moment that Giovanna turned a dagger on herself. The way she apologized to a tiny Cielo before plunging it deep. "She took her own life. Through *the brilliant death*, her magic fell to Cielo."

That magic, stolen from the Capo's court, had taken my strega years to learn, to shape with the help of the book, to gain a measure of control over. I had the same stolen magic in my blood now—but I didn't have years.

We walked in silence, the early dark of the season bearing down on us.

"A Capo, a strega, and a priest," Vanni muttered. "That sounds like the beginning of a tavern joke, not someone's family tree."

A little more than an hour later, we reached a small forest of what seemed to be stunted trees but turned out to be composed entirely of tents. We ducked out of view, and I grabbed Cielo's hand and pulled him aside, not wanting the other streghe to see the fear that crawled through me, claiming territory. My throat. My lungs. My heart. "What happens now?"

"I know you wanted to fly in on the wings of victory," Cielo said. "But perhaps it's better this way. If you came in here with a portion of the Capo's army on your side, but you hadn't bested the Capo himself, you would have a skirmish on your hands. But if you sneak in and overtake him first . . ."

Cielo's strategy was elegant, and I wanted to believe I'd taught him this skill from my store of di Sangro lessons, but there was a much more obvious possibility. "This plays into your own schemes somehow, doesn't it?"

A moment came back to me, the meaning fully visible now that I didn't have a battle clouding my view. *I am not the one who came here to stop a war.*

"Why did you come to the Neviane, Cielo?" I asked. "And if you say that you did it out of love for me, I'll know you are lying, because you can love me and disagree with me as easily as you can walk and preen at the same time."

Cielo cast a quick eye at the encampment. "I want to pay a visit to the soldiers of Erras."

"Why?" I asked. "Are you trying to steal those knives?" My throat was healing, but my magic stung at the memory.

"I'm not after the Bones of Erras," Cielo said.

"Then what?" I asked, remembering Dantae's offer of a place with the soldiers of Erras. I didn't truly believe my strega would defect, but it didn't stop worry from trampling me like soiled boots on fresh snow.

"It has occurred to me," Cielo said, "that if the Bones of Erras are real, other things might be real as well."

I grabbed Cielo's arm when I sensed movement in the camp, pulling us back to the heavy darkness of the pines. "Such as?" The words came out as glittering and sharp as the icicles that clung to the branches above us.

The hood of Cielo's cloak was flecked with snow, the points of white nearly all I could see in the darkness. His voice came from some depth in his chest I hadn't plumbed before, a place of ancient hopes and fears. "There is a story of what happened to Veria after she called the sea to swallow Erras. She was more than just the one who killed him, you know. They had been allies, once. Great friends. Some of the stories . . . well, some believe they were lovers."

A chill moved through my bones, slowly, like the shift of shadows as the moon nudged them.

"Why would Veria love such a terrible god?" I asked. "He killed everyone they both knew."

"Erras believed he was righteous, but Veria saw the truth. And those are not always the same thing." Cielo's hand went to his pocket, the one I knew concealed his book. "Before that rift, they must have understood each other. There weren't many in the world like Veria and Erras. Imagine how lonely it must have been." I looked to the tiny band of streghe I'd gathered, each one looking deeply alone as they faced the great woods, the wide mountains, a camp full of men who did not understand who—or *what*—they were.

When I thought of the old gods, I had only been able to see an existence of worship and power, but distrust and fear were just as likely.

Cielo's voice drew me back to the slashes of darkness that passed for a hiding place. "Whatever the truth of their love, Veria's heart broke when she killed Erras. To contain her grief, she worked a vase out of moonlight and cried into it for days, emptying her body of a sadness so heavy it almost dragged her into the sea. Those tears are called Veria's Truth. Whoever drinks them will see whatever is real but hidden and change what they thought of as forever fixed."

"You want to use the tears of a goddess to reveal the truth of the Capo?" I asked. "To unseat him? There must be simpler ways."

"You are thinking in miniature, Teo," Cielo said, breathing on his fingers that had almost been frosted to death. "I want to look into the heart of magic and find a new way to pass it from strega to strega." Moonlight flitted over his face, drawing deep green from the wilds of Cielo's eyes. "I want to change the death inheritance."

The magic inside of me stirred, though I could not tell if it was in favor of the idea.

I did not care.

Cielo carried the same heavy truth I did. As long as magic

was passed through death, we would always be hunted. I dared to think of a future when our magic was only a source of art and beauty, and no longer had to be used as a weapon to keep us safe.

But a practical part of me, the di Sangro part, didn't understand how we could be focused on a hope as old as the empire when there were so many wrongs in front of us that begged to be sorted. "So we are in the business of chasing gods now."

"*You* are not," Cielo assured me. "At least, not while the Capo still rules Vinalia. But he will be deposed before dawn, and then perhaps we can turn our eyes elsewhere." The casual air that breezed through Cielo's words proved how firmly he had dug his heels into this idea.

There would be no talking Cielo out of this errand. What's more, I did not want to. But there were still arguments to be made. "I can't let you pay a visit to the soldiers of Erras alone."

"Remember the twenty-seven-part favor you promised me?" Cielo asked.

I'd agreed to this endless string of favors before we left Amalia, and Cielo hadn't invoked it since we left that city in a burning rush. I touched his face, warm fingers against icy marble. "I had thought parts three through twenty-seven could be delivered in a certain . . . specific form."

"We can talk about the remaining, ah, bits when I get back," Cielo said, his breath telling and quick, each white scratch of breath a hope written on the darkness. "For now, you have to trust that I will survive another chat with Dantae, as much as I trust you to face my uncle alone."

A single mention of the Capo drew us apart like two halves of a curtain.

I wanted to tell Cielo not to trust a word from a strega so willing to punish her own kind. I wanted to ask how I was supposed to overtake the Capo if he was still wearing a ring that deadened my magic. I wanted to grab Cielo away from the shadow of this camp and kiss him with enough heat to thaw the mountains into an early spring.

But Cielo was pulling away from me, drawing out his book, losing himself in its rustle. He looked up at me, the blank white pages reflecting the moon, throwing light on the nervous twist of his smile.

"In the mouth of the wolf," he said, offering the traditional Vinalian words for luck. The dash of added cleverness did not escape me—the Malfara family crest bore the image of a running wolf.

I nodded and gave the customary response, my words icy with intent. "May the wolf die."

Cielo turned the page and became a sleek winter fox.

My strega trotted into camp, and if a few men noticed an unexpected creature among their ranks, they only gave a quick glance.

꘠

"WE WON THE BATTLE AT ZARISI FOR THOSE PEOPLE!" VANNI shouted after I told him I would be sneaking into camp. "We should be able to stride right in and tell everyone we saved their frozen asses from the Eterrans."

Xiaodan shook her head. "A soprano could hit the highest note that has ever been sung, and it wouldn't matter if no one was there to hear it. We have no witnesses in the Vinalian camp to swear that we stopped the war."

"These people won't believe a bunch of streghe," Mimì added.

Each word of defeat was a stone tossed at me. I flinched, over and over, but I refused to turn back. We had come too far to have our victory stolen from us. Words were as powerful as wars, depending on who spoke them. If the Vinalian troops wouldn't believe streghe—what kind of person would they believe?

"The Capo is going to tell everyone himself," I said.

The streghe stared at me as if I'd loosened my hold on the reins of my mind and perhaps dropped them altogether.

"I'll turn myself into a soldier in the Capo's army," I continued, "and deliver a few boring papers. We'll have the Capo sign, in blood if you like, and then the second I leave his tent—*after* they're signed and his magic-negating ring can't ruin things—I'll change the papers into a written confession and abdication. It will be in his own hand, which I can forge magically once I have something to go by, and the signature itself will be perfectly real. The papers will state that the battle at Zarisi was won by powerful streghe. There will be a bit about how he has not proved to be the ruler Vinalia needs. It will be full of the Capo's sentiments about the good of Vinalia and how it comes first at all costs."

"Brilliant," Vanni said. "Mirella told me you were smart, but this is . . ." Vanni formed tiny fireworks with his hands.

"A very pretty plan," Xiaodan agreed.

Mimì's smile burned with borrowed moonlight. "Do you think you can work in a bit about Salvi's independence?"

"Of course," I said, handing out a sizable promise before

I had a chance to think. A second later, fear caught up with me. I wondered if I would have enough time, and enough control over my magic, to make so many alterations.

I distracted myself with more plotting. "When you hear the announcement, can you throw a few light bombs, some fire in the sky? Nothing to hurt anyone, just a bit of pageantry. You know how Vinalians love a good show."

Vanni and Mimì shared a look of delight.

I turned to face the dark fringe of the camp as torches were lit. "Now all I need is a soldier's uniform."

"Oh," Xiaodan said, fiddling with the furred hood of her cloak. "Costumes are important."

"And not easy to come by in the middle of a mountain range," Vanni said.

I thought of my cousin Sofia, the strega seamstress killed at the urging of a bone knife. Murdered by the same people Cielo was paying a little visit to right now.

My thoughts stumbled, and I could not seem to pick them up again. I turned back to the streghe to find Xiaodan sizing me up with her eyes. "What happens when you shift form?"

"She gets broader in the chest, with stockier legs," Mimì said with a startling confidence. I had almost forgotten that she had met me when I was in a slightly different body.

"Boy Teo is an inch or two taller," Vanni added.

Xiaodan cocked her head, nodded once, and then strode directly into camp. I almost cried out for her to stop, but Mimì grabbed my hand and pressed it tight. "Don't give her away," Mimì whispered. "Let the artist work."

Xiaodan swayed on her feet, looking mildly lost and very young. She grabbed the arm of a passing soldier, a youth with fine features, freckles like a generous dusting of nutmeg, and a habit of nervous swallowing. "Can I . . . can I help with something?" the boy asked in a lovely tenor.

"My name is Elettra, and I'm here to sing for the pleasure of the Capo and his troops," she said, the story striding off her tongue as if she'd been practicing it for weeks. "Do you happen to know the way to his tent?"

"Yes, you walk a bit farther down here, and then turn left at the heart of the camp. That path will end at the Capo's tent. Though you might want to pay a visit to the Capo's wife first. She'll be delighted to know culture has found us all the way out here. She loves opera and fine things."

I grasped for the image of a woman the Capo could have taken for his wife—and found myself empty-handed. He didn't seem like the sort to play at romance, even for the sake of spectacle and pleasing Vinalian crowds.

I only knew one thing. She would have to be someone easily reeled in by promises of power.

"I would love to visit both the Capo and his wife," Xiaodan said, unfurling a shy smile. "But first, well, I'm terribly cold from coming up here in a sleigh. If you don't mind, can we share something hot to drink in your tent? Or perhaps a warm blanket?"

The soldier looked around, trying to discern if he was caught in a dream. Then he looked back to Xiaodan. "Of . . . of course." He offered her a hand and drew back the flap to his tent.

When I turned to the other streghe, Vanni's eyes were wide with impressed shock. Mimì put her hands together to clap, though she kept the sound muted.

Xiaodan emerged a half hour later, alone, with a small bundle under her arm. She hurried to the edge of the woods and set down the clothes. I rushed to pick them up. "How did you . . . I mean, *did* you . . . ?"

Xiaodan's face flared with satisfaction. "We mostly kissed. And talked in hushed voices. And then I helped the poor thing realize how exhausted he was, and he fell asleep. Don't worry, I made sure I tucked the blankets up high so our soldier won't die of cold."

"Yes," I said. "That was definitely my first concern."

"You made love to a man to steal his clothes?" Vanni asked.

"I made love *and* stole his clothes," Xiaodan corrected. She grabbed my shirt and started stripping me with the efficiency of a young woman who had been dressed and undressed backstage thousands of times.

"How did you know to choose him, of all the men in that camp?" Mimì asked, bundling up my traveling clothes as Xiaodan threw them off.

"Oh, that's simple. When I sense emotions, I can feel which resonate with my own. It causes a lovely, shimmering harmony. That's how I knew it was fine to join a group of strangers on a trip into the frigid north. That's also how I was certain the young man I approached would be not only friendly, but lonely and inclined to talk. And just so you know, sentiment against the Capo is already turning in the camp. Some want his second-in-command to take over, but others don't think that's a good idea."

Xiaodan shucked off my traveling skirt in a single motion. I almost yelped as the mountain air pierced my skin, finding its way past all of my boundaries and working deep into my bones.

Vanni turned his face up to the moon and pretended

none of this was happening. A moment later, I looked down to find that I was outfitted in green and black.

Xiaodan had changed me into a soldier.

Now it was my turn to keep my promises.

༜❀༜

I WALKED AWAY FROM MY LITTLE BAND OF STREGHE, TOWARD THE camp. Torchlight mottled the darkness; cheers roughened the air. I wanted to head straight for the Capo's tent and face him before my courage drained away. But first I needed a mirrored surface so I could change myself. I didn't think many Vinalian soldiers kept such things in their tents. I crept to the edge of the camp and looked around for a source of water—a barrel for the men to drink from, perhaps.

That was when a soldier caught sight of me.

From the startled look in the unfeeling shallows of his eyes, I could tell what he saw. The quick, futile movements of an animal caught in a snare. The riotous curves of a woman's body stuffed into a soldier's clothes.

This wasn't a reflection of the sort I would find in a mirror or a glassy stream, and yet seeing myself as this soldier saw me gave me enough distance to work a reversal. I called on my magic, less afraid this time.

If I was going to use these shattered and stolen bits of other streghe's magic, I might as well use them against the man who had killed to force them together and shape them for his own use. I had always been good at punishing men who took what was not theirs.

This was my gift, and for the first time since I'd left the di Sangro castle, my magic rose without pain. It still felt impossibly vast—as harsh as the sea, as wide as the sky. It took all of the focus in my body to pinch it back down, to give it shape.

Change Teo into a nameless, faceless boy. My body shifted, whispering in new ways against the soldier's uniform.

The man stared at me in horror.

"I know you've probably never seen a bit of magic in your life, but that reaction is a little much, don't you think?" I asked.

I grabbed the man by the neck before he could reply, digging through muscle for a point Father had taught me about. My fingers clamped down, and the man fell into the snow. A few other soldiers turned to see what had happened, and I shrugged. "I think he choked on something."

Perhaps his own stupidity.

"I'll go get help," I added.

I moved away as other men gathered around his body. It was a good thing Xiaodan had already found out the way to the Capo's tent. One long stride at a time, I worked my way through the camp. My face felt strangely numb, but I assumed that was the result of being out in the cold for too long. The entire camp was still humming with the victory at Zarisi, and I nodded heartily as I passed, trying to look as if I belonged here.

Brow after brow furrowed, until I wondered what was wrong.

When I finally passed a water barrel, I stooped over, broke the skin of ice on top, gathered some frigid water in my hands, and used it as a makeshift mirror.

I dropped the water, stunned.

The magic had taken the word *faceless* literally, and where my features used to be, I saw only smooth lumps. My lips were papered over with plain skin, my dramatic nose all but gone. My eyes were a familiar dark brown, but there were no lashes fringing them, and where my eyebrows should have been were two barren ridges of bone.

No wonder I was drawing so much attention. People had a nasty habit of pasting their eyes onto anyone who seemed different. I rushed toward the Capo's tent, only a few hundred feet away.

"He must have been in the battle at Zarisi," a man behind me said, as if I couldn't hear him.

"I heard it was a massacre," another offered. "No survivors."

I paused, in the grip of a new idea. If people believed I was the lone survivor from Zarisi, it played into our plan.

"I was there," I said, my voice turned thick, words blunted by the state of my lips. "I ran up to the mountains to see if I could take out a few Eterrans from above. That's the only reason I survived." Men were drawing in from all directions now. "Their forces were laying waste to ours, and then streghe appeared on the mountainside, like angels." I was playing it broadly, but war was not a time for understatement. "They used magic to change every single Eterran soldier in the town to snow."

". . . snow?" one of the men asked.

"I believe it," another one tossed in. "Those two in Amalia changed themselves into wind and fire, remember?"

Those two in Amalia.

They were talking about me and Cielo.

"I have to go report to the Capo," I said, walking away from the soldiers with a long stride, a delicious swagger that came from learning I was as infamous as Cielo believed.

I ducked toward the Capo's tent, pulling out the papers I'd drawn up on loose pages Vanni had folded neatly in the bottom in his pack to write a letter back to his mother if he got the chance. He'd even brought a small pot of ink and a pen with a nice, wide nib.

"God bless Signora Moschella and her over-packing tendencies," I'd said as I wrote up a quick, false report from the southern provinces. Making it from the Uccelli had seemed a little too bold, like it might somehow draw attention to my true identity.

The lines I'd inked were now running with my sweat. Of course, it didn't matter what the paper said. I would change it as soon as the Capo had signed and I'd gotten safely away from his ring.

He wore that shard of magic always. It kept streghe from hurting him, but I believed his reasons for seeking it out went deeper. He spent so much time around dying streghe, and he didn't want *the brilliant death* to turn him into one of us. We were tools, not true Vinalians. We were there to be used and discarded.

A man like the Capo dreamed of becoming an emperor, not a strega.

I ducked inside. As soon as I'd entered his tent, my body shifted seamlessly, without my permission.

I was back in girlish form again, my reversal undone. I spun to leave, but I could not cross the boundary. I cursed until I ran out of breath, and then I cursed silently until I ran out of satisfying words.

With my plan shattered to pieces, part of me wanted to sit down and give up, but I hated the Capo far too much to curl up and wait for his return. I started ransacking his tent for something I could use against him, but he kept his battlefield home as sparse as his rooms in the Palazza. A cot for sleeping, a porcelain basin to wash, a bar of soap that prickled my nose with the surprising scent of lavender. Perhaps this was his new wife's influence.

On the Capo's desk there was a mountain range of important papers, but just as I went to rifle through them, I noticed something more interesting sitting to the side. The ring the Capo usually wore, crafted from gold and stolen magic, was sitting in a bowl of water. The water cast the shine of the ring up and across the canvas of the tent, gilding it.

I reached for the ring, thinking I might steal it before the Capo returned, but my magic balked. It didn't wish to be so near an object whose sole purpose was to unravel its working. Trying to touch the ring again felt like putting my hand to a flame—the drawback was instantaneous. In that moment of hesitation, the Capo drew aside the flap of the tent, smiling at me as if I were some long-lost cousin.

He beckoned to a soldier outside the tent and said, "Tell my second that Teodora di Sangro has returned to the fold." The soldier saluted and spun, but the Capo cuffed his arm before he could start off. "If this strega is here, my nephew— or niece—can't be far behind. Inform the men to keep a sharp eye for a young person with long black hair and a pampered air."

"Pampered?" I asked as the soldier set off and the tent closed behind the Capo, sealing us in together. "I thought Cielo's lot was fairly difficult after you destroyed Giovanna's life."

"She made her own choices," the Capo said mildly.

"So you didn't drive her to death and your brother back to the arms of a strega-hating religious order?"

"I thought my soldiers killed you in Castel di Volpe," the Capo said, no longer amused by my presence.

"You must have been too busy losing a war to notice that I was still alive."

"There is that wit," the Capo said. "I had forgotten how well matched we are, Teodora. Together, we could have doubled our greatness. Who knows? In time, I might have asked you to be queen of Vinalia." The thought slithered over me as the Capo took a seat in his canvas chair. "All of that is unimportant now that I've found the perfect wife. Strong of body, mind, and will. A good Vinalian woman, Fabiana. The people love her. And they don't have to worry about whether or not she'll turn them into thimbles when she gets angry."

He should be a tapestry that you can pick apart, thread by thread, my magic chanted, but no matter how much of it spilled out of me, nothing happened. My eyes went to the bowl on the desk. The Capo tracked my attention easily.

"Do you like that trick? A ring that protects me from the touch of magic can be used to cast a wider ring, with the same properties." He picked up the gold band and slipped it on. "The soldiers of Erras gave me the idea. They know all about shards of magic. I do wish they were slightly less obsessed with those bones, though."

I must have twitched, because the Capo gave a rich, heavy sigh.

"Please don't tell me *you're* interested in the Bones of Erras. You always seemed a more reasonable sort."

Part of my mind snagged on the idea that the Capo

believed he knew me so well—but the rest moved on. "The bones are shards of magic?"

I thought about the way they'd whispered to me, the judgment that dripped along their blades. *Of course* they were magic. I'd just been so wrapped up in thinking they were godly in nature that I hadn't seen it.

"You didn't know?" the Capo asked, leaning forward on a fresh wave of excitement. His enthusiasms were as catching as ever, but I knew they could be a death sentence. And that knowledge gave me a kind of immunity. I leaned back, arms folded as he rambled on. "Those figures that some called gods were powerful streghe."

If the Capo was right, the old gods were still with us, left behind in pieces, their magic stored and waiting.

My mind scurried back to what Cielo had told me about Veria's Truth. The tears in that vase carved of moonlight weren't some brittle old tale. They were strega magic, as real as the iron necklace I'd worn to Amalia.

I worked to throw a cloak over my hopes so the Capo wouldn't see their naked shine. If he wasn't already searching for Veria's Truth, I didn't want to give him any new ideas to steal from the streghe of Vinalia.

"The old gods brought the first age of magic," he said, still storming down the path of his own interests. "It's no wonder they existed at the same moment as the only empire this land has ever known. Magic and power have always been tied together."

One last piece of the Capo's plan for Vinalia slid into place, like an intricate puzzle box that I'd finally unlocked, revealing the darkness inside. The Capo had learned of the connection between the old empire and the streghe known as gods. Whether it was the beginning of his hopes for a new empire or only one step along the path hardly mattered. As soon as he could manage it, he had enlisted magic, risking the displeasure of the church to do the one thing that he believed would bring a new age of glory.

The Capo worked off his black leather boots with twin sighs. His feet were bare and pale with winter and confinement. He waved to the canvas chair opposite his. "Since you can't leave, you might as well sit. You and I keep meeting for a reason, Teodora, and I'm sure we can come to some kind of—"

The tent flap rustled. I held my breath, sure Cielo was about to be pitched headfirst in front of the Capo's bare, sweating feet. When I looked up, everything inside of me went dangerously still.

The orange torches of the camp set the edges of a young man's body alight. His eyes were the same dark brown as mine, but they had a searing quality that traveled through skin and muscle.

"Sister," he said. "I thought I would have to hunt all over Vinalia for you."

"I'm sorry to deprive you of that pleasure, Beniamo," I said.

My brother had the same deceptive loveliness that had come to his aid so many times as a child. He had been able to flutter his long black eyelashes at any adult until questions about the bruises on my legs dissolved. As he grew older, he had simply gotten better at placing my injuries where no one would notice them.

Any traces of softness that hid his cruelty had been stripped away by his time as an owl. The intensity of his face never waxed or waned now, but stayed at full, glaring strength. He wore a cloak of pelts and feathers, only a thin pair of trousers beneath. I wondered if he truly didn't feel the northern cold or if he was trying to train himself to care even less.

My brother moved between me and the Capo without a sound. I remembered what Luca had told me about owls, when Luca was still alive, before Beniamo ripped him from the world and left a ragged hole in my life.

Owls were silent as they flew. Prey didn't hear the great birds until they were already striking.

"Thank you," Beniamo said. His voice was low and hollow, and it scraped against my bones.

"Of course I was going to let you know that your sister had been caught running around camp," the Capo said. He gave me an apologetic shrug. "When you abandoned me, I was in need of new allies. Your brother was all too happy to swear his loyalty."

"I was thanking my sister," Beniamo said. He moved in front of me, taking up every inch of space in the tent, every crevice of my mind.

I knew that feeding him a scrap of interest was dangerous, but the question asked itself. "For what?"

"The victory at Zarisi. A *di Sangro* victory." I did not like how his voice lingered on our shared name. "I've been waiting for this moment."

"We all have," the Capo said. "Vinalia—"

"Needs a strong leader," Beniamo finished smoothly. "A man who will not lose his first war."

"Which is why it's such a good thing we've won," the Capo said, but his laugh sounded sickly.

"Yes," Beniamo said. "We have."

In that moment I remembered the stories Xiaodan had brought back from her soldier's tent, stories of a second-in-command who desired more power and might be too dangerous to wield it. I should have seen my brother mirrored in those words.

Without taking his eyes off me, Beniamo lifted his right hand to show that his nails had been replaced with long talons of some silvery metal. I did not know if this was magic, or if he'd grafted them himself.

He pulled his hand back in a swift arc and plunged his talons into the Capo's gut.

The Capo's eyes went shiny-wide, then dimmed. With Beniamo's hand still stuck in him, he fell to the ground. My brother huddled over the Capo's body, talons ripping fast, tearing him apart, until the Capo was no longer a man, or even a corpse, but a mass of blood and flesh and the soiled white of bone.

Beniamo stood up, his bare chest laced with blood.

"Now we are alone again, sister. How long has it been?" For years, I had been so careful not to be caught near my brother without someone else in the room. But this was not the di Sangro castle, and there were no doors to close, no one left to hide behind.

I shrank from him. Beniamo tracked my movements as if he knew where I would step before I did. He crowded my body with his against the rough canvas of the tent, leaning over me, the salty-hot smell of blood sticking to him.

He uncurled his fist, talons poised over my face.

I waited for white-hot streaks of pain. "Not yet," Beniamo said. "I don't want to rush things."

He flicked his wrist and caught me across the face with the back of his hand, knuckles bold against my cheekbone. "Do you know how long I've waited to hurt you without having to hide it?" he asked, backhanding me again.

I could not scream. Beniamo loved it when I screamed.

My temples felt like they would burst. My right ear hummed a metallic whine and then went strangely dull. I tried to stuff my pain back into my body, but it would not fit. I shoved and shoved, handfuls of pain, nowhere to put them.

As the first scream pulsed out of my throat, my brother leaned over me, smiling.

"That's a good start," he said.

It took every bit of will to keep from passing out, to stay on my feet when all I wanted to do was collapse. "Start to what?" I asked, trying to sound defiant, even as blood ran down my face like hot tears.

"Vinalia needs a leader who will not lose," Beniamo said, tracing the words with hungry lips. "And *you* are my war."

Three

A Garden of Fallen Stars

9

I was forced through a trapdoor into my childhood, crouching in the corner of the nursery, waiting for Beniamo's cruelty to pass like a wind off the mountains. He raised his hand so many times I learned every chapped line between his knuckles. He thrashed me with hateful words as often as he struck me, but I stayed silent.

It was the only way I knew to survive.

Magic did not rush hot through my blood, clamoring to save me. I'd stopped it from hurting Beniamo so many times, barely avoiding the fate of turning on family when he felt no such need. The pain inside of my head hardened, splitting into several sharp hopes. Rescue. Revenge. Escape.

My magic wobbled and struggled to right itself.

Do something, I told it. *Before he kills us.*

Beniamo turned away and walked with his back to me, the slight hunch of an owl lingering in his posture, his shoulders perched high. "You are not going to use magic against me."

I winced at fresh pain. Beniamo knew me well enough that I did not even feel safe from him inside my mind. I could not bear for him to see through me, like so much leaded glass, weak and wavering. Easy to break.

Stilling my thoughts, I silenced myself down to the marrow.

He bent over the mound of flesh and blood that had been the Capo and came up holding the ring. Beniamo licked the Capo's blood clean.

"Do you know how many of my kills I used to eat?" he asked as he shoved the ring onto his finger. I had been careful not to think too much of the time Beniamo had spent as an owl, the ways his humanity had been broken and put back together. It had left marks, though, as if he had never fully transformed back. "Most of those animals went down whole, and I vomited up their bones." I writhed, which only made him glow with satisfaction. "I ate other owls, too. Did you know about that, Teodora? Is that one of the scientific facts our brother told you?"

Without thinking, I raised my hand and slapped his mouth before Luca's name could pass through it.

Beniamo smiled as if I was finally playing with him. Then he grabbed my face between two fingers, pushing until my entire skull ached. "I've killed *so many* of your kind. Since magic is passed through death, I had no other choice, but I can't say I disliked the task." For all of the pain in my head, it was nothing to match the one that ripped through me now, a tide of mourning for streghe I would never know.

"No matter how many I torture, or slay, or tease the last breath from, I stay this way," Beniamo said, pressing a hand to his bare stomach. "The way Father and Mother made me. The way *you* made me." A darkness passed over Beniamo's face, like shadows smothering the moon. "Magic won't have me, Teodora. Tell me why."

"Your soul is too weak to feed it," I said, a guess spun from pure spite. Magic made its own choices, and even though I'd been a strega for years, many of its workings were mysterious to me. Still, I felt some grace in the knowledge that magic had passed over my brother.

Beniamo stroked my hair, a sickly playacting of the brotherly love he'd never felt. "You're the most powerful strega in Vinalia. Maybe I just haven't been killing the right people." He stood back and studied me, and the pain in my head grew. When he spoke, the words sounded off-kilter, far away. "It's fairness I'm after. You probably think of yourself as a good daughter, a good strega—if there is such a thing. But you took me from home and family. *You* did that. And so it is fair that I will take this land and everyone you love. You changed me with magic. If I can't have magic, I will tear it from the throat of Vinalia."

His words left me shaking.

But I would not speak. I would not think.

I would not give him *any* weapon to use against me.

"I might let you think you're safe for a while," he said, throwing himself down in the Capo's canvas chair. He sat impeccably still, only the burning centers of his eyes shifting with each tiny movement I made. "A few years to build your life, one nervous stone at a time, always looking over your shoulder when you hear an owl's call." For the first time I noticed another legacy my brother's time as an owl had left behind—a ring of orange around the dark di Sangro brown in his eyes. It burned with delight. "And then, oh then, I will swallow you whole."

It was all I could do to clench the vomit and muscle it back down my throat. Beniamo smiled at my struggle as I choked a few thin strings into the dust. "Of course, that's after I disembowel that black-haired strega boy. Or is it a girl?"

My head snapped up, my eyes meeting Beniamo's. He had played his strongest move. Now it was my turn to do what I always did.

Lose.

But I could not hold back this time. If I failed to stop Beniamo again, it would be after spending every bit of strength I had.

"*Now*," I said, in the hard, clipped commands of the old language.

Magic roared out of me.

I could not touch Beniamo while he wore the ring, but the circle cast by the bowl of water was no longer in place. Anything else could be changed. My magic met the canvas of the tent in a great crash, and it became a thin pane of glass. In a ripple that covered the entire camp, all of the tents became just as transparent and breakable.

"Is that all you want to do?" Beniamo asked with a laugh that sounded achingly familiar. He'd stolen it from Father. "Or maybe you can't even control that magic?"

The magic inside of me was the sum of a hundred deaths, too large for any single person to hold from moment to moment, but my rage was a force large enough to match it. I could feel it growing, spreading, pushing certainty into every corner of my soul. I knew what I had to do.

Stop my brother, at any cost.

The shouts of confusion from the soldiers around us were growing. With glass walls, the men in camp could see what

Beniamo had done to the Capo and what he was doing to me now. Beniamo had been allowed to hide behind closed doors for much too long.

"Look," I cried. "Look!" I wished that my voice didn't sound so high-pitched and fragile, but at least it drew more eyes.

Beniamo pounded to his feet. My magic had set the stage, and now he had a thousand men as his audience—an army of Vinalians at his mercy. I could feel the tide turn against me before a single wave hit the shore.

"The Capo is dead," he said. "By my own sister's hand. She has been given the power of many streghe, and it has turned her into a danger." His words sounded flimsy, empty, but men listened to him nonetheless. "She won a great victory for Vinalia today, and I wish I could help her, but she has no way of keeping her magic in check. We will have to stop her if we wish to keep our country."

I screamed at his lies, a wordless, raw sound.

And my magic screamed with me.

The sound broke the glass of the tents. Men knelt to take cover, shards lodging in their arms and throats. I slipped and fell to one knee, looking down to find that my magic had iced the floors, turning them to cold, clear mirrors. Here was my face bloody and bruised, my mouth misshapen by a scream, my arms raised.

I had kept my silence for too long, and now I could not stop filling the air with my howling, because if Beniamo spoke one more word, I would destroy everyone in the camp and myself in the bargain. And if he was the only one who walked away from this, with the Capo's ring on his finger, there would be no one to stand against him. He would kill every strega in Vinalia.

Starting with Cielo.

Help, I told the magic. *Help me leave this place alive.*

I looked down at my reflection trapped in the glass beneath my feet, and felt a reversal work itself even faster than last time. Before, I'd been trying to keep the power of this great magic from unraveling me. Now I urged it on. The screams that had passed out of my lips became the howls of a great storm. My body unlaced itself into gales of wind. I battered the camp as I went, but there was nothing left to break. I could only hope that Vanni and Mimì and Xiaodan—the streghe I had dragged to this place—had run away.

And then there was *my* strega.

I saw Cielo on the ground, a tiny figure running. He spotted me and vanished. A moment later, smoke rose from the camp, unfurling its long fingers where Cielo had stood. The smoke moved fast, beckoning me across the southern stretches of the Neviane.

Cielo and I left the camp behind as Beniamo howled at the sky, his rage and delight impossible to pick apart.

꓿꒰꜀꜂꒱꓿

I FLEW FOR HOURS, FOLLOWING AS MY STREGA DREW A DARK streak across a sky as pale as a fevered brow.

I had always thought storms looked swift from the ground, but in this form of clouds and wind, I proved to be a great, lumbering thing, unable to move without noticing every disturbance I caused below. I rustled trees, toppled carts. The men and women of the northern provinces squinted up at me through distrusting eyes and I thought, *This will only worsen when Beniamo's message spreads.*

My brother would slander us—tell stories of two streghe with magic grown ravenous and wild.

And people would believe him.

My anger rattled down as rain, lightning, thunder, until I had nothing left. I traveled in an emptied-out quiet.

Vinalia shed her skin, the raised flesh of hills giving way to smooth fields. From this height, I could see—no, I could *feel*—the roads. So many of them, built of dark and enduring stone, sliding people and goods toward a single point. This was how the ancient empire had poured blood into its heart, by creating roads unmatched throughout the world, all leading to a single point.

Prai.

The ancient capital burst into sight, prickly and glorious, clad in every material imaginable: brickwork, stone, tile, painted wood. The white and pastel marble found in so many Vinalian cities was here, but it had competition. Along each lively, jumbled street, homes and churches and shops shouted their existence to keep from disappearing. At the center of Prai stood the vain but undeniably grand dome of the Mirana, home of the church. At the outskirts of the city, the markets and temples of the old empire, slighted by time and weather, kept watch.

From so high, I could sense how this place was different from Amalia. The Capo's chosen capital had been laid in straight lines and squat arches. This place held a little bit of everything, the best from all corners of Vinalia stolen and tossed together. If Amalia was an earnest soldier, Prai was a pickpocket.

I thought we would fly straight over the city, but as we drew close, Cielo wound around the tops of the buildings. I followed, doing my best not to blow tiles off roofs and crosses from the tops of churches.

People tilted their necks, confused by the strange and dangerous dance taking place in the sky. Cielo slid toward the ground and I followed, calming my winds as best I could, but even so, women's skirts fluttered and water in fountains trembled at my touch.

We came to a street lined in tall houses, a proud few painted in persimmon or marigold. Their sides were furred with dark green vines, which shushed me as I tossed their leaves. When we slipped into the alley, I tore a great deal of laundry off the slanting lines.

Cielo slid through a second-story window. I blew open the curtains and tumbled, naked, onto a hard wooden floor.

Cielo had come back in girlish form and was somehow half-clothed in an underskirt and a linen corset with none of the stays done. She kept one eye on me as she dug through a trunk and tossed me the first thing she found—an overlarge silk shirt. I brought it to my nose. It smelled of garlic and the rose perfume of the last person who had worn it. I pulled the shirt on slowly, silently.

"Are you . . . all right?" Cielo's voice was a smoky rasp. It sounded far too quiet.

"Where are we?" I asked.

"Prai," Cielo said.

"Be more specific." I was being blunt. Harsh. But now that I was back in the body that Beniamo had attacked, I could feel every spot he'd touched me, and there was no room in my body for tenderness.

Instead of giving me more clothing, Cielo sat behind me and covered me with her arms, pressing her chest to my back. Her tenderness melted a reserve of tears, and they flowed out of me silently. "We are in a nameless house that certain streghe know of, where both travelers and those who are in danger might stay for a time."

"The Order of Prai doesn't know this place?" I asked roughly.

"Of course they do," Cielo said. "We have them over for anise biscotti every Tuesday."

Another fear wedged into my heart, which I had thought was full. "Do you think the streghe made it out safely?"

"I'm sure they did. Beniamo didn't know they were there, and they should have been able to vanish back into the woods without being discovered. Remember? They were waiting for our signal, which never came."

I breathed raggedly at the thought of my failure, and the whole ridiculous plan, which felt so tiny and easily crushed now that Beniamo had returned. I put my head to the floor, my cheek against its rough grain, overwhelmed by misery that had chased me all the way from the Neviane.

Cielo rubbed my back, her hands moving in large, generous circles. "What happened in the camp? In the Capo's tent?"

I told her.

"I'm sorry," she whispered. Or maybe she was speaking at her usual strength, and that was part of the problem.

"I will not let you take one drop of blame for my brother," I said, forcing my tears to a stop.

"Not that," Cielo said. "I thought I understood about Beniamo. I knew you used magic against him once, but you were so protective of Luca, and he had thwarted your brother's inheritance. I assumed Beniamo's bout of violence was a spectacle, a one-night-only engagement, if you will. A show of foul manly behavior as well as disgusting owlish ways. I never imagined . . ."

"How bad it truly was," I finished.

It had taken this much time for Cielo to see my brother. To understand the kind of terror I'd grown up with, gnawing at my days and infecting my nights. Of course, Cielo's ignorance was partly my doing. I had never wanted to speak of what Beniamo had done to me. I had wanted to shove my memories of him to the side, in the hopes that his life would never touch mine again.

"I was so upset over my lack of a family that I might have been a bit foolish about yours," Cielo said. It was true that the strega had never been able to understand that my deepest hurts, as well as my greatest pride, came from being a di Sangro. "I might never have figured it out unless I saw . . . unless . . ."

"Don't worry, at some point you would have talked until you crashed into an understanding," I said. A small smile awakened the muscles deep within my face, the ones Beniamo had dug into with chapped fingers.

Cielo's hand flew at the first sign of my pain, touching my bruises with feathered gentleness.

It did not surprise me that Beniamo had started out with marks that proved he could hurt me, but would fade in time for him to add a fresh set of wounds. There was one injury that might not heal itself, though, as if my brother had left an invisible promise of what was to come.

"My ear . . ." The skin around it was burning and tender, but that wasn't the worst part. On the inside, it felt like a mattress stuffed with too much ticking, sound muffled to the point of vanishing.

"What's wrong?" Cielo asked, the worry on her face coupling with the anxiety I felt at her faint, faint voice.

"Maybe it's not permanent," I said. And then I remembered what Cielo had told me: how any loss would persevere no matter what form I took. I stood and slipped into the more boyish version of myself that I'd been in the Capo's court. The reversal slid out of me seamlessly. I no longer needed to stare at myself from a distance to know that the girl in the reflection wasn't my only possible form.

Whatever happiness came with that knowledge was torn in half when Cielo announced, "It looks like you're becoming fluent in the language of reversals." Her words felt miles away. My hearing was as dull now as it had been before.

I raged to one end of the room and back again, finding myself caught against Cielo's chest, wound in her long, bare arms. She stared down at me, her eyes as wide as open doors, sadness passing through freely. "What?" I snapped. "Stop giving me that funeral look. I'm hurt, not dead."

"I have twelve decent reasons to kiss you right now, Teo, but I'm not certain I should." A new desperation fastened onto my thoughts. If Beniamo got his fingers around the way Cielo felt about me, and strangled it, I would never recover.

A kiss came on with such force, I didn't even feel our lips on each other at first. I was a gale, rushing into her. Then my mouth opened against Cielo's, the way the sky cracks wide at the start of a tempest.

Cielo needed no more convincing. She tugged at the shirt she'd given me a few minutes earlier, and I worked her up against the wooden walls of the house. As we kissed, groans brewed in her throat, so strong I could feel them rumbling in her skin.

"I thought this place was a secret," I said, plastering her neck with kisses. "I can only imagine what that sounded like with two working ears."

"I don't care if every single priest in Prai hears us," Cielo said. "In fact, it would do most of them good."

"I think everyone heard you, and that includes the retreating Eterran army."

"I haven't seen you this way for months," Cielo said, slipping around me and taking full stock of my body, a quick but obvious glance measuring the effect she had on it.

"I didn't know it was something you missed," I said, unable to hold the distance between us. My mouth found its way to her back, pressing along the wrought-iron lines of her shoulder blades. "You don't mind if I keep changing sometimes? You like when I take different forms?"

Pleasure rubbed against unexpected worry. It had been one thing to work a reversal in Amalia, but what would Cielo think if I used my magic to change forms, not because it was needed, but simply because it felt right? My strega had always changed outward shape, flickering in and out of forms. What if my reversals seemed different to Cielo, less natural? The wrong way to live outside of the world's strict boundaries?

"I like it when you are Teo, whatever that means," Cielo said as she fingered her undone corset laces. I felt the worry in my chest ease, and then slide away as easily as the cloth that bound Cielo's breasts. "There are times when you are more a storm than a girl, and I'm not speaking of the Capo's camp."

As she let the corset drop to the floor, I pressed in to cover the newly bared territory. Cielo poured out approval in warm, wordless sounds.

I closed my eyes and entered a place that was only darkness and pure feeling, and there I discovered a truth: the forms that pleased me most were the freest ones, with no boyish or girlish aspects. I had come to love my girlish body, but it was not the whole of me. I found comfort in this boy's form, but I couldn't imagine swearing off every other just to please a world shaped by men.

Cielo reached back with her fingertips, running them up and down my sides, drawing out deep shudders that felt like the frayed ends of my pain. "When we met, I'll admit it bothered me you had to appear a certain way for other people, in order to hold power that should have been yours in the first place."

"That is the way of the world," I said.

"That may be true." Cielo's voice skipped darkly over the words. "But if we cannot change the ways or the world, why bother with magic at all?" She spun around, pushing me against the wall, the strength in her slender arms blazing. "You and I have already scratched out a few rules that I'm sure most people thought were inscribed in stone."

She worked my legs open and settled herself between my hips. When she lifted the hem of the shirt, my body leapt to greet her hand. I strained forward into her loosely closed fist as she poured a river of kisses down my neck, the strong lines of my stomach, and lower.

And then I could do nothing but cry out, as loud as Cielo had done, and louder.

I stepped into the feeling as if it were a steaming bath, the first few moments almost scalding with pleasure, which settled into a deep, soothing warmth. My hands skimmed through Cielo's hair as my hips canted forward. With each long sweep, my worries and fears faded. They would return soon enough, but I would not live without this feeling. I would not live without Cielo. This, our brilliant life.

I tapped on her shoulder, politely first, and then urgently.

"Do you still have the vials?" I asked.

"Mmm?" she asked, more than a little distracted.

"From the strega in Pavella. *The vials*."

She shot up between my legs. "Oh . . . I'm not sure I would need . . . I mean, it's hard to know what to expect if I were to . . . I'm not certain I can become . . ." I expected a long discourse on the subject, but Cielo nodded and said, "Best not to spit in the eye of fate." She scampered half-naked across the room, rummaged through her cloak, and downed a small vial of milk.

Then she threw off the rest of her clothes as if they were enemies, the only things standing between us and victory.

I pulled more clothes from the trunk to soften the blunt floors, and we knelt together. I did not reach for her at first, and she did not rush past this moment either. We were stilled by a vast feeling, as if we had both rounded a bend in the road and found an ocean that had not existed the moment before. Cielo gathered me in her hands and pulled me closer, lifting herself up, until I moved out of the world and entirely into her.

I did not know what to do at first, and panic threatened to put a stop to everything, but my body stepped in with its own understanding. I saw myself, two small versions of my striving caught in her clouded-over eyes. My fingers coupled nicely with Cielo's ribs, her breasts brushing the tops of my fingertips. I felt a storm gathering through my body, a lightning strike that wished to pass through my hips. I tried to hold it off, but lightning was not easy to tame.

Cielo tipped back and lay down, giving me a startling, complete view of her body as I resettled on my sore knees. I was frozen by the sight of her, afraid to move. Afraid that some disaster of my life or magic would shatter this long-awaited moment. She grabbed my hand and settled my thumb on the softest part of her breast, where pale skin shaded into milky brown.

She had always been an impatient tutor.

"I'm afraid," I admitted.

"Of my breast?" she asked.

"No . . . I . . . no. I have a more *general* fear."

"I don't," she said, her eyes settled on my face. Cielo had always looked at me that way, as if staring directly at my face was as good as rummaging through the cupboards of my soul. "I'm not afraid, Teo. We are the only ones in this room, and there is no piece of you that frightens me." I thought she meant the forms I could take, or the fact that I might spontaneously destroy the safe house with magic, but she was not done. "Your anger, your power. Your sadness." That last one slowed me. "In fact, I will only be upset if you hold anything back."

My hand traveled down between us with a startling confidence. Having touched myself there many times, I knew it would add brightness and depth to Cielo's feelings. Her breath became as rich as oil, and her body arched into a deep crescent. She turned her face to the ceiling and swore in every dialect of Vinalian.

I got so tangled in the glory of watching that it came as a

surprise when my own body doubled its strength and speed, flying into a whirlwind as Cielo clutched at my waist and closed her eyes.

"You are safe here," she muttered. "You are safe."

I did not know if she was speaking of the house for traveling streghe, or something much larger than that. But those words, in her throaty alto, broke me. I slid my hands to get a firm hold underneath her, and I held nothing back. One more great strike of our bodies, and we rocked together in the wake of my finish.

With a pitted groan, I withdrew. Cielo stood up suddenly, as if important business had come to her attention. I watched her retreating backside, raw happiness already spinning into the fine threads of memory. But when she bent over, she flipped to a well-worn page in her book, took on a boyish form, and crawled back to me.

My wanting picked up, an eager wind. As Cielo's body clashed with mine, another truth came clear.

Only the sky can hold a storm.

10

I woke to a stream of noise bubbling through one ear. People shouted in Vinalian, laced through with several other languages and the gritty cries of babies. Prai was fully awake.

So was Cielo. He sat near my ankles in boyish form, his face cast in a honeycomb of light by the tattered curtains. He was spreading out a heap of food, arranging and rearranging with long, careful fingers. "You must be hungry after . . . well . . . I believe it would save a great deal of breath to call it *everything*."

That felt like a challenge, and my mind slipped new ideas between the cracks of my memories.

"How long did I sleep?" I asked as I stretched muscles whose limits had never been quite as thoroughly tested as they had been last night.

Cielo rolled his wrist several times as he said, "Exactly as long as it takes to recover from a march into the snowy mountains, a battle against an entire army, and a surprise visit from your brother." My chest pulled at the mention of Beniamo. Still, I was glad to find the strega back to his traditional habit of honesty, not combing through his thoughts and picking out the offending ones before he spoke.

I sat up slowly, finding myself back in girlish form, having changed so many times I lost track. There were leftover wisps of feeling all through my body. I set my fingers to working out the worst of the snarls in my impressively destroyed hair.

"What are those?" I asked, nodding at Cielo's bounty: small fried globes that were giving off a lovely smell.

"A small miracle in edible form, one that I miss each day that I am away from Prai. They're called supplì. First, rice is rolled together with beef ragù and mozzarella, the whole of which is coated in . . ."

Whatever else Cielo had to say melted away as I bit into one, the thin fried coating giving way to savory, salted warmth. I groaned in a way that made Cielo's face take on a distinctly helpless look.

I leapt to my feet and crossed to the trunk, on fire with the knowledge that if I did not leave now, I would spend the entire day in this room, vigorously forgetting about Beniamo, the future of Vinalia, anything but the way Cielo stroked his lips as if they were newly lined with gold.

After pulling on a linen shirt and woolen skirt, I added a man's half cape and sturdy leather boots. If people were going to stare at the streghe no matter what, I figured I might as well dress however I wished.

We ate the rest of the supplì in a rush, and Cielo led me onto the streets to find a bottle of wine.

"How can we be worried about our appetites when Vanni, Mimì, and Xiaodan are missing?" I thought of them climbing down the iced slopes of the Neviane with Beniamo—and his stolen army and his penchant for killing streghe—not far behind.

"I promise I will fly back north and find them soon," Cielo said, tucking his arm through mine with little care for the looks that followed us. "There is a small matter to deal with first."

It was one thing to swirl over Prai at a great height, and another to be cast into the froth of people and horses and carts on the street. Piazza after piazza burst forth, each with its own fountain. They were adorned with a dizzying array of statues: animals, angels, naked men and women, God in the flesh. It felt a bit as if Prai had gotten drunk and pointed wildly at everything it wished to have.

Once we had found our wine, a white from the central provinces that bloomed in my mouth like flowers, Cielo let me take all of three sips before he grabbed my wrist and kept moving. "Why am I starting to think we're not in Prai only because of the safe house?" I asked.

"Because you are always trying to assign slippery motives to people, even ones you know and trust," Cielo said. A smile threatened his features. "And because we are not in Prai only for the safe house."

We turned the corner and entered a neighborhood where a new blend of spices scented the air, and carts sold everything from blessed oils to fried artichokes. I'd heard of this place, a ghetto in Prai, home to believers of the Evracco faith. I watched them closely as they went about their days, taking comfort in the fact that their religion was older than the empire, as old as streghe, proof that some in Vinalia had never been converted to the church of Prai.

Cielo smiled at everyone we passed, but the face he turned to me was drawn in straight, somber lines. "When I spoke to the soldiers of Erras in the Capo's camp, they gave me assurances that Veria's Truth was real."

"Apparently, it's a shard of magic," I said, tired of being two steps behind in Cielo's search for a way to change the death inheritance. "Did they also tell you that the old gods were streghe, or have you always known?" I would have tossed in the disgrace of learning such a fact from the Capo, but his death dampened my outrage.

I thought of his body: muscle exposed, blood spreading, steam rising.

"I'd heard rumors, but I had no way of knowing if they were true," Cielo said. "Think of the strega stories Fiorenza told you as a child. Streghe have turned out to be gloriously real, but does that mean you now believe every detail of those tales? Or are you slowly picking the flowers of history from the weeds of myth?"

"I always liked weeds," I said stubbornly. "They grow without anyone giving them permission."

Cielo gave me his best smile then, one that was not a flourish of script but a simple, quickly jotted truth.

"So we are in Prai to find Veria's Truth," I said as we passed out of the Evracco neighborhood and into one that seemed to be composed entirely of bakeries. From every direction, the smells of butter, chocolate, and toasted nuts crowded in.

"It's not that simple a dance," Cielo said. "Dantae can tell us where to look, but I have to provide her with payment first. As you rightly pointed out, the soldiers of Erras didn't care for the Capo nearly as much as they appreciated what he was willing to give them."

"The Bones of Erras," I said. "But they already have those, don't they?"

"Dantae wants the full set," Cielo said. "She knows that

a time of open magic means that her people are in danger from all sides, and she wants them protected. According to legend, the magic of the knives is strongest when they're united. Turning people's worst fears against them is a powerful weapon, and in the end it means *less* killing. Dantae is brilliant and brutal, but she's not bloodthirsty." Cielo's tone wobbled, as if he wasn't quite sure he believed that last bit. "The soldiers of Erras were getting a bit desperate since the Capo had cut them off until they supplied a military victory."

"You promised them another bone knife," I said, the words cutting against the sugary sweetness of the bakeries.

"Three, actually."

"Did you think that was a good idea, considering what those knives can do?" I asked. "To us?"

Cielo's silence formed a rickety bridge between us. The soldiers of Erras weren't the only desperate streghe in Vinalia.

"Besides, how are we meant to find three tiny godly bones in a city this massive?" I asked. "We've walked through a string of neighborhoods, and we haven't come to the center of the city or even glimpsed one of its edges. We could spend the rest of our lives searching for them and never—"

"They said the Capo was given his information by a priest," Cielo muttered.

The Capo had only one priest to call his own. He had been told the location of the bone knives by Oreste, Cielo's father.

We turned a corner, sharp as a caught breath, and the Mirana came into view. Its dome was colored grayish blue in a striking match with the air above Prai. The gilded lines that segmented it ran in seams down the sky, as if showing that it, too, was a construction of God. The white marble body of the great church was lined with fluted columns and ornate pedestals, bolting heaven to earth.

"My father will never tell me a thing without . . . coercion," Cielo said. "And seeing as that is on the menu of di Sangro specialties . . ."

Cielo believed I would do anything to help him, but I still hadn't told him what I'd seen on his father's face in the square in Amalia, when Cielo and I left with a rush of magical flame. "Oreste remembers your mother."

Our steps had pulled us across the great open circle in front of the Mirana where crowds gathered on holidays. When I reached the building, I dropped to my knees and hung my head, a motion that came as thoughtlessly as breathing.

Cielo knelt beside me. "Of course Oreste remembers my mother," he said. "He hates her."

"I believe your father remembered the truth of their love, at least for a moment," I whispered. "When he tried to kill the kitchen strega, her magic overcame Oreste and gave him back the rightful memory, the one that Giovanna had pasted her magic over."

"My mother's magic couldn't have made my father believe he was tricked into loving her without his help," Cielo said, pushing up from his knees. "He provided all the raw materials."

My magic hissed at me, angry that I'd done the same as everyone else, pointing a finger toward a strega's magic instead of where it should have been aimed—at human failures, fears, and weakness.

"You're right," I said, to the magic as much as to Cielo. "But perhaps he can still be won over."

"If that's true, it adds to the list of reasons you must come with me," Cielo said. When I did not move, he sighed viciously. "You gave your word that we would seek to change the death inheritance after the Capo was unseated."

"He wasn't unseated by us," I said. "He was torn apart by Beniamo. You have to see how that changes things."

As much as I wanted to believe in Veria's Truth, the story paled when I thought of the pain Beniamo had heaped on me in the Neviane. It would spread to all of Vinalia if I did nothing to stop it. I paused on the steps of the Mirana, hoping I looked like a hesitant pilgrim instead of a nervous strega. "My brother . . ."

"You think this is different, Teo, but it's the same terrible story," Cielo said. "Beniamo is one more man who wants to rid the world of us."

On a quick heel, Cielo turned and stormed into the heart of the church of Prai, abandoning me to an impossible choice.

To follow or to leave him.

꒰✤꒱

INSIDE, THE MIRANA WAS EVEN GRANDER THAN I EXPECTED, the painted ceilings split with gold, each curved section decorated with a riot of saints and angels and God in his many forms. It looked as if a church had coupled with a palace, and the Mirana was their child, dressed in finery and made to put on a show for visitors.

"Where do you think they keep the priests?" Cielo whispered as we passed through yet another archway. "Are they cowering far away from these paintings? Perhaps having God grimace over them in twenty different strains of agony inspires them to keep those vows of celibacy."

Pilgrims to the Mirana turned to gouge us with disapproving stares.

My magic guttered like a flame in a strong wind, wanting to take this entire place down in one violent blaze of change.

I thought of *the brilliant death* and the dozens of streghe whose power I carried. How many of those had been forced into hiding, hurt, or even hunted by the church of Prai? Were they pushing me toward revenge—or was my own anger at what the church had done to Cielo's family enough to make me burn?

They had killed a beloved teacher as Cielo sat there, bound. They had turned Oreste's heart so completely against streghe that there was no place in it for his own child.

"Do you think my father is hiding in the walls like a church mouse?" Cielo asked, his fear bubbling up his throat and coming out as endless chatter. It drew the stares of a solemn set of guards in white and gold, flanking a set of interior doors.

Prai was within the bounds of the Otto territory, but a deal struck with the Capo had kept it independently ruled by the church. The Mirana was allowed to raise a small, mostly ceremonial army. Most of the men hailed from Prai, but some came from as far away as the island country of Celana in the north, which had been part of the old empire and still swore fealty to the church.

"You might want to keep your thoughts inside your head," I said, splashing into the stream of Cielo's constant chatter. "Those men at the doors aren't simply decorative. Those are soldiers. They protect God against blasphemy."

"We're *walking* blasphemies," Cielo pointed out. "What do they do with those?"

That question seemed to draw the interest of the two closest guards. They looked back and forth between us, solemn faces betraying the smallest bit of excitement at finally having more to do than guard a door from eager pilgrims.

"Who are you?" one of the soldiers asked, stepping forward. "Declare yourself and your intentions here."

The man's eyes had just enough time to flash with true fear before both guards dropped to the ground, brightly painted spinning tops.

"You couldn't have made it something more showy?" Cielo asked.

"You were just complaining about the gaudy nature of the Mirana," I said.

"Strega!" one of the pilgrims cried.

Another set of guards rushed around a corner, their boots ringing on marble. They both had the pale-moon complexions, freckles, and light hair of Celanese.

"Stop," Cielo said, "or she will turn every one of you into a prayer bead and wear you around her neck all strung together."

"We wish to see Oreste," I said. "Father Malfara."

"You are prisoners of the church," the guard said in a curiously formed accent, although he did not take a step closer.

"No, *you* are prisoners of the church," Cielo muttered. "We are passing through on our way to more interesting places."

I picked at the cape on my shoulders, acting as if we barely had the time to deal with such trifles as being caught by the Mirana guards. "Tell Father Malfara the streghe from Amalia will see him in his private rooms," I said. "Unless, of course, he'd prefer something more public. We could meet him at the altar if he prefers."

My audacity pulled gasps from the crowd.

"Showy enough?" I muttered to Cielo.

A field of silence stretched, wide and fallow, as we waited for the guards to rush away and back again. When the Celanese returned, they had gathered an entire flock of guards, which only turned the streghe from Amalia more impressive and dangerous in the eyes of the crowd. To be honest, I could have made them all into wooden playthings with a single command in the old language.

Part of me longed to do precisely that.

"Father Malfara says he will see you in his rooms," the guard told us, his head bowed as if he didn't dare to meet our eyes. Was he afraid that we would hurt him, or was looking at us a sin?

The ring of guards opened to swallow us, a sort of living cage that we would be carried in, all the way to Father Malfara. "Here's a bit of advice," I told Cielo as the circle sealed around us, and the air filled with the threat of fearful men. "Family gatherings are always twice as disastrous as you think they'll be."

❦

WHEN I'D LAST SEEN CIELO'S FATHER, ORESTE, HE HAD BEEN carving a public spectacle out of the death of a strega.

Now he stood in a small ornate box of a room, pouring espresso into tiny blue-and-white Ovetian cups, and laying out tea cookies. I had seen enough terrible men in quiet moments not to be fooled into thinking Father Malfara was harmless. It only proved that he could clothe his hate, hiding it from the world, and even from himself, before he stripped it back down.

"Will you take a cup?" he asked me. Fingers of pale, luring steam rose from the liquid.

"After you pour one for Cielo."

"Of course," Oreste said. He managed to push a cup of the vivifying drink at Cielo without looking his child in the eye.

I sat and poured the espresso down my throat in a single motion. Its bitterness stayed with me long after I glimpsed the bottom of the cup.

Father Malfara sat, his charcoal robe wrinkling darkly. "Why have you entered the house of God?"

I could see Cielo visibly restrain himself from making a thorny comment. He didn't bother to take his espresso, or the seat his father waved at in a meager show of generosity. "You'll be glad to know I'm not here to make some great, magical scene or shout the specifics of my bloodline. I need one thing, and it's fairly simple. Then I can vanish from your life as quickly as I came."

"There is no need—"

Cielo put up a hand to stop him from making any planned speech. "Tell me how to find the Bones of Erras."

"I can't possibly," Oreste said, as if those three words were the beginning, middle, and end of the matter. "What if the church knew I'd handed over such a powerful tool to . . ."

"Streghe?" I supplied. "Or the child you fathered by one?"

"Giovanna stole my reason from me," he shouted, as if his excuses had been waiting years to burst from their cages.

"I don't know what happened between you and Giovanna,"

I said, forming my words with the care of manicured hedges so I would not grow wild with loathing. "You do, though. That day in Amalia you saw the truth. You *felt* it."

"It's useless, Teo," Cielo said, collapsing into the chair across from his father, looking as surly as a small child. I clearly hadn't done enough to warn him about the difficulties of having a father.

"There is no reason the church needs to know that you're helping us," I said.

"And how would I explain my meeting with the two most powerful streghe in Vinalia?" Father Malfara asked.

Cielo perked at the compliment, even if it came snared in a web of disappointments.

I poured another drink from the silver press, but as soon as I downed it, my thoughts leapt in every direction. "Tell them we forced you into it," I said. "You have every reason to fear us, after all. We *are* able to change your form and your fate in a single moment."

My magic heard the opportunity in those words and slid through me, putting me dangerously off balance. I brought it to heel, knowing Cielo would never forgive me if I used my abilities against his father.

Even if he *would* make a fine tasseled footstool.

But Cielo's family—even the dregs of it—meant far too much to him.

"If I reveal the location, will you use the Bones of Erras to hurt people?" Father Malfara asked. "They're grisly tools."

"Very different from the Order of Prai's legendary chambers of torture," I said tightly.

Father Malfara raised an eyebrow at me. I drew back, burnt by his resemblance to Cielo.

"We won't use the Bones of Erras for any dark or magical deeds," I chanted flatly. I neglected to add that I was unable to supply any such promise for Dantae and her leather-clad streghe.

Oreste plucked a baci di dama from the tray. It passed through his mild tan lips, leaving a shine on his fingers. He let us wait as he chewed, scattered the crumbs from his lap, and wiped his fingers on his robe. "You've heard of the bone roads, I assume?"

"Yes," Cielo said, revealing far too much eagerness. I gave him a stern look cast in the mold of Niccolò di Sangro.

"I thought all roads that lead to Prai are called bone roads," I said.

"After the name was coined, the use spread," Father Malfara explained.

"Vinalians do love a bit of death in their whimsy." Cielo leaned forward over his crossed leg, giddy with interest now that we were getting somewhere. "Or maybe it's the other way around. . . ."

"The original bone roads were laid late in the empire," Father Malfara continued. "They have fallen into disuse, but they are still there, hidden under dirt and stone."

A shiver worthy of midnight crossed my skin, even though great blocks of sun fell through the Mirana's windows. "You're telling us that Erras's bones are buried beneath the roads."

Father Malfara nodded, the lines of age in his neck meeting the dark collar of his robes. "Where the roads meet the city. The power of Erras rings this place . . . if you believe in that sort of thing."

Cielo flew to his feet, unable to sit now that he had a

destination, a new line to stitch onto the map that would lead us to Veria's Truth.

I set down my cup. "Wait," Oreste said, his hand on the table, falling just short of my wrist. "Are you . . . in danger?"

"Always," I said.

Father Malfara nodded again. "God walk with you."

"He's never kept me company before," Cielo said, stacking three baci di dama between long fingers and disappearing out the door.

I was stuck in a whirlpool of thought, unable to break away. The Order of Prai would not have approved of what Father Malfara had revealed to us, or the blessing he'd offered, but it had not stopped him.

He was able to stand up to great power, even if he was not brave enough to stay on his feet for long. It took me a long moment to understand that I was taking Oreste's measure, the way I had with every man I had changed for my family's sake in the Uccelli. And while it was true that Cielo's father was cowardly, there were worse things in this world than a disappointment.

Beniamo was one. He had killed this man's brother. He would kill every one of us unless the right person rose against him. And if Oreste was not brave enough to stand for long, perhaps he only needed more strength to prop him up.

"What is it?" Father Malfara asked, no doubt worried by the length and depth of my stare.

There was no way the news from the Neviane would have reached him yet. The fastest messenger, traveling on foot, would still be crossing the Otto territory. Cielo and I had gotten here ahead of the miserable truth.

"The Capo is dead," I told him, to begin with.

"Cristoforo?" The name tumbled out of Father Malfara's lips, soft as prayer. For a moment, it turned the Capo back into what he had been at the start: a loyal brother, a bright and hopeful young man. I did not need to forgive what he had done to Vinalia—to me—in order to understand the shadows that moved across Oreste's face. My brother Luca was gone, and my soul knew the heavy gray feeling that came with such a loss.

There were more people to save, though, and that would require a great deal of magic. I would start by changing Oreste, not into a footstool but into the next leader of Vinalia.

"What do you know about Beniamo di Sangro?" I asked.

"My brother took him on as a second-in-command," Oreste said. "The man wished to become a strega." He could not quite hide his disgust at such a plan. And I could not quite hide how much I pitied his fearful heart.

But in this case, he was right to be afraid.

"What Beniamo wants is power, any way that he can have it," I said. "And now he's brought the Capo's army to heel."

Oreste stared into the distance, as the steam from his untouched cup of espresso twisted through the air.

"What if there was a way for you to step back from the Order of Prai without losing a drop of honor? What if it was not a disgrace, but a call to another form of duty?"

Father Malfara seemed to follow my logic without a detailed map. "If I say no, I suppose you will reveal my past."

"No," I said. "I will let you die knowing that you could have done something to save thousands of God's children, and one of your own."

11

As soon as we stepped out of the Mirana, Cielo looked up at the gray sky strewn with the rubble of clouds. The sun had gone into hiding, and it was almost impossible to tell how long we'd been inside.

Cielo looked so pale, I was surprised that I could not see the working of his blood beneath his fair skin. If a single talk with his father could do so much, I wondered how long it would take before he became wispy and transparent.

Before he faded away altogether.

I put a hand to the tempered blade of Cielo's shoulder. "No need to act defeated now that we are finally gaining ground," I said. "We know the Bones of Erras are beneath the city, and . . ."

Cielo spun on a choppy heel. "I cannot believe you are planning to make that man the leader of Vinalia. He's an invertebrate creature who can't take care of one infant, let alone a nation." Cielo paced in tight circles, as if chasing himself down. "Oreste will run away the first time Vinalia cries."

"And Beniamo will bash Vinalia's head against the stones," I said.

Cielo had seen what happened at the camp in the

Neviane. He'd watched Luca die at the hands—or talons—of my brother. But I'd seen Oreste's cowardice, too, how it drove him away from Amalia in the same hour that he finally saw his child. Cielo and I stared at each other, our pasts locked in a silent battle.

Father's words broke the stalemate.

Family is fate.

This time, one of our families would shape the fate of an entire nation, and I could not have it be mine. "You have always accused the di Sangro family of being too friendly with violence," I said. "You don't have to agree with my argument. You can use your own logic against yourself. Your father might not be a good king, but will he be a catastrophic one?"

"From useless to catastrophic," Cielo muttered. "That's the scale on which we measure things now?"

I knew the exact depths to which we'd plunged since the Capo died. All the more reason to act, before that possibility was taken away from us, along with everything else. "You know the Capo's bloodline is the clear one to follow for succession. Otherwise the Vinalians will never accept a new leader quickly enough to stop Beniamo's ascendance. As far as I know, the Capo has only one other living relative." I used the oldest trick, throwing my winning card out with a careless shrug. "If you prefer to run Vinalia yourself . . ."

Cielo leapt away from me slightly, as if my words had bitten him. "Oreste it is." But as soon as he'd agreed to my scheme, he thrust an accusing finger back toward the Mirana. "Your plan might as well be a piece of cheesecloth, though. It's fashioned entirely of holes. You know that man won't last against your brother for five minutes before we find him huddling in the cellars of the Palazza."

"I'm aware of what we'll need to keep him upright. I'll start searching out the bone roads, but I need you to—"

"Deliver messages to the five families, the streghe, and any other allies you've concocted?" Cielo asked.

My hands lodged on my hips as if those were their rightful homes. "Am I that easy to predict?"

"Knowing you in many forms is quite the advantage, Teo. I can always feel the way your winds are blowing," Cielo muttered lowly. My throat stuck when I tried to swallow, and a faint dimple graced Cielo's cheek. "But even without the help of magic, you are predictable. I could write an epic poem on the subject, but I'm afraid all the verses would be the same."

"You can skip the poetry," I said. "But I will be needing paper and something to write with. And I'd rather not use magic in Prai, at least until I know it's welcome here." The idea of facing yet another set of men who didn't know what to do with a strega, and therefore did whatever they pleased, was less than tempting.

"We are in the greatest city in Vinalia," Cielo said. "You can have paper from any corner of the world. Paper of every weave, every weight, every shade, and edged however you please. Paper fine enough to eat for supper."

Cielo walked me past a row of shops filled with furnishings and ironwork to a stationer's, a rarefied place of dark wood and brass fittings that gleamed from constant oiling. Stacks of ledgers wrapped in creamy leather sat next to handmade paper with rosemary pressed into the pages. There were loose leaves made from untouched groves across the virgin continent, while the innards of one journal came from an ancient tree in the mountain countries near Oveto. I passed squat bottles of ink in unexpected colors: a serpentine green, a violent mauve. On one shelf, the proprietors of the shop had set out little cards with samples of their work.

Cielo stopped in front of a wedding announcement. The names were left blank, to be slotted in later.

"Fine work, don't you think?" he asked, pointing out that one. He turned to me, studying my response.

"Do you ever . . . think about such things?" I asked.

"Becoming a calligrapher? Never," he said, looking down at his hands. "I have nice enough script, but I don't always have fingers, which would be an impediment."

I rolled my eyes and moved along, but Cielo was stuck on that little card, one finger touching the weave of the paper. I looked back and found all mirth cut away from the strega's expression.

"That is not on our path, Teo," Cielo said. "It is miles away from our destiny of changing magic."

"It shouldn't matter," I agreed. And yet, from some reason, it did. Not because I'd dreamed of a wedding all my life. Perhaps it was because I'd *never* dreamed of one until I had Cielo, and the spark inside of me lit. Since Mirella's wedding, the untended fire had grown into a blaze.

Cielo's fingers moved from the wedding announcement to a nearby stack of wares, tucking away a pen, followed by paper and ink. I was outraged—and slightly relieved at the distraction from my hopeless thoughts of marriage.

"You're taking those?" I whispered hotly. "People think streghe are nothing but magical criminals at best, and you're stealing?"

"There are men dashing off with entire countries," Cielo said, sotto voce. "A bottle of ink and a pen are hardly the problem."

Another one of Father's sayings arrived in my head. *A thief steals his own sense of right and wrong first, which makes the rest simple.*

"We'll pay the shopkeeper back," Cielo said, probably because I was still glaring at him. The spindly shopkeeper was now glaring at both of us, whether because we looked suspicious or because we were now acting that way to match, I couldn't tell.

I imagined the basket of olives that would appear on his step several months from now.

We left quickly and worked our way over several streets before I sat down in a brightly tiled piazza, under the beatific smile of a mermaid who spouted water from her pursed lips as well as both breasts.

I wrote as quickly as I could manage, spreading the paper across my lap to keep it from growing wet or grimy on the stones. As I wrote of Beniamo's deeds in the Neviane, and what he had promised to do next, fear sent my letters sprawling.

Cielo walked the stone lip of the fountain, back and forth, back and forth. "It's not right to leave you here, Teo. You don't know the city."

"Prai is not a person with whims and ways that have to be worked around," I said, my spoken words breaking the flow of the written ones.

"Of course she is," Cielo said, his frown implying that I'd learned nothing in all of our travels.

"I'll be fine here," I insisted, although I did not like the idea of wandering Prai alone. It meant leaving myself open to attack. What if Beniamo came for me first before declaring himself the new leader of Vinalia?

No. He had promised to hurt me before I died.

It was not much comfort, but I knew that Beniamo would not skimp on any kind of torture. I was safe for the moment—but nothing else was. Cielo would be fine as a bird, I assured myself. Beniamo was no longer able to track him in the air. My brother didn't have magic. He was limited to a single, terrible form.

"You'll have to move as quickly as possible," I said, handing off the first two letters. Cielo held them out for the ink to dry, since he hadn't stolen any powder. "At my guess, we have less than a week before Beniamo reaches Amalia with the Capo's army."

"I'll take all of the messages at once," Cielo announced.

"In bird form? Is that possible?"

"I've spent a fair amount of time as a flock," Cielo said. "Though streghe are not meant to be carrier pigeons."

"And you can fly in three different directions at once?"

Cielo studied the sky as if it held all of the answers and only needed to be looked at from the correct angle to give them up. "I've never really tried before, but . . . three?"

"One of these is going to the five families at Castel di Volpe, and the other two are headed back toward the Neviane."

"I'm assuming one is for the streghe we left behind," Cielo said, rolling the first two letters into scrolls.

I bent over the third, bearing down hard on the stolen pen. "I have written one for the soldiers of Erras."

Cielo plucked the paper from my hands even as I was finishing off my signature. He looked over what I'd written. "It's a bit brief. And biting."

"That woman slit our throats, and you want me to offer

her my best social graces?" I asked, springing to my feet, my hands leprous with ink. "Do you think Dantae will answer the summons?"

Cielo traced a few lively steps in the piazza, and the passersby looked at him with twice as much confusion as I did. "I think she'll dance a Celanese jig if we give her those bones."

"I'll have them," I said, making one more impossible promise. I pulled three threads from the bottom of my borrowed skirt and used magic to turn them into thick twine, a change that, for once, drew no unwanted eyes.

Then I tugged Cielo in by the elbows and undid all of my attempts at invisibility by kissing my strega. I leaned over the papers so I would not crush the delicate letters as our mouths sought new angles, and great depths.

"Fly fast," I whispered.

"So I can put us at the center of yet another festival of enemies?" Cielo asked.

"So you can come back to me." I kissed Cielo once more, so quickly that it cast me to the clouds and back down to earth in a single, dizzy moment.

Cielo grabbed the book, turned a page, and split into a trio of birds braiding through the air. They alighted on the edge of the fountain. With shaking fingers, I tied a message to each. As the birds took to the sky, my left ear caught the beat of Cielo's wings but I refused to watch as my strega left me.

I kept my eyes on the ground, as if they could cut through the skin of Prai, to the bones beneath.

I WALKED BACK TOWARD THE SAFE HOUSE, TRACING OUR PATH. As I headed down the gauntlet of bakeries, I wished I had Cielo's long fingers or reversible morals. When I was nervous, my appetite swelled. I could have eaten a dozen of the delicately layered sfogliatelle or the raised, puffy bombolone piled in the windows.

But the sugared tops of the pastries only reminded me of the snowy Neviane and the streghe I'd dragged there in the hopes of making Vinalia safer for them—only to place them in my brother's path and then immediately storm off.

As I passed through the Evracco neighborhood, my boots hit the cobbles like flint. Hearing that hard sound in one ear and not the other left me feeling unbalanced.

I found myself missing Cielo, missing my family, missing everyone I could imagine, from my sisters all the way down to Favianne Rao.

Of course, she'd never actually become a Rao. Who would know the truth about what had happened to her after I vanished from Amalia? Vanni, most likely. The five families traded gossip with more vigor than old men before confession. I would have to ask on his return. Not that Favianne and I had been close. We'd only circled each other once or twice before I realized she was eager to use me in her endless search for power and pleasure—and the feeling was a bit too mutual for comfort.

Still, I was curious to know what had become of her. We were matched in ambition, and she was the only other person I knew who had slipped the hold of the five families. What did her new, handpicked fate look like?

Was it as strange and dire as my own? Or had she kept to a well-trodden path?

When I reached the safe house, I kept walking, marking its location from all directions so I would be able to find my way back. Then I left behind the building clad in shadows and vines, pressing toward the edge of Prai. Oreste had told us that the Bones of Erras would be found where the bone roads met the city.

I walked past so many doors painted in bold shades, so many people on their daily rounds of butcher and baker, a hundred packs of wild children. All I could think was how much this place would be changed if Beniamo had his way. I felt like I was seeing two cities at once—the one that existed now, and the one that would replace it if Beniamo was allowed to rise to power.

He would bleed Vinalia of color and life. He would not stop until every one of these people was as nervous as I had been as a child, casting glances over a shoulder, afraid of the moment when he noticed my happiness and crushed it underfoot, like that crown of violets. He wouldn't do it for his own gain, or any kind of glory. Beniamo lived for the simple delight of watching my eyes go wide, and then empty.

He wanted me to have nothing.

To *be* nothing.

With this much distance between us, I could see a new truth: that was how Beniamo felt every moment, and he wished the rest of us to feel it too. No matter how much he had, it never gave him satisfaction. No matter how much power was gifted to him—through his birth or his life or the death of others—it would never be enough to fill the hollow in his soul.

Prai came to a sudden halt at a neighborhood composed of pale brick and nervous mothers. They churned through errands, dunking clothes into charcoal water in wooden buckets, none of them noticing a strega skirting around the edges of their homes. I walked to the line where the city dropped away, and it felt like being back in the Uccelli, standing at the edge of the Storyteller's Grave.

Behind me, life and noise and chaos reigned. The countryside, in comparison, was stunningly empty. There was only silence and a slight wind running a finger along the folds of the hills.

I cast my magic away from me. If the Bones of Erras were below the city, I should be able to feel them from here. The power of a godlike strega had to be strong enough to travel through layers of earth, to survive the long, slow burial of time.

"*Find them,*" I said, letting myself speak to my magic out loud, hoping the old language would help orient me toward the bones.

My magic worked its way into the earth like a stain, moving down and outward at the same time, covering a great amount of ground, finding nothing but earth and brick and dull, dead shards of the past.

"*Try harder,*" I said, my heart railing against the effort, as if I were running miles instead of standing in a single, unimpressive spot.

My magic filtered its way down through layers of Prai, each one shed like a skin the city had outgrown. I could feel the shape of what lay underneath me: walls and buildings and waterways. There were no glints of magic in this heap, nothing that whispered or shouted in the old language, nothing that begged or commanded to be pulled from the earth.

If Oreste was right, the Bones of Erras should have

surrounded the city, and finding one shouldn't have been difficult if my magic had any sense at all. There were so many bones in a human body. So many tiny, fragile pieces that somehow added up to a person. So many different ways to break.

My magic rushed down until it hit hard rock, then recoiled.

Nothing.

Frustration stabbed at me. Oreste could have lied. What if he sent us on a foolish journey simply to get Cielo away from him? Why would he give up the church's secrets to streghe? Why would he finally choose to be helpful after so many years of denying his family, picking up the hem of his robes and running from his fears and failures?

I walked the rim of the city: one mile, then two. The sun made a slow, dramatic exit from its place of honor in the sky. Stars appeared, fighting to be the brightest in the sky, to outstrip each other with their silver offerings.

I grew tired and hungry, and the only thing that kept me moving was knowing how much this meant to Cielo. I did not have to believe it was as important as stopping Beniamo. I only had to remind myself that Cielo was in the sky right now, soaring toward my family and our band of streghe.

If Cielo could have faith in my schemes, I could have faith too.

The fields that had been uninterrupted for so long finally gave way to the sight of ruins just outside the city, the hobbled temple to the old gods and the glorious ancient marketplace stripped of everything but a few splintered walls.

There, my magic said, pointing me in a new direction—not down, but forward.

After all of my dark mutterings, the truth came like the dawn, bright and obvious. The edges of the ancient city were in a different place.

I ran, breaking the invisible line between city and countryside. My magic guided me. I had never been talented at finding other streghe, but these shards of magic were so powerful that even I could sense them, a dull aching throb. It felt like the aftermath of being cut, like the legacy of a wound.

Where are they? I asked my magic. *Where are the bones?*

I ran to the stairs of the temple, looking up through the smooth columns that ended in ruinous points like the ribs of a wrecked ship. My magic pulled me through the temple, which stood open to the air. Worship in ancient times had moved freely as breath. My steps carried me to the far side, where I cast myself to my knees.

What was it like, to be worshipped as a god, when you were simply a person with great magic? Was it a tide of constant adoration? Or was it the wash of loneliness I felt now, without Cielo nearby? Perhaps it was both, like magic and its reversal: two things that looked different but were actually the same.

My magic pressed down through layers of tight-packed earth. What they found made me shiver in restless bursts.

They are here. They are here. They are here.

I dug with my hands and my magic, both at once, working in a kind of jagged harmony. First I stripped away a section of earth with magic, changing hard-packed clay to air. Then I sifted with my fingers. Raw earth came up in my hands, and soon I was removing the rubble of another world, forgotten pieces of pottery and brick. Prai used to be here, but it had migrated, like some great bird that flew as slowly as the mountains rose and the oceans bit away at Vinalia's shores.

Why did you come here?

The whisper in the old language slithered up through the earth. My hands scraped with a new frenzy, and as the moon rose over the hills in the distance, it caught on the scarred white of old bone.

You don't believe magic can be changed. You know the ways of the world. The cruelties of men are never-ending. A circle you cannot break.

I picked the bone from the dirt, shook the dark crumbs free. It could have been any part of the god known as Erras. I was not familiar with anatomy like my brother Luca had been. I could not name what I held; I could only feel its magic rushing through the halls of my mind, throwing open doors that I kept locked.

You are here for nothing. You are nothing. Magic has not given you the power you seek. You will spend the rest of your short life chasing it, then fall into a grave, forgotten.

You have no god to claim you.

No friends who will come for you.

No family who will mourn you.

No love strong enough to save you.

12

The night grew darker, clouds making a slow journey over the moon and dulling its glow. I didn't stop digging until I found three bones. Where the first was slender and curved, the second looked small enough to be part of a finger, or a toe. The last sat heavy in my hand, scratched dark at both ends.

After listening to the bones whisper their insults for hours, I would have happily turned the large one on myself simply to gain a minute of silence.

But I had to be back at the safe house when Cielo arrived, so I tucked the bones in my pockets and carried them back into the living city. When I'd studied the neighborhoods of Prai I had dug the trenches of memory deep, and my body found the vine-covered house without much help from my thoughts.

When I reached the little room on the first story I dropped onto a pile of clothes and fell into a chasm of sleep. I woke expecting to find Cielo at my side.

All I had were the bones in my pockets, whispering.

Your strega is gone. You have already lost.

I waited for an entire day, only leaving the house long

enough to barter for another heap of hot, oily street food. It did not taste nearly as delightful as it had the first time, with Cielo's hand sometime brushing mine when I reached for a bit of baccalà.

As night crept near again, I spent every minute thinking of the ways Beniamo might have tracked Cielo, hurt Cielo and left my strega without help, killed Cielo and waited for me to discover it.

I imagined Beniamo's smile, slick with moonlight.

I imagined his talons, raised and glinting, then crushing through Cielo's slim body with a sickening sound.

I felt the heat of Cielo's blood rising as steam. I smelled death on the wind.

I lived the moment when Cielo passed out of the world, and then started over and lived it again.

My mind lost its ability to tell the difference between a real death and one that it drew with its own crude hand. I railed against the wooden floor, cried out, crushed my body into painful shapes. This must have been one of the tortures Beniamo had devised for me. It was as keen as any blow he'd ever landed.

A knock sounded at the door downstairs, bold enough that even with my near-deafened ear I heard it right away. I flew down the narrow staircase and flung it open to see a woman, clad in leather and a deeply notched frown.

"Dantae," I said. "What do you want?"

"You dead on the doorstep, but I'll settle for the Bones of Erras," she said. "Your strega told me you were working on some kind of elaborately stitched plan, and I would find what I needed here."

Elaborately stitched plan sounded exactly like a phrase Cielo would conjure, and for a moment my heart sparked with hope. Cielo had made it all the way to wherever the soldiers of Erras had gone after breaking camp. Cielo had delivered my letters. My hope did not catch, though, and light the fires of true comfort.

"Cielo should have returned by now," I mumbled.

"You love that feral strega, don't you?" Dantae asked.

"Who told you that?" I asked, defending my deepest feelings from yet another person who might try to turn them against me.

Dantae nodded at where I was clutching myself across the middle. "It's all over your body. You might as well be screaming it."

The whisper of the bones drifted down the staircase, cold and certain, finding me even from a distance. *You have lost the one person who knew you. The only one who truly cared. You have sent Cielo to greet death.*

I brought Dantae upstairs and gathered the Bones of Erras, unsure of whether I was doing the right thing but glad to be rid of them. "Why do you worship filthy pieces of a strega you never knew?" I asked, thrusting them away from me.

"We don't," Dantae said simply. She took one bone at a time, studying them with the eye of a scholar. "The old gods aren't a religion to us. They're . . . more like our elders. The Bones of Erras make it easier to defend streghe against the many people who seek to destroy us. The Bones of Erras keep us alive. And they don't work against my own men and women, which is part of the appeal."

"I'm sure your people are pure as November snow," I said, sarcasm crusting over my tone.

"Not a bit," Dantae said, sitting down with her knees pointed at the ceiling, the bones in a heap between her legs. She took a knife as long as my shin from a sheath at her side and started to whittle the long, slender bone, leaving chips of an ancient strega on the floor. "Others are free to judge, but the soldiers of Erras don't give their judgments power over us."

I tried to picture what that would be like, but it felt impossible, like trying to spot the sun at night.

And my mind was somewhat busy, taking in the sight of the knife that Dantae was creating in front of me, one long stroke at a time. "Now that you have the bones you wanted, are you going to kill me?"

"Why don't you answer that yourself?" she asked without looking up.

I felt the question I'd asked open up slowly, like watching a flower unfold into bloom. "You want to," I said. "It's not because you hate me, though. It's . . . my magic. Something about my magic. You want it back. You think it belongs to the soldiers of Erras. To *you*." I took a step backward, as if that would stop me from running into more truth. "How did I know that?"

Dantae chuckled. "My magic spins a question into an answer."

"So, you agreed to kill me and Cielo because you want to reclaim the magic of dead streghe," I said.

Dantae bent over the bone, working hard as she flayed the point, her lips set. "There is only one dead strega whose magic I care to steal back."

The rest of the story came without help from Dantae's magic. Memory carried it to me on a silver tray. "The man who came to the Uccelli years ago, the one that Father killed. The one my magic came from—you knew him?"

I was about to ask if he was her brother, her cousin, her friend—but the look on Dantae's face hit me in a tender spot. I thought of Cielo, and how I would look if I knew someone else carried my strega's magic inside of them.

"He was your lover, wasn't he?" I asked.

Dantae's face betrayed nothing, but her fingers tightened on the handle of her knife, as if she could throttle the truth. "Niccolò di Sangro was his end? Hardly seems fitting. I figured you did away with Mirco yourself."

"When I was nine?" I asked.

"Children are less afraid of death. Less afraid of their own power, too. We start training ours young. There's no point in pretending they're helpless little creatures. If you tell them that story, they start to believe it."

I thought of how many times I'd been told I was powerless, that what I most wanted was farthest out of my reach. That story had become as deeply twisted with my soul as magic.

"Why did Mirco's magic . . . why did it choose me?" I asked.

Dantae shook her head. "You're asking the wrong question. The answer won't come."

In a fit of desperation, I grabbed the long bone and held it out. It wasn't sharpened yet, but it could still raise a decent bruise. "Why don't you rephrase it for me, then?"

Dantae looked up, her interest whetted. "I have a better game. We fight. Whoever wins gets what they want."

Cielo never would have let me agree to such a vicious bargain, but Cielo wasn't here, and I needed the soldiers of Erras on my side. I couldn't use magic against Beniamo, which made having an army to face his even more necessary.

"You want Mirco's magic," I said, laying out the terms clearly, as Father would have done. "I want your undying loyalty."

"You think I'll answer to you after I'm dead?" Dantae said with a rough smirk. "I'm afraid that'll cost extra."

"I'll have to settle for the rest of your life, then."

Dantae rose to her knees and leaned forward, brushing her lips against my cheek. Her lips were strangely hot, and she still smelled of death, but I found that I was growing used to the deeply salty odor. I kissed her cheeks, so tanned by a life spent in the woods that her skin was covered in a web of tiny lines. The aging of wind and weather made her look at least five years older than she was.

She must have been a young woman when she lost Mirco—perhaps the age that I was now. If I lost Cielo, how far would I go to find a piece of my strega? To keep part of Cielo with me, at any cost?

"Begin," she said, without the showy smile she'd flashed in Castel di Volpe. Her eyes were hard and unblinking.

"*Give her a reason to fear me*," I told the magic, the old language leaving me on a thunderous breath.

I wanted her to hear those words coming from my lips. I wanted her to understand how well I knew my own magic.

It changed the leather clothing on her body to a hissing wreath of snakes that moved over her skin, keeping her tightly wound in scales. Dantae glanced down and laughed. "I like that," she said. "It will make for good stories."

"What if they're poisonous?" I asked.

Dantae shrugged. "Then you'll be down one partner in battle with no one to blame but yourself."

"*Show her we are strong*," I said, but the magic felt stuck. "*Hurt her, if you have to.*"

She is already hurt, it promised me. *There is nothing we can do to her that will leave a deeper mark.*

As I battled my own magic, Dantae gripped my arms below the shoulders. "What would happen if you died today?"

I opened my mouth to answer, but Dantae's magic was already at work, digging out answers. "Your brother will become the leader of Vinalia," she said. "I don't care about that, little one. Kings and rulers don't care for us any more than we care for them." Her fingers gripped harder, and my body remembered all at once that her closeness could mean death. "Here's something worse. Your brother wants to kill every strega he can find. He'll start with the weak ones to send a message to the strong. Then he will let our fears prey on us until we are half-dead. That man will hunt streghe like wounded animals."

"He wants magic," I said. And then, since she could probably get her hands on the truth anyway, I added, "He wants whatever is mine."

Dantae's first concern was keeping the soldiers of Erras safe. That was what she wanted the bone knives for. I should have known that it was the one thing that would win her over to my cause. But I'd gotten caught up in wanting to fight her—in craving a small portion of revenge for what she'd done at Mirella's wedding.

"I've seen your brother in the Capo's army," Dantae said. "He'll never inherit magic, but that will only push him harder, like a stallion with spurs driven into its sides." She stepped back. "You don't have my eternal vow, or whatever you noble types swear to each other. But you have me on your side in this fight, and that should be enough."

"What about Mirco's magic?" I asked.

"I can always kill you later," she said with a shrug. The snakes that used to be her vest shivered up and down her skin.

꧁❀꧂

WHEN CIELO ARRIVED AT THE SAFE HOUSE, HOURS LATER, SHE was weaving lightly on her toes, as if she were dancing the lead role in a difficult ballet after swallowing a great deal of liquore genziana.

"What happened?" I asked as Cielo stumbled into my arms.

"Flying in three directions at once was . . . Dantae, you made it! . . . harder than I supposed . . . Teo, did you . . . not my favorite way to travel . . . must talk to my father about his role in all this . . . get the bones?"

Her words kept weaving as her feet tried to carry her all over the room. Apparently, she had pushed too far with this latest magic. "I got the letters where they needed to be, but I couldn't stand the separation for another minute. I had to be whole again, or I would never have made it back to you." Cielo's speech finally glued itself together, and her feet carried her in a straight line to me.

Dantae looked pointedly away as Cielo pressed herself against me.

"Is anyone else here?" Cielo asked. "I hate to think I went through all of that pain for nothing. It was like a headache that had the power to split my mind into three pieces." I rubbed Cielo's temples at the place where the roots of her dark hair tugged at her skin. She sighed into my touch, closed her eyes, and kept talking. "The streghe were behind me, so they might need another day, but the five families received my message first and had the least distance to cover. They should have been able to make it to Prai in less than a day's ride if they were moving with adequate haste."

"Only Dantae is here," I said, trying not to let those words pitch me into despair. Oreste would never be able to rally the church to our cause unless I gave him the backing of the five families. He would disappear into the safety of his robes if the only ally I could offer was a begrudging strega.

Cielo spun as if noticing Dantae for the first time. "Teo, did you put snakes all over our guest?" I tried to come up with a way to explain our little rissa incantata, but Cielo wasn't waiting for my response. She pointed to the bones on the floor. "I see that Teo has filled our half of the promise. Now, what do you know about Veria's Truth?"

Dantae gathered the bones, her vest hissing at Cielo. "Why don't you answer your own question?"

Cielo's head tilted slightly, her eyes narrowed. "You don't know where to find it but you have heard of a place that should point us in the right direction. It's called the Buried City. It's underneath the very center of ancient Prai." Cielo shook her head as if trying to rattle a marble out of a wooden maze.

"You can thank Dantae's magic for that," I said.

And because I could not stay in that tiny room waiting for my father, I grabbed Cielo's hand and drew her toward the stairs.

Cielo's whisper hooked into the softest parts of my body. "I've barely returned, and you want to work at your schemes all night?"

"I want to work at *your* schemes," I said, pushing Cielo against the railing as soon as we were out of Dantae's sight. "And there are plenty of hours before dawn."

᚛᚜

WE RETURNED TO THE EVRACCO NEIGHBORHOOD, THE OIL LAMPS in the windows like a set of low-hanging stars. I heard the rasp of boots on the cobbles behind us, but I knew enough not to turn.

"We're being followed," I said, sliding my hand onto Cielo's arm.

"That's the point," Cielo whispered.

She spun, and I followed, to find a girl whose dark eyes were touched with gold from the lamps.

"Are you lost, traveler?" she asked.

"We are all lost," Cielo said.

"Can I help you find your way?"

This exchange made me think of a scrap of music that had been played an uncountable number of times, a well-worn passage.

Cielo stepped closer, and the girl flinched away, but I saw no fear in her eyes. It felt more like she wasn't allowed to stand close to us, at least not when someone else could be watching.

"Where is the center of ancient Prai?" Cielo asked.

"Under the fountain of the maidens," the girl said, in a voice that seemed familiar with the weight of secrets.

Cielo nodded, and the girl went on her way. We continued our walk past the shuttered shops. I resisted the rising urge to look back.

"Is she a strega?" I asked.

"Rivka? Yes, and no. She was born and raised in Vinalia, but the Evracci have their own name for those who hold magic. Chisappe."

I wanted to ask a hundred questions about Rivka, starting with how—and how well—Cielo knew her. Jealousy rushed through me, as certain as magic and twice as sharp. "Is the magic of Chisappe the same as ours?" I asked.

"Again, it's a matter of yes and no mixing together to create a different shade of truth. Chisappe can work magic and a reversal at the same time. They don't see the two as opposites. They believe all things come together, hand in hand, without sorting them first the way other Vinalians do."

"I don't understand," I said, feeling like Cielo and I had taken a step backward in time, to the days when I was first learning what it meant to be a strega. The magic inside of me still longed to know more. It was never done with seeking out knowledge, with answers that split into fresh streams of questions.

Cielo offered me her arm, in the same courtly way she had in her boyish form. "Magic is bound up with a person, and a person is bound up with everything around them. The way they are raised, what they are taught to believe. If you change the way people think, how they live, their magic has to change."

The night air rushed with a thousand small messages about the people who lived in this city: what they had eaten for dinner, where they spent their daylight hours. I felt the stirring of new possibility. "So, if we change magic with Veria's Truth, it might change the way people live in turn?"

Cielo's arm tightened around mine, and for a rare moment, I let Cielo's hope flow into me. Then we turned a sharp corner, traveled down the dark slit of an alley, and emerged into a piazza.

The fountain of the maidens was nothing like the bombastic creations scattered through Prai. While newer fountains had been carved of marble, this one was dark gray stone, slicked green with age. A single, deep bowl was ringed with young maidens kneeling. Their hair ran down their backs in waves of stone. Tears dribbled down their stone faces.

"Who would build this?" I asked, the words a low scrape in my throat.

"Most fountains are made to flatter and please," Cielo said. "But this one is clearly made from a different sort of raw material." Cielo turned to me on the fresh wind of an idea. "Do you think you can use your magic to change all the murderers of the world into fountains? They can spurt water wherever they've stabbed people."

"I don't know if there should be monuments to people like that," I said.

"There are *only* monuments to people like that," Cielo reminded me.

"This is different, though," I said, running my fingers down the cold stone skin of one of the girls, from shoulder to elbow, as if I could take her by the arm. Studying her face felt as intimate as staring into a mirror. I knew that expression.

They're mourning, my magic told me.

"We have to find a way underneath this," Cielo said. "The water flows down. Shall we flow with it?"

"I think we can make it easier than that," I said, pointing to the grate beside the fountain. I knelt beside it, and using night as a blanket to cast over my magic, I changed the metal bars into a set of dark twigs and then snapped them.

The hole that opened up beneath us was wide enough to slide down, and I sat down in the middle of the piazza, slipping into the world beneath. Iron staples bolted into the stone formed a ladder that led me below the city.

Cielo followed me down. Moonlight came with her, forming a column as white and solid as any made of marble. As I reached the bottom of the iron ladder, I stepped out of the light, into the darkness beneath Prai.

I picked up a broken bit of stone.

Light, please, I told the magic.

It flared, and the stone in my hand softened to tallow, the end springing to light with a single point of flame.

Cielo skipped the last few rungs of the iron ladder and leapt down, landing on the ground beside me with a skittering of stone. I turned in a full circle, thrusting the candle in every direction, hoping it would show us what we came to see.

Not that I knew precisely what to expect.

"What are we looking for?" I whispered. The ancient silence down here needed to be dealt with delicately. "The Buried City could be enormous." Ancient Prai was probably smaller than its newest incarnation, but that could still mean miles of tunnels.

Cielo put a steadying hand on my wrist. "Start here," she said, leading me toward a chamber that opened up at our left.

I was about to launch a thousand ships of argument, but the moment I took a step, I saw what lay behind the crumbled remains of a stone door. It had most likely been sealed once, but now it was a heap on the ground, and behind that, a dozen raised mounds of earth, set with stone tablets, each the length of a body.

"The Buried City isn't just another layer of Prai," Cielo said. "It's a great deal more literal than that."

I walked first, the candle bringing the crypt to life, one illuminated patch at a time. Now I understood what the fountain above meant. Those maidens mourned the passing of the old gods and marked their burial chamber.

"Look," Cielo said, touching one of the stone tablets set on top of a burial mound. "These are their stories, spending eternity with their bodies."

The first stone set near the entrance of the room featured paintings of Melae, the goddess of death, usually depicted as a woman. But the flaking images reminded me that she was known to transform into a man once a year, when death came for the summer and the harvest was reaped, as well as into a bird who bore her favorite souls directly to heaven on large black wings.

Now that I knew the old gods were streghe, I felt a kinship with Melae. I wondered if Cielo felt it, too. For my part, the connection only grew stronger when I thought of the magic I carried, which was able to send so many to their deaths.

I had feared Melae's powers as a child. Would others in Vinalia grow to fear me?

"Here is Cecci," I said, moving on to a safer tablet, running my fingers over faded paint. In a few images, an artist had rendered the story of a strega who adored wine nearly as much as lovemaking. For a tribute to a god, the stone did nothing to hide Cecci's bawdy nature, with more than a few images of Cecci and his lovers in positions that tugged at the limits of belief.

"I suppose that could be a sort of magic," I mumbled.

"Looking at this, I'm beginning to feel like it's the only magic worth having," Cielo said.

At the bottom of the tablet was a very different image, of a man with righteousness in his eyes and a knife in his hand. The final picture was Cecci's body letting out rivers of blood, the waves washing red. Under the picture, a single word was set down in the old language.

Prai, the magic told me, translating the markings.

"Does this mark where the stone was made?" I asked. "Or where Cecci died?"

Cielo looked from tablet to tablet. "They all have different places filled in, so probably the latter."

I moved on, knowing what I would find and yet stuck to the sight of the blood at the bottom of each tablet, washed to a dull pink by the centuries. But time scrubbed away none of the terror. "All of these stories end the same way. Erras kills the gods. His family, his friends, his lovers."

"Look," Cielo said, drawing my eyes to the end of the chamber and two burial mounds that didn't match the rest.

One was empty.

"Erras," I said. "He's buried all around the city. Those worshippers were like wolves, scattering him."

"He deserved it," Cielo said darkly. She moved to the final burial mound, her fingertips resting on the stone tablet. "It's her."

I stood across from Cielo and tipped the candle closer. Veria's burial mound told the story of a strega whose magic stripped away lies and left the truth shining. Wherever she went, hearts glowed with it, like small suns trapped in people's chests.

At the bottom of the tablet, Erras appeared again, but this time Veria slipped away from his knife. The final picture showed her huddled in a cave as waves rushed in to claim Erras. She was crying, crying, her tears mingling with the sea. Some of them trickled into a vase that glowed so brightly I thought it must have been magic, but when I touched it, there was only flaking old paint.

There was a single word under the picture. *Drowned.*

"The vase of moonlight," I said. "It must still be in that cave."

"Why wouldn't they bring it here?" Cielo asked, impatience ripening and bursting all at once.

"They must not have been able to find it." The water in the cave gleamed a shade of blue that was nearly purple. I knew only one place in the world that looked like that. "It's somewhere along the Violetta Coast."

Cielo sighed, setting her weight against the burial mound. "The Violetta Coast covers a hundred miles, more if you take into account every nook and cranny and cave. I was hoping for something a bit more specific."

Drowned, the magic said.

"I know *she drowned*," I growled in the old language.

Drowned, my magic repeated.

I looked again at the word on the burial mound, and my heart didn't quite glow, but it did flush with heat. On the other burial mounds, the word did not give a description of how the person died.

It named the place where death came for each god.

"Have you ever heard of the drowned grottoes?" I asked.

Cielo looked up with a vague, unformed recognition on her face, like clay that had been palmed but not yet molded.

"Fiorenza, my stepmother, is from the Violetta Coast. She used to tell us a story about a place where pirates would go to hide their treasures, and girls would go if they cared to make love to pirates. Parts of it were flooded by the sea, and the tides ravaged it each day. There were secret ways in and out, known to only a few who lived nearby. Fiorenza called it the best hiding place in all of Vinalia. That's where Veria's Truth is."

Cielo's defeat did an about-face, and suddenly she was rushing toward me, leaping and shouting. "We can do this, Teo. We can change things. Finally." Her smile spread out wide and whiter than the moonlight vase on the stone tablet.

I wanted to believe Cielo, but I knew that changing magic would not be enough to stop my brother. He had already been molded and set. If we managed to change the ways of the world, he might simply burn the whole thing down.

Cielo leaned in to kiss me, but my lips wouldn't rise to the occasion. They felt as cold as stones in winter, and all I could think of were those girls above us, weeping silently, and forever.

Cielo and I climbed back through the grate as the bells in the Mirana chanted the hour, peal after peal until twelve had piled up. Cielo and I walked to the safe house and found it dark, but at least it was familiar. It gave off that wafting sense of *home* that I hadn't felt since the day I left the Uccelli. It was as strong as Fiorenza's favorite orange-and-anise powder, as sudden as a flash of Mirella's dark hair moving through the leaded windows of the tower.

And then I realized that the feeling wasn't coming from the house itself, but something inside of it. A magic I knew as well as my own.

He's here.

I pushed past Father's magic and found more waiting. Mimì, Xiaodan, Vanni. Dantae was still there. I was getting better at recognizing power at a distance. The rest of the five families, those poor souls without magic to light their way in this dark world, must have been packed tight in the narrow house too.

"They're all here," I whispered to Cielo, hope getting a stranglehold on my voice. "They heard the call to stop Beniamo from taking Vinalia by force, and they came."

When I was a child, I had tried to tell my parents that my brother was dangerous. They had done nothing to stop him. Fiorenza hadn't been able to rein in a di Sangro boy born to another woman. When I dared to tell Father, he had frowned at me like I was causing trouble, instead of being harmed by it. Beniamo had doubled my punishments as soon as he had me alone.

I wasn't alone anymore.

I had the five families, and now a sixth, as well as the soldiers of Erras behind me. I was no longer a little girl, taking off my slippers so I could move silently down the stone hallways of the di Sangro castle, afraid to be caught.

Tears rimmed my eyes, and the press of Cielo's hand in mine almost shoved them over the edge. "Go in," Cielo said. "Your family is waiting for you."

No matter how strongly I felt, this moment also set the practical clockwork of my scheme in motion. "We go to Oreste," I said. "This minute. He needs to know that our plan has powerful backing."

"Otherwise he'll disappear on the first boat to the virgin continent?" Cielo asked.

"Only if he's being predictable," I muttered. "We need your father to renounce the priesthood and ask the church to join us so we can bring our forces together for a great meeting tomorrow. If we don't leave Prai by the day after, we'll never cut off Beniamo as he marches the army into Amalia."

"Which gives us a single day to unite the squabbling powers of Vinalia," Cielo said, the slanting of her inky eyebrows just as effective in the dark.

"Think of it this way," I said. "If you give a man any longer than he needs, he will invent problems he doesn't have."

"Is that one of your father's sayings?" Cielo asked.

"No," I said. "It's one of mine."

Cielo grabbed my other hand, so we were doubly linked, and laughed as she said, "I never thought there would come a day when you'd choose the Malfaras over the di Sangro family, even for an hour."

I cast a look at the safe house, my heart straining toward the people I loved. My magic had other plans, though.

"Let's move fast," I said.

"As long as there are no feathers involved," Cielo said. She drew out the book and flicked a page, becoming the wind I knew almost as well as the strega's boyish and girlish forms. I watched Cielo slide into the sky above me.

With a liquid reversal, I rose into the night.

At midnight, Prai was fiery thread stitched on a background of velvet darkness. Cielo and I skimmed over the bristle of tile roofs and parted around the curve of domes. We flowed together, branching and weaving in so many combinations that I could not tell which bit of air belonged to me and which was Cielo's.

Hope urged us forward with reckless speed. We knew the location of Veria's Truth. We had our allies gathered. If both of our plans worked, we might be free to live. We might have the chance to love each other fully.

I'd had no idea how much fear was holding me in place until I left it behind, ripped away by the cold wind.

The Mirana slid into place under us, and Cielo and I tumbled down, over the fretted roofs and into a series of wondrous gardens, each one like a small jeweled box set with flowers in a hundred different shades. We came back to the world, naked and already twined, grass biting into my bare skin everywhere it was not fortunate enough to be pressed against Cielo's smoothness.

"We can't do this here," I said, the presence of the priests like a set of eyes pinned to my back.

"What will they say?" Cielo asked with a rough smirk. "Two streghe were caught in a headlong embrace in their own gardens?"

"So, we're safe because they don't want to admit their failures?" I asked.

Cielo answered by kissing me. His lips offered the same heady freedom I'd felt when I was flying. I could think of no more reasons to hold back, and so I poured with a generous hand, fingers and lips streaming over his skin without pause. I used his shoulder blades to draw him closer.

Stop yourself, my magic said. *Before your enemies stop you.*

Heat built around our bodies, the white heart of a bonfire. The feeling pushed me forward, eyes consuming every bit of Cielo's skin, kisses searing. I did not care about the priests, the constant parade of dangers.

I needed Cielo, only Cielo.

"Teo," he said, tapping on my shoulder so politely, it stopped me in the midst of reaching for him. "Teo, are you by any chance angry at these flowers? Have they done something to bother you?"

I looked around to find that the garden was on fire. Every bloom had ripened, not with life, but with flame. Delicate petals burned with a steady blaze. Fruit trees crawled with yellow and orange, a hunger that threatened to devour them. Flakes of ash latched on to the wind, falling like impure snow. The heat that I'd felt was not only a matter of rubbing skin and the rush of eager blood.

It was magic, burning a small patch of the Mirana.

"Well," said a voice that made me cringe, a voice that did not belong to this moment. I looked up to find Oreste standing in an open doorway, looking as if he'd just tossed on his robes, the collar left undone. "This is quite a scene."

"*Stop,*" I told the magic, but it only flared brighter at Oreste's sudden appearance. The garden was being swallowed. I did not know how far my magic would go, if it would claim all of the priests, every inch of Prai.

"I can only protect you for so long," Oreste said. "Someone else is bound to notice this little show. I suggest you do away with the hellfire if you don't wish for people to start drawing comparisons."

Oreste's dry wit was so much like Cielo's that I couldn't decide whether to cringe or laugh. The frantic need to stop the flames did nothing to help me control my magic.

"Teo," Cielo said, his words fractured by smoke. "Perhaps some water, to put this out?"

Cielo was right. Stopping my power wasn't the point. Giving it direction would work just as well. I took a breath, smoke crowding my lungs.

"*Water,*" I cried.

The flakes of ash became rain, sizzling the fire into nothingness. The garden went dark.

The silence that came over us was laden with trouble.

Oreste sighed. "You must leave. You never should have come here."

"What?" I asked, standing up with one arm slung over my chest and the other hand covering the feature that I thought a priest would most object to.

"It is one thing to help my child, even if such a child

should never have existed in the first place. That is my sin to bear, not . . . anyone else's." Oreste looked briefly at Cielo, then away, as if the sight of his own family burned. "But to help that child sin . . ."

A small, rough laugh escaped me.

Did Oreste truly care about this degree of sin? While some young people pretended to be virtuously untouched, it was true for few in Vinalia, and everyone simply nodded along while they lied. It was like calling the land across the sea the *virgin continent*. There had been colonists from this side of the ocean on it for nearly two hundred years—and whole civilizations there before they arrived. And yet we kept calling it untouched.

Of course, I couldn't argue any of these points with Cielo's father, especially not while trying to fan my hair over my breasts with the hand that wasn't covering the spot between my legs.

"Do you deny that you two are sinning?" Oreste asked, his voice taking on the shiny heat of coals.

"Yes," Cielo said.

"Do you deny that you are lovers?" he asked, hotter still.

"Not a bit."

"What if we were married?" The question flew out of me, doubts flocking darkly behind it.

Should I have said that? Did I wish for Oreste to marry us here, now, as part of a desperate bargain to save Vinalia from my brother's rule? Would Cielo believe I'd only come up with this plan to soothe his father's God-fearing heart?

And then, when I saw the strained, questioning look on Cielo's face, new fears troubled the skies of my thoughts. Did Cielo want to be with me forever? Had I been afraid to ask because my strega—ever the cynic about people's hearts—might have less trust in lifelong love than most Vinalians had in magic?

"*Are* you married?" Oreste asked.

"Not presently," I admitted. "But you are a priest, and therefore the only person who can help with that part."

"A wedding would be an acceptable solution," Oreste said.

Cielo flung his hands in the air and turned from his father, letting him see the dimples of his buttocks. When he thought Cielo was no longer watching, I saw Oreste take us in with a gentleness that made me wonder. Was he remembering what it was like to be in love with his own headstrong strega? Did he see that love mirrored in us?

"We'll get started at once," Cielo's father announced.

"You're going to perform the ceremony in a burnt garden?" I asked. "Doesn't it have to be in a church?"

"If you'd prefer," Oreste said dryly. "Though you're not exactly dressed for church."

I felt my blush grow, branching out in several directions.

"I prefer the gardens," Cielo announced, standing up to prove that he didn't care if Oreste, the entire Order of Prai, or even God saw him strolling around naked. "It's a better story, altogether. Everyone gets married in a church. How many people can say they have gotten married under the moonlight in the Mirana gardens, after setting the whole thing ablaze?"

"This is about pleasing God, not improving on your legend," Oreste reminded Cielo.

"Here's something more important than proper setting or costume," Cielo added, ignoring his father. "We have no one to prove that we're married."

"I can go fetch witnesses," I said, thinking of Father and Fiorenza in the safe house, just across the city.

"No," Oreste mumbled. "This will have to be a secret, at least for the moment. I can't have the church leaders knowing I've done this. Or the five families dangling it over my head." He sighed and headed back into the Mirana.

"I can't believe he agreed to it," I mumbled. A priest of the most infamous strega-hating order in the land had just agreed to marry Vinalia's most powerful streghe in God's own gardens.

"Is this the *good* sort of disbelief or the magic-will-start-leaking-out-of-you-at-any-moment sort?" Cielo asked.

"The first one."

Cielo took my hands, his fingers still warm from the flames as they played over mine. "Did you only offer to keep Oreste on our side? Or . . . is this what you want?" The strega looked up at me with an impenetrable stare.

"Is this what *you* want?" I asked, spinning the question around to face Cielo.

"Teo." Cielo's hands gripped mine, a hard clench. "Please. I need to know why this plan sprang to your lips so easily."

"I want to be with you in every way that the world can devise," I admitted, chasing the words with a dry swallow of fear.

Why did it worry me to say that? Cielo and I had taken on a great deal together. We had peeled away layers of safety and certainty along with our clothes. And yet admitting such a deep and constant need for the strega made me feel more vulnerable than being in the church's stronghold, naked and pouring magic.

Cielo's lips quirked. I expected a long speech that pinwheeled from subject to subject, ending in my strega's acceptance of my rather odd proposal. But all he said was, "Then it's settled."

"If Oreste is off to find more people, I'm going to need something to wear," I said.

Of course, the magic answered, as the air around my body tightened and thickened into a simple, elegant dress, as green as the most verdant spots in Cielo's eyes. I ran my fingers down the fine cloth, shocked into a laugh by the obviousness of the solution.

I asked my magic to give Cielo something to match.

"How have we not thought of this before?" he asked, appreciating his clothes by running his hands over his shoulders and chest.

"Perhaps I've never been terribly interested in clothing you," I admitted.

Oreste reappeared and waved two guards into the garden. They looked around at the dark, crumbled remains of the flowers and fruit trees and said nothing. Their eyes were stuck halfway across the bridge between wonder and fear. One had a fair Celanese complexion, complete with a hail of freckles. The other had the famous Prai nose, a long straight ridge, and looked barely older than Luca should have been.

"MacCartaigh and Cinquepalmi are two of the church's soldiers," Oreste said. "If the time comes when you need to prove this took place, they will swear to it."

"Were you and my mother married?" Cielo asked, tossing out the question as if it hardly mattered. Here was another thing these two had in common—both child and father were not particularly skilled at making their true feelings vanish from sight.

"No," Oreste said numbly. "That would have been against my vows."

"I thought you had promised to give those up," Cielo said. "Or was that a lie to entice her into bed?"

"Cielo . . ." I warned, not wanting his father to snatch back his offer now.

But Cielo's stare did not let up, even if his questions did.

"I intended to leave this place for Giovanna," Oreste said, the hard clang in his voice fading. "But life did not honor my plans."

"*You* did not honor them," Cielo corrected.

"Well, you have a chance to put some salve on the wounds of the past," I said, jostling my way into their argument. "The five families have united with us against Beniamo. With the help of the church, we can keep a man even more tyrannical than your brother from the throne. We have to move fast, though. Can you promise a meeting tomorrow morning?"

Oreste looked stricken, but he gave me the barest nod.

"Look at you, Teo, scheming even in the middle of your own wedding," Cielo said with a smile that would not be held down.

Oreste cleared his throat and held up a book of prayers. The words of the ceremony, spoken in the old language, drifted over us like the slightly burnt smell of greenery on the night wind. And even though I knew the Order of Prai hated streghe, and the church did not trust them with a power they believed should be God's alone, that did not stop the prayers Oreste spoke from sneaking into my heart.

I watched Cielo's eyes on me. I could not read their color; the moonlight forced everything silver. For once, Cielo was not allowed to speak, unless he wished to stop the wedding. At the end of the last, solemnly intoned prayer, Cielo kissed me. Not a polite, ceremonial kiss. Cielo's lips delved deep, and I swam down into a dark, shining place.

When I came back, I was gasping.

Cielo smiled at his father. "Teo and I did not require a wedding, but I thank you."

Oreste looked from Cielo, to me, and back again. "Now, even if life does not honor your plans, you have each other."

҉

WHEN WE REACHED THE SAFE HOUSE AGAIN, THE BELLS IN EVERY church in the city rang in chorus. Once. Twice. The darkness around the streetlamps seemed to huddle and grow even stronger as night threw its long shadow over the start of the new day. I looked up at the lean house, its windows unlit.

"Go ahead," Cielo said, nodding me toward the door. If we had not just been married at the Mirana, I would have. But if I opened the door, climbed the squealing stairs, and woke everyone inside, I couldn't imagine the next time Cielo and I would have this chance to be alone together.

"Let's not spend our wedding night with di Sangros around us on all sides," I whispered.

Cielo snuck me in through a door to the cellars. We could find nothing to lie on but a rough old blanket, and yet I couldn't find a single complaint in the stacks that I usually kept close to hand.

"Do you think we can celebrate without burning or breaking anything?" Cielo asked, running a nervous finger down my stomach. "Our allies are sleeping above us, and if we fry them up, your scheme is going to suffer."

"The only scheme I care about right now begins like this," I said, kissing the strega's long, pale neck.

"Where does it end?" Cielo asked.

"It doesn't," I said. "That's what makes it the best scheme I've ever come up with."

"You are very good at strategy," Cielo said, "but I have a few notions of my own." Starting on his knees, he slid over me until he was unraveled at his full length. "Since we're husband and wife tonight, I thought we might try something . . . traditional."

"We're not good at holding fast to the ways of other people," I said, pushing his dark hair behind his shoulders so I could keep his face in full view. "Even our wedding was as odd as possible."

"That's what will make it so interesting," Cielo said. "I'm sure we'll come up with our own embellishments." This arrangement, with Cielo's boyish body hovering over my girlish one, might have been traditional, but nothing about the way he skimmed his entire body up and down mine felt obvious. This was new, and bright, and so full of hope that it hurt. He pressed closer, coupling our skin, then our lips. Cielo's body blazed into mine, a streak of sudden brilliance moving through me, a star falling.

I thought Cielo would be eager to repeat the motion, but he stayed where he was, staring down with the same expression I'd found so inscrutable in the garden. "What did you mean when you said we don't require a wedding?" I asked.

"I don't need a priest to bind us," Cielo said. "I have been yours since you asked me to teach you magic, and you taught me how to belong to another person. I have tied the knots and invented the prayers myself."

And with that, Cielo and I were married.

We celebrated many times that night, and no houses were burned, and the spines of no mountains snapped. When the fear of losing this feeling stormed through me, I was prepared. I let magic have its way, set free when I had kept it close and careful so long. It turned everything it touched into flowers with silver petals, so that a cellar in a nameless house in Prai became a garden of fallen stars.

❦

WHEN I WOKE THE NEXT MORNING, IT WAS WELL BEFORE DAWN, and the flowers were still glowing softly.

"Cielo," I said, pushing on his bare shoulder.

He grumbled softly in his sleep.

"Cielo! The meeting with the church! Your father told us to bring everyone to the southernmost hall of the Mirana."

"I suppose you want to go muster your troops," he said, turning over and pulling the blanket over his head.

I thought of climbing the stairs and facing everyone like this, with a hurricane of hair and sleepless eyes.

"No," I said, shaking Cielo with a little more vigor. "You go up and tell them where we're meeting. I'll see you there. I have a few things to attend to before we start this whirlwind of planning."

Cielo did not respond but burrowed under the blanket until he was little more than a silent, stubborn hill.

"They need to listen to me as they would to any leader," I said, "and no one will do that now. If the first glimpse everyone has is of me at Oreste's side, with the power of the strega-hating church at my command, it will force a needed change in perspective."

Cielo's voice rose through the weave of the blanket. "I already see you as powerful in the extreme." His head emerged, and he blinked with the fussiness of a newborn. "Does that mean I get to keep sleeping?"

I cast him a glance that could have turned all the water in his body to ice, and then cracked it.

"All right, all right."

I left Cielo to his work and crossed the waking city. I barely saw or heard the scenes that Prai staged all around me. I could only think of the morning ahead, the elaborate dance that must be done to keep the Order of Prai from killing the streghe, and the streghe from lashing out against the church.

And then there were the five families, who had no love for the Malfara line.

The southernmost hall of the Mirana was a quiet place, not nearly as ornate or gilded as the rest of the edifice, but I found it suited my purpose. I didn't wish to draw too much attention to our meeting in case Beniamo already had men loyal to him scattered throughout Vinalia.

When I pushed in the door to the chosen rooms, I found a sideboard laden with wine, bread, cheese, and a few sweating grapes—and only two men waiting. I recognized them as the guards who had witnessed my wedding. If they were surprised to see a young woman enter the meeting alone, they did not show it. Of course, they had seen much stranger things only the night before.

"MacCartaigh. Cinquepalmi." They dipped their heads. "Where is Oreste?"

The men stared directly in front of them without meeting my eyes. "He told the high council of priests of your plan," MacCartaigh said, his Vinalian salted with a Celanese accent. "Then he said he needed time to prepare himself."

I couldn't imagine what preparations would take so long unless they included baking a sense of honor from scratch. "I will have to hold the room until he arrives," I said. "Has he sent any priests to represent the church?"

MacCartaigh looked to Cinquepalmi frantically, as if trying to hand off a heated stone. "The high council will not allow any priest to sit in such close quarters with a strega," Cinquepalmi said, "but they have vouched their army to your use in stopping Beniamo's coup from reaching its full potential. They believe that God means for the Malfara line to continue its unbroken rule of the nation."

"I'm sure that God was in no way swayed by the fact that the next Malfara up for succession had been a priest for the last twenty years."

Neither of them answered.

"So . . . *you* are the delegates of the church?" I asked.

The two men saluted with brisk hands. I went to the sideboard and, instead of sighing or raging, poured a glass of wine to the brim, even though it was far too early and I hadn't even had espresso to spark my senses to life.

So this was how the church chose to play the game: by winning a round against Beniamo while proving that they did not have to directly condone the existence of streghe.

As long as they were not burying us up to our necks as the Order of Prai had a reputation for doing, I would have to take it. I spent a few minutes making the most of the soft cheese and ciabatta laid out on the sideboard as I drew battle plans in my head. They were the only things that calmed me, as familiar to my di Sangro senses as a lullaby.

Then the doors crashed open and the five families, the soldiers of Erras, and the streghe were upon me.

Cielo slid in while everyone was taking a seat and posted himself in a corner, making it clear that he did not seek a place at the table. I left one open at my side, but there was no way I would begin this meeting with what could only sound like a lovers' quarrel.

"We will begin as soon as our leader arrives," I said as every side of the table filled to bursting.

Mimì, Xiaodan, and Vanni sat together, with Mirella and the baby serving as a bridge to the five families. I'd seated them the farthest away, for the sake of being sure my dull ear didn't miss anyone's comments. The five families tended toward shouting even when the matter at stake *wasn't* one of life and death. Father kept company with the oil-and-water duo of Lorenzo and Pasquale, as well as Signora Moschella. The third side of the table played host to the soldiers of Erras, a half dozen arrayed with Dantae at the center. She stretched her legs up and let her boots fall to the table with an impressive thud.

She was still wearing the vest of snakes I'd created at our last meeting.

Father pursed his lips. MacCartaigh and Cinquepalmi shot each other the cannons of meaningful looks, as if they weren't sure whether Dantae's boots displeased God enough to remove them from the table by force.

The fourth side of the table was mine alone. I could feel Oreste's absence, like the darkly rotted place where a missing tooth should be. I glanced to Cielo, who shrugged, as if he couldn't be expected to herd his father, along with everything else I had asked.

There was a great knock, and MacCartaigh disappeared for a long moment. When he returned, he looked flustered. His cheeks were two hothouse peaches. "Signorina di Sangro, there is someone waiting outside who wishes an audience with you."

I trapped a sigh of relief in my throat so no one would know how close we had come to ruin. "Of course, of course." It all seemed ridiculously formal since everyone gathered knew who we were waiting for.

The double doors flung wide, the gilded panels splitting to reveal a young woman in a ragged dress that had once been as white as the snows of the Neviane, trimmed in gold thread and set with a fur collar and cuffs.

Our unexpected guest was Favianne—the girl who had offered her lips up to mine when she thought I was a son of the five families.

Cielo stared at her like she was a bowl of bitter grapes he was being asked to stomach. My strega had never particularly liked Favianne.

"Aren't you going to bow?" she asked as she ripped through the room to the sideboard and filled a tiny plate with as much food as she could grab. "Really, people showed more respect in towns where they had only one goat. This is the great city of Prai, and most of us in this room are old friends. I thought I would find a better reception."

"Why would we bow to you?" I asked, though the answer was already naked in front of me.

The Capo had gotten married to a young Vinalian woman who was possessed of beauty and a strong will, who loved opera and culture and all fine things. The last time I'd seen her, Favianne had been engaged to Pasquale, and at the same time flirting her way through the Capo's court.

Now Pasquale was staring at her as if she had died and come back to life.

"As long as this country has no ruler, I'm still the Queen of Vinalia," Favianne said, whirling to face me. "And I'm here to save you from your vile brother as well as yourselves. I only want one thing in return." She looked my body up and down, and I remembered the way she had tried to claim me.

"What's your price?" I asked, stifling a thousand other questions.

Favianne patted her elaborate crown of amber braids, lifting her arms in a way that showed off her breasts to perfection. "Isn't that part obvious?" The smile she thrust at me was as blinding as sunlight on snow. "I want magic."

14

It felt as if several pistols had been fired at once, shattering the peace, filling the room with the smoke of argument.

"You can't just stroll in here making demands," Mimì said.

"I didn't stroll," Favianne corrected. "I hiked miles in a gown and completely unsuitable shoes."

"The Capo's widow has no place in these proceedings," Father muttered.

"Why?" Signora Moschella asked with a leathery bellow. "Because she's a wife, instead of a husband? If I'm sitting at this table, so can she."

"Get her out of here," Pasquale said, standing and pointing a trembling finger that would have been at home in a cheap ballad of love and revenge. "Favianne can't be trusted. She will break any vow, take any man by the balls and . . ."

"I have to agree with Pasquale," Cielo tossed in. "Which is so unsettling, I'm dizzy."

Dantae let her feet drop from the table. All eyes swept to her as she pushed to standing and approached the former Queen of Vinalia as her vest of snakes writhed. "How clever," Favianne said, running a finger along one with scales the color and sheen of blackberries. "I'm sure this would catch on in Vari. They're so far ahead of us in fashion, and not afraid to wear any sort of animal, though they're usually dead first."

"How do you imagine we're going to hand you magic?" Dantae asked. "It's passed by blood, and I don't mean fancy lineage."

"Give me a knife, then," Favianne said, holding out a blunt palm.

No time for fighting, I told my magic.

Every glass of wine in the room iced over with a cracking sound. Vanni pouted at his, tipping it slightly to see if he could still drink. "No one is attacking my allies to gift themselves power," I said, now that I had everyone's attention.

Favianne's lips formed a frown that was somehow no less charming than her smile. "And yet you've just proven how useful magic can be. Everyone knows you, and what you are capable of, Teodora, and you didn't have to fasten yourself to a man with all the subtlety of a pond leech. I thought that if anyone in Vinalia would understand why I'm tired of living that way, it would be you."

It struck me that I was doing the same thing in a different way: I had fixed my hopes on Oreste so he might wield the power I could not. I didn't admit that to Favianne, of course. I wanted her to see me as she did now, as a strega beholden to no one. Her blue eyes worked their way back into my graces, lashes beating swiftly.

"You're flirting with Teo *as we speak*," Cielo said. "You don't seem ready to give up your old ways."

"Well, I can't help breathing, either," Favianne said with a hand clapped to her chest. "Do you want me to train myself to stop breathing? It seems a waste of time, considering that

Beniamo is marching to Amalia *as we speak*. Have you heard what he's getting up to along the way? I walked here from the Neviane, stopping in several towns he'd already ravaged. How do you think he treats the women there? Do you suppose he spares the children?"

Mirella clutched Luciano tighter, and his cry filled the room.

"I was the only woman in a camp of five thousand men. How many times do you think Beniamo tried to slither into my tent when the Capo wasn't looking?" Favianne asked. "If you imagine that I walked here because I fancied a bit of fresh air and a stab at magic, if you *truly* believe I have no quarrel of my own with your brother, you aren't sharp enough to best him. And you certainly aren't the friend I believed I made in Amalia."

Silence came for us all. Even Luciano's cry thinned to a watery gruel.

Xiaodan stood, shaking out her skirt, and moved to Favianne's side. "Are you hurt? I can help you feel . . . less. If that's something you need." I realized, with a dull stab, that Xiaodan was offering to perform a reversal of her magic for Favianne. To lessen the ache of whatever horrible things Beniamo had done to her.

"No magic will be performed in the Mirana," Cinquepalmi recited from his place at the door.

Dantae shook her head and sputtered with indignation. "You invited us to a feast, yet all these priests offer are stale crumbs."

"Teo just did magic a moment ago," Cielo reminded the guards.

"No *more* magic will be performed, anywhere on the grounds, including the gardens," Cinquepalmi said, splitting a meaningful look down the middle, offering half to Cielo and half to me.

"It won't be necessary, in this case," Favianne said, gifting a smile to Cinquepalmi that made him blink as hard as staring directly into the sun at noon.

Then she slid her arm through Xiaodan's, treating the girl like they were already great friends. Xiaodan blushed a gilded pink. "I was Fabiana Malfara for less than a year. Favianne Rao should have lived a comfortable life, but the girl I once was, Favianne Compagnari, wasn't even a noble let alone a queen. I grew up in the darkest reaches of the Oscurra Valley. Do you know that place?"

Xiaodan shook her head, upstaged for perhaps the first time in her life.

"I shouldn't think anyone of your talents knows the Oscurra Valley," Favianne said, doling out the overly sweet compliment like a bit of candied orange. "There's not much call for opera there. No cities, and only the poorest of towns. Most of us lived in a stretch of woods where the trees are as twisted and ugly as the hearts of the people. The branches there are fingers, throttling the sun. It creates a sort of false night and closes girls in with all sorts of monsters. I learned how and where to strike a man until he couldn't perform any sort of aria, if you see what I mean. Of course, no one expects a queen to kick and bite. It was probably the surprise alone that saved me." Her face brightened several notches, and she turned to Dantae. "Oh, does Beniamo have magic? I'd be more than happy to slice it free."

"No, and we must keep it that way," I said.

"You're the most ruthless woman in all the provinces," Pasquale spat as he leapt to his feet.

"Why do you think the people love me?" Favianne asked.

I stepped between them, not willing to let a quarrel between former lovers crumble an entire nation. "Why were you called Fabiana?" I asked.

"Oh, Cristoforo thought my name wasn't properly *Vinalian* enough," she scoffed. "My mother chose it because she spent time in the countryside near Vari as a girl, but I'm as Vinalian as the soil beneath this blessed building."

She hung her head in a show of piety. It didn't fool me, but it seemed to be enough for MacCartaigh, who hung his head with her, and Cinquepalmi, who looked ready to burst into applause.

"Oh good, she's got a new set of fools," Pasquale muttered.

I spun around to face him. "Pasquale, if you'd prefer to live your days as a barn cat, that can be arranged, but if you mean to stay here, please stop scratching around for trouble and sit down." Pasquale returned to his chair with a scrape of wood against marble, trying desperately to make it look like his own choice.

I turned to Favianne, aware that how I handled her now would set the tone for a great many negotiations. "If you want to help us, you can sit, too. Though there will be no more talk of killing streghe to claim their power. That was the Capo's chosen path, and if you follow him down it, only God can help you, because I certainly won't. However . . . *if* you win the Vinalian people to Oreste's cause, I'll find some way to give you what you ask."

Favianne's eyes gleamed as if I'd promised her a hoard of gold, or something she valued even more highly—secrets. "If magic is passed through death, nobody has to be *murdered*," she said reasonably as she claimed the seat at my side that

I'd reserved for Cielo. "There must be some old strega lying around Prai, simply waiting to fly to heaven."

"The greed in your eyes is not the last thing a strega should see before dying," Cielo said. "Not if she wants to rest peacefully. And you needn't worry about your inheritance. Teo and I will arrange that ourselves."

"*After* we stop Beniamo," I slipped in.

Cielo's stare grappled with mine, but I did not give way. We couldn't go after Veria's Truth until Beniamo's rampage was ended. Otherwise we would split our forces, and my brother would have a greater chance of killing the people in this room. The people I loved.

Cielo's mouth worked, chewing the gristle of a response. Before he could spit it out, I turned back to the table.

"Now we come to the part where we plot our next move," I said.

"Which everyone knows is Teo's favorite sport," Vanni added.

Mirella blanched. "This is not a game, Vanni."

I pushed on, past all of these small indignities, to the point. "We need to stop Beniamo before he takes the Capo's place. As soon as people see him as the rightful successor, we lose our claim and Oreste becomes the usurper. Right now, we can still twist the story, bend the path."

"Toward another Malfara," Father said, playing the music of displeasure with a series of stiff taps against the table.

"The answer seems clear to me," Lorenzo said, in one of his rare but welcome bouts of speech. He stared openly at Mimì. "We must use magic to overcome Beniamo. Our streghe are powerful. Why would we deny them the chance to use that power for the good of everyone in Vinalia, and Salvi?"

Mimì stared back at him, history and passion swelling to the point that half of the people at the table noticed their locked stares. It did not escape me that Lorenzo had listed Salvi separately from Vinalia—an issue I hadn't even brought up with Oreste, who might not be able to talk the priests into relinquishing their grasp on the largest island in the Terrano.

Dantae tapped her boots on the table, and several sets of eyes jumped to her. "I like the way this lordling thinks. But here's a problem. The Capo had a ring that made it impossible to touch him with magic, and my guess is that Beniamo has no trouble stealing from the dead."

I saw my brother's dry lips open, his tongue searching out the Capo's blood along the curve of the metal. "He does wear that ring," I said thinly, as if my voice had to travel all the way from the Neviane. "Which means that whatever magic we spend against him will be wasted."

The streghe shook their heads, a ripple of doubt moving through the room.

This is what he always wanted, my magic said. *To be untouchable.*

I feared that my magic was wrong this time.

Beniamo is only starting here, I pointed out. *Now he can take everything he wants, without a single consequence.*

A dry, hollow sound pulled me away from my thoughts. Mirella was tapping on the table in a perfect imitation of Father. I had spent so much of my life counting and sorting the ways that I was like him that I'd skipped clean over the fact that Mirella practically *was* Father in a younger, girlish form. "He can't use that ring to protect an army. And if you take them away, my brother won't have any toys to play with."

"I thought this wasn't a game," Vanni said with a sour note.

"It's not," Mirella said. "And neither were our childhoods." She nodded at me, and I felt close to her again for a brief, bittersweet moment before she turned to face the table. "Beniamo is the same now as he was then."

"Which means he is most dangerous when he has nothing," I reminded her.

Father pushed back his chair and stood.

He will fix things, my magic said. It wanted Father to make some kind of grand statement, to release a flood of healing and stitch the broken world back together. But I already knew that would never come to pass. When it came to my father, I no longer drew from the bottomless trust I had as a little girl.

He hadn't always protected me, even then.

"My daughters are right," the great Niccolò di Sangro said, his voice snapping in several places. The words came out broken, but a broken offering was better than none at all. "My son must be stopped. I will do it with my own hands if I have to."

Father could drain the life from a man with a reversal, which meant he'd always had the ability to stop Beniamo. But how could Father make that choice? Should he have fractured his own family to heal it? When should he have known that it was right to break a bone to set it, instead of sitting back and hoping time would do the hard work on its own?

"No magic, remember," I said, laying my hand on Father's arm.

A shadow crossed his face, as swift and threatening as when they moved over our mountains. "I don't need to use magic."

WITH OUR PLAN TO MARCH TO AMALIA IN PLACE, THE MEETING broke. All anyone could do was ask about Oreste and worry over whether he was losing the backing of the church as we spoke. They agreed to wait for him together, but I had another reunion in mind. I walked over to my sister on soft feet.

Luciano slept at her breast. His miniature eyelids pinched in a way that made me think his dreams were already filled with enemies. Mirella and I both kept our eyes on him so we would not have to face each other.

"Thank you for saying what you did," I told her in a low voice. "It came at the perfect moment to draw everyone together . . ."

"I'm not here for you, Teodora," she said, bobbing the baby up and down to keep him from waking. "I came for my son. I won't let him live in a world where Beniamo is allowed to rule."

She held on to Luciano so tightly, I worried she would keep her promise—that she wouldn't allow this tiny child to go on breathing if our brother was named leader of Vinalia. I wondered what I would do if I had a child to care for, a new life to tend to in the middle of so much death.

Vanni appeared at Mirella's elbow. "Let me hold him for a minute," he said, gentling the baby out of her arms into an awkward, loving grip. Vanni took a great deal of joy in counting Luciano's toes several times over, as if he might eventually come up with a different sum. Mirella pushed her way past both of them to wedge distance between us.

"Do you think you can convince your wife to hate me slightly less?" I asked.

"She's afraid, Teo," Vanni said, smiling at the baby as he woke, though his words were grim. "We all are."

"Did you have any trouble getting the streghe out of the Neviane?" I asked.

"Oh, nearly the opposite," Vanni said. "Mimì kept us warm with her snow magic, and Xiaodan plumped up our best feelings until you could have confused us for a merry band of travelers. For an opera singer, that girl can coat her lungs in brass and belt out so many lewd ditties that a nun would burst into flames."

I looked over at Xiaodan, trailing Favianne's steps as the former Queen of Vinalia praised her bright brown eyes and her straight black hair and gave advice on how to tighten her corset to its full throttling potential. Was Xiaodan trying to curry favor with a powerful noblewoman, or was she that starved for friendship? I realized I knew little about the famous soprano besides her magic.

"The only bad part was . . . well, at times we thought we were being followed," Vanni admitted. "We heard broken twigs, crunching footsteps. I assumed it was Beniamo but he never showed himself. Now that I see her in that dress that she clearly hasn't washed since breaking camp, I think Favianne was tracking us."

My eyes skipped away from Xiaodan and landed on Favianne, who took notice of my attentions at once and curled her hand in a wave, each finger crooked like an invitation to come closer.

"Teo," she called out. "Aren't you going to come take up our conversation where we left off?" She turned to Xiaodan and leaned in closer. "Teo and I used to have the most intimate talks in Amalia. I've missed them."

"Help," I whispered.

Vanni offered the baby, but I shook my head. If Mirella saw me holding Luciano, she would undoubtedly come and grab him away from his dangerous godmother. Besides, I felt uneasy near Luciano. He was new to this world, and strangely clear-eyed, as if he was judging me more harshly and fairly than the grown men of the five families ever could. I felt freshly relieved that I'd swallowed that magical milk after leaving Pavella. I could take on a room full of the most influential and magical figures in Vinalia, but the thought of a single infant terrified me.

Cielo stepped in and accepted Luciano in my stead. He drummed his fingers on the baby's stomach, making his lips burst into a wide show of gums, his smile edged with spittle. Cielo didn't appear to share my reservations—and in fact seemed to prefer Luciano's company to that of anyone else in the overstuffed room. I drifted away from this stolen moment of happiness.

Toward Father.

He looked stiff from travel, dusted with the grit of the roads and the heaviness of our talk. He stepped closer and drew me into his arms. Things had been so strained between us since I left the Uccelli that the only reason I could think Father might embrace me so deeply in public was if someone we both loved was dead.

"Where is Fiorenza?" I asked.

Father cleared his throat. "Well . . ." he said, beginning a story instead of giving me an answer. My fear folded over on itself, doubling in strength. "When your summons came, I wanted to believe that the matter with Beniamo would take care of itself. But your stepmother took one look at your letter and she . . ."

I waited as my heart screwed tight.

"She left us." Father pressed his hands together. "She went back to the Violetta Coast and took the girls to hide them."

"But she loves you," I cried. In the wake of my own wedding, I could not fathom the idea that Father and Fiorenza's marriage was crumbling. Their love had always been unquestioned in my mind—even though some practical part of me knew that Fiorenza had done well to get Carina and Adela out of our brother's path.

"She'll come back after we've won, won't she?" I asked.

Father rubbed the spot on his forehead where his hairline was pulling back, slow and steady as a tide. "I don't know. She said that I would keep trying to live as if Beniamo wasn't dangerous because that was what I had always done. Your stepmother believes . . . she believes that going was the only way for me to understand how serious things have become."

Father studied my face, and it took me a moment to realize he was tracing the bruises on my cheeks and jaw from Beniamo's cuffing. "She is always right," he added. "No matter how much I argue with her."

Then he whispered a story, simple and true, and I felt the ache and tightness I'd grown used to over the last few days fade, disappear.

"Thank you, Father," I said, touching my relieved cheek.

My lopsided hearing remained, the conversations in the room muffled in the way I'd come to expect. Apparently, my ear couldn't be healed in the same way as a cut or a bruise.

"I should have done more to keep you out of harm." He pulled his stiletto from his sleeve. There was no grand, sweeping motion. Only a knife in his hands one moment, and mine the next. "This is for you, Teo."

The night he'd offered it to me in the ruins of the di Sangro castle came back all at once, as ruthless and clear as the light of a full moon. He had told me that I should keep the family stiletto, along with the boyish form that the men in Amalia respected. "I told you I can't accept . . ."

"There are no conditions," he said.

I ran my eyes along the edge, which looked as sharp and promising as ever. "If you're going to face Beniamo yourself, you still need this."

Father shook his head with great force, which meant I had stepped over a line from simply wrong to willfully so. "Your stepmother called this stiletto my favorite piece of art. Your mother teased me for being in love with it. My father chose me as his heir and offered me the di Sangro blade when I was a year younger than you are now. Every one of those memories is worked into the metal. It is a weapon, Teo, but not *only* a weapon. It would be wasted on your brother. Please, take it. I don't care if you use it to cut apples for the rest of your days."

"She prefers pears," Cielo said, striding over with the contented baby in his arms. "Red ones, if they can be had."

"Of course," Father said, his voice clouding with memory. "I knew that." His disdain snapped back into place. "I see that your . . . friend . . . is still with us."

"You're not the only one with family here," Cielo said, looking at me pointedly.

I felt certain he was about to bring up our marriage.

I trembled, wanting and fearing those words in equal measure.

Cielo slipped the baby into the crook of one arm and held up his other hand, flicking his fingers and scattering my expectations. "Now that he's giving up the priesthood to rule Vinalia, I suppose I can reveal the shameful fact that Oreste is my father. Though at this point I can't remember whether I'm supposed to be ashamed of him or he's meant to be ashamed of me."

"*You're* a Malfara?" Father asked. He narrowed his eyes, as if that made it easier to see the truth. "You're as tall as a Malfara, though you don't have their vices stamped all over you."

Before this could go any further, I looped my arm through Cielo's free one and steered him back toward Vanni, returning Luciano to his father. "Wait here," I said, spinning back to mine. "We'll bring Oreste, and you two can sew up the rest of the plan."

"It looks like you have done the hard work yourself," Father said. "Fiorenza would be proud." As I nodded, he added in a dusty whisper, "So would your mother."

Heat flowered in my chest, unfurling petals of orange flame. Both Luciana and Fiorenza di Sangro would understand this scene far too well. I had brought everyone in this room together, streghe and soldiers, church and five families. There hadn't been a single splinter of violence to break the discussion.

I looked around, from the former Queen of Vinalia chatting with a magical opera singer to the head of the soldiers of Erras standing in close quarters with the powerful family whose newborn heir she had tried to float down an underground river. I had brought this moment into the world, a difficult birth that easily could have left more than one of us dead.

Now Oreste would sweep in and claim everything, as if it was his right.

"The new leader of Vinalia will be so glad to see that his subjects are getting along," I said, with an empty smile and a heart to match.

༄❀༅

THE ROOMS ORESTE KEPT WERE ON THE FIRST STORY OF THE Mirana, which meant we had to climb a nautilus of stairs to reach him.

"How do you think it went?" I asked Cielo. A skin of worry had formed on my thoughts, and I could not seem to pick it away.

"You've worked a miracle," Cielo announced to the empty stairwell, his voice hitting cold stone and bouncing. "I'd call you Saint Teodora, but you have to die for that, and martyrdom doesn't suit you any more than it does me."

"Dying for what you believe in isn't a fashion that comes and goes, like high-necked dresses," I said.

"Isn't it?" Cielo asked, sounding more distracted with each step that we took toward his father. "Both look pretty in a certain light and are uncomfortable in the extreme."

We reached the door, and I managed a polite knock, when all my magic wanted was to break the wood to splinters so I could stride through without stopping. "Now we just need Oreste to take his place in all this."

We waited, but there were no footsteps.

"You don't think we're going to open this door to find a carefully inked letter explaining all of the reasons he can't possibly be the leader of Vinalia, do you?" Cielo asked with a nervous tremolo of laughter.

"He is probably having a quiet moment to himself," I said, though lies did not suit me any better than martyrdom did.

"You mean he's hiding under his desk and shaking like a rabbit in a hutch," Cielo said.

"If that's something he needs to do at the moment, it really is better for him to take care of it privately."

"He's a priest of the Order of Prai," Cielo said, setting his hand to the knob. "I'm sure he knows how to hide his sins."

"Shouldn't he simply . . . *not* sin?" I asked.

Cielo sighed. "Sometimes I forget that you spent the first sixteen years of your life hidden away under a pretty pile of rocks."

"The di Sangro castle is *not*—"

"A pretty pile of rocks? Fine, it's a menacing pile of rocks."

He pushed the door in. The small table at the center was set for tea, its tiled surface covered in half-filled cups that had taken on an oily sheen. I walked over to find the pot of black tea with bergamot gone cold. Cielo looked over Oreste's desk, but there was no letter pinned to the ink blotter, not even a loose scrap of a note.

A wind troubled Oreste's papers. My eyes went to the window, cast open though the once-fine day had retreated, and the dark gray of rain was advancing.

The weather was the least of our troubles, though. There was a rope, tied to the leg of the desk, snaking over the ledge.

"My father escaped out the window?" Cielo asked. "That seems childish, even for a man who has run away from every one of his worldly duties so he can pretend he is God's special son."

A pit of dread from some bitter fruit lingered in my stomach. "I don't think he escaped."

I walked to the window, following the line of the rope as it dropped. A nearly naked man, stripped of his robes, swung at the end, bruised where he had bashed against the wall of the Mirana, purple lines scratched into his skin where the rope had left him burned.

The next leader of Vinalia was dead.

And so was my plan to save us.

Four

The Last Malfara

15

Oreste's body swung lightly, moved by the urgent hands of the wind.

"What do we do?" Cielo asked as rain started pouring misery all over Prai. I stepped back from the window, and not simply to keep dry. I did not want anyone in the Mirana to notice my place in this tableau and blame me for the death of yet another Malfara.

There was a tap at the door. I leapt back, and before I could summon magic and escape, we had company.

It was Cinquepalmi, his strong features pinched with contrition. "Signorina . . . I'm meant to tell you . . . I have a message."

"Who is this message from?" I asked. He stepped back slightly as if I'd battered him with the words—now that my ear was dulled, I had a tendency to speak with greater volume and pointed articulation.

Especially when my emotions were rushing in every direction.

Had the church killed one of their own, a known lover of streghe, to show that they were never going to be on our side? Was standing against magic so important that they would sacrifice the rest of Vinalia to my brother?

"These are the words of Father Malfara," Cinquepalmi said, clasping his hands behind his back. He went into the singsong voice of rote memorization. "I'm meant to tell you that he offers his apologies. He says he wishes for God to be with you on your mission against Beniamo, but there is too much guilt in his soul to make a good ruler, and now that he remembers the . . . manner in which he broke his vows . . . he can no longer remain a priest in the Order of Prai."

Cinquepalmi let out his reserves of breath, looking relieved and more than a bit pleased. I doubted that he knew Father Malfara was hanging outside the window, and that he had just delivered the man's final words.

I sank into a crouch, setting my head in my hands, seeking out darkness—wishing I didn't understand.

This wasn't the church's doing. This was Oreste's choice.

I looked up at Cielo, and from this angle I could see something inside of him break. It was less of a clean snap, and more like watching a city crumble.

Cinquepalmi ducked his head. "I'm sorry I didn't say anything sooner, but Father Malfara asked me to wait until you came up here to find him. He didn't wish to make a scene." I thought of everyone waiting downstairs—the impossible peace that I had knitted together. "Shall I go and let everyone know that circumstances have changed?"

"No," I said, pushing to my feet. "Nothing has changed."

"Nothing has changed?" Cielo asked in an incredulous voice.

"Has anyone else heard this message?" I asked. I could hear myself going through the steps of keeping this plan alive. I felt like a doctor must when a patient is beyond saving, working hard while the possibility of life retreats into the distance.

"Only MacCartaigh," Cinquepalmi said.

If Oreste really did wish for us to stop Beniamo, he'd done one good thing. He'd arranged for the church to lend us an army, and we couldn't ruin that now.

"Good," I said. "Go back down and tell everyone that we'll be there soon enough."

My anger drove me around the room in sharp lines. Oreste was meant to be our savior, but he could not face the upcoming battles, or Beniamo, or even the disappointment of his child. Cielo had been afraid that his father would run away, and he had done exactly that, flying to the one place we could not follow.

My mind turned up the memory of Cielo's mother, driven to kill herself when the Capo's troops closed in.

Cielo had no parents now.

But he did have family—the one he'd married into.

Had Oreste thought of that as he married us in the garden?

Even if life does not honor your plans, you have each other.

"He was thinking of doing this the whole time," I mumbled.

When Cielo finally stopped struggling against the truth, he sank deeper into sadness. He stared over the stone lip of the window as the rain fell on his downturned face, sliding down his forehead and beading on his lips.

His profile was absurdly noble. His fingers were slick on the stone but poised, ready to act. He looked more like his uncle than his father in that moment. Traces of Giovanna stuck to him, always. It was easy to forget that Cielo had not made himself from long strings of words and great volumes of magic. He might have spent most of his life estranged from his family, but he was a Malfara.

A new plan came like lightning, hitting the ground before I even saw it, illuminating the skies on its way back to heaven.

"This doesn't have to be our ruin," I said, cuffing Cielo's arm with a gentle hand and pulling him away from the window. "There is one thing we can do, but it must be done quickly. Study the papers on the desk. Write a note in Oreste's hand, explaining that he wishes for his child to take over the great work of leading a unified Vinalia. We'll go downstairs and tell everyone *you* are the heir to the Capo's line. It helps that we already told Father you are a Malfara. And there is your recent marriage, of course. That will get the five families to swallow the situation a bit more smoothly."

Cielo blinked a few times. Rain had turned his dark eyelashes into a shining set of spikes. "You misunderstood me. When I said *what do we do*, I meant should we cut him down or pull him up? Not, from what new angle we should scheme now that my father is dead."

I sighed, but even my breath was chopped short by my haste. "I wish we had time for proper mourning, but . . ."

"No, you don't," Cielo pushed out.

"Do you want my unvarnished thoughts?" I asked, pointing to the rope. "That man has abandoned the people he loves at every turn. Vinalia could have been a much better place if he'd stood against his brother all those years ago. Think of the suffering that could have been stopped before it ever came to pass." I took a deep breath, scouring my lungs.

"You wanted to change things, Cielo, and now you will. You can be the leader that Oreste never could."

Cielo stared at me with two fingers digging into his knotted brow, as if he'd gone mad and somehow that was the least of our problems.

"You are suited to this!" I cried. "I know you to be loyal, strong-minded, fair . . ."

"Are you describing me, or yourself?" Cielo asked. "You seem to have gotten us tangled up, and not in the good way."

My strega was skilled at evasion, but I would not let him slip away from his fate. "You are capable of withstanding the great loneliness and pain that come with being a leader. At times, you can be so clever that it almost hurts," I said. "What is more, you are not so hungry for power that you will rip it out of the hands of those who starve."

I crossed my arms, locking the vaults of my reasons. I had given him plenty and now he would have to agree.

There was no other way.

"Even if all you said is true, you're missing an important detail," Cielo said, his voice growing cold as the rain outside. "I want to save Vinalia from the scourge of great men, not become one."

"If you love Vinalia half as well as you love me, the world will be better for it," I said.

Cielo went over to his father's little table, still set for tea. He braced himself and took a sip, wincing against the overbrewed leaves. He mumbled something into the cup, but it was too low, and with my dull ear, I could not hear it.

"What?" I asked.

Cielo's voice leapt, skipping over reasonable volumes and rising to a shout. "I will not do it."

He reached for another cup, but my magic was ready. It changed all of the cups on the table to crowns, so that wherever Cielo reached, he found the same answer waiting for him.

Cielo sighed. "There is no amount of flattery or magic that will change my mind, Teo. You think you only have to talk me into it, and that I will be happy. But the life I want has a different shape altogether."

"Most people never face such a moment. You simply aren't thinking it through. This is a call to greatness."

He sat down at the tiny table, picking up one of the crowns I'd made. The gems gave off the green fire of emeralds, but from the way he held it I could tell it didn't have the convincing weight of gold.

"We should have a baby."

Ice entered my veins, pushing its way through my heart. "What? This is not the time for a child."

"And yet I think you should bear one," Cielo said, leaning back, letting the crown dangle from his finger and drop to the floor.

"You're being ridiculous," I said faintly. "What about the milk from the strega in Pavella? We agreed on that."

"We agreed that a cave wasn't the right place to start a family. I love babies," Cielo said. "Or haven't you noticed?" I thought of Cielo holding Luciano, drumming fingers against his tiny stomach, helping my nephew invent his first laughs.

But as lovely as that moment had been, the truth remained. "I don't want to carry a child." It had little to do with present circumstances and nothing to do with Cielo. That was how I'd felt for years.

I couldn't understand why we were talking about this

now, with Oreste hanging outside in the rain. Anger circled back for me. "Why did you choose this moment to make such a demand?"

"We're newly married, and isn't that when most people have children?" Cielo asked. "Besides, I think you're suited to motherhood. It's a decision I've made by myself, with no real need to consult you. If you love the baby half as well as you love me, the world will be better for it. And don't worry if you've never wanted to be a mother before this moment. Calls to greatness *must* be answered."

"You've made your point," I said. "Although you didn't have to twist the knife quite so hard."

"You weren't listening to me, Teo," Cielo said. "You haven't been listening for some time." He stood up, scattering the crowns I'd made.

"What do we do now?" I asked.

"You do whatever you believe you must," Cielo said. "I'm going after Veria's Truth."

A hundred arguments welled up, a hundred reasons Cielo couldn't leave me. "But—"

"I've been searching this whole time. Did that factor into your plans? Did you tell your father about it?"

I lowered my eyes.

"You pretend you care about the fate of Vinalia," he added, "but it has always been di Sangro business. You must defeat your brother. You must win back the love of your sister. And by all means, you must make your father proud."

"What of our marriage?" I asked. "*You* are my family. My strega."

"You did not claim me, did you?" Cielo said, breaking toward the door. "You did not tell your family about us."

I caught him by the wrist. "Oreste told me to keep it secret."

"And you honored his wishes without a second thought." He picked my hand off his wrist and dropped it. "You sway to the tune of powerful men."

I raised my hand and drew it back.

I put it down just as quickly, but the true damage didn't come from slapping Cielo: it came from being willing to do it in the first place.

Cielo groaned and drew his hand across his lips, as though the words he was about to speak were sickening him but he had to let them out. "No one knows about our wedding but those two soldiers. It would be easy enough to disavow."

Now it was my turn to rush for the door. "I will go and tell everyone we are married right now."

Cielo drew out the book, flicked a page, and became a black-furred wolf, running ahead of me, curling into place so that I could not pass, then stalking back and forth. I took a brash step forward, and the wolf let out a howl that went through my muscle and bone.

Cielo came back to girlish form, still pacing in long strides, her eyes glinting with feral instincts. "You want to tell everyone now that it's to your advantage? Now that my marriage to a di Sangro daughter will put my bid for the throne in a better light? I could always show up in this form—how do you think they would like it?" Cielo tried to smile, but it became a snarl, lips drawing away from her teeth. "You call me your strega, and I am yours, but you are not mine. You are a di Sangro. Always."

"What does that mean?" I asked, wanting to touch her, afraid to take a step closer.

Cielo flung an arm toward the window. "You forced my father into your schemes. He is dead because you backed him into a corner."

"He is dead because he is a coward," I shouted.

Cielo ran a finger along the edge of the book. The pages slipped against each other, releasing a dry rasp. "So, everyone who kills himself is a coward?"

"No! *He* is. Your mother—"

"Is also dead at her own hand!" Cielo shouted. "What a fine moment to bring that up."

I gritted my teeth and kept on. "Your mother wasn't always right, but she was brave. She loved you. She died believing it would keep you safe."

"She was wrong," Cielo muttered. "Does that mean she died for nothing?"

Cielo flicked page after page, changes coming on with a fury. Wolf and wind and girl and boy.

"What are you doing?" I asked. "Come back."

Cielo settled into girlish form long enough to look around the room with a touch of dizzied confusion. "I used to do that when I was little. Change and change, wondering if I could find the shape that would bring them back."

"That man is worse than no father at all," I said, rushing to the window. Now I was furious with Oreste not just for ruining our plans and thrusting our lives closer to danger, but for hurting Cielo. For never being there for my strega—and leaving the world behind, the moment he got a second chance.

I cast my magic down, along the line of the rope, dropping heavier than the rain. I pulled Oreste up, hand over hand.

I walked back over to Cielo and slapped a small block of unfinished marble in her palm. It was cream white, veined with charcoal gray. "Here," I said. "It will be less of a weight to carry."

Cielo stared at me like I was some new breed of monster. "Are you going to change me next? Remember, I can't rule Vinalia as an olive." She slid the marble into her cloak and grabbed for the book, which she'd set down on Oreste's desk. I knew that the moment she flipped to a new page, I would lose her.

Keep Cielo here, I begged.

I could not touch the book, but the magic was clever enough to come up with another way. The desk became a seamless chest of granite in the darkest possible gray, and the book vanished into its stony heart. Cielo ran and threw herself into opening it, but the large box had no lid, no hinges.

"You would keep me here by holding my book captive?" Cielo asked, looking amazed and disgusted. "You know I don't need it to change."

"You need it for control, though. Without the book, all of that magic your mother stole from other streghe will run wild."

Cielo nodded, pursing her lips with decision. Then she flung herself forward, sliding into the air, becoming wind. Unfettered, Cielo pushed me back, and I hit the stone box that held the book. My head cracked against the edge, leaving a line of blood.

Cielo came back to boyish form on the windowsill, poised on his toes, ready to leap. But when he looked back, he saw me holding my head, red seeping between my fingers. He ran back, cradling the wound in both hands. "Are you all right, Teo?"

"Please stay," I said, kissing him once, then twice, as though it would patch over the things we had just done. I needed the strega, and that need was as terrifying as anything else I had to face. "Please stay with me."

"I can't," Cielo said.

"Then you truly are your father's son."

"Look at that." He lifted one corner of his lips, a smirk weighed down by sadness. "Our fates finally match. You are your father's son, too."

Cielo grimaced as he pulled the di Sangro stiletto free from my sleeve. I thought I would face down the point, but the handle was spun toward me, an offering instead of a threat. "Is this what comes next? You hold me here by force? Tell me I must play this role? That there is no other way?"

Cielo pressed the stiletto toward me, the blade pointed at his chest.

I would not take it.

The knife dropped to the floor, and as my tears followed, Cielo grabbed the cloak and crossed to the window. For a moment I thought he might stop there. He held a hand up, and when his fingertips met the rain, he changed into a dark burst of droplets, tumbling along with the green-purple silk to the courtyard below.

❧❦❧

I RETURNED DOWNSTAIRS ALONE.

"Where is Oreste?" Father asked.

"Did the church bury him for sitting so close to streghe?" Dantae added with a knowing squint.

I had no responses prepared. "No." My voice doubled over on itself, thick with pain. My breath trembled, as if every time my lungs worked, it reminded me that another moment had passed without Cielo near.

Xiaodan was tugging at my sleeve, asking a question, but she was pouring words into the wrong ear.

"What?" I asked, slipping so I stood on her other side.

"Is something wrong with Oreste?" she repeated.

I saw MacCartaigh and Cinquepalmi, still flanking the door, lean farther into the room to note my answer. If I admitted that Oreste was dead, I might lose the church's army, which I needed, since magic could not get me close to Beniamo.

I had to pick up my answer with delicate fingers. "Oreste has passed on his right to lead," I said. "He believes he is not the right man to rule a young nation. He has chosen his only child—Cielo—to take his place."

I needed to keep this alliance whole, at least long enough to stop Beniamo. The question of succession could be settled after he was dead.

My brother had taken Cielo away from me, just like he had promised, by making the world an impossible place for us to live in without constant fear, terrible choices, the threat of unhappiness sticking to us like a shadow.

Beniamo deserved to die. I did not care if it lit the spark of another war, as long as my brother was not there to blow on the flames.

"We march for Amalia today," I said. "This very hour."

"Where is Cielo?" Vanni asked.

I thought of my strega chasing a shard of magic in the drowned grottoes. "Cielo has gone to seek the blessing of the old gods," I said. "A pilgrimage of sorts."

"Oh, good," Favianne said mildly. "I'm sure Beniamo will wait politely on the outskirts of Amalia while Cielo prays."

"Cielo won't be gone for long," I said, knowing that was probably a lie, my lips clenching tight around a last wisp of hope.

"Who is going to lead us until the last Malfara returns?" Dantae asked as MacCartaigh and Cinquepalmi threw open the great paneled door of the Mirana only to prove that it was raining so hard that the sky had turned white as a scar.

"You are going to lead yourselves," I said. "And I will be here in case anyone needs a reminder of how *not* to kill each other."

Vanni claimed a place at my side as we headed out into the drowning day. "Won't the heir of Vinalia be in danger traveling alone?"

I scoffed to hide a fear so strong, I almost retched instead. "Cielo is a strega of nearly limitless power," I said. That seemed to satisfy everyone in the room, but I was left with the acid touch of fear at the back of my throat. If Cielo was grand and reckless with all of that magic, it would only turn my strega into a target. And I had stolen Cielo's control by sealing up the book.

I told myself that Cielo would be fine.

And my magic answered me:

Liar.

Strega.

Thief.

16

The march to Amalia took us through the muscle and bone of Otto territory. The Otto family ran the central provinces of Vinalia, though Amalia was widely known to be a stronghold of the Malfara family, and the church had long held dominion over Prai. The rest belonged to Ambrogio, and the farther we walked through a collection of small towns and wide fields, the sharper the memory of his betrayal.

From the look on my sister's face, I could tell I wasn't the only one slicing herself with the rusted knife of the past. Mirella had trusted Ambrogio once. She had taken him into her bed. And then there was the vile possibility that she had loved him.

The thought of love brought Cielo back in a harsh, vivid stroke.

I bandaged yet another invisible wound and kept walking. I kept my eyes on Mirella, who cast far too many glances down every path when we came to a crossroads. She was walking through Ambrogio's lands with only the hope that he would not claim a father's right to her child.

He has no such right, my magic hissed. It had already changed his heart to wood once, and that was before I'd

taken on the power of the Capo's streghe. I wanted to promise Mirella I would protect her, but after the hand I'd had in
tearing down our home and ruining her wedding, I did not
think it would be a welcome vow.

As dusk slithered over the hills, Vanni, who had stayed
locked at Mirella's side, let himself fall back to walk with me.
"She looks worse with every step," he said. "Another day of
this might kill her. Why wouldn't she stay in Prai? Or better
yet, Castel di Volpe?"

"A di Sangro woman does not like being left at home," I
muttered.

"I am not going to treat her like a piece of Ovetian porcelain, I promise," Vanni said. "But . . ."

"You misunderstand me," I said, pulling my cloak against
the damp. It had stopped raining shortly after we left Prai,
as if the sky was spent. But now the water seemed to be
trapped in the air, hovering. "When I was in Amalia as a
di Sangro boy, Mirella was left at home to watch Father
waste away. And when we were younger, Father was gone
for months at a time. We always wished to be with him."
Not the least because when he wasn't at home, Beniamo had
the run of the house, even if Fiorenza did what she could to
keep him from us.

How much did Father know about Beniamo's little
tortures?

How much did he look away from?

I watched his back from his place at the head of the column. Father had insisted on taking the lead, saying he knew
the roads that led away from Prai like he knew the sight of
his own feet beneath him, but he'd set the pace of an ancient goat. I had subtly asked Xiaodan to walk at his side,

where she spoke to him of her time in the opera, and he worked hard to keep up with her broad, even steps. Mimì and Lorenzo followed behind them at the same brisk pace, so Father wouldn't flag, and Favianne and Pasquale brought up the rear of the party, Pasquale looking at everything in creation but the woman he had once been sworn to.

If it weren't for the church's army trailing behind us like a wisp of smoke, it would have been easy to mistake this for a gathering of the five families.

"I remember how happy Mirella was at being sent to make the rounds of the five families," I said. "It brought me dangerously close to hating her. The only thing that stopped me was the knowledge that she was being sent off to fetch a good marriage, like goods being carted to market."

Thoughts of marriage turned swiftly, obviously, to thoughts of Cielo. I had chosen the strega for myself, and that hadn't turned out much better. The truth scorched, so I doused it with worries about my sister.

"That's not how it seemed to me," Vanni said. "Mirella once said she loved seeing Vinalia that way, dancing from ballroom to ballroom. Every time she came to Castel di Volpe, it was like spring coming back."

I had forgotten that Vanni and Mirella's history was not as shallow as the last several months, a hurried courtship ending in a marriage of convenience. Vanni had memories of Mirella that stretched as long and deep as the riverbed of the Estatta.

"Did you ever try to court her before . . . ?" *Before Ambrogio stole her away? Before she made the wrong choice and ruined her life?* That's how the Teo of a year ago would have put things. But when I looked at Luciano, his little body bundled in a lemon-colored blanket I remembered from my own child-hood, life didn't feel ruined at all.

Another thought of Cielo intruded.

I love babies. Or haven't you noticed?

"Oh, I knew better than to court your sister," Vanni said. "Until recently, I don't think Mirella saw me as anything but a red-haired nuisance." His smile faded like a tapestry that had soaked in too much sun. "I *was* a red-haired nuisance."

"You are a different man now," I said, tugging him close with my arm around his shoulders, one of the habits I'd learned in a more boyish form. "And it's not only the throw-ing of light."

"Mirella is the same, though," Vanni insisted.

"Perfect and impossible?" I asked.

We stopped at the edge of the night's encampment. There was no use marching until morning, not if it wore holes through our resolve. Mirella helped pitch tents with one arm, baby in the other, as if she'd been doing things that way her whole life. Between quick and purposeful movements, she gave Luciano smiles, each one like a secret that she un-folded just for him.

My sister was the same as she'd always been, and she was also different. As a child, I'd felt her holding back, always a little fearful. Beniamo had taught us that anything we loved was in danger from the moment our hearts dared to beat a little harder. My solution had been to hide, to do everything in secret. Mirella's had been to harden the defenses of her heart. But I could see her changing now, the way she lavished kisses on Luciano.

"She is not afraid to love her son," I said. "She is only afraid to lose him."

I was glad that Mirella had chosen to come with us. She had my protection, even if she did not wish to acknowledge it. And she had Father, Vanni, and half a dozen various Moschella in-laws who had chosen to make the journey from Castel di Volpe. I recognized the nervous boy who'd stood across from me during Luciano's baptism. Signora Moschella had stayed behind in Prai, declaring that she was too old for battle, and someone had to keep an eye on the priests.

When Mirella crouched to light the campfire, flint in one hand and the baby in the other, Vanni rushed to her side. "You do have to let someone else hold Luciano at some point," Vanni said. When Mirella gave him a di Sangro glare, he added, "In the hazy, distant future."

"You could hand him off to me," Dantae said.

"Ha!" Vanni shouted so violently, I thought he might fall

over backward from the force of it.

Mirella struck the flint, a dry chipping sound that beckoned flame. "Yes, of course, now that we're in Otto territory I'll hand you the baby to make your job easier. Ambrogio is probably waiting for you behind that tree."

Even the mention of his name turned my steps stiff and wooden.

"The offer was genuine, Signora," Dantae said.

"Why, in any ring of hell, would I let you touch Luciano again?" Mirella asked.

Dantae's magic went to work, opening Mirella's question like a ripe fruit so she might search for the seeds of an answer.

"You've borne children," Mirella said.

"I believe I'm the only other one in this party who has," she added.

Mirella tucked the flint back into its roll of cloth and left Dantae staring into the fire. Instead of handing Luciano to any of us, she laid the baby in a special traveling crib that Signora Moschella had given her, the posts carved into foxes.

"There are people who call you *mother*?" Vanni asked, sounding far too fascinated to stop himself from prying.

Mirella marched back to the fire, facing off with Dantae across the fire's grasping orange fingertips. "If you want to help Luciano, the least you can do is change that . . . thing you're wearing. Your snakes are drawing attention. I'm fairly certain someone recognized us in the last town because we were standing too close to your adder-skin vest."

"Fair point," Dantae said, shedding the vest all at once so that her breasts touched the fire-warmed air. "Is that better?"

"Don't answer," Vanni said, though I felt he was warning himself more than anyone else.

"The soldiers of Erras aren't afraid to walk through the world the way we came into it," Dantae said.

"Where does a woman sign up?" Favianne asked, sliding into the ring of light, the fire casting a little more of its brilliance on her than it did on the rest of us. Xiaodan followed, looking tired from a day of setting the pace and shepherding Father.

"We'd be too humble for your tastes," Dantae said, with a mocking bow. "Your Highness."

"Did you not hear my entire speech about my humble origins?" Favianne asked. "Or was it too hard with your boots stomping on the table every other moment?"

I could not help it—I grinned. Favianne returned the smile with startled grace.

"Everyone in Vinalia thinks you know a person at first glance," Xiaodan said, nearly pasting herself to Favianne's hip. "It's stifling."

"No doubt Cielo would agree with that sentiment," Vanni tossed in. "I first met Cielo as a servant, and now our secret Malfara is about to become the king of Vinalia. These are either strange times . . . or they're normal times and I'm not nearly strange enough."

"Where *is* our illustrious new leader?" Favianne asked, making a grand show of gazing to the copse of trees in one direction and the hills in the other, even though layers of fog and darkness sifted over the land.

I thought I saw my strega's shape tossed against the night, but it was only a long, lean shadow.

I had been waiting, giving Cielo every chance to change direction before I came up with a way to patch the crumbling plaster of this plan. But we were more than halfway to Amalia, and there had been no sign of Cielo in any form. I hadn't felt the littlest stirring of my magic to make me think Cielo might be returning.

"If this young Malfara truly wishes to run Vinalia, he is not off to a good start," Father muttered, his voice rising out of the darkness before he stepped into the firelight. He did not look pleased, and soon doubt rose to the surface of every expression, so thick and heavy that I half expected it to smother the fire.

I had to produce Cielo quickly.

"I'll be right back," I said, splitting away from the group.

"Are you not feeling well, Teo?" Father asked. Once he got hold of a question like that, he wouldn't stop until it was answered. "Teo?"

I kept rushing on numb feet, toward the nearest rise in the hills. I was not well, and I wouldn't be until Cielo came striding back to me. But my strega had chosen another way. And I would have to keep moving down this path, or else I had given up a great love for nothing.

The irony struck me, cold and bloodless. I had lost Cielo at the moment that I needed my strega more than ever.

These people need a Malfara, the magic corrected. *So give them a Malfara.*

"*Can you do that?*" I whispered.

The magic buzzed through me like a host of wasps.

When I'd worked reversals in the past, I had not demanded a specific form. I had given my magic a loose idea and let it fill in the details. But I had studied Cielo in painstaking detail, and as it turned out, love was a thorough tutor. I knew Cielo's body, Cielo's face, all of Cielo's forms. And now I had the magic of dozens of streghe running through me. If all of that stolen magic was going to be good for one thing, maybe it was saving Vinalia.

First, I had to summon up a picture of the strega in boyish form, which was painfully easy.

Then I drew magic from every quarter of my body.

But before I could give a command, I found myself running back toward camp. When I'd left, there had been the sounds of tents being raised and food being rustled from packs, the strands of a dozen different voices spinning into a single hearty rope.

Now there was something else. Silence.

My magic worked as I ran. It knew exactly who I needed to be. It turned my feet longer and thinner, breaking my stride. My clothes sighed and popped as Cielo's height challenged every seam. *Change the clothes as well*, I reminded my magic.

Lastly, Cielo's long hair slid behind me, swaying like the pendulum of a clock. It swished with every strike of my feet—Cielo's feet. When I broke back into camp, I looked exactly like the last Malfara. But I was still Teo.

And Ambrogio was dangerously close to my sister.

Dantae and the soldiers of Erras had drawn their bone knives, but the Otto men that Ambrogio had brought with him were holding them at a stalemate, pistols drawn. The church's army was trudging miles behind the five families and the streghe—we'd been sent ahead to scout. Even if I screamed, and they heard me, they would never reach us in time to help. And Ambrogio might start killing people in a frenzied haste if he thought we had reinforcements behind us.

Our party was bound by the hands and feet, which meant that Mimì, Xiaodan, and Vanni couldn't use their magic. Vanni looked on with a haunted air, and I felt certain the last few minutes had been etched deep in his mind and would never fade. On the other hand, Luciano still lay in his crib, sleeping as if nothing in particular was happening.

The Ottos had used their knowledge of the land to overcome us without a fight.

Take Ambrogio from them, my magic whispered. *Take one of theirs. And don't give the bastard back this time.*

But if I used my magic—Teo's magic—and changed Ambrogio into a barrel of slimy fish, I would immediately give away my disguise.

The entire camp, including Ambrogio and the Otto men, were staring at the figure that had just split the darkness. I had one more moment before the surprise wore thin, and I would not waste it.

I flew at Ambrogio. The fire stood between us, and I leapt when I reached it, changing to a wind. When I came back in Cielo's boyish form on the far side, my fists were already striking Ambrogio.

Mirella ran as far as she could before one of the Otto men grabbed her and pulled her against his chest. I looked away long enough for Ambrogio to land a single decent blow, then I doubled my attack.

"That man won't harm her," Ambrogio said. "Why would he hurt my wife?"

Fury flowed from me like fire, eating at me even as it burned Ambrogio. My hands struck him, open and closed in fists. I did not care how I hit him as long as he was in pain. I pummeled and kicked him in places that would have made Favianne proud. His whimpers lodged in the air.

Ambrogio had come to take my sister as his prize. He hadn't only been attempting to steal back the baby. I vowed to give him twice the pain, for trying to take two people from me after the world had already taken so much.

Ambrogio's lovely face painted itself red under my hands, his nose cracking and his lips engorged, chin dripping with blood. I wanted to feel triumphant, but my stomach seemed to have a false bottom. It dropped away, leaving me sickened, as I remembered how Beniamo had turned a man to a mass of blood and bone.

Remember, I heard in a voice that sounded suspiciously like Cielo's. *You already killed this one, and it didn't fix matters.*

I stepped away.

My breath came back in harsh strokes. Cielo was stronger than I'd realized. The force of my intention had traveled down the long, tensed wires of my strega's body. He was quick to dodge and quicker to strike. The truth was that Cielo could win a fight, but the strega chose not to start them.

Shame turned the last of my fire to ash.

Then Ambrogio leaned toward one of his men and through his ruined lips said, "Bring me my son." My rage rekindled. There had to be another way to show everyone what kind of foul creature Ambrogio was.

A price that did not have to be paid in blood or death.

"You are harboring a traitor," I told the Otto men in Cielo's cool voice. "Ambrogio profited from the death of his father and admitted to me that he felt no loss when that great Signore left this world. All he cared to do was line his pockets with wealth, whether it was inherited or stolen." Ambrogio opened his mouth to argue, but my voice climbed over his, stomping it out. "He conspired against the five families, betraying them at the first chance, and there is no reason to believe he will not do the same again." I almost spat out how he had used Mirella, treating her bed as a rung on the ladder to greatness, but that story did not belong to me. And besides, there was plenty to damn him without it. "If you have wondered why there is no room for you at the table of the five families anymore, look to Ambrogio. And if you wish to keep control of these lands when I am king of Vinalia, rid yourself of him now. I would suggest digging a large pit and keeping it well guarded. If he climbs out, he will stab whoever is nearest."

The Otto men looked to each other, and then someone thought to glance at Father. They respected his word, even if they'd tied him up with the rest. Niccolò di Sangro nodded at me. "Everything the Malfara says is true."

The entire party of the five families and streghe looked at me—at Cielo—with approval.

I blinked, dizzy.

For a few heated moments, I had forgotten who I was meant to be. I had spoken as Teo, without giving any thought to convincing the people around me that I was someone else. But when I stared down at my blood-spattered hands, all I saw were Cielo's fingers, the ones that had touched me with great care, and then greater recklessness.

I would never feel that again. Even if we beat Beniamo, and I let this disguise fall away, I would not have Cielo back.

"If you'll excuse me," I said, stumbling into the nearest tent. I collapsed under the full weight of what I had done.

I had crafted my own ring of hell, and I would be the king of it.

It took Favianne three minutes to rip open the tent flap and come after me. The sky behind her was smoke and darkness, and it clung to the deep curvature of her body in ways that banished decency.

"You'll be happy to know that the Otto men took your advice," she said. "They just left with Ambrogio tied in the same ropes they'd been using on us. And a few stayed on to join our little Beniamo-hunting party."

I nodded, waiting for Favianne to leave, but she lingered.

"Aren't you going to thank me for the report?" she asked.

"Leave me alone," I said, the words caked with disgust. I was not in the mood for Favianne and her infinite beauties. I wanted Cielo, and the sight of someone who had tried to flirt her way past the strega and into my bed only made matters worse.

"I never pinned you as an angry sort, Cielo Malfara," Favianne said, bent slightly to fit inside the tent's confines. "Whimsical, irrelevant, as rude as the night is dark. But angry? At women?" She used her fingers to brush the thought away. "It doesn't become you."

"I'm sorry," I said, although I wasn't truly sorry for anyone in the world but myself. Favianne smiled in a way that made me realize she'd just worked me into the position she wanted.

"Does that mean I can stay?"

"Don't plan on a long visit. I need to rest before the battle tomorrow."

"Really?" Favianne asked. "I would think Teodora keeps you up well into the night."

I looked down to escape Favianne's insinuations, only to find Cielo's body waiting. Memories of being stretched against it came in a flood, rushing away before I could get a decent grip on any of them.

When I looked up again, Favianne was directly in front of me.

"That was prettily managed outside," she said. "Well, the part *after* you pounded Ambrogio into beef carpaccio." She claimed the canvas chair nearest to me and sat down at one of the only two distances Favianne knew: close and too close.

"Yes, well, all I did was tell the truth," I said. I wished that Cielo had been there to see it—how I'd stepped away, changed course.

Favianne leaned in. "You told the truth at the right moment, in the right way, to people who were willing to listen."

"None of that should matter," I said.

"And yet it does." Favianne looked me over, inch by inch. It was impossibly strange to feel the hair on Cielo's neck rise. "You'll make a fine king."

"And you love kings, don't you?" I asked, with a bitterly mocking blink. At least that was flush with Cielo's character.

"I love sensitivity even more than strength," Favianne admitted, everything she said molded to sound like a confidence. "My last husband had very little to offer me in that regard. He courted me in a fever but once we were married, all he wanted to do was bed me, over and over and over again. If there hadn't been a war in the way, I doubt we ever would have left his chambers." I tried to swallow but failed spectacularly. "Don't bother looking scandalized. You've met your uncle. He was trying to create an heir. It wasn't the most attentive lovemaking."

I worked hard to keep the image of the Capo atop Favianne from forming too crisply in my head.

"He was a horrible man," I said. I would not turn him into a hero now that Beniamo had murdered him. I could regret the manner of his death and the way that he'd lived his life, all at once.

"We didn't agree on a number of things," Favianne told me, another whispered truth. "But I can't imagine that you and Teo always do either."

I choked down her words. "Teo is not here to defend herself, so do not take wild stabs at her character, and do not question our love." Even if it was broken, Favianne had no right to pore over the pieces.

"That very answer proves that you are sensitive. Not a man who will lead with his weapon," she said, pinning the spot between my legs with her gaze. "You seem less interested in a knife than in the velvet box it is laid in." I unfolded the layers of meaning around her words and found myself blushing. I knew what Cielo's blushes looked like, bright as poppies to match my strega's lips.

"Do you really believe you can sleep your way onto the throne twice in one lifetime?" I asked.

Favianne laughed broadly. "Twice in a year would be a

real feat. And no. That's not why I came to you tonight."

"Of course," I said. "You want magic, and you think I can give that to you."

"Two guesses, and neither come close to my true aim," she said. "I thought you were cleverer than this."

"I'm not clever enough to throw you out of my tent at first sight," I said. The words came out well fortified, but that only proved that Favianne had breached my defenses.

"Cielo, Cielo," Favianne said, putting her hand down in the territory between my thigh and groin. "When are you going to tell Teodora about us?"

"*What?*" I asked, leaping up, my head brushing the canvas.

Favianne leaned back and studied me as if I were a flawed painting. "Don't act like you have no idea what I'm talking about. The Palazza? Our favorite little spot in the courtyard?"

I picked frantically through my memories of our time in Amalia when Cielo had barely been able to look at Favianne and certainly had done nothing to court her as far as I could see. Of course, what I had read as jealousy might have been something else entirely. It might have been guilt.

No—that was impossible.

And yet my breath came faster and faster.

"Settle, my love," Favianne said, her voice firm under all of that plush lining. "I promise I won't tell Teo anything. You must do that yourself."

I shook my head, the long black strings of Cielo's hair whipping. The ability to speak had flown away from me on dark wings.

Favianne stood up, grabbing the open neck of my linen shirt and running her hand over my skin—*Cielo's* skin. "Are your memories of me fading? Do I have to kiss you, to remind you of what you enjoyed so much?"

I took a step back, running into the wall of the tent. Favianne pushed forward, her lips brushing mine as softly as the night breeze, passing onto my left ear, the one that worked well enough to carry her whisper straight to my heart. "You have never looked more like Teodora di Sangro than you do at this very moment."

My eyes flew open.

I should have denied it to my last breath. Giving in to Favianne's doubts would be like handing her a pistol she could fire at any moment. But I could not keep up this deception; it was too costly.

I let myself slip out of Cielo's form, shrinking back into Teo's girlish skin. Letting someone else—even Favianne—see one of my true forms bludgeoned me with relief.

"I knew it," she said with a snappish glow in her eyes. "If you want to convince people you are truly Cielo, it's going to take a lot more work, and you can't break this easily. I was barely trying." When I didn't push back against any of what she'd said, her eyes dimmed. "Is Cielo dead? Is that why you're using magic to take on this likeness?"

"No!" I shouted. But she had pushed too close to my worst fear, and it was going to leave a bruise.

Favianne's jaw worked back and forth. "You haven't paid him off and sent him far away so you can rule the country in his stead, have you?"

"That sounds more like *you*." I crossed my arms.

"Two guesses, and I'm nowhere close." She sat down with a sigh. "I give up. Where is Cielo?"

"Gone," I said. The word came out as a single, short

scrape. "We fought, and Cielo left. The strega believed all I cared about was forcing a Malfara to be king of Vinalia so we could stop Beniamo."

"Is that true?" she asked.

"No," I mumbled. "Well, stopping Beniamo *is* necessary."

"Necessary? I might be a horrible paragon of love, but even I can see that's not a good sign. Maybe you two aren't as suited as I thought." She cocked her head. "What do they say? There are many eels in the river, and most of them will eat you alive, so choose carefully. And if you see a glint of teeth, toss it back."

"That must be an Oscurra Valley saying." I sat on the ground, gathering my knees to my chest. "I do not want to lose this eel."

Favianne knelt in front of me. "Well, this is not going to do. What will happen when Cielo comes back and finds out that you've been using this body, puppeting it all over the central provinces?"

Guilt rubbed me to a raw state as I remembered my strega's words. *I like it when you are Teo, whatever that means.* That definitely did not include impersonating Cielo to keep yet another scheme from falling apart.

"Cielo's not planning to return," I said. Heat coursed through me, melting a reserve of tears. "The Violetta Coast," I pushed out. "Cielo went to the Violetta Coast to find a shard of magic in the drowned grottoes. It's all my strega wants in this world."

"That's a bold lie," Favianne said. She rocked back to her heels so we were sitting in matched positions. "I've never seen two people who adore each other more fully and maddeningly. I've had dozens of men, and at least one woman, tell me they love me. And perhaps some of them did, but what they wanted most was to prove their worth, to sate themselves, to make their lives more convenient. Nothing about great love appears to be convenient. You and Cielo prove that point, too." She stared me down, and this time there was no false sweetness in her eyes. "In a life of troubles that were thrust on you, loving this strega is the trouble you chose."

The words rang deep and true, like the bells at Mirella's wedding.

Favianne rose, dusting off her dress.

"Where are you going?" I asked. Cielo might have sent her rushing back to her tent, but I needed someone I could be honest with. I was in no danger from Favianne anymore. Her loveliness was as obvious as it had always been, but it no longer opened a door in my heart and let in temptation. Even with Cielo so far from me, my strega was in my every step, my every thought.

"I'm off to bed." Favianne patted at the tender skin below her eyes. "I require a certain amount of sleep."

"You aren't going into battle tomorrow," I said.

"I am always going to battle, Teo," Favianne said, with a tired twist of a smile. For a moment, her beauty existed for its own good, instead of being put to work flattering and convincing men. It felt like I was truly seeing her for the first time.

"When did you first know it was me?" I asked. "I mean, how long did you know, before . . . ?"

"Before I decided to repay you for that near kiss in Amalia? Oh, I could tell from the moment I had you in sight."

"How?" I demanded. If there was something I needed

to do to convince people I was Cielo, I would have to learn quickly. There was still a battle to get through before I could let this disguise fall away.

Favianne ran her hands down the rich cloth of her dress. "Let's say I could feel the difference. I've been attracted to a certain di Sangro since the first time we spoke. And when I look at the strega you've chosen to love . . . well . . . I could not be further from ecstasy."

"It must have been a challenge to pretend you two had a secret history, then," I said, relieved I had not misread their feelings and impressed at how easily Favianne had tossed together this little scene.

Favianne ran her fingers down the tent flap as tenderly if she were touching a lover, and sighed. "The things we do for Vinalia."

⟡

WE RODE THE CREST OF THE DAWN, APPROACHING AMALIA FROM the west. Its great domes and endless marble greeted me coldly, not that I expected a great flush of nostalgia. It felt as if my entire life had done an about-face since the first time I'd seen the city.

Back then, I had thought the Capo was my truest and deadliest enemy, and Beniamo would spend the rest of his life as an owl, dangerous only to those who were unlucky enough to cross the Uccelli when he was hunting.

Now the entire country was in his talons.

And then there was the matter of my body. At that time, I had barely learned to change form, and now I was a perfect imitation of another person. But that didn't feel like a triumph. It felt like twisting a great deal of magic, stolen death by death, to do something that never should have been done. Favianne was right—Cielo would have hated it.

Amalia did nothing to help matters. It heaped memories into my helpless mind. The first time I'd kissed Cielo. When I'd dared to call the strega mine. The moments when I allowed myself to dream of a life shaped by Cielo's long fingers and mercury whims—as much as my own stubbornness and quick-rising passions. And then there had been our escape: when our magic gripped the city and we grew infamous.

We had turned into a story, and I was not ready for it to end.

"Do not worry," Lorenzo said, clapping a hand to my shoulder. "Teo would never miss a good fight."

Cielo would have scoffed, so that was what I did. "*Good fight?* I believe that's a contradiction of terms."

"That's why you need a di Sangro at your side," he said.

Lorenzo was trying to help, but for someone who rarely spoke, he had chosen a deeply imperfect moment.

"Perhaps Teo is tired of fighting," I said, staring out at the army encampments clustered along the Estatta like burrs.

"Are we talking about the di Sangro women?" Vanni asked, joining us. "Mirella just tried to convince me that she should join us on the battlefield. *With* the baby."

My sister was currently breaking stale bread and handing it out to the Otto men and the church's army while she and Father muttered about the upcoming battle. I took my place in line, suddenly aware of how hungry I was.

She broke off a portion of the loaf and handed it to me as if I were any man, not a powerful strega or the future king of Vinalia. She treated everyone in line with the same brisk kindness.

The scrap of food looked miserable at first glance, but then I remembered when Mirella and I were little, pretending that the rations we had to get us through the winter were our favorite foods. Strawberries doused in dark sweet vinegar, clouds of mascarpone, the creamy flesh of pears.

"It's perfect," I said. When Mirella looked at me, I was certain she would see through my disguise—I almost wanted her to—but her squint did not catch on the truth.

I tore my bread, the crust as hard as stone. As I broke my teeth against the first piece, Father came over and clapped a hand on my shoulder.

"Glad to see that you are not in rough shape after dealing with Ambrogio." He looked Cielo up and down, a dry scrutiny that sent me scurrying to hide my most blatant di Sangro qualities. My mouth even ground to a halt in case I was chewing too much like Teodora. Father finished by nodding approval—the same look he'd given Cielo after the fight.

I swallowed, pushing the bread down my throat with a scratch. "That was less than a scuffle," I said in Cielo's raw honey tones. This voice stung at me, and keeping in this shape for so long pulled at my magic.

"Well, today we are in for far more," Mimì said, pointing at the encampments on the Estatta River. "There were either more troops left in the Capo's army than we thought, or Beniamo has been picking up reinforcements."

I looked over at the tents, hundreds of tents, with smoke rising from cookfires outside. The men I saw moving about looked as small as beetles from this distance, but I knew they had homes and families, stories that would be cut short today if we won and unraveled more slowly if Beniamo did.

"Xiaodan, can you tell us what we're facing?" I asked.

She walked slowly, with a deep sway, toward the edge of the camp, as if following a trail of scent. Her hands lifted into the air, then parted it. "Those soldiers are afraid," Xiaodan said. "They joined Beniamo out of fear."

I did not wish to believe the Vinalians we faced today had the raw materials for redemption in their souls. It would make fighting them—killing them—so much harder than if they were simple villains.

"Most of these soldiers did not join Beniamo's army," Lorenzo said, shaking his head. "They were only there when he took the reins."

And the others were men from the villages he'd plundered along the road to Amalia. The ones who were given one choice—join him or die. Did he threaten their families if they did not fight for him? Did he burn their homes?

Did he smile as he hurt them?

Xiaodan fell to her knees. I ran to her side, to see if she had been felled by some kind of sickness, or perhaps even an attack on her magic. "I know this fear," she whispered. And then words flowed out of her, as smoothly as the notes that rushed from her lips during a song. "My parents were artists, paper and ink mostly, and I was small and silly enough to look forward to the days when men came from all over the world, asking for Father and Mother's wares. But one day they did not have enough to satisfy the Vinalian men who came all the way to our country for fine goods. They threatened to take Father and put him to work, but . . . one of them heard me sing while I was dusting the shop. I knew songs from all over the world, even at eight years old. He said that Vinalians would be delighted to see a little Ovetian girl spill out an aria or two."

She took a deep, studied breath, controlling her voice, careful with her pitch. "The music was beautiful, and I believe it is the one thing that kept me alive. It took months to travel here, and every time we stopped they chained me so I wouldn't be able to run. My parents had taught me what to do with my magic. Every time those men thought well of me, I increased the feeling tenfold. But there were moments when they had nothing in their hearts but hate for the world, and a belief that it had not given them enough. I was never very good at taking feelings away, except for my own. So, when they hurt me, I . . . I took away everything, until I was completely blank inside. As blank as fresh snow."

She looked up at me with her eyes glowing far brighter than I'd ever seen before. "Please don't ask me to make their fear stronger."

My mind worked to understand, but walls stood between my youth and Xiaodan's. There were people who had faced more hardship than I could imagine, even with Beniamo for a brother. I'd grown up with Fiorenza and Father, my sisters and Luca. I'd spent my days surrounded by those who loved me.

I'd known moments of wild fear, but Xiaodan had lived knee-deep in it.

"No," I said. "No, of course." The soldiers' fear might put us at an advantage in the battle, but I wanted nothing to do with the dread Beniamo inspired. I would not use it as a weapon. "All I need you to do is give us strength during the battle. And for that, you will need your own."

Xiaodan nodded, her hands bolted to her lap, retreating further into herself.

"Leave those men to their feelings. Do not hurt yourself more than the world has already hurt you," I whispered. Then I stood and walked to the rest of the streghe.

"You cannot be so soft with your soldiers," Dantae said.

"Xiaodan is not my soldier," I said, thinking about trying to change into the wolf Cielo had become so many times, so she could see how I was bristling. "She is my sister in magic."

Dantae's eyes narrowed until they were two splinters in a wooden expression.

But I would not relent. Azzurra and Delfina had been made into soldiers by the Capo. I was not here to do the same. I hadn't been able to save the strega sisters who had been pitted against me, but I would never be so ruthless with my people again.

"You are welcome to join the sixth family," I told Dantae, flinging the invitation at her soldiers as well. "My name might be Malfara, but that is not my allegiance. All streghe will be taken in without needing to bleed for it." I turned to my father. "We could use a healer, Signore. And you know what they say. Family is fate."

Father blinked hard, as his own words had traveled from the past and finally caught up to him. "If anyone on our side of the battle is injured today, I will do what I can to heal them," he muttered.

He offered me his hand, but Dantae slipped into the space between us, slithering like an eel. Or perhaps I was only thinking of eels because of Favianne's words. "You are a strega, aren't you, old man? Seal your bargains like one."

I brushed Cielo's lips against both of Father's cheeks, and he had to stand on his tiptoes to do the same.

Vanni did his valiant best to stifle a laugh.

I turned to Vanni and Mimì and started making plans for the use of their magic in the upcoming battle. "We will need you to break their ranks so the church's army can get us to Beniamo."

"Beniamo will be out front, leading his troops," Father said—proving that, once again, I knew his own son better than he did.

"With all respect, I believe he will want us to spend ourselves, waste our magic, and face him weakened. If he doesn't hurt us before we die, Beniamo can take no pleasure in it." I shivered, Cielo's shoulders caving slightly.

"And what of the soldiers of Erras?" Dantae asked. "We are Vinalia's best fighters, and you've left us out altogether."

"Don't worry," I said. "I have a particular task in mind for you, and it involves those knives you love so well. Speaking of the Bones of Erras, do you think you can spare one for the battle?"

Dantae snapped her fingers, and one of her soldiers brought a leather roll filled with knives. She plucked out the one that had been carved from the long bone I'd found at the temple to the old gods. "I can't believe I've lived to the day when the future king of Vinalia wields a magical knife." Dantae offered it to me with a flourish, one leg extended in front of her as she dipped down in a bow.

"Oh, it's not for me," I said. "Favianne is going to use this to defend the camp." Favianne rushed forward as if she had been waiting for just such an opportunity. She plucked the bone knife from Dantae's hands. The older woman's weathered scowl did nothing to scare her off.

"Be careful with that," I said as Favianne carved the air with the knife. "It will whisper the worst of you, and you will have to hold strong."

"I'm more than acquainted with my flaws," Favianne said. "The first is being far too perceptive." Her darkly golden eyebrows pushed up an inch. She was clearly proud that she was the only one who had seen through my disguise.

"Why are we making all of these plans without Teodora?" Mirella asked, snapping my thoughts like twigs underfoot.

"I thought your sister was out of your favor," I said, the words tumbling out.

Mirella bounced Luciano against her hip as he grabbed for her rippling hair, dark as tree branches in winter. "She is. But that doesn't mean I've forgotten her strengths. I am thankful for your help with Ambrogio. Luciano and I are in your debt. So here is my advice. If you want to win today, find Teo at once."

"Don't worry," I muttered. "She is closer than you think."

"I, for one, am glad to see that our new leader is versed in strategy," Father said. He took a step to the center of the gathering, and all eyes made their way to his solemn face. "There is something that needs to be said."

I stood with Cielo's fingers in loose fists, brittle and waiting. Whatever Father said now could shatter our plan.

He turned to me, facing the strega he believed was Cielo. "I have misjudged you. Since leaving Prai, you have shown that you have the makings of a fine leader." I flushed with relief and anger, the feelings running deep as magic. It did not escape my notice that Father still needed to see me in a boyish form to believe I was fit to rule.

But Niccolò di Sangro wasn't done. He cleared what sounded like a pile of rocks from his throat. "What is more, you are clearly in the favor of my daughter. I offer you my blessing to marry her."

Anger pushed its way past relief, and I took a single step toward Father, Cielo's motions quick and twitching. "Did you just *offer* her to me? And what, exactly, changed your mind? Was it the moment when you learned my noble last name? Or was it when you saw me using my fists to mangle another man?"

"Neither," Father said, defensive to the last. "It was your ability to send Ambrogio off like a chastened dog *without* further violence. It was the way you have held such a large assortment of Vinalians together, many of them enemies."

It was true that my father had never gloried in blood. My anger slackened. "Yes, well . . . I learned a great deal of that from your daughter," I said. "The truth is . . ." I almost told them who I was, revealed the whole lie in that moment. But I knew this group would never take to the battlefield without a leader.

I could not break.

Favianne watched me carefully. "The truth is, Teo and I are fighting."

Father and Mirella nodded as if they understood all too well.

"Oh, that's bound to happen," Vanni added.

I almost pounced on their reactions.

"When Teo returns, send her to me," Father said. "We must be the ones to face Beniamo."

"Because I am the heir, and she is disposable?" I asked. I had started flinging out truths, and there was no use stopping now. Besides, this was how Cielo lived. Even if the strega changed form with each breath, nothing about Cielo was a lie.

Mirella stalked up to me, her finger pointed at my chin. "I know you are making a point, but *never* speak of my sister that way."

My smile unscrolled, and I could only imagine how Cielo looked.

"Why are you delighted by what I just said?" she asked.

"Because Teo would be." Favianne sucked in her cheeks, a subtle reminder that I was being unsubtle again.

"My daughter will want to be there when Beniamo answers for his many crimes," Father said.

I clapped him on the shoulder, like he had with me, a bit of mocking built in. "You're right, Father." Confusion turned him paler, one shade at a time, until he was nearly white. Favianne sighed as if I'd ruined everything—but there was one truth she hadn't dug up. "Oh, didn't I mention that bit? I'm glad you are feeling kindly toward the match because Teodora and I are already married."

Vanni embraced me so quickly and fully that the air left my lungs. Xiaodan and Mimì clapped. Favianne looked at me with her eyes wide as oceans. I'd finally surprised her.

Father shook his head, but he could not undo what Cielo and I had done.

I walked away, the wind of victory at my back. I had done one of the things Cielo most wanted me to—shared the news of our marriage—and I found myself laughing up at the sky, the sound rising from Cielo's throat both bitter and satisfying. It felt wondrous to let everyone know and agonizing to let them know when Cielo was already gone from my side.

Father came over to me and laid a hand on my arm. I glanced up to find his dark eyes mirrored by the brightness of the day. But when I looked past the doubled reflection of Cielo, I found respect waiting. I was learning a lesson that I suspected Cielo had always known. Truth was so powerful, it could turn every other weapon to dust.

"What happens now?" he asked, nodding at the encampments. At one time, I'd felt a childish delight when my father turned to me for help. Today, I only wished to know the answer for my own sake.

I looked to the army and found that the smoke from the cookfires was thick, but I could no longer see the men moving through it. Beniamo must have known we were coming and called his men to arms.

I knew it would not be long before we saw him. Beniamo did not just want the throne of Vinalia—that was not enough. He wanted streghe to fight him. He longed to write the tale of his victory in our blood. Above all, my brother wanted me. He believed that I owed him more pain.

He was there somewhere, stalking through the camp, his orange-rimmed eyes tracking our moves.

"Now we stop acting like hunted animals," I said. "Now we stand in the open and fight back."

I would have marched at that moment, but one more piece had to fall into place before we could leave. The church's army met us as the sun made its timid way toward noon. From a distance, the long, tired trail of men looked like the mark a snake left on dust.

When MacCartaigh and Cinquepalmi reported to Cielo as their leader, I was ready with my orders.

"Have your men carry buckets of water from the nearest stream," I said, "and be ready to light campfires when we stop marching."

"Why?" MacCartaigh asked.

"A strega has her reasons," Mimì said, cracking her knuckles and warming her fingers for battle.

Cinquepalmi squinted at the view of the tents in the distance. "Why hasn't he just marched straight into the city? He's clearly beaten us here."

"Beniamo wants to fight us," I said. He longed for it, a desire that had a long, dark history. I had lived in its shadow for years.

"He must have known there would be opposition to his coup," Lorenzo said. "In the streets, even a handful of streghe would give us an advantage. Those men are trained for the battlefield."

Cinquepalmi made a rude noise. "They're barely trained at all. Told to play soldier for Vinalia. There's no reason to think you're going to survive to see one day sprawl into the next. I got so good at praying that when we won the battle for unification, I figured it might as well join the church's army."

MacCartaigh let out a high, shimmering laugh. "He told me he didn't want to tumble around in the snow with Eterrans."

"Oh, good," Mimì said. "We've inherited all the men who weren't brave enough to fight in Zarisi."

I shook my head, cutting off any further complaint, although my heart darkened as I thought of leading such men against Beniamo.

I arranged our forces into two long lines that would march at the same time. The first line of defense was composed of the soldiers of Erras, the sixth family, and Lorenzo, who insisted on fighting at Mimì's side. The second was mainly the church's army, with my father at one end, ready to heal any wounded soldiers, and Pasquale at the other, looking as if he'd been brought here with his hands and feet tied, screaming the whole way.

We needed all the hands we could get, but I would not drag men against their wishes to pain and death. "You can stay behind in camp," I offered.

"With the women and children?" Pasquale asked, sneering enough to let me know that he was the same coglione I'd met in Amalia.

"I'm sure the women and children would protect you," I said. "Even if you've done little to deserve it."

"I can't just sit there alone with . . . *her*," Pasquale said, stepping around Favianne's name like a great sinkhole.

"Then you will have to stand with us."

Pasquale shifted his weight but stayed put. "You forget," he said. "I've met Beniamo Di Sangro. He wasn't fit to lead a boar hunt, so he shouldn't be leading Vinalia."

I walked away shaking my head, amazed that for all of his faults, Pasquale was standing on my side of the battle instead of rallying forces against me.

Once I had checked over our army, I took my place at the center of the front line, and we began to move. For the first time, I had an army to command—but it was nowhere near the force that began to spill around the tents, a dozen men at a time.

Vanni grabbed my arm, his fingers like needles. I thought this was finally it: the moment when everyone gave up on my plan and scattered to the winds. I would hardly be able to blame them.

"I owe you a drink if we both live through this day," Vanni whispered.

"And if we don't?" I asked, with Cielo's airy concern.

"Then I owe you a drink in heaven." He kissed his fingers and raised them to the skies. Behind us, I noticed MacCartaigh and Cinquepalmi repeating the motion.

I looked to Xiaodan, who stood on the other side of Mimì. "Is their fear too strong?" I asked.

"I'm keeping my hands very still," Xiaodan said. "I . . . I only hope that the friend I made in the Capo's camp deserted after the Capo was killed. I would hate for him to die at the end of a bone knife. I'm afraid he wouldn't go home, even if he had the chance to slip away."

"Why not?" I asked.

"He joined the army because no one in his village understood that he is truly a boy, and he doesn't have the sort of magic that you do, Cielo, that allows a person to shift outer form easily. All he could think to do was change his clothes and bind his chest and run away."

I thought of Cielo—off on the Violetta Coast, searching for Veria's Truth. What would the strega's life have been without magic?

What would it be now, without me?

Xiaodan turned to me as if we weren't in the middle of the battlefield. I knew that feeling, the one that blurred everything but the memory of the person I loved. Xiaodan's brown eyes glowed, and not from fear this time. "Massimo—that's his name—Massimo said he would try to come see me in *Il sole e la luna*. It's a story of two lovers who are torn apart each day and brought back together each night. I promised I would sing the words for him until I saw him again." Xiaodan's hands tightened their hold on each other until they were a choked white.

I wanted all of us to live long enough to make our ways back to those we loved. But the closer we marched to Beniamo's troops, the less likely that grew. "These soldiers are not to blame for Beniamo's sins," I said. "They should not have to die."

"And yet they will." I heard Father's voice behind me. For once, it was not trapped in my head. But we weren't reunited, either, not in the way I'd dreamed of. I was standing before him in disguise. Our family was scattered, fighting, less whole with each passing minute. "No one wins a war, Cielo Malfara."

"There is only a side that loses less," I finished.

His forehead took on the trio of lines that meant he was puzzled, or displeased, or both. "Did my daughter tell you that?"

"How else would I have plundered the treasure trove of di Sangro sayings?" I asked faintly.

I looked out at Beniamo's army. I knew, from the camp in the Neviane, that some were loyal to him. Perhaps a few were like him, believing that destruction and cruelty would even the scales for slights against them, both real and imagined. But most of Vinalia's soldiers had joined the army to save us from invading Eterrans. They had gotten picked up by a storm and set down here. They deserved a world without Beniamo on the throne as much as we did, but how could I separate them from the soldiers who backed him?

I thought of my failure in Zarisi, a great drift of snowflakes returning to the sky because I had not been able to save anyone.

I thought of the streghe who had volunteered their lives to make a better Vinalia, the ones who had been sacrificed.

I was tired of watching people die, tired of the way powerful men broke our lives as thoughtlessly as a child breaks toys.

I motioned to Dantae, who stalked over from her place in line. Her vest of snakes was back in place now that we no longer needed to be stealthy. The darkly scaled creatures looked calm today; it seemed marching into battle soothed them. They slid and overlapped and made the sound of troubled paper as I whispered a new plan.

"Are you sure?" Dantae asked, sticking the bone knife against my chest. A single push and it would be deep in the workings of my heart.

Vanni and Mimì turned to disarm her, but I gave my head a minuscule shake. "Don't hurt anyone," I said. "Dantae is testing me, which is her right."

The bone knife's whispers made their way into me, an icy stream. *This is a foolish plan. You are a foolish strega. You have come so far and you will risk everything. There is a clear path to victory.*

But I knew that the path was only clear because someone else had walked it before me. Killing everyone in Beniamo's army until they surrendered was the old way. If we wanted a new path, we would have to break off in a new direction. We would have to pound the dirt down and lay the markers and draw the maps ourselves.

"I'm sure," I said, without a tremble this time.

Dantae pulled back the knife, tossed it in the air, and caught it in her teeth as she took two more out of her pockets.

She was ready for the show.

I cleared Cielo's long, beautiful throat and threw the strega's voice as far as I could. "Raise your arms." Swords and pistols, bone knives and the hands of streghe took to the air in a single motion.

The other side mirrored it. I waited for the crack of a pistol shot or the cry of a soldier charging. There was only the smallest rustle of feet as Beniamo appeared, splitting the sea of bodies.

I hadn't expected to see him until later, when he could claim some kind of victory over a field of men cut down as blithely as poppies. When he could grin at death and gloat at my loss and force me to my knees again.

But I'd been thinking as Teo—not as Cielo.

Beniamo wanted a chance to intimidate the strega I

loved. Perhaps even to kill Cielo before the battle could properly begin.

Beniamo seemed to glide forward. His eyes took me in as if he were already swallowing me.

"So we finally meet," he said, his voice pitched only for my ears. I was in more danger in Cielo's form than I had been in my own, but alongside that truth came a sense of relief. By taking this shape, I had kept the real Cielo safe, with a bit of help from the old gods. I imagined him clattering down a cliff on the Violetta Coast, diving naked through beautiful grottoes.

"*Thank you, Veria,*" I muttered in the old language.

Part of me expected Beniamo to fly straight at me, the way he'd dived for Luca on the mountains. My fist ached as I watched his hand, remembering those talons plunging straight through the Capo.

I would not wait for Beniamo to enjoy my anticipation, my fear. And I would certainly not wait until he claimed me or the people I cared for.

"Now," I said.

With two fistfuls of Vanni's light thrown down, the battle began. Everyone on our side had been warned to cover their eyes when the brilliant bombs struck, and we marched forward with our arms cast over our faces, eyes closed.

A few moments later we were emerging from a haze of white as Beniamo's army staggered and blinked. Beniamo himself had used the opportunity to disappear into his ranks. My brother was not brave, but he was not a coward, either. He was a di Sangro, plotting out every move.

"Don't give them time to recover, Mimì," I said. "Hit them again."

She nodded, and with a hand outstretched toward a campfire the men behind her had just lit, she twisted flame into water. It rose into the air in great streams, then crashed down. Water hit the troops, splitting their forces as newborn rivers divided the battlefield. If Beniamo was going to use the Estatta against me, I would have to bring rivers of my own.

Mimì wiped sweat from her brow as Lorenzo rubbed her hands, which were still a bit singed from the flames.

Vanni took up the slack, throwing light bombs at the nearest soldiers. And then a great cloud rolled over the sky. Cielo would have turned into a wind and blown the cloud away, but I could not imagine stretching my magic in another direction when it was already working so hard to maintain the tiniest details of Cielo's form.

The soldiers were coming nearer, their pistols almost in range. I looked up at the cloud, lined by a single thread of gold, like the pages of a fine book.

Vanni closed his eyes, and I thought he was preparing himself to die. I shook him by the shoulders.

"Cielo, if you don't mind, I'm working on something," he muttered.

I stepped back as his hands lifted, palms deeply cupped. Instead of light, he gathered darkness. It snaked down from the sky, one smoky thread at a time, and gathered in the hollow of his hands until they were filled with two small swirling clouds. Then he cast the darkness away, and it spread like a great sigh, blanketing the people it touched. It wrapped them tightly so they could not move, could not speak. A hundred men went down. The rest were surrounded by a weeping black fog that dripped slowly toward the ground.

Again, the magic said.

"Again," I commanded.

"I'm not sure if I can," Vanni said, staring at his hands as if he'd find them coated in sticky darkness.

We can win with that magic, my own said. *Kill him if you have to and take the power for your own.*

I blinked against the terror of my own thought and pretended it was only the strangeness of the fog, which reached our ranks and turned everything grainy and dark. The one thing I could see in the blackness was Vanni's pale, nervous face. "If your magic is spent, go back to camp. Check on Mirella and the baby."

Vanni gave me a hasty smile and started running. "Thank you, Cielo," he called over his shoulder. "I always knew that you were the reasonable one."

I watched until he reached the edge of the battle, safe from Beniamo and pistols shot in the dark, as well as my own greedy magic.

One of Dantae's soldiers cried out. Behind me, Cinquepalmi took a ball to the shoulder.

"Go see Signore di Sangro," I shouted.

When the gloom lifted, a fresh round of soldiers headed for us, stepping around the men on the ground, wrapped in darkness.

"What now?" Mimì asked, on to her second round of water, carving the rivers deeper and longer so they would join the Estatta. Once that happened, they would continue to flow on their own.

I pointed to Dantae, who had barely been able to restrain herself. She loosed her soldiers on the battle with a cry. *"Magic is all,"* she cried in the old language.

"All is magic," the soldiers of Erras called back as they

locked into combat with Beniamo's army. The streghe fought in two ways at once, their magic fending off attacks, their bone knives close at their sides. They moved like dancers, a lifetime of readiness exploding through their bodies as Beniamo's soldiers grunted and swore.

As soon as the soldiers of Erras had tilted the fights in their favor, they thrust the bone knives toward their opponents, and the great judgment began. The knives whispered about what these people had done in life, and what they had failed to do. Some of them sat down on the battlefield, shaking, refusing to fight. Others brought a fresh and hardened fury, but they were so busy battling inner voices that they struck out wildly.

I had been clear with Dantae that every soldier in Beniamo's army was to be spared. Those who sat down were treated as stones, soldiers parting around them like the flow of a great river. Those who fought were dealt blows that felled them without stealing their lives.

"No killing," I reminded the soldiers of Erras, who were growing a little frenzied in their attacks. The great show that was being put on at the front of the ranks seemed to confuse and frighten the rest of Beniamo's troops, who would not charge, even though orders were being shouted.

"Mimì," I said. "It's time."

She dipped her hand into buckets placed at her sides, and with her arms raised to their full height, she blew and blew, sending a nightmare of flame into the sky. "Let's give them a taste of the hell they're narrowly escaping," she said, sweating but glorious as she threw and shaped fire.

Lorenzo looked on, glowing with admiration.

The church's army stepped forward, filling the spaces

between the streghe in our ranks. If we followed the plan I'd set this morning, it was time for them to charge and carry me and Father to Beniamo, wherever he was hiding.

But that would mean soldiers cut down, lives lost.

I held up my hand and the church's army went still.

"Are you sure you don't want us to go in?" MacCartaigh asked. "This is the minute, if there ever was one."

"Wait," I said.

This was exactly the lack of honor I'd expected from my brother. He knew that we either had to give up or cut our way through his soldiers.

There is only a side that loses less.

"What's wrong, Signore Malfara?" Cinquepalmi asked.

I looked out at the battle with Cielo's eyes. My strega would never let people die like this. We were here to defend Vinalia, not to murder Vinalians.

"Xiaodan, come here," I said.

"Do you need me to increase the bravery of these troops?" she asked, casting a pointed glance at the church's army.

"No," I said. "I need your voice."

Her eyes went wide, and this time it was with love, not terror. "Should I sing a high note to grab everyone's attention? I've been stretching my range."

"It is not only their ears I need," I said, looking out at the soldiers, some of their faces grim with the anticipation of killing, others flooded with the anticipation of death. "I want their hearts."

"If you're looking for a battle hymn, we could use the anthem," Cinquepalmi offered. "It's fairly catchy."

"That belongs to the Capo," I said. I had no desire to build on the bones of his would-be empire.

"I know what to sing," Xiaodan said. "Trust me."

MacCartaigh and Cinquepalmi offered Xiaodan a hand, so she was standing with a foot on each of their thighs. It resembled a sort of living throne. Even in the midst of battle, her smile curved, brightening the edge of her voice as she began to sing. Her tone lacked the hollow purity and high gloss of opera. She was letting out something new this time—or something very old. It was a Vinalian folk song, as trusty as the stories of streghe, its roots winding as deep through our childhoods.

The soldiers on the battlefield, both fallen and charging, looked up. Xiaodan's voice carried like wind and fell soft as rain.

In that moment of surprise, when we had everyone's attention, I stepped out in front of my troops, hoping that none of the drawn pistols would be too quick to remember their purpose.

"This is not a war," I said. "Which means there will be no losses."

Even my own streghe and soldiers and family were looking at me as if I had just announced that the sun would be lighting the night from now on, and the moon would shine by day.

Cielo would have enjoyed that look.

"Today, the sixth family has shown that we will stop every false battle waged for control of Vinalia. There is no fight here. There is only a usurper who must be stopped." I looked for Beniamo's slick movements and his glowing eyes, but I could not find him.

"All we ask in return for sending you home with your lives is that you welcome the sixth family of Vinalia. We are tied to you by blood, by love, by this land. We will not fight Vinalians, for we are Vinalians." After a pause I added, "And Salvians."

Mimì took my hand and squeezed it, her palm still hot as coals from conjuring fire.

"We won the battle at Zarisi in your name. We sent the Eterrans back to the north without their spoils. Our magic is powerful, but we have no wish to turn it against our families and neighbors. The truth is that we are already part of your story. The great ages of magic have come and gone, but we were always here."

I waited for Xiaodan to finish her song, the last note shivering in the air, as delicate as the peace I had just created.

"You are free to go," I said. Father stepped forward, and I pushed past the wonder of this moment to what must come next. I raised my voice and added, "All but one."

‍‍‍✠‍‍

THE LAST OF THE SMOKE FROM MIMÌ'S FIRES CLEARED AS THE battle formations broke, and Beniamo's soldiers went wandering off in every direction. I waited for my brother to scream after them, to force them back together with the glue of threats and violence.

Instead, a single figure ran toward us. I reached for Father's stiletto, but the soldier I would have pointed it at ran straight into Xiaodan's arms. When she kissed him, the sight of two people's hands clinging, their lips sliding open, lit fires that I could not feed.

I had to turn away.

I found myself facing Mimì and Lorenzo. It looked as if they were saving their romantic celebrations for later. Mimì was kneeling and breathing hard, working to regain her strength after carrying so much of the battle in her charred hands.

"That fire took everything she had," Lorenzo said, too nervous to play the role of noble protector. The brown of his eyes looked melted with worry. "She's hotter than Amalia in July."

"Get her to the stream," I said.

"It's a good thing we didn't end up needing that army," Mimì told me as Lorenzo helped her to her feet. "They're as useful as a bucket made of holes."

"Perhaps, but it will be good to have a force at our back when we're facing Beniamo. Speaking of which, I should fetch Teo," I said.

"How are you going to find her?" Lorenzo asked. "Especially if she doesn't want to be found?"

"I'm certain she's tired of being parted," I said, voice straining over the truth. I wanted nothing more than to see Cielo again. Favianne had been right—there was nothing practical about our love. It was intense and wild and I needed it far more than I needed to face down Beniamo.

I might as well have called what I felt for Cielo magic, because it was threaded through my soul, and it changed everything.

Lorenzo was looking at me strangely.

"Don't worry about Teo," I said. "I've always been able to feel when she's near."

I left what remained of the armies, sliding back into my

girlish body when I was out of view, every di Sangro feature in its proper place. All I wanted to do was run to the Violetta Coast, but I was not abandoning Vinalia now that I'd come this far. I would go after Cielo the second we were done here. I braided back my hair, waiting as long as I could before I returned to the field as Teo.

Father's face shone at me from the battlefield, a beacon of relief and impatience. "Teo," he said. "Where is Cielo?"

"Checking on the camp," I lied. "Cielo said that this moment is di Sangro business."

Father nodded. "Let's go, then."

"Are you sure that Beniamo will meet us?" I asked.

"This is a direct challenge to his rule," Father said. "If he does not face us, he admits that he is a usurper. His claim to the throne just weakened, and he cannot have it weaken any more if he wishes to take power."

I waved my hand, taking in the army that had been broken by my words. "He is not going to be delighted by any of this." I tried to sound confident and uncaring, but I knew how much sharper his rages grew when he was disappointed.

"Well, that boy cannot have his way anymore," Father said, more like a scolding parent than a man who was trying to save his country from a tyrant.

We walked to the center of the field, facing the river and Amalia beyond.

"Beniamo!" Niccolò di Sangro shouted. "You cannot hide from this moment forever."

"You have no right to claim Vinalia, brother," I added in a voice that carried as far and spread as thick as battlefield smoke. "You have no right to anything you've taken, and yet you grab with both hands."

"You have not faced me for Luca's death," Father said, digging up the feelings he had given a hasty burial when Luca failed to return over the mountains.

"Come here, Beniamo," I cried, my words harsh on the wind. But it was blowing strongly, and it tossed them aside.

Father and I waited, the remnants of the church's army, the streghe, and the soldiers of Erras behind us. The silence stretched long, rubbing away at my certainty. "Do you think he's made a break for the Palazza and tried to finish off the coup?"

"He can't hope to hold the throne by himself," Father said.

I pictured Beniamo pushing me off Father's walnut chair.

Stop him, now, my magic said.

It had been telling me this since I was nine years old, and I had always stopped myself instead. But now my silence was broken.

"This is your final moment," I said in steady, even tones. "You say that I have stolen away the life that should have been yours, that I turned you into a vile creature, but neither of those are true. You took my childhood long before I ever touched you with magic. And you have *always* been a vile creature."

I waited for Beniamo to appear. In a strega story, I would find some clever way to change him, even though he wore the Capo's ring. But a shard of magic held great power—and unlike the magic in our bodies, anyone could use it.

"Teo." I felt a tug at my sleeve. "If your brother is making you wait, there should be anticipation in the air. A sense of waiting, wanting, bloodlust." Xiaodan's fingers picked at the tapestry of emotion hidden in the air. "There is . . . nothing."

I looked to Father. "We need to cross the Estatta and get to the Palazza. While we've been standing here, naming his sins, Beniamo has gone for the throat of Vinalia."

The direction of the wind changed, blowing in from the west with a roughness that startled my skin. Xiaodan's hand covered her mouth. "I'm afraid it's worse," she said, looking back to camp.

"Mirella," Father said, the worry in his voice a creeping stain. "She's there with Luciano."

In a breathless reversal, I became a wind, which was like being a storm, but quicker, lighter, with less fury to gift me thunder and more fear to drive me across the sky. I split the seams of my clothes when I forgot to remove them, and they fell to the ground in tatters. I rose only a little above the ground, following the line of the hills, pushing my way back to the camp.

When I tumbled to the ground, I saw the red heaps of bodies.

The moments we had spent staunching the blood flow of battle Beniamo had spent gutting everyone we had left behind. Our victory was the beginning of a massacre.

Five

All Is Magic

19

I walked naked into the ruin of the camp, every cord of muscle and pinch of nerve aware that Beniamo might be waiting for me in one of the tents. New clothes appeared on my body as if my magic needed no prompting on this subject.

A black dress. A blood-red cloak.

The first dead man I came upon had bright red hair. A member of the Moschella family—the young man who had been named Luciano's godfather.

I counted. Five men dead around the campfire, and one more in a tent, marked with bloody furrows where Beniamo's talons had struck.

These must have been the men sent back to camp carrying the news that we had won the day. I did not know if they had been killed before reaching Mirella or if they had delivered their message and spent the last few moments on this earth in celebration.

I did not know which was worse.

The day was dwindling, and the camp felt too still in the dusk. The fire flickered with a weak imitation of life. I looked everywhere for Favianne and the bone knife I'd left behind, but there was no sign of her sunlight hair. My only hope was that she'd run to the tent to protect Mirella and the baby.

"Vanni," I whispered. I'd sent Vanni back, his magic drained, so he could be with them. A stone of guilt sank through my terror.

As I stood at the verge of Mirella's tent, every prayer I had ever been taught rose like the weak, wispy smoke of votives. I didn't speak the words, though. There were no gods left who could stop Beniamo.

I took a step inside, my eyes closed. I knew that once I saw whatever horrible truth the tent held, it would change my life, and I wanted to keep it the way it was for one more moment. Mirella, my sister. Vanni, my brother. Luciano, their baby. All alive.

All mine.

There, in the darkness, I felt a sigh of hope. Magic thickened the air, like the promise of rain.

Vanni, my magic said.

I opened my eyes and just as quickly tried to close them again. The picture pressed into my mind. It would be trapped there forever. The red-haired boy I'd met in Amalia on the ground, both hands stabbed through, a great dark stain in the center of his chest. The brother I had chosen, the one who had fought and changed and muttered nervous jokes at my side. Beside him, my sister, one arm flung out like a broken-winged bird, her mouth trapped in a silent cry, her body so torn from the neck down that her innards dribbled out.

"Mirella," I said on a half-formed breath. "Vanni."

On the far side of the tent, I saw smears of blood in

Luciano's crib. The sheets were blank, the baby missing.

"Luciano?" I asked, as if the tiny child would answer. Maybe I was waiting for Beniamo to emerge from some hidden fold of the tent with the child in his arms. For my brother, no nightmare was out of reach.

But I was alone. Completely alone.

Vanni, my magic said. It kept insisting that my brother-in-law's magic was here, that he was still alive.

"*You're wrong*," I said, the blunt words my only comfort.

I walked over to the crib, trying to imagine what had happened without losing the last fragile slivers of my mind. Beniamo must have taken the boy—to raise him? To swallow him whole? Both were equally terrifying. My heart took flight and threatened never to land. I fell to my knees, desperate for breath, but all I found was blood, Vanni's and Mirella's.

I grabbed at the leg of the crib.

The edges of the ornate decorations bit into my palm. They brought me back to the world, and I found myself staring at foxes. Wooden foxes stacked on top of each other, a tiny dark space between each carving.

The crib had holes in it.

I thought of what Signora Moschella had said, about her talent for keeping her children alive. I pulled myself to standing and tore up the blankets, exposing the long, flat board underneath. I pried until crimson rose in the beds of my fingernails and pain came back to me like an old friend. The board pulled up, splintering at one edge.

The sound woke Luciano, who was sleeping safely inside a small compartment lined with blankets. He looked up at me with a deep frown, distrustful from the start.

I could not blame him.

Vanni, my magic said.

It had not been wrong—Vanni's magic was here, as strong as ever. *The brilliant death* had gifted it to his son. I picked up Luciano in his little white gown and pressed him to my chest so he would not see what had been done to the people who loved him. As I rushed past the ravaged bodies on the ground, I clutched Luciano and whispered his parents' names.

🜁✤🜂

WHEN COMPANY CAME, I WAS SITTING AT THE EDGE OF THE fire, holding Luciano as tightly as Mirella ever had. At the rustling sound in the trees, I flinched and pulled out Father's stiletto.

"It's us, Teo," Mimì said as she and Lorenzo rushed over to me.

"He's coming back," I said, a rattle snaring my breath. "He's coming for me. He promised he would take everyone and then come back for me." But that wasn't quite right— he had told me he would make me wait until the moment I felt safe before striking again. So I would do the only reasonable thing.

I would never feel safe.

"Your sister . . ." Father said, putting a hand to my curls. His sadness was so thick, I could have carved into it with his knife and served it up to everyone for dinner.

Pasquale and Lorenzo carried the bodies of the messengers to the edge of the camp and began digging. Mimì said prayers over their bodies in Salvian, a dialect that sounded like another shade of Vinalian, the vowels pressing deep into her throat. I hadn't been able to move any of the bodies, not with Luciano in my arms. He was a quiet baby, but his heart-beat troubled me. It seemed to flit at an impossible speed and nothing I did could slow it.

"What happened, Teo?" Xiaodan asked.

"He did not care," I whispered.

"About what?"

There were too many answers. Beniamo did not care about the men he let die. Or our family. Or anything in this world, except causing me pain. "The throne," I said. "It was a distraction. I should have known better. I should have seen—"

"If you had stayed here, he would have marched on us and killed everyone," Father said.

"Do you think that kind of reasoning *helps*?" I cried. He was trying to make the losses acceptable, but I could never accept them. His own daughter was dead, and yet he was trying to force his way back to calm. Soon all of his children would be dead or gone, all but one. "Beniamo is coming back for me," I said, and my fingers felt slippery, and Luciano nearly fell. I shook my head at my failure as I patted the soft, silken hair on his head. "He will always come for me."

His words returned on a vicious wind.

You *are my war.*

Father looked helplessly at my state. My heart turned so numb that my hands would no longer obey even the simplest order. Dantae appeared at my elbow. It would have taken a true twist of fate for Mirella to let Dantae hold her child, and yet I found myself sliding him into her waiting arms.

"Wait," I said, "your vest . . ."

But Luciano was already holding his hand up to the snakes. Their constant motion and slight hissing seemed to delight him. It proved exactly how little I knew about babies.

I thought of Cielo, who would have taken the child from my arms in an instant and discovered some new way to make him smile. My strega had inherited magic when Giovanna died, when Cielo was as small and soft and unformed as Luciano was now. It had been an overwhelming inheritance, as much of a curse as a gift.

Luciano needed Cielo as much as I did.

"Why did Vanni's magic fly to Luciano?" I asked. "He was hidden away, and Beniamo was . . . well, he was right there." I tried not to picture my brother, hovering over Vanni as he pushed those long, silver nails into his body.

"You tried to ask this once before, but the question wasn't worded right," Dantae said, pursing her lips. "You asked me why magic wouldn't *choose* him. Magic might feel like a person of its own, but it's not. It's part of you." Those words echoed what Luca had used his scientific mind to guess, long ago. He had been right about magic, and I had the bright flash of a desire to run and tell him. But my brother and my sister were both gone.

"There is no magic without a strega, Teodora," Dantae explained. "It doesn't make its own choices."

"Why won't magic take root in Beniamo, then?" I asked.

She nodded as if I'd gotten a better hold on the question. "Besides the fact that he wears the Capo's ring?"

"He would have taken that off," I insisted. "Beniamo wants magic of his own. He wants everything I have."

It was Mimì who answered, wandering over after she

finished her prayers. "Your brother caused those deaths, but he doesn't carry them."

She pointed to the small scar on her face. "I was chosen to inherit the magic of the foremother, the most powerful woman on Salvi. Every generation, she picks a girl to teach, and train, someone to pass on the old ways. Even though I knew her death meant that I would finally take on magic, I wanted her to live to a hundred and twelve. But she flew to heaven when I was only twelve. I remember sitting there, watching her tired fingers stir a bowl of water, the last of her flames rising. When they stopped, I started to cry, and my first tear for her turned to fire."

"My aunt died suddenly," Xiaodan said, putting her hands out to the fire, turning her palms bright. "Her heart gave way while she was climbing a ladder in my parents' shop. I was there when she fell. She told me not to run for anyone, that I was all she needed. She was always able to feel when people were coming, even from a great distance. It made her like a living map. Of course, there were people who feared her, and no man in the village would marry her. She never had children of her own, though she wished to. When she died . . . I felt the change. Not just in our lives, but here." She ran her hands down her sleeves, all the way to her wrists.

Mimì held up her hands, as proof of where her magic lived. Dantae touched her temple and then swept back her hair.

My magic was in my blood, always moving through me.

It had been there since I saw a strega die in the di Sangro castle when I was nine, but now I carried more than one death. I had the memories of Azzurra and Delfina with me always. I cared about every strega who had died in the Capo's dungeons, killed for his dreams. I wished I could tell Cielo, who thought I did not care for anyone but my own blood.

Pieces of all of those streghe lived in me, a collection of magics that glinted silver like knives, silver like a restless sea.

"Beniamo does not feel it when he kills anyone," Dantae said. "No piece of them becomes a piece of him." In one clean motion, she sat and started to jolt the baby up and down on her knee, an abrupt motion that somehow seemed to soothe him.

"You are good with him," I said.

"He is easy, this little di Sangro," she said. "Mine were not so mild."

"How many . . . ?"

"Three," she said. "The first was with Mirco, and the other two . . . well, I was still young when he died."

That meant that when Father killed Dantae's lover, there had been a child whose father never returned. I found myself looking at that night from a new angle, not my own view in the di Sangro kitchen, but another home, another set of eyes wide and waiting.

A different sort of fear, and change.

"So that is why I have Mirco's magic," I said. "Father doesn't carry that death with him . . . but I do." At that point, Father had already welcomed violence into his life, even if it was an unwanted visitor. He had told himself that there was no other way. But when he was younger, and his heart still had open doors, one of the first people he'd ever killed for the five families must have been a strega.

If I had killed a strega today, would the magic have flowed

to me? How many deaths would it take before I could no longer feel what I did?

There was a sound from the trees, and the entire camp turned to face whatever approached us in the dark. I was not alone anymore, and yet it would take more than an army to make me feel safe from Beniamo.

Favianne staggered into the camp, her skin yellowed by the firelight, her eyes dull and the rest of her face shining with sweat. Through the cloth of her fine dress, her chest had been raked in long, bloody furrows.

I should have been angry that she'd taken the bone knife and left Mirella and Vanni to die, but the only feeling that pushed up through my shock was relief that someone had survived Beniamo's attack. "You're alive," I said. "I thought—"

"Your brother came quietly," Favianne said. Her words were crisp and unbroken, but she could not stop blinking, as if trying to shatter whatever she was seeing in her head. "He'd killed three of the men before I even noticed. And then . . . he had me in his hands and . . ." She turned to me, brave and blunt and beautiful, which proved to me that she was still Favianne, no matter how terrified. "I lied, Teodora. I told him I hated you. I said that you had ruined my life, and I was only trailing along waiting for a chance to take revenge. He . . . he liked that answer. It made him laugh." She wiped her lips, smudging the last of the makeup she wore. "His mouth was slicked with blood."

Beniamo had started eating his kills.

"I'm glad you kept yourself alive," I said. Favianne had used her cleverness to survive. She knew that Beniamo wanted to kill people who loved me. And, despite all of her bravado and demands, I knew that Favianne did care. She'd been able to hide it, though—to push it down some trapdoor in her soul. "But then . . . why did he hurt you?"

Favianne looked down at her bodice. The cuts did not look deep, but they must have been painful. My fingers rose to the sticky red edges of the wounds, as if I had the power to take this pain away. I was no healer, though. Death and pain followed everywhere I stepped.

"Beniamo said—" Her voice gave way. She took a long moment and then spoke in a whisper, rough as granite. "He said he remembered how I'd treated him in the Capo's camp. He told me I thought too highly of my beauty, and he would be happy to fix that." She ran her finger down a line, dark red and crusted. "And then . . . Teo, he promised he would kill your sister and Vanni in front of me if I didn't give him what he wanted."

A thousand possibilities lit in my head, torches along a hall that led to a terrible place. But after a moment, there was only one left, a terrible burning truth.

"He wanted to know where Cielo was, didn't he."

"But he'd just seen Cielo on the battlefield," Pasquale said as he joined us. He clapped his hands together, dusting the feeling of dead men off his fingers.

Favianne finally looked up. "He knew it was you." All eyes in the camp came to rest on me, but there was no time to explain. Favianne's face cramped with disgust. "He said . . . he said he'd know your scent anywhere."

"Did you lie to him about where Cielo is?" I asked, frantic with hope.

Favianne's breath came in hectic bursts. "I wanted to save

Vanni and Mirella. But once I told him, all Beniamo did was walk off to their tent, laughing at how clever he'd been. He didn't kill anyone in front of me. He let me get away." Her shame was a palpable force. I took Favianne's hands in mine, trying to settle it.

"That was not your fault," I said. "He . . . he wanted me to know what happened here. He left a survivor on purpose."

I had been so distracted by Beniamo's move toward Amalia and the threat of my brother in power that I hadn't paid attention to the words he'd given me in plain Vinalian. My brother had told me that he would not let me die until Cielo was dead. And there was no pleasure in killing my strega in the drowned grottoes unless I lived through the pain of it.

I needed to get to Cielo. Nothing else mattered.

The strega needs us, I told my magic.

No animal I knew was fast enough to track Beniamo if he'd left nearly a day earlier. A wind would take me to the Violetta Coast quickly, but it could not tell me where the drowned grottoes were. Their hidden nature worked against me.

I need to see, I told the magic. *I need to see* everything.

And the power of a hundred streghe answered, soaring through me, working together to save us all.

ᚠ⚶ᚴ

WHEN I BECAME THE SKY, IT DID NOT HAPPEN ONE PIECE AT A time. I blinked, and I was spread out against the heavens, the whole of Vinalia stretched beneath me. We were locked this way, a marriage of solid earth and woven air.

I felt the rapid, pushing fingers of rivers underneath me, and the crawl of mountains, moving and growing and chipping away so slowly, a person would never notice. The towns were knots of life, and the cities were great, grasping fists.

Oceans pushed their waves onto shore, and shores accepted them with grace, changing with each kiss of water to land.

Winds and birds moved through me freely, and they were mine to hold in a loose, loving grasp. The sun moved through my skin. The clouds were my breath. The storms were my rage and beauty.

Yes, my magic said.

If I was going to carry this much magic inside of me, I could not think of a better way to use it. A smothering burden lifted, and I rose and rose, with nothing to stop me. I would have been happy to stay as the sky forever, but Cielo was down there, and I could not let my strega die thinking that I did not care. From this distance, life and death and love shouldn't have mattered.

Magic was all.

All was magic.

But no matter how much I had taken on, I was not *only* magic. The part of me that was Teo, the sorely human part, strained to find the black-haired stranger I had met on a mountain, the one I knew as well as I now knew the country beneath me.

I searched everywhere at once. I felt every inch of Vinalia, and it brought on a flood of truth. This land needed new paths: the old ones had led us to dark places. Still, no matter how difficult this moment, no matter how dangerous the choices ahead, this place was so beautiful that even the sky held its breath.

Somewhere along the Violetta Coast, I felt the pinprick of magic that meant *Cielo*.

And I poured myself back down to the earth.

20

I arrived back in my girlish form at the edge of a ribboned cliff on the Violetta Coast. But I could not seem to fit back inside of myself. It felt like trying to force an ocean into the shallow curve of a spoon.

I looked around in a daze.

I had been to this part of Vinalia only once, when I was ten, and Father carted all of us on one of his long trips after Mirella and I begged until we lost our voices. We feasted on pasta dotted with tiny clams every night and swam in the sea every morning when we woke.

Fiorenza had told me so many stories of this coast, its seaside villages a clash of turquoise and coral and sunbeam yellow bright enough to rival the greenery that draped itself over homes and cliffs alike. Some of the beaches were filled with volcanic sea glass instead of sand, but even those could not approach the beauty of the water. Instead of a single constant shade, it was alive with a swapping and melding of blues and greens and the sea's namesake, a deep inky purple.

The salted air moved through me as freely as the wind had when I was sky, teasing my hair into knots. But this breeze did not bear Cielo's magic.

My own magic pulled me down toward the beaches, which made me hope that Cielo had found the grottoes—and perhaps even Veria's Truth. Maybe I would discover the strega emerging lazily from the water, glistening from a swim, the vase of moonlight lodged in the sand.

I ran down the cliffside path at a foolish pace, my steps almost sending me pitching into the open air and then the sea. Below me, waves broke against rocks, rabid with foam. As I rounded a sharp downward turn I slid on one heel. My imagination spilled over the edge and sent me to my death, but I clung to the earth, gripping the roots of the lavish green vines that spilled over the cliffs. I thanked God—all the gods—for a childhood spent on the steepest mountain slopes.

When I reached the bottom, I realized that I was still naked.

"*Clothes*," I demanded in the old language.

The nearest patch of wildflowers, cloudy blue and tangerine and hardy red, became a tunic with those colors all mixed together, the fabric softly scented. I pulled it on, already missing the play of wind across my skin. But I did not have time to mourn each tiny loss, when such a large one loomed overhead.

I ran up and down the beach, coating my feet in dampness and grit, but Cielo was not in any of the coves, and I did not see the strega's pale figure among the scrolled edges of the waves.

I turned away from the sea and faced the cliffs behind me, a series of great dark holes, as if some giant thing had burrowed inside the rock and made itself at home. In a way, it had. The sea was a creature that breathed tides and hollowed out grottoes.

When I picked up my feet and ran toward the nearest of the great openings, the magic balked. It scratched and hissed like an underfed cat. *Here*, it said, directing me to-ward a dark keyhole in the rock. I didn't hesitate to push myself through.

In that moment, it became clear that I trusted my magic the same way I used to trust Father's voice.

I pushed myself into the earth, scraping on teeth of stone, and emerged ankle-deep in water. A grotto opened around me, but beyond a few sun-pierced inches, it was dark. I could see no bridge leading onward, no puzzle path of stones to fol-low. There was only water.

Farther, my magic said. *Do not hesitate.*

I trudged in up to my shins, my knees. Eddies washed around my thighs, the tide sucking me closer as it took me by the hips. It was cold here, away from the blessings of the sun. I shivered, slowing as my tunic pooled and tugged. The sea was striking into the cave with far more confidence than I was. Soon the water was so deep, I could not skim the bot-tom with my toes.

I had to swim.

A lifetime spent in mountains meant that I could push across a fast-moving stream, but I had barely one month of ocean swimming to guide me. The only thing that helped was the tide at my back, pushing me farther in.

It pushed so fast, I grew less and less certain I would be able to fight my way back out. I kept my arms outcast, searching for rocks. There was no certainty that I would come to a new resting place, only the faith that my magic would not lead me here without reason. Only the hope that soon I would find the strega perched on a dry spit of rock, eating a lunch of bread and olives from the nearest fishing town, Veria's Truth cradled in one hand.

Far off, I heard the thick shushing of wings. My reason, and everything I knew about grottoes, told me that those were the sounds of bats.

Look up, my magic said.

Overhead, a stray beam of light showed me birds rather than bats. The black of their wings, banded with di Sangro red, was a color as beautiful as any shade of the sea. My heart lifted painfully.

Cielo.

I almost turned back, wanting to follow in the wake of Cielo's flock. But my magic kept me pointed in the same direction. Maybe Veria's Truth was still here in the depths of the grotto. Maybe Cielo hadn't been able to find it.

I could fix that. I could mend every broken thing between us.

Rock bashed into my foot as I reached a new series of shallow pools, leading me one by one toward a grotto, where I stood on a thin ledge in front of a deep, rocky bowl filled with water. The walls were pitted with tiny holes that sucked in light from the outside world. The surface of the water grabbed for that radiance and cast it on the walls, creating veins of light and color.

I was so taken with the strange, secret majesty that at first, I didn't notice Beniamo standing at the far end of the grotto, holding one black bird in each of his fists. He had seen me, though. The cold of the water that I'd been keeping back with eager movement sliced into me like a thousand tiny knives. I wondered how long my brother had been standing there, savoring the last of my hope.

It would be a small and pointless victory, but I did not want him to speak first. Beniamo always claimed the room with his voice before he followed with other means. "You must have killed your horse to get here so quickly," I shouted. The words hit the stone walls, harsh.

"She was a determined creature," Beniamo said, sniffing at one of the birds. "You would have adored her. Now she is rotting on the cliffs."

"Your forces have been defeated," I said, but the words rang hollow.

"Did you like your moment of playing queen?" Beniamo asked. "That daydream has always been your weakness. I thought it should be stripped from you before you died." Beniamo had fought his battle against me on as many fronts as he could. Everything my brother had done had been arranged to hit me in the tenderest places. Beniamo wanted more than one death from me.

My wonder, my will, my body.

"It was never enough for you," I cried out. "Being the chosen di Sangro son. If you couldn't have everything, neither could we."

Beniamo's patience was one of the most maddening things about him. It remained smooth and glassy, unbroken by my rage. "I'm glad you caught up to me, Teodora," he said. "Once your lover is dead, we can move on to the final stage of things." His hands curled tighter around the birds, and they rustled and writhed in his grasp. "I will take the magic that should have been mine."

No, my magic said.

I could not use it, though. I could not risk my brother taking pieces of Cielo in return.

I was nearly felled by my own fear. But I stayed on my feet, and I summoned my voice. I had spent so long throttling it when Beniamo was near that it was hard to set it free. "You will *never* have my magic. You don't carry the death you cause."

As the words met the rocks and resounded, I questioned whether they were true. Beniamo hadn't cared about the other people he had killed, and yet in a twisted, foul way, he cared about me. Would he carry my death with him like a trophy? Would that be enough to transfer my magic to him?

"I'm sorry," I choked out.

Beniamo's laugh pulled up a shiver from my depths. "Do you really think apologies will have any effect—"

"*I'm not talking to you,*" I said. My voice shook hard enough that the ripples sounded less like a wildflower giving way in a strong wind, and more like the beginnings of an avalanche. I finished what I needed to say to Cielo—the words I could not die without saying, the ones that were bound so tightly in my breast that I could barely release them. "The thing we needed to do most was right there, and all I could see was what stood in the way."

We needed to change magic so men like Beniamo would never be able to claim it again. I looked around the grotto for Veria's Truth, a vase of pure moonlight that held the tears of a god—or a strega.

If I could get it, I would drink the water inside of that ancient shard of magic, the tears infused with Veria's power. They would show me the truth: how to use my stolen magic to do the best thing for all streghe.

I would know how to change the death inheritance.

I searched the water and found nothing. Beniamo was laughing at my struggle, enjoying the sight of me growing cold and desperate. I closed my eyes, true black spotting against the weaker darkness of the cave.

Keep looking, my magic insisted.

"It's over," I muttered.

But I felt the slightest wind of hope, and when I opened my eyes, they went to the water swirling around my calves. The ever-changing colors reminded me of the endless hues caught in Cielo's eyes. I knew this magic. It was just like the feat the strega had pulled off in the Neviane.

Cielo had become the colors of the Violetta.

Or at least, the parts of Cielo that weren't clutched in Beniamo's hands. I almost scolded the water beneath me for being so reckless, for stretching Cielo's magic so far. For coming back when this was my fight and always had been.

"*Di Sangro business*," I muttered. "Remember?"

But the water was already changing, leading my eyes as a lively braid of deepest blues drifted and sank to the bottom of the cave. Here were more colors: the rich green of pines and the violet of plums. If I hadn't been looking straight at them, they would have blended with the shimmering water.

But I knew the ripple of that luscious silk. I knew what those green and purple hues looked like as they flew in a mountain wind or hung around my strega's ankles. Cielo's cloak was weighted down to the bottom of the pool.

It fluttered, revealing the brightest shard of white pottery that I'd ever seen, and then it settled back into place.

A new scheme leapt to my hands, my fingers desperate to hold Veria's Truth. I slid my eyes over the cloak, taking care not to tear my attention away too quickly. If I drew Beniamo to that point, he would find what Cielo had worked so hard to dislodge from the layers of time.

I would not disappoint Cielo again.

If I died today, the last thing I would do was change magic.

"Well, sister," Beniamo said in a teasing tone. We were back in the nursery, and he wanted to play a game. "What are the chances I'm holding a piece of your lover that he can't live without?" His predatory instincts snapped into place, his eyes moving over the shining feathers of each bird. "His liver? His heart?"

There were so many pieces that Cielo could not spare— and Beniamo knew that making me guess was half of the pain.

"Which should I eat first?" He held them out, keeping his thumbs hard on their necks as they churned in his hands. "Your choice."

But that was no choice at all, and I would not speak if it only fed into his brutal games. I pulled Father's stiletto from my sleeve. I rushed at Beniamo, my blood pushing me forward, forcing open the pathways of my heart until it ached.

Beniamo nodded sagely, as if he'd seen this coming.

Good, the magic said.

Let my brother think that all I cared about was killing him.

With the tide at my back, I thought I would reach him in two flying steps, but the water spun into a thick pool and slowed me.

"Poor choice," Beniamo said. I was caught watching as the bird in his right hand disappeared into his mouth with a crunch of bone.

I pushed forward with everything I had left in my exhausted body, screaming and plunging the stiletto into Beniamo's left shoulder just as he turned to the second bird.

It flew up to the heights of the grotto, smacking itself against the stone ceiling in its haste.

"Go," I shouted to Cielo.

Beniamo pulled me close, his talons biting into my back. He didn't spear them straight through, but dragged them down, deeper with every inch. "I wondered how long it would take before you fought me with your own strength and lost with honor." Even though I was gritting my way through intense pain, the notion that Beniamo was the bastion of honor made my mind truly riot.

"Father's knife will not help you now," he warned. "Neither will his little sayings. The weak die, and the strong live." Beniamo laid the words out slowly and thoroughly. "*You* proved that to me when I became an owl. It is the way of nature."

On the other side of the grotto, at a safe distance, Cielo came back together, the color magic flushing her like a chameleon for a moment before she returned to her usual complexion. "Magic is entirely natural," Cielo said, flicking water from her skin, droplet by droplet.

"You will have to start fighting it now," I whispered.

With Beniamo distracted by Cielo's sudden appearance, I stabbed him. I did not go for his heart or his guts or the arteries in his neck. I ignored every one of the killing blows Father had taught us. I aimed down, at Beniamo's leg, letting him believe I was choosing to injure him so he could not follow me as I escaped.

When his hand came down to swipe Father's blade, I grabbed him by the wrist. His other hand answered far too quickly, talons stabbing into my stomach. I did not change course. I kept my grip on his wrist and aimed for the top of his palm, carving away several fingers in a single motion.

Pain rushed to Beniamo's face, but I took no delight in it, only exhausted relief as I staggered back, curving around my wound. Beniamo fell to searching for the Capo's ring. He could not sink to his knees, though, because the water had risen too high. The tide was bold now, scattering froth up to my chest.

I started backing away, but I could not move very fast.

I tried to call on magic, but it was draining along with my blood.

"Please," I said. "Change him into something small, something helpless." But I could not find enough strength in that moment.

Cielo dove into the water, and I feared that she would try to stop Beniamo. She came up, naked and glistening, holding the vase that had been at the bottom of the pool. Understanding what Cielo meant to do, I scraped out a cry.

Veria's Truth could not be spent on Beniamo. He was just one horrible man, and the world was full of them. If the only shard of magic powerful enough to show us how to change the death inheritance was gone, we might never get another chance.

Cielo was already unscrewing the lid, releasing the musty breath of ages and a trickle of water. "No!" I shouted, but there was no force behind my words. Cielo flung the contents of the vase at my brother and the drops spattered his face, dribbling down his chest, anointing him.

"Let him see the truth of what he's done," Cielo muttered, tossing the vase away and coming for me.

Beniamo's eyes slid from us and did not return. He looked off into some unknown distance, his brow taking on the three deeply carved lines of di Sangro confusion, while his hand drizzled the dark rock with blood.

The water below me had taken on another color—red. It did not join the rest but kept to itself, like a vein in marble. I could not stop staring at what my life looked like as it left me.

I had the same cold feeling as I'd had when Cielo left me in the Mirana.

Beniamo started screaming in pain. When I looked back, he appeared to be standing in the water, unmoving. It was up to his chest now. The tide had crept up on us, but now it was turning with a vengeance.

"What's happening?" I asked Cielo, shaking from the cold of the water and the weakness in my limbs. It was moving inward, toward my heart.

Cielo grabbed me by the arms, pushed a hand through my wet hair, and looked off toward my brother. "Veria's Truth is giving him a guided tour of his own life. It's showing Beniamo the truth of everything he's done. He has no choice but to live through every torture, every moment of pain. He can't turn away."

My body slipped into a state of shock as I watched my brother's face lose its vile certainty.

I watched as he grimaced and ground his teeth together, as he pushed against invisible ties that held him in place.

"We have to go," I said. "While he's still caught."

"I think your brother might be here for some time," Cielo said. Then he took one look at the onrushing tide, and another at my bloodied stomach, and added, "Let's move quickly, though."

Cielo turned into a wind, cracking a hole in the side of the grotto where the pinholes let in light. The entire wall crumbled and let in a rush of sea air. I pushed, one faint step at a time, onto a shelf halfway up a cliff.

Cielo sat down next to me, girlish again. Behind us, Beniamo's screams and the water rose, each one fighting to fill the grotto. The water must have won, because soon it washed over his voice, and my brother was finally silent.

Cielo and I stood on a ledge, overlooking the sea, but its glories could not wrestle my eyes away from Cielo. The strega looked stunning in a determined sort of way. "My apologies are late in arriving, but . . . your brother did have to be stopped. I could not see it on that day in Prai."

"We were both right," I said. "Magic still needs to be changed."

"Don't forget the part where we were both horrendously wrong," Cielo said. "I should not have left you."

If we'd never parted, the story would have been different. But there was no use wishing it into a new shape now.

"What did Beniamo take from you?" I asked, sweeping my eyes over every inch of my strega's body, expecting a stain of blood, something missing.

"I can't feel anything wrong," she said. "Though I *did* feel it when he treated one of my birds as an antipasto."

The strega's light, tripping humor stumbled. She flinched, and I grabbed her by the shoulders, running my fingers down her sides, unable to keep myself at even this distance after so long away.

I pressed onto my toes to kiss her, my calves like two hard stones, but with an inch left, I stopped. In my rush, I had been looking for lost limbs, showy bloodstains. At such a close distance, I could see what Beniamo had taken.

The many shades of the strega's eyes, that constant swirl,

was gone. Cielo's irises were a pale, nothing color. I brushed a thumb along the soft skin of her cheek. "You will live."

Cielo was looking at me as if she wasn't so certain she could offer the same words in return. "We have to get you back to your father," she said. But I was still bleeding, and even the idea of making it to Amalia was so exhausting, I nearly fell. Cielo pulled me against her, the top of my head buried in her lovely neck.

I was too tired to think of a life that went on like this, from one stepping stone of near death to the next. "I want to stay here," I said. I meant in the crook of Cielo's neck. The sandy ground beneath me also looked tempting. Even the sea below would be a beautiful place to die.

"You have to change now," Cielo said, shaking me. "Use a reversal."

My magic was faint and far away. A reversal would take more than I could possibly summon. I had only a small measure of life in my body, and I knew what I wanted to do with it. I pulled Father's knife out of my sleeve, Beniamo's blood still crowning the blade.

I'd barely looked at the stiletto since the day I'd fought with Cielo.

"What are you doing?" she asked, catching my arm before I could toss it in the sea below.

"No more knives passed down from fathers to sons," I said. "No more magic passed death to death. Promise me you'll find another way to change the inheritance."

Cielo looked at me with a sadness that I could not possibly bear, along with every other weight.

"*Promise*," I said.

The strega dipped forward, her lips hitting mine with a

warmth that crackled and glowed as sure as sitting by the hearth on a winter's morning. The sun above us shone cold and measly compared to this.

The world seemed to tilt, and I believed it was sliding me toward whatever sort of heaven or hell awaited. Then something deep inside of me *flicked*, and a strange and magnificent feeling came, like turning to a blank page in a story I'd thought was fully written.

When Cielo pulled back, he was in boyish form.

"Don't worry," I said, pushing forth a smile for my strega, even though I couldn't feel it. "I'll miss you in every possible way."

"Teo," he said, standing back with the huddled features of a stranger. "Let me try something."

I laughed, which was a mistake. My guts seared with pain. "Do you really think we have time for that?"

Cielo's fingers touched the line of my shoulder, brushing my skin, the motion as smooth and tight as turning a page.

Another *flick*.

Cielo was in girlish form again, looking down at herself with something like wonder.

"What did you just do?" I asked. This could not be *the brilliant death*—not yet. I was still alive. But it seemed that when Cielo touched me, Cielo changed.

I thought about my strega's book, that collection of leather and blank pages infused with magic, how I had locked it away, even though I claimed to love Cielo. The memory of the fight left me aching, wanting to cry out. It felt like pressing on a barely healed wound.

Our hearts had broken that day, leaving splintered pieces everywhere.

I carefully uncurled my palm from the stiletto, the handle leaving a harsh indentation as if I'd been gripping it for years instead of a few pitiless minutes. I looked at the dark twist of the handle, spiraling and then sliding down to the point. "You put this in my hand the day we fought," I said. "The day you left me."

"I started with the apology, if you'll remember, but we can circle back to that if you need to hear it again . . ."

I put my hand to Cielo's lips, quieting her for one single, necessary moment.

"This is a shard of magic," I said. "*Our* magic."

Cielo's eyes blasted wide with understanding.

"Your magic changes the forms of things outside of you, and mine changes the form of the caster," she said, speaking at a rate I'd never heard before, even from Cielo, words pounding faster than a fearful heartbeat. "Magic is something inherited from the outside world, twined up inside of each strega . . ."

"And this shard of magic holds both of our powers."

"And we're stronger than any streghe in ages."

Neither of us was bold enough to speak the hope that together, our magic was enough to change the death inheritance. That perhaps we had taken the deaths of so many streghe in Vinalia and spun them into something better.

Something new.

Cielo looked at her fingers, which were trembling slightly. "I think I could change when I touched you, because . . . I changed you. Into the book." She cocked her head. "Well, more like a human form of the book."

"You're saying that we traded some of our magic."

"But if not through death . . . how?" Cielo asked.

As soon as I heard the question, I knew. If magic could be passed only by a change as potent as death, the answer was clear. Besides, I had felt it. I knew the truth in my body, my rushing blood. "It happened when we kissed."

"Can you take on a different form now?" Cielo asked, hope riding high in her voice.

I was afraid to try—afraid to be wrong. But the only other choice waiting for me was death.

I tugged on all of the strings of my magic, and it came together smoothly. This did not feel like a reversal. It was as simple as breathing.

I tried to think of the fastest way we could return to Amalia, to Father and his healing magic. I didn't need to be the sky this time. I only needed to be fast. As my dying mind wandered the halls of the past, I remembered that long ago, my brother Luca had told me the fastest way to travel.

343

"Come with me," I told Cielo.

After so much cold, I became a burst of light.

21

Traveling as light was nearly instant, a searing that cut my breath to pieces. At first, I thought I had died and was imagining one last journey back to Amalia. But I woke naked, damp with blood, lying on a battlefield.

If this was life after death, it was a cruel joke.

Cielo leaned over me, cheeks drawn tight, apologetic and pleading. "Your father is coming. I don't suppose you can whip up some clothes?"

My neck rusted over with pain, and I could not even shake it. "Try it yourself."

"Can I do that?" Cielo asked, worry seasoned with delight. Our trade of magic was a discovery worthy of feasts and celebrations, parades and dancing, but all I could manage was a wincing smile as Cielo pointed at a trampled patch of grass, and then tossed a green-brown cloak over me.

He helped me up to sitting, the pain in my stomach shading quickly into numbness as it became too much for my body to fight.

I faced the same view as I had the day before. Mimì's rivers were unmistakable, and so was the green stripe of the Estatta separating us from the city. Amalians were crossing the bridges to see what had become of the armies, to make a hasty peace with their new fate.

And Father was approaching.

"Teo," he said, his breath spent in running. I hadn't seen him run in years. "I thought I saw you. . . ."

"I'm here," I said, forcing the words out past the overwhelming urge to faint. Talking to Father made me feel like everything might be fine, that my life could still return to its former state.

But when Father looked to the wounds in my stomach, his face fell into grim, helpless lines. Still, he threw himself down at my side, telling me stories, pouring the words into my nearly deaf ear.

I strained to listen, but there was little comfort here. These were not the calm, measured stories Father told other people who were sick or wounded. They were strega stories, yes, but the sentences were choppy, the plots half-remembered.

His magic was faded.

I had come all the way back from the Violetta Coast, and Father couldn't save me. He must have used up too much power after the battle, saving all the wounded soldiers like I'd asked him to.

"It's fine," I whispered. "You don't have to keep trying."

I didn't want the last thing I heard to be his frantic misery. I looked up at the sky, the brightness burning behind the clouds.

Father kept throwing useless words at me. Tales that should have felt true, but all rang empty. My hands went to my stomach and slid around in my blood. Words. More words. They didn't mean anything.

All I could think about was how the streghe in those stories were dead and gone.

While I was dying, the past was like a half-opened door, and I found another truth beyond it. Father had feared a moment like this since the day I was born. This was the way he must have looked when he could not save Mother, when no amount of magic could put back the life she bled away after pushing me into the world.

"Death is not your greatest enemy," I said, giving Father the words though each one cost me another clawing second of pain. Father had left so much of life untouched out of a potent mixture of fear and tradition.

"Do not be sad for me," I said, one last di Sangro demand.

I had used my magic. I had loved my strega.

My eyes closed. There was an abyss waiting, a ravine as dark as the Storyteller's Grave on the mountain at home.

I was no longer afraid to fall into it.

Cielo's voice leapt with urgency, a silver fish traveling against the tide. "Signore, you must kiss your daughter."

"I would prefer not to take orders at this moment," Father said with a gruffness I could not help loving—and a stubbornness that I knew all too well.

But even after those words, I felt the dry brush of Father's lips.

My magic lifted and rose through my body like dawn, banishing the darkness. Everywhere I hurt, it spread brilliance. Everywhere I bled, it dried up the rivers. And where I was broken, it mended my skin.

I opened my eyes to the rarest sight of all—Father's amazement. Instead of us looking like him, Niccolò di

Sangro looked like one of his children: Luca bent over his specimens; Mirella caught in a rare unguarded moment of translating a mountain scene with her thick, oily paints; me when I had my first magic lessons from Cielo.

"How?" Father asked.

"I had plenty of magic, but no way of healing," I said, the pain stepping away from me like a dance partner as the music stopped. "You gave me what I needed to do it myself."

The trade of kisses that Cielo and I had done on the cliffs of the Violetta Coast was not a onetime matter.

This was the new inheritance.

This was a new age of magic that would not be a bloody echo of the others.

I wondered if that meant Father had just taken in a little of my magic too—some of the strength that he needed to use his powers openly and freely. I rose to my feet, as wobbly as a kid goat. Cielo steadied me, setting my face between his hands. His eyes were solemn, the missing colors calling to my memories, but I did not wish to spend the rest of my days mourning tiny losses.

Not when there was so much beauty here.

"Your eyes are clear as water in a mountain stream," I said, finding a new way to admire them.

Cielo's focus was so intent, I wondered if the strega had even heard the compliment. "Because you survived, I am going to do something foolish."

I cocked an eyebrow.

"I have a scheme," Cielo said. "But I'm not a di Sangro, so it is stuck together in the most careless fashion, and a great deal of it rests on your newly mended shoulders."

"Good," Father said, with a laugh that still had a last bit of fear clinging to it. "If you don't give Teo a challenge, she will slap one together in the next four minutes."

❦

WE GATHERED THE REST OF OUR PARTY AT CAMP, AND IN THE midst of bittersweet greetings, I gave Cielo several looks that should have pried the truth from his lips. But my strega would not speak a word of this new scheme.

While Mimì and Xiaodan embraced Cielo, I rushed over to Luciano. My godchild was wailing in Dantae's arms. He was the one person who felt the lack of his mother more keenly than I did. I patted his head, and he stopped crying for a moment, though he gave me the same suspicious glare he had earlier.

Then he cried harder, his entire face blotching di Sangro red.

"He'll need milk soon," Dantae said. "It's the one thing I can't give him. There's a woman back at our camps who's just had a baby of her own, and she could be here in less than a day."

"We're close to talking Dantae and her soldiers into joining the sixth family," Mimì said.

"Her feelings are resonating closely with ours. I told her there won't be any sticking of knives to anyone's throats, though," Xiaodan said. "That made her frown a bit." She hooked one arm through mine, and Mimì claimed my other elbow.

As they told me everything I'd missed while I was on the Violetta Coast—mostly the fact that the Amalians had heard of our victory and were waiting to see what happened to Vinalia next—I noticed Favianne across the camp, standing near a twitchy Pasquale and looking thoroughly left out.

The church's army had started the long march back to Prai, but I was surprised to find MacCartaigh and Cinquepalmi sitting around the campfire. They both leapt up to greet Cielo.

"Good," MacCartaigh said, pounding on Cielo's back and offering him a tin cup that could have held anything. "You're back."

"Father Malfara would not have liked us to leave without seeing his child safely returned," Cinquepalmi added.

"My father didn't care what became of me," Cielo said, sipping at the drink. I could smell it from where I stood, and judging by the piercing odor, it was as purely distilled as a vase made of moonlight.

Cinquepalmi shook his head, his great nose cutting the air. "You were all he spoke about in the last few months. He came back changed after Amalia. He couldn't talk to the priests about his past with a strega, but he took us into his confidence. Why do you think we were at your wedding?"

"*They* were at your wedding?" Father asked, looking more than a little slighted.

"We can have a di Sangro celebration," I said, but the words lingered on the air like smoke. I did not know who would come to such a feast. The di Sangro family had dwindled, one loss at a time. I could hope to change Fiorenza's mind, and bring her back, but if she chose to stay on the Violetta Coast with my sisters, I would honor her decision.

When I looked around the fire, I could see another family,

stitching itself together. It eased the grief in my chest, though it could not banish it completely.

I took a quick drink of Cinquepalmi's liquore. After facing Beniamo in the drowned grottoes, this moment still required all of my courage.

I took Father's hands between mine, as if I were teaching him to pray. "There is a place for you in the sixth family if you're willing to accept it."

Father's brow folded. He didn't answer yet. I found I didn't need him to.

The offer stood.

I walked over to Cielo, who swiped the cup from me and tipped it so gravity gifted him the few last droplets. "Come," he said. "We shouldn't keep all of Vinalia waiting."

After I had used magic to add a few more items of clothing to our outfits, Cielo led the sixth family and the remains of the other five into Amalia. I walked at the strega's side, the cloaks he had made for us flapping around our legs like the wings of birds. He had already taken to the pageantry of clothing magic—perhaps a little too well. We looked regal, and yet not in the way of Vinalian nobles. A people of our own.

As we walked, the Amalians stared and traded bits of stories.

They spoke of the streghe who had saved Vinalia from a madman.

They spoke of the di Sangro who had saved Vinalia from her own brother.

"These people are following us like stray cats," I said as the crowds grew, inviting curiosity and yet more people.

"Let them stare," Cielo said, flicking a hand to draw them

all closer. "I find that I don't mind being a sensation. After so many years of hiding, the whole thing is refreshing by comparison."

We stopped in the square in front of the Palazza. The statues of the Capo had been charred by Cielo's magical fires, or pitched over, a few chunks of marble left as the only tribute to the greatness of Cristoforo Malfara. But some of the statues of the old gods stood, proud and lasting. Melae, with a robe that hid the sight of a person's death in its folds. Veria, with her solemn gaze. Erras, with his knife.

As we came to a stop in front of the Palazza, the crowd perched on every bit of open space. A nearby conversation turned to the battle and the already infamous speech Cielo had made on the battlefield.

"What are they talking about?" Cielo asked with a clear-eyed squint and a heavy frown. "I didn't make any speeches. I would have a memory of that."

I coughed, pretending it was caused by the dust. "Yes, well, I might have borrowed your body for a brief time," I said. "But your scheme?"

Cielo squinted. "Ah, yes."

He stepped in front of the crowd of gathered Amalians, and they went silent. I savored this moment—the last before another war inevitably broke out to decide who would rule when Cielo stepped aside.

"You require someone to lead you," Cielo said. "And it would seem that I have the right blood in my veins, as well as the traditional anatomy between my legs." There were confused stares but no laughter. Cielo looked disappointed, but pushed on. "I accept the honor, and honestly, the tremendous burden, of being the next king of Vinalia."

My hand raised to grab Cielo's arm. I did not want the strega to turn his life into a string of grim, unwanted responsibilities. Cielo had given up so much to Vinalia, and I would not ask my strega for more sacrifice.

But just as my hand met his sleeve, he spoke again. "I will not be running this country, however. I have other plans, starting with giving a great deal of magic back to Vinalia, magic stolen by the previous Capo. No, I will not be able to cut your deals and scheme your schemes. That is the calling of Teodora di Sangro, who I have married, which I believe makes her your queen."

The crowd looked more than confused now. They shifted, unsettled, as if we had faced a calm sea and then a storm had broken the sky.

"I imagine that some of you are already writhing like squids in a net," Cielo shouted. "However, I would like to point out that other countries have put queens on their thrones. In Eterra, there is one ruling right now. And there have always been those who helped shape countries quietly, standing at the elbow of a man on the throne. Also, I would remind you, quite forcefully, that you have already followed Teodora's rule before today. She has proven herself in battle, if you care about that kind of thing. She was the general of the strega forces who held the pass at Zarisi, and she kept all of you from cutting each other open just yesterday." The people looked to each other, sure of themselves when they shouted that no such thing had happened.

Cielo sighed. "Teodora felt the need to borrow my likeness, otherwise no one would have listened to a single word she said. I would appreciate if that wasn't necessary. It would make kissing her entirely awkward. And while Teo does have a delightful boyish side, I will not stand for anyone making demands on how we must appear."

Cielo grabbed my wrist and changed into girlish form with a great *flick* that stilled the crowds. "You can continue to lie to yourselves if you need to believe that I am only a man, and only a man can rule. But here is the truth, and refusing to see it will not change things."

Cielo touched my cheek. "I believe it is your turn," she whispered.

Father put a hand on my shoulder and urged me forward.

I faced the uncertain crowds of Amalia. They did not know what to expect, and to be honest, neither did I. We had gone off the edge of all known maps. No one knew where to step. But I thought of a small girl with brambles for curls who had dreamed this day, and I imagined all of the girls who must have done the same. For their sake, I cleared my throat. Even if I did not know what to say, the di Sangro daughter sitting on Father's walnut chair making decrees did. I set my hand over my heart, where she lived. "This moment seems to have come out of nowhere, and yet it has taken us ages to arrive." With nothing to stop it, my voice ranged far. The marble of the buildings sent back my words, doubling their strength. "The Capo led you with false hope. My brother would have led you with fear. I will treat you as family.

"Your fate will be mine."

᛭

"WELL, THEY LOOKED RIPE FOR MUTINY," FAVIANNE SAID AS THE crowds parted. She was resplendent in a summer-green dress with golden vines a shade darker than her braided and coiled hair. I had assumed she would cover her chest, but she wore her battle scars with the same pointed pride that she did everything else.

"I think Teodora did well enough," Pasquale said grudgingly. All eyes snapped to him. "For a woman."

I wondered how he could have made it this far and yet learned so little.

"Tread with care," Lorenzo said. "Teodora can still turn you into a boot and wear you to her coronation."

"Teo, you already know that you were splendid," Favianne said, tacking the words on to her earlier statement. "But Vinalians don't change quickly." The stare she aimed at Pasquale could have shriveled off several of his favorite body parts. "Some don't change at all."

I did not know if men like Pasquale would ever see me as their ruler. I did not know how they would respond when I looked past them, to the Vinalians whose lives often unfolded in their shadows. I didn't know what I would do on the days when I was a storm rather than a queen.

The greatness of the task before me unrolled like endless, shining fields to be sown. "I will need time, and help."

Favianne looked me over. "I will give a tour of Vinalia, extoling your virtues." Her voice took on the velvet of her coquettish ways. "Of course, it would be best to have you with me, but . . ."

Cielo's stare could have sent Favianne's most intense one scurrying.

"But you will be kept busy here, I'm sure," she added.

Cielo folded her arms around me, as if she needed to keep Favianne at bay, and yet the way she pressed me gently made it clear that she was only looking for an excuse to touch me in company. I surrendered all of the tension in my body and slid into a state of pure contentment—which lasted only a moment.

There was something missing. I broke through Cielo's hold and crossed to Dantae at the edge of the square, lifting Luciano gently from her arms.

I brought my nephew back to Cielo, doing my best not to cry at the many reminders of Mirella that dwelled in his face. "You've made me Queen of Vinalia, my love, so here is the impossible thing you wanted in return," I said softly. "We have a baby."

Cielo's head turned a fraction, as if she was doing impossible sums. "That was . . . instantaneous."

I passed Luciano off to her, and Cielo took the offering with surprised grace. My strega looked down at the tiny boy in her arms. The light around the baby's hands seemed to take on a different quality than everything else around it, dark as amber and nearly as solid. I wondered if Luciano would grow up to carve things from light.

I thought of the vase that Veria had kept her tears in, hidden for so long.

I was still figuring out the truth of what had happened in the grottoes. Judgment was a sharp blade, with a single cutting edge. Truth had many faces, and each one shone. Truth was a gem: a beautiful thing, one that came at a price.

Today, the price was that I finally understood why Beniamo had chosen me as his favorite partner for his vicious games. If I was being honest, it had started well before I had used magic to turn him into an owl.

When he'd looked at me, Beniamo had seen ambition and anger, his own strongest qualities. He'd prodded me further and further, believing that ambition must lead to greed, and anger had no choice but to harden into violence. But I did not have to turn my qualities in the same direction as Beniamo had.

I did not have to use them against people, as he chose to.

"The first thing I'd like to do is move the capital back to Prai," I said to the small gathering of people around me—my first advisers. "Its history runs the deepest in Vinalia, and there will be fewer complaints from the church if they believe they have a close eye on our pack of wild streghe. Of course, we should also keep one eye on them."

Cielo held up a resolute finger. "And there will be gelato in the summers. Prai has the world's best gelato."

"The things I have to teach you," Mimì muttered. "Gelato was invented by a fisherman from Salvi."

"Well, we can't move the capital to Destinu," I said. "If Salvi chooses independence, you will need a capital of your own."

"Prai will have to do, then," Mimì said as Lorenzo put an arm around her waist. I found myself trying to imagine what would happen the next time they kissed.

"My opera house is in Prai," Xiaodan said. "You will come every opening night! And closing night. And whenever you feel like it. I will save you a box seat."

"What about your soldier?" I asked. "Shouldn't he be given pride of place?"

"Oh," Xiaodan said, with a telling blush. "Massimo will be waiting for me backstage."

I could not help turning to Cielo and found that my strega had beat me to it. Cielo's eyes were hard and fast on my body.

I knew that the best thing I could do was start strengthening my rule so Vinalia would have time to heal. Part of me wanted nothing more than to call a meeting of allies to the newly claimed throne. But there would be time, and I would not be kept from what mattered most.

"I will make a decree in the morning," I said. "Tonight is for more pressing business."

꒰꒷꒱

CIELO AND I SPUN AWAY FROM THE SQUARE, HEADED THROUGH the great arch of the Palazza and into the main courtyard. Everything was chipped and torn by the last time we'd left Amalia in a hurry. The Capo hadn't been able to fix things before leaving for the Eterran front, and it was odd to find our last visit preserved. It felt like only a moment ago Cielo and I had been running through these rooms, tripping over our vast feelings for each other.

By the time we reached the stairway that led up toward the Palazza's bedrooms, my hands were on Cielo's waist. When we reached the first landing, my body was so bursting with possibilities, I could no longer stop myself. I pushed my strega against the wall, halting us before we could reach our destination.

Perhaps this *was* our destination.

Cielo kept looking at me strangely, her eyes pale to match the rest of her, hands falling on my neck like long bars of moonlight.

"You tried to be gentle with me once after I was hurt," I said, pushing into Cielo with the force of my curves, ending with my hips. "I thought we agreed on not repeating our mistakes."

357

"Does that mean we won't be away from each other again?" Cielo asked, wincing at the tender question. It looked as though I should be gentle with my strega—at least for the moment.

"It does," I said, kissing Cielo until there could be no more doubt. "We are together in a way that cannot be undone."

Cielo's hands ventured under my grass-green cloak, through the gaps between my shirt buttons. I wanted to blink and move straight to the part where we were unclothed. At the same time, I wanted to savor the moment when each button slipped its mooring.

It was my turn to pull away, though. "Do you think we can stop saving each other's lives and just . . . live?" I asked.

"All I wanted was a life where we could have *this* without the constant threat of it being stolen away," Cielo said. "The concept felt so simple and yet it turned out to be the most difficult thing in creation."

I looked around at the utter lack of people stopping us.

"Let's not call it official," I said, "but I think the world is already a slightly different place."

I had seen from the sky above Vinalia how slow certain things were to change. The land and the seas moved in a way that they seemed to be eternal from our everyday vantage. But I had felt that they *did* change—that everything, even the slowest mountain, was in motion and could not be stopped.

And then there were the things that transformed with the *flick* of a page or a well-placed kiss.

"Will we keep trading magic every time we do this?" I asked, my lips pressed against Cielo's even as I spoke.

"I feel the same as I did on the Violetta Coast, when it

first happened," Cielo said, taking on the tutor's knowing air that I had found so infuriating and attractive when we first met. "I think that perhaps the kiss of inheritance is a very particular one."

"So, the rest are for our purposes alone?" I asked, liking that idea very much. I packed the force of my delight into another kiss, melding Cielo to the stones of the Palazza, one hand against her shoulder and the other moving toward the waist of her pants, seeking out other parts of my strega that I had missed.

"I have an idea," Cielo said, breathless as my hand perched lightly over the front of her pants, closing her eyes as I bore down.

"Only one?" I asked.

Cielo concentrated as if she was summoning either magic or a great force of will. And then she took my hand and pulled me away from the landing. For once I felt sure that no great disasters would interrupt, and my hopes would be satisfied, but they still caused a finely tuned ache.

Cielo led me down a vaguely familiar set of stairs, a path that my body had traced at one point but could not remember in its entirety. We came out into a secret courtyard that I'd first seen from within the cage of memory: a courtyard where many streghe had died. Where Cielo's mother, Giovanna, had been pushed into killing streghe to gain their powers, and her father, Oreste, had spoken words that split a family into pieces.

Now it was a silent place, the trellises overflowing. I knew that the blooms on the flowers were too young to remember what had happened here, but I wondered if they drank the sadness from the air.

"What are we doing here?" I asked.

"This is the place I come to, often, when I'm dreaming," Cielo said, touching the walls and the flower petals as I walked alongside. She put a hand to mine, and I felt the deep movement, the *flick* that turned the strega to a slightly different form. His eyes were still clear as quartz, and his dark lashes framed a bright, fractured gleaming. "When I come back, there are no streghe being killed. There is no man waiting to pit us against each other."

Cielo reached for my face. The backs of my strega's fingers stroked the blunted point of my cheekbone. The touch bore his intentions, like the sweet, unfolding scent of almond blossoms on the wind. "I thought perhaps we could add a new layer of meaning to this place."

When Cielo touched me, the shifting came on faster—my strega kissing me with each change from boyish to girlish, plunging me deeper into my own feelings until I no longer noticed the blur of changes and only rode them like a wave breaking on the Violetta Coast. One of my hands skimmed over my strega's heart, as the other turned more fervent in its stroking.

My strega's face tipped up to the sky, and rich sounds left Cielo's throat.

We fell to the grass, and I set myself stubbornly beneath Cielo's legs, pushing apart the strega's thighs and holding them in place as I bent to give back several of the best feelings Cielo had given me.

And then Cielo was reaching for me, pulling me ever closer, finding all the ways that we matched each other. I changed once—back into the boy that I'd first shown to the court of Amalia. That di Sangro boy, Teo of the broad shoulders, had always been part of me. And so had the storm that grew inside of me.

It raged beautifully, setting us both to shaking.

Cielo rested against my chest, looking up at the great dark wound of the night sky, salted with stars.

"You meant what you said, about giving back our magic," I whispered.

My body pulled me in different directions: my magic urged rebellion, while my muscles craved the relief of carrying less, setting down the burden that came with Azzurra's and Delfina's deaths.

"Not to the point that we'd stop being streghe, of course. That would be foolish and tragic. You and I could never be plain Vinalians." Cielo shuddered at the thought. I'd spent so much of my life dealing with the difficulties magic brought that I'd never counted the blessings of being a strega—so many that the stars seemed paltry.

I could see the faint shimmering of another truth that had been hidden by brighter worries until this moment. I'd struggled with the great magic inside of me, not because it was broken, but because I had felt broken. Leaving my family and being a part of the streghe sisters' deaths had fractured my heart, shaken my confidence loose.

My magic echoed me, always.

Now I was coming together in a new shape. I was going to serve Vinalia in ways that had once been stories I told myself, but were quickly becoming real. I felt stronger, surer, ready to put the magic inside of me to good purpose. "It took so much to learn how to wield this," I said. "Giving it up now won't be easy."

"Still, the magic we carry should be spread out a bit. One

strega was never meant to hold so much," Cielo said, bracing for the onrush of argument.

"I know," I said firmly enough that my magic would not immediately stage a coup. The best sort of good would be giving some of this power away. My past as the hidden strega of the di Sangro family—and the days I'd spent without Cielo in the wake of our fight—had taught me that being powerful and alone was not an existence I wished to return to.

Cielo squinted as if I'd stolen Teo and come back with another strega altogether.

"Don't worry," I said. "I'm sure that we'll continue to disagree on a stunning number of topics."

"That's part of the enjoyment," Cielo said, touching the smile that had bloomed on his lips like a flower out of season. My strega touched my lips, gifting that smile to me.

I drew the strega's finger into my mouth, and Cielo gasped.

"Before we give most of our magic away, I do have an idea," I said.

"Only one?" Cielo asked, cocking a perfect eyebrow. That, at least, would never change.

"I've never liked the Palazza," I said, pulling myself atop Cielo, my body flush with the strega's, our chests together, our hips grappling. I sat up, rising high in my seat so that Cielo could take in the sight of me, exactly where I wished to be. I let the wind swirl its way over my bare skin, the glorious Amalian night touching me at the same time my strega did. Cielo's hands rose to my breasts, hips lifting in a manner that released a sharp-winged cry from my throat.

"Well?" I asked. "Should we take this place down? For the good of Vinalia?"

"It helps that we've crumbled a mountain. As practice," Cielo said.

We started up again, and this time I invited my magic to twine through each moment. It would not be easy to let go of so much power, I thought, as the walls started to split in branching lines, and stone became powder all around us.

But as I leaned down to kiss Cielo I felt as far from powerless as I'd ever been.

Through the night, Cielo's hands and mouth and skin left their marks on me, and so did our magic. It felt like there was no end to what we could be, and who we could be together. Cielo and I turned and turned and turned, finding each other's empty pages, writing on them until nothing was left blank. This was a story always worth the telling, every kiss a brilliant truth.

The End

When I was the Queen of Vinalia, I spent a great deal of time traveling, seeing in fine-tipped detail what I had noticed in broad strokes as the sky. Vinalia was a glorious place, but it had been rattled by decades of war, and centuries of intolerance had seeped into its bones. People were tired, fearful. After each round of visits, I hurried back to Prai, hunched over a desk sheeted in endless papers, signing treaties and making decrees.

Cielo was nearly always at my side, carrying Luciano for as long as it was still possible, and then longer, until the boy tumbled out of Cielo's arms and started scurrying across the rare, red-veined marble.

"His magic is coming along nicely," Cielo said as Luciano ran from the hall, chased by Mimì, who was staying with us on one of her long visits from Salvi. She sent sprays of water after my nephew, making his small voice split with laughter.

That sound had been late to arrive, but now we heard it more and more often.

Cielo took care of the boy every day, teaching him with an impressive patience. Luciano loved all of Cielo's forms, and was particularly attached to the black-furred wolf, treating my strega's most fearsome incarnation as no more than an overgrown pet.

At night, I sat with Luciano in his narrow bed, telling stories—sometimes the strega stories I'd loved when I was younger, but more often tales of siblings who lived in a mountain-clad castle, and the red-haired boy who fell in love with one of them.

I did not leave out Beniamo, but I did not linger on him either.

Golden beams slanted their way in through tall windows, and Luciano grabbed one, twisting it into the shape of a cat, and held it out, a present for Mimì. "It's mostly cats these days," Cielo admitted. "Though he did make me a small boat out of the sunset."

As Luciano and Mimì disappeared down the hall, I thought about the task that hung overhead like a low-bellied cloud. I had not yet started handing off my magic. Cielo was tracing the families of the streghe killed in the Palazza under the Capo's rule. We had decided that my magic would be spread to new streghe, but in the thick fog of running a country, I could not see where to start.

"You know, you never sit on this thing," Cielo said, looking over at the throne. It had nearly as many battlements as a castle, the whole thing carved of black walnut from the Uccelli. In building the new capital, this was the one demand

I'd made, and then I ignored the uncomfortable perch in favor of a more practical desk.

Cielo put his hands to the arms of the throne, and lowered himself delicately, as if the chair might balk at his presence. When it remained a common chair, he settled in, looking like he meant to stay.

I got up at once. "You can't refuse to rule *and* claim the throne," I said. "That's not how it works."

"I thought you were a fervent believer in new traditions," Cielo said, pursing his lips with challenge.

I tapped my foot against the marble, ticking off the moments until I removed him by force.

Cielo smiled up at me, the bottomless mischief returning to his eyes.

"Usurper," I said, climbing atop him.

"Fine," Cielo said. "You sit in your rightful seat, and I will sit in mine." In an impressive move, my strega somehow spun me so that I was sitting, and Cielo was lounging across my lap, one hand in my loose curls.

I felt a presence in the doorway: something that I would always be good at, a dark gift from Beniamo. For a moment, I thought that everything was beginning again, that my brother was standing there watching and waiting.

But Beniamo had died on the Violetta Coast. Fishermen had found his body in the grotto, and Father and I interred him outside of the di Sangro graveyard. The sea and the rocks hadn't been kind to him, and yet I felt the need to glance at my brother before he was buried, simply to be sure he was gone. He no longer looked angelic or even cruel. His cheeks were eaten away, his curls lank. Death had been the only one strong enough to pry the smile off his lips. Thank all the gods, Beniamo didn't have magic. If his bones had become shards of his power, I could only imagine what horrors they would have held.

I turned to find that the person waiting for me was Favianne. Her tour of Vinalia—extoling my virtues—had proven such a success that she'd done it three times.

"What would the Vinalians think if we told them their rulers can't stop making love all over Prai?" she asked, her true exasperation only half as strong as she pretended.

"They would applaud us, I should think," Cielo said. "Perhaps we should kiss in public more often." These were the sorts of helpful ideas that my strega came up with for running Vinalia, and Cielo had them in abundance.

But today I would not be deterred from my task. "There is the matter of your payment, Favianne."

She dipped at the knees. "No payment is needed, my queen." But from the depths of her curtsy, she looked up at me with a dark blue glimmer, a stare that held the power of a girl who knew precisely what she wanted.

"We made a bargain," I said. "And now you'll have to kiss me."

Favianne looked to Cielo in slight bewilderment. "I cannot kiss you, Teo," she mumbled, all formality sliding away. "Is this a trick?"

"It's simple, really," Cielo said, shifting with irritation. As he was still on my lap, that made things rather uncomfortable. I nudged him to standing. "This is how the magic inheritance works."

Favianne took a step forward, then another, and when she

reached the throne, all of our near kisses came into season. Her lips were gentler than I'd expected, with a tenderness that she did not wear on the outside. I kept my mouth against hers to make sure that magic passed. When she pulled away, she blinked dizzily and touched her face.

The strict architecture of Cielo's frown collapsed. "I'm not sure why I was quite so opposed to that."

Favianne looked down at herself, as if magic should be springing from her in great fountains. She waited. And waited. "Nothing is happening."

"You might have a subtle ability," I offered.

"That's exactly the word I would choose for Favianne," Cielo said. "Subtle."

Favianne touched her face again. Perhaps that was where the magic had taken up residence. "I do feel different," she whispered.

I felt a change too. I was lighter.

I folded my hands and put on my best queenly manner. "Whatever your magic turns out to be, I have an idea of where you will use it."

"You're sending me away?" Favianne asked, slightly bewildered.

"You are so well loved in the provinces that you could topple my reign at any moment, now that you know the Vinalians will accept a queen on the throne," I said.

Favianne preened a bit, tucking a sunbeam of hair back into the deceptively complicated knot that she wore. I felt sure it was all the rage in Vari. "That's probably true."

"I need a spy in Eterra," I said.

"Have there been northern grumblings?" Cielo asked, all

of the strega's concerns waking up, as if I'd fed him several cups of espresso at once.

"Worse," I said. "There has been a pallid sort of silence. I think they're plotting something. I've chosen the very best to deal with that. Favianne will have to charm and magic her way through every castle on the continent."

"Don't forget the islands," Cielo added helpfully.

Favianne nodded, her solemnity touched with delight. She had accepted my challenge, just as I knew she would.

"Now, if you don't mind, the king and queen have to finish what they've started," Cielo said, flicking a wrist and sending her off.

Favianne turned, showing us the low dip in the back of her river-blue dress. "Eels," she muttered.

"What is that about?" Cielo asked.

"How I claimed you and refused to let you go," I said.

"You are going to have to prove that last bit," Cielo said, helping me up from the throne.

"Is this the twenty-seven-part favor again?" I asked.

Cielo spent a moment counting on long, lovely fingers. "We're only up to part nine."

"The rest will have to wait," I said. "We have a country to run, a small strega to raise, and magic to restore."

I was inventing excuses—the truth was that I never wanted the other eighteen parts to reach their end. "You once told me that we would be doing this until the day we died," I admitted. "I plan to hold you to your word."

"I would never cross a di Sangro," Cielo murmured, brushing those long fingers across my hand, pulling me away from the papers on the desk that I seemed to hover

over constantly. I started scheming all the favors Cielo and I might trade as we left the confines of the throne room, stepped into the amber heart of the day, and became a part of Vinalia once again.

Acknowledgments

The true life of a fantasy series is not found in silent pages. It's made up of every hour someone spends walking away from the mundane, down a path cobbled in words, not knowing where it might lead. Thank you for coming with me to Vinalia. I hope you found something worth the journey.

Kendra Levin, you believed, and belief is always where magic starts. Aneeka Kalia, Maggie Rosenthal, Jennifer Dee, Kate Renner, Theresa Evangelista, Karen Dziekonski, and the whole Viking/Penguin Young Readers team, your efforts lifted up these stories and shaped their path.

Sara Crowe, you make every word possible.

Leilani Bustamante, thank you for the art that graces two impossibly glorious covers. Carlotta Brentan, thank you for lending your (perfect!) voice to this story. Zoe Keating, you might never see this, but thank you for the spellbinding music that I listened to over and over as I wrote every chapter.

Love to my family, always.

Cori, you surprised me with Italy, and understanding who I am in all ways.